Curtis

The Walkers of Coyote Ridge, 1

BY NICOLE EDWARDS

ALLURING INDULGENCE
Kaleb
Zane
Travis
Holidays with the Walker Brothers
Ethan
Braydon
Sawyer
Brendon

THE WALKERS OF COYOTE RIDGE
Curtis
Jared
Hard to Hold
Hard to Handle
Beau
Rex
A Coyote Ridge Christmas
Mack
Kaden & Keegan

BRANTLEY WALKER: OFF THE BOOKS
All In
Without a Trace
Hide & Seek

AUSTIN ARROWS
Rush
Kaufman

CLUB DESTINY
Conviction
Temptation
Addicted
Seduction
Infatuation
Captivated
Devotion
Perception
Entrusted
Adored
Distraction

STANDALONE NOVELS
Unhinged Trilogy
A Million Tiny Pieces
Inked on Paper
Bad Reputation
Bad Business

NAUGHTY HOLIDAY EDITIONS
2015
2016

Curtis

The Walkers of Coyote Ridge, 1

NICOLE EDWARDS

Published by Nicole Edwards Limited
PO Box 1086, Pflugerville, Texas 78691

Curtis
The Walkers of Coyote Ridge, 1
Nicole Edwards

COVER DETAILS:
Image: © Wander Aguiar | WanderBookClub.com
Model: Sebastian Skinner
Back Cover Image: © Lindsay Helms (36305261) | 123rf.com
Design: © Nicole Edwards Limited

INTERIOR DETAILS:
Formatting: Nicole Edwards Limited
Editing: Blue Otter Editing | BlueOtterEditing.com

ISBN:
Ebook 9781939786593 (ebook) | Paperback 9781939786609

SUBJECTS:
BISAC: FICTION / Romance / Contemporary
BISAC: FICTION / Romance / General

Note to Reader

Although you've spent time with Curtis and Lorrie throughout the Alluring Indulgence series, I wanted to give you an insight into their lives before they had children. Their love story is one that I think many of you have seen or even lived. I believe we all hope to meet our soulmate one day and even some of us are lucky enough to have met that one person who completes us. I hope you enjoy Curtis and Lorrie's story from the very beginning.

Throughout this book, you will see passages from Lorrie's journal as well as letters written from Curtis to Lorrie and Lorrie to Curtis. I hope you enjoy them as much as I've enjoyed writing them.

Lorrie's journal passages are reflected with
dates formatted like this:

♥ *From Lorrie's journal* ♥

Dedication

JACK DeNORMANDIE

Without you, this book wouldn't have been written. Thank you from the bottom of my heart for sharing so much of yourself with me. (And thank you for Chancy, too)

Prologue

"POP!"

Curtis Walker glanced around, looking for the face of the person calling him. He recognized the voice, but for the life of him, he couldn't place it. The last few hours had left him jittery and frustrated, making it damn near impossible to think about anything except his wife.

Lorrie.

God, baby, please be okay.

His chest hurt so much that it was difficult to breathe. His lungs felt ten times too small. As though a band was cinched tightly around his ribs, squeezing, suffocating.

Damn it.

He needed air. Needed ... something.

A firm hand touched his shoulder, and he focused long enough to realize his oldest son was standing at his side.

Shit. Where am I?

"Dad? You okay?"

No. No, he wasn't. Not even a little bit.

Then it all came back to him in a rush of noise and light mingling with the stench of disinfectant and disease. He was in the emergency room waiting area because they had taken Lorrie back for some tests. He remembered the nurse had kindly asked him to wait out here because he was a nervous wreck and he was making the doctor uneasy. At first, he'd considered arguing—for a brief moment, even throwing a punch at the surly doctor—but when he'd looked down at his wife, so pale, so weak, lying in that bed, her lips thin, eyes dim from the pain she was enduring, he had relented.

And yeah, damn it, he was a fucking nervous wreck. How could he not be? His wife was sick. Sicker than he'd ever seen her in her life, and he'd been by her side through plenty of illnesses over the past fifty plus years they'd been together.

"Where's Mom?" Travis asked, his tone gruff, his face a stony mask of concern.

Curtis met his oldest son's gaze, those hard, blue-gray eyes identical to his own. "Tests," he forced out, noticing that Travis's wife, Kylie, his husband, Gage, and their daughter, Kate, were with him.

"Dad, you need to sit down," Curtis's daughter-in-law stated firmly, her hand curling around his arm as she led him toward one of the empty chairs.

He hadn't even realized he was standing. *Shit.*

He needed to pull himself together.

Although he towered over Kylie by a solid foot, outweighed her by God only knew how much, it seemed she had more strength in her hand than he had in his entire body.

Lorrie.

"Breathe," Kylie stated delicately. "Just breathe."

Not so easy when there were ten tons of emotions sitting on his chest. Not knowing what was going on with Lorrie made it damn near impossible to function, but he forced himself to draw air into his lungs, exhaling slowly.

"Where're your brothers?" Curtis asked Travis, doing his best to clear the fog from his head.

"They're on the way. I called them as soon as I hung up with you. Did the doctor say anything before they sent you out here?"

Curtis shook his head. Hell, he couldn't remember half of what the doctor had said. "Something about infection..."

Travis's hand was once again on Curtis's shoulder, giving him comfort. "From the kidney stone?"

"They said that shouldn't have caused it." In layman's terms, the stone was gone, so technically it was no longer an issue.

Oh, God. Curtis put his hands on his face, tried to gather his composure, but it was futile. The riot of emotion was tearing him apart. He just needed to be by Lorrie's side. It was the one place on earth that he belonged, and they had sent him away. Banished him to the godforsaken waiting room.

He knew Lorrie would be fine on her own, but he wasn't so sure he'd be fine without her.

"Hey, Trav. Pop."

Curtis looked up to see more of his boys coming toward him. Ethan and his husband, Beau, along with Kaleb and his wife, Zoey. Not far behind were Sawyer and his wife, Kennedy. He knew the rest would be along shortly, especially if Travis had told them that their mother was sick.

"What sort of tests are they doing?" Kylie asked, her hand gently resting on his forearm.

"Blood tests and a CT scan." At least that was what he thought they'd said. He really wasn't sure.

"What happened?" Kennedy questioned.

Curtis sat up straight, gripped the arms of the chair, and took another deep breath. He tried to ignore the incessant pounding of his heart as he looked at his daughter-in-law, then around at the others. "She woke up this mornin', said she felt horrible. She couldn't eat, and if she tried, she couldn't hold anything down. Her temperature was one-oh-three..." God, she'd looked so pitiful. It had broken his heart to realize he couldn't do a damn thing to help her, either.

Ethan squatted down in front of Curtis, placing his hand on Curtis's knee. "When did this start?"

"When she went to bed last night, she said she didn't feel well. Thought maybe she was coming down with the flu."

"The flu?" Ethan frowned. "But she's been better since Friday?"

Curtis nodded. "For a bit, yes. Then this morning, her skin was kinda ashy. Finally, she told me to get her to the hospital." That was when he'd known it was bad. Lorrie hated hospitals, so for her to suggest it meant there was a serious problem.

"Be right back." Travis patted Curtis's shoulder, then headed over to the nurse's desk as more people moved toward him.

Braydon and Jessie, Brendon and Cheyenne, Zane and Vanessa. Now all his boys and their significant others were there, along with his nephew, Jared, and Jared's son, Derrick. Not far behind them, Curtis saw his sister, Maryanne, and her husband, Thomas.

Looked as though word had gotten out.

"I need to see her," Curtis mumbled to himself, not thinking about all the people who where there watching him lose his shit.

"You will," Kylie assured him. "Travis'll make sure of it."

"She'll be okay, Pop," Ethan said, his voice low. Curtis heard the concern in his boy's tone, though. He knew everyone was as worried as he was. Lorrie was the backbone of their family. Without her...

No, he wasn't going to think about that. She was going to be fine.

She *had* to be.

LORRIE WALKER FELT LIKE CRAP WARMED OVER. Her entire body hurt and she had no idea why. It was as though every fiber of her being was being pricked with tiny needles, then squeezed with pliers. She couldn't stop vomiting, either, but they'd given her something to help with that, or so they'd said. The only thing she wanted to do was sleep until she could wake up and be well again.

They'd been poking and prodding her for the past couple of hours in an attempt to figure out what was going on with her body, but no one seemed to know. And the worst of it was, they had sent Curtis out into the waiting room because he'd been looming over them, making the medical staff nervous. She hadn't wanted him to leave, but she knew it would be best for the doctors and for Curtis if he didn't have to sit and watch.

Now that the CT scan had been done and she'd given more blood than she'd thought she had in her veins, Lorrie was settled into the bed, and they had promised they would go get him, but twenty minutes had passed, and she could hardly keep her eyes open. Still no Curtis.

When the bubbly blond nurse walked in, Lorrie shifted her legs, trying to get comfortable. "Is my husband coming?"

"Oh, right. I'm so sorry, Mrs. Walker. I'll go get him in just a minute. You should probably get some rest in the meantime."

For most of her sixty-seven years, Lorrie had been described as kindhearted. Non-confrontational. Loving even. And yes, she was usually all of those things, including the easygoing woman everyone suspected her to be, but there were a few things in the world guaranteed to set her off. One surefire way was if someone messed with her boys. Another was when it was clear they were trying to keep her away from Curtis—or vice versa. At that point, the gloves came off and a different side of her came out. A side most people didn't want to see.

This nice young woman should've been warned. Too late now.

"You need to go get him," Lorrie said, keeping her tone as polite as she could while she breathed through the pain that was currently tearing apart her insides.

"We will, Mrs. Walker. Just close your eyes and rest."

Lorrie smiled, and based on the way the nurse was looking at her, she knew it wasn't a pleasant one. "I'm only gonna say this one time. And it's more of a warning for you than anything else. If my husband finds out that you're purposely keeping him away from me, the outcome is going to be unlike anything you've *ever* seen before."

And heaven help them all if her boys were out there, too.

The men in her life did not take kindly to someone attempting to keep her away from them. Especially Curtis.

The woman's smile faltered, her forehead creasing. "We understand, but—"

"No, I really don't think that you do." If she did, she wouldn't be standing there gawking at her.

"We thought it might be best if you got a little rest without him here."

Lorrie plastered a fake smile on her face. "I highly suggest you don't tell *him* that."

Lord have mercy. Was it that difficult to understand?

Thankfully, the nurse nodded and rushed out of the room. Within a couple of minutes, Curtis was walking in, his face hard, his beautiful blue-gray eyes reflecting the fear she'd expected to see in them. She hated that he worried so much, but the truth was, she was worried, too. Never had she felt like this before, and she couldn't even pinpoint exactly what the problem was. She hurt *everywhere.*

"What did they say?" Curtis asked, his voice deep but soft as he leaned over and kissed her forehead.

"Something about high white blood cell counts from the preliminary tests," she told him, trying to remember exactly what they'd said. She was having a hard time focusing as it was. Nodding toward the IV in her arm, she continued, "They've put me on antibiotics while they wait for more tests to come back."

Curtis eased into the chair beside her bed and rested his hand over hers.

"I'm so tired," she told him.

"I know, darlin'. Close your eyes and rest. I'm right here."

"You won't leave me?"

"Not in this lifetime."

Knowing he meant every word, Lorrie succumbed to sleep, instantly drifting off, knowing Curtis would keep her safe. Just as he always had, since that very first day...

Part One

"Love isn't something you find.
Love is something that finds you."
~ Loretta Young

One

I can't believe Daddy made me go over to the Walkers' place today. On my way over there, I hoped that no one would be home, and I could come back and tell him so. I didn't get that lucky.

Of all people, Curtis Walker answered the door. The nerve of that boy. If I didn't think he was cute, I would be really mad at him right now. Not that I like him. I'm still on the fence about that. He's… I don't know what he is. Stubborn, maybe?

When I got to his house, he was the last person I expected to see when the front door opened. I figured if anyone would answer when I knocked, it would be Carol, the lady who works for them.

I should probably mention that the Walkers aren't like the rest of us. Granite Creek is such a small town. We've got one school, one pharmacy, one gas station, a diner, and a tiny little grocery store. It's more of a farming community than a town, and it's no secret that people aren't rich here.

And then you've got the Walkers. Not only do they live in one of the nicest houses, they've got people who work for them, and I'm not talking about on their ranch. They have a housekeeper and a cook, while we have to do all the work ourselves. With so many people doing things for them, I'm surprised Curtis even knows how to answer the door.

That wasn't the worst, though. When he joined me on his porch, he nearly pushed me out of the way, not even saying he was sorry. Then again, he's a Walker, and everyone in Granite Creek knows that the Walkers are big shots. They're arrogant and rowdy, even mean sometimes. Especially Mr. Walker. But he's dead now, so at least I didn't have to talk to him. That would've been bad.

I heard that Mr. Walker's funeral was a big to-do with most of the people in town showing up to say good-bye even though no one really liked him. We didn't go, of course. Daddy didn't like Mr. Walker, and he makes sure everyone knows it. Which makes me wonder why Daddy wanted me to go over there in the first place. I heard him and Momma talking about Mr. Walker's death wishes. Something about land and money, I think. I tuned it out because Daddy is always talking about how hard it is that we don't have money and everyone else in town has more than we do.

I don't care about their money. It don't make no difference to me. Not that I can tell Momma or Daddy that. They wouldn't like it much. Maybe tomorrow I'll ask Mitch or Kathy why I had to be the one to go. They might know.

I'm actually writing in this notebook because of Curtis. Something tells me I should start writing down my thoughts. Maybe it'll be important one day, I don't know. What I do know is that I hope no one finds my new diary. I wouldn't want them to read any of it. I'll have to think of a good hiding place. ♥

Curtis

"CURTIS! JOSEPH! ONE OF YOU BOYS ANSWER the damn door!"

Curtis Walker frowned, his mother's intoxicated shriek grating on his nerves as he moved through the big, empty house, heading for the *damn door*. The Patsy Cline record she'd been playing nonstop skipped momentarily, then, unfortunately, found its groove again.

Although there were ten of them who lived there—well, technically eight now—for some reason, the place felt hollow these days. Aside from the depressing music drifting throughout, plus the numerous liquor bottles that had become decoration as of late, there was a void that had taken up residence.

Could've been because his father had died, or because his older brother, Gerald, was a year into his Army career, stationed elsewhere, or perhaps it was his mother's recently acquired drinking problem that was causing everyone to stay out of sight. Regardless, ever since Frank Walker Sr. had suffered a massive heart attack and gone and died on them just a couple of weeks back, Curtis's mother had been on a downward spiral, becoming more and more irritable with every passing day. To the point Curtis didn't want to be here, but he didn't have anywhere to go today, so here he was.

He had no clue where his brothers and sisters were, and he didn't much care. Still, he didn't understand why the hell Carol couldn't answer the damn door. She was the housekeeper. Wasn't that what they paid her to do? Or was Carol taking care of the little ones, keeping them a safe distance from Mary Elizabeth and the bottle of hooch she'd commandeered from God knew where?

"I'm comin'," he announced to the door when more knocks sounded.

Figuring it was another person bringing some foil-covered crap for them to eat now that his old man had kicked the bucket, Curtis steeled himself for an uncomfortable conversation. Not that he didn't miss the old bastard, but truth was, with Frank gone, life wasn't quite as bad as it had been. Even the little ones seemed less stressed.

A bottle crashed in the other room, jarring him momentarily. For a fraction of a second, he considered going to check on his mother, but thought better of it. She'd been drinking for the better part of the day, which meant she was close to passing out if they would leave her be.

Another knock had him gritting his teeth.

With a little more force than necessary, Curtis grabbed the doorknob, twisted, and then jerked it open, coming face to face with … air.

He glanced down and frowned, confused.

There, standing on his front porch, was the last person in the world he'd expected to see. Since most of the townsfolk had already been by—some more than once—he had figured the visitors would've stopped by now. But he suspected this blond-haired, blue-eyed girl wasn't here to bring them food. It wasn't a secret that her old man despised the Walkers. Still, he said, "If you've got a casserole, you can take it on back home. We don't need no more food."

Lorrie Jameson stared back at him as though he were speaking a foreign language.

He eyed her suspiciously, noticing her hands were empty. "You didn't bring food?"

She shook her head.

"Then what d'ya want?" he grumbled to the girl now glaring back at him as though he'd kicked her dog.

She still didn't answer.

"Come on, girl. You came to my house. What d'ya want?"

"I don't like you," she said haughtily, hands on her narrow hips as she pinned him in place. "I don't know why I even bothered."

That made him smile as he gave her a good once-over, starting at her poufy, golden-blond hair that sat atop her shoulders, and then slowly letting his gaze travel the length of her body. She was... She wasn't the typical girl who caught his eye, but he liked what he saw. She was on the short side, and not as filled out as he would've preferred, a tad bit too skinny, too, but as he let his gaze roam up toward her face once more, he paused to admire her great boobs. A little small but nice. He fleetingly wondered what she would look like in a bathing suit, instead of that boring yellow dress that hid most of her and hung past her knees. Yep. He definitely wanted to know what she'd look like in a bathing suit. One of those two-piece numbers.

"Quit lookin' at me like that," she hissed, her soft voice laced with venom, eyes glittering with what he could only assume was frustration. Or perhaps hatred.

Nonetheless, she was feisty. He liked that.

He let his eyes travel up to meet hers, and she wrinkled her nose up at him. A laugh rumbled up from his gut, spilling out of his mouth as he stepped outside before his mother could get all nosy and ask who it was.

"How'm I lookin' at you?" he asked, stepping right up to her, his much bigger body forcing her backward. Last time he'd been to the doctor, they'd told him he would be taller than his old man. That had been two years ago, and he'd succeeded last year after he'd turned sixteen, already six foot five. She had to have been a full ruler shorter than him. Maybe more.

Lorrie didn't answer, but the irritation remained in her eyes, intriguing him.

"Why're you here?" he asked, reverting to his original question as he moved over to the railing that surrounded his parents' ranch house. Well, it was now his mother's, he guessed.

As she watched him, he pulled out a pack of cigarettes and tapped one out, then put it between his lips.

"Because my daddy *told* me to come over here."

"To do what?" The cigarette bobbed when he asked.

Lorrie shrugged, watching as he pulled a lighter out of his pocket.

The way her little nose flared amused him. She didn't look at all happy to be there. Or maybe she didn't like the fact that he smoked.

"So your old man forced you to come over here?" Curtis lit his cigarette and inhaled.

"Yep."

"To see one of my sisters?"

"Nope."

"My mom?" He exhaled slowly.

"Uh-uh."

"My brother?" Curtis knew that she couldn't possibly want to see Gerald, because he was off in the Army. And he doubted she wanted to see Frank Jr. or Lisa or Maryanne because they were still little brats. But everyone knew his brother Joseph had a mad crush on Lorrie. They were almost the same age, he guessed.

"Wrong again."

"Then who? Me?" *Surely not.*

"Mm-hmm."

That didn't make any damn sense. "Well, what the hell for?"

"Didn't you hear me the first time? I. Don't. Know."

Although they went to the same school—Granite Creek, with a population of 470, had only one school—Curtis hadn't ever talked to Lorrie before. She was several grades beneath him. He'd sometimes had words with her older brother, Mitch, but never with anyone else in her family. And because their town was so small, he knew them all. He knew that Lorrie had two brothers and five sisters, the youngest only a few months old. He knew that her old man was a ranch hand at one of the places outside of town because he was too good to work for the Walkers, or so Curtis's father used to say. And he knew the old bastard had a heavy hand with his kids and that her momma was too timid and quiet, and she got knocked around quite a bit, too. Well, the last part was a rumor, but some of her bruises had been talked about before.

"How old are you?" he questioned curiously when it was clear she wasn't going to enlighten him.

"Why do you wanna know?" she snapped.

"It's a safe question, don't ya think? It ain't like I asked what color your panties are."

21

Lorrie's cheeks went from pink to red in a heartbeat, and it was in that moment that Curtis realized how pretty she was. Huh. Strange that he'd never noticed. Maybe not as pretty as Helen Jenkins, but she was definitely a close second. Then again, he didn't much like Helen because that girl wouldn't leave him alone.

"How old are *you*?" she countered, ignoring his question altogether.

"Sixteen," he said proudly. "But I'll be seventeen in a coupla weeks."

"Well, I just turned fourteen."

"Fourteen, huh?" If he hadn't already suspected she was the same age as Joseph, he never would've guessed. Lorrie Jameson definitely didn't look fourteen. Curtis grinned to himself, leaning against the railing, bracing himself with one hand while bringing his cigarette to his mouth with the other. "You're just a baby," he goaded before taking a drag.

"Quit teasin' me, Curtis Walker."

"If you don't want me teasin' you, why the hell'd you come over here?"

"Don't you swear at me!" Lorrie exclaimed. "And I told you. My daddy told me to."

"I heard you the first time," Curtis bit out. "But that don't make no sense. What for?"

Lorrie shrugged, but Curtis got the impression that she didn't want to tell him the truth. Or maybe, just maybe, she really didn't know.

LORRIE JAMESON DIDN'T KNOW HOW TO ANSWER Curtis's question because she honestly didn't know why Daddy had wanted her to come over. Rather than repeat herself, she shrugged her shoulders again. Although she'd asked him, Daddy hadn't explained his reason for wanting her to go visit the Walkers, but ever since Mr. Walker had died, he'd been insisting that she talk to Curtis. Why Curtis and not Joseph or David or even Daphne, she couldn't figure out. The only thing he'd said was that it wouldn't hurt for her to get to know him.

The thing was, Lorrie didn't want to get to know Curtis. Or any of the Walkers, in fact.

But when Daddy had threatened to get his belt (far more drastic an action than she'd been expecting), she'd known he was serious, so she'd promised him that she would go talk to him when she could.

And here she was, in an attempt to get this out of the way so she could move on with her life.

"Well, if you ain't got nothin' to say, I'm goin' inside," Curtis drawled, exhaling smoke as he spoke, his deep voice laced with irritation as he pushed off the rail.

"Fine. Go inside then." Lorrie turned to head down the steps, but Curtis stopped her with a hand on her arm.

"Hold on, girl," he grumbled, as though he hadn't expected her to hightail it out of there so fast.

"What?"

"You really don't know why you're here?" His gravelly voice was a little softer, his blue-gray eyes studying her face.

He really did have dreamy eyes. All the girls said so. Lorrie hadn't ever paid much attention, but his irises were a rich, smoky blue, and his eyes were ringed with long, dark lashes. His skin was smooth and tan from being out in the sun, but she couldn't see his hair because of the cowboy hat he wore all the time.

Finding herself unable to speak, Lorrie shook her head.

"But your old man wanted you to?"

"My daddy said I *had* to," she clarified. "Said if I didn't, I'd get a whoopin'."

"Well, that's just stupid," Curtis argued, then nodded toward the porch. "Sit down."

Confused, Lorrie plopped down on the top step. When Curtis sat down beside her, she moved over so that he wasn't too close. He took another drag on his cigarette, then flicked the butt into the dirt.

For some reason, she couldn't stop looking at him as he propped his elbows on his knees and stared out into the yard. She wasn't sure she'd ever been this close to him before. Sure, she'd seen him at school and she'd seen him at church, but never had she spoken to him.

"Why aren't you here to talk to Joseph? He's in your class, right?"

Lorrie didn't like Joseph Walker. Ever since the third grade, when he'd put bubble gum in her hair, she hadn't liked that boy.

"Yes," she answered. "He's in my class."

"So it makes more sense for you to come see him."

"No, it doesn't," she disputed, though yes, she had to agree, it kind of did.

"Yeah, it does."

"Curtis Walker, quit arguin' with me."

"If you don't want me to swear, and you don't want me to argue, then tell me why you're here," he insisted crudely, his gaze slamming into hers.

Without a second thought, Lorrie hopped to her feet and skipped down the stairs, furious that her daddy had said she had to come over here. Curtis Walker was impossible, which made the idea of talking to him stupid. Especially since she didn't know what she was supposed to say or do, and it was obvious he couldn't have an intelligent conversation.

"Hey! Don't go." Curtis's deep voice rumbled from somewhere behind her.

Lorrie waved over her head, refusing to turn around. She made it all the way to the end of his gravel drive before she realized he was following her.

"Leave me alone," she hollered.

"No way. You came over here to see me, I wanna know what about."

When Curtis's big hand touched her shoulder, she spun around to face him. "I told you. My daddy said I had to," she snapped.

"But he didn't say why?"

"No." *Why was this boy so dense?*

"So what're you gonna do now?" he asked, glaring down at her, his big body shielding the sun from her eyes.

As she stood there staring up at the boy who had infuriated her so, she noticed several things about him. One, he was tall. *Really* tall. Taller than his brothers. The top of her head didn't even reach his shoulder. He was big, but he was also skinny. Too skinny. Like he didn't eat enough food or something.

But still, he was cute with his dark hair and dreamy eyes. She even liked his nose, which was a little crooked on the bridge. Then, of course, there was a dimple that winked every now and then in his cheek.

"I'm gonna go home," she told him simply.

"What'll you tell your old man?"

"That I came over to your house and talked to you."

"What'll he say?"

Lorrie shrugged. "That all depends on why he wanted me to come over."

"Does your momma know you're over here?"

"Yes." Her mother had encouraged her to come over, as well. Said it wouldn't hurt for Lorrie to get to know the Walkers. But her mother *always* reinforced whatever her daddy said to do.

"She ain't worried about your virtue?" Curtis's grin was devilish.

Goose bumps broke out along her arms as she thought about the implications of his words. The kind that made her want to take a step closer to Curtis, although she remained right where she was. "Are *you* worried about my virtue?"

Curtis's full lips tilted into a smirk and Lorrie knew that look. It was the same way a lot of the boys at school had started to look at her once she'd started developing. Until now, she hadn't liked it when they looked at her like that. But for some reason, she didn't mind when Curtis did.

"Maybe." His voice was low, the reverberation racing across her skin.

Curtis Walker had a reputation. Everyone knew he was rough and rowdy, always had been. There were rumors about him. Lots of them. About how he liked all the girls and all the girls liked him. And he especially liked to go necking in his daddy's old farm truck down by the lake.

Lorrie didn't know whether any of that was true. But she knew he was cute and funny—apparently not all the time, though—and according to Helen Jenkins, he was a good kisser.

She didn't want to think about Curtis kissing Helen.

"Why don't we take a walk down to the creek," Curtis suggested.

"Why?"

"To talk," he said, still smirking.

"About what?"

"Hell if I know, girl. We'll figure it out as we go."

She stared blankly up at him, a battle brewing in her head. She should go home and get as far away from Curtis Walker as possible. She should tell Daddy that Curtis was mean to her, but that would be a lie. He was a little rough around the edges, sure, but he hadn't exactly been mean.

For some weird reason, her desire to leave was no longer as strong as it had been moments ago. Spending a little time with this boy wasn't necessarily a bad thing. After all, her daddy had urged her to.

Maybe they could talk. About what, though? They didn't really have much in common. They were from opposites sides of the railroad tracks. Literally. As it was, his family owned land in Granite Creek, and the Walker's ranch was definitely the biggest around. Her parents lived in a small house with barely enough rooms to put all the kids, which meant Lorrie had to share a room with two of her sisters. Their yard was small, and her daddy owned an old, beat-up truck that didn't start half the time. Complete opposites they were.

For some reason, that didn't put her off the way it seemed to put off her parents. She didn't care about Curtis's money, or the fancy cherry-red Chevy truck in the drive, or that he didn't have to wear clothes that his mother made for him, or even whether or not he had nice things in his house. None of that had ever mattered to her.

Still, there was something about him ... something Lorrie hadn't really noticed before. Perhaps it was the devilish twinkle in his eye or that smirk that made her insides quiver. When he was near, there was a strange flutter in her belly, and when he'd put his hand on her shoulder, a million little sparks had entered her body and flowed straight down to her toes. It was both exciting and scary.

The exciting part was now winning the battle over whether or not she should stay or go.

"Okay," she finally said.

"Okay, what?" Curtis frowned.

"Okay, I'll go down to the creek with you. To talk."

Curtis's devious smirk set loose a billion butterflies in her belly, but Lorrie ignored them—or tried to—as she started toward the creek, not waiting for him.

"Wha'd'ya wanna talk about?" he asked, falling into step beside her.

"I don't know." He'd been the one to suggest they talk.

"Fine. Tell me why you don't like my brother."

"Which one?" she asked, knowing good and well which brother, but not wanting to answer the question.

Curtis chuckled. "How many of 'em do you not like?"

Lorrie shrugged.

"Girl, you ain't makin' this easy."

"Maybe you're just not askin' the right questions," she countered.

He chuckled again, and Lorrie found she liked the sound of his laughter. She wasn't sure she'd ever heard him laugh before, not up close, anyway.

"Joseph," he said. "Why don't you like Joseph?"

"I like him just fine," she lied. Curtis growled, and she was the one now laughing. "Okay. I don't like him. He's not very nice."

"What'd he do? Maybe if it's bad enough, I'll take him out back and beat him up for it."

"That's not necessary," she told him, not sure if he was making fun of her or stating a fact. "And it was a long time ago."

"So, you *do* like him?"

"No," she answered quickly.

"But you like me?"

"I didn't say that, either." Lorrie focused her attention on the ground, keeping an eye out for snakes and such that slithered through the tall, dry grass.

"What'd I do to you?" he inquired.

"I don't know you," she admitted.

"But you want to?"

Lorrie looked up at him, meeting those smoky blue eyes. "Maybe."

Curtis nodded, his grin growing wider, but didn't say anything more as they trekked down to the creek.

As they neared the water, Lorrie spotted a coyote standing by the stream, its head cocked as it watched them. There was another up on the ridge behind it. She stopped for a moment, taking in the sight, admiring them. She'd seen plenty of coyotes in and around Granite Creek, but most of them were scraggly and small. These two were beautiful.

"I shoulda brought my shotgun," Curtis grumbled.

Lorrie put her hand on Curtis's arm when he went to move forward. "No, don't scare them away."

"You like coyotes?"

"I do." She wasn't sure what it was about them. Something majestic and beautiful that had fascinated her since she was little. "I think they should've named the town Coyote Ridge. Makes more sense than Granite Creek."

"You're a weird girl, you know that?"

Feeling a tad defensive, Lorrie turned to face him. "I am not."

Curtis was grinning again. "You've got a fire in you. I like that."

For some reason, that made her blush, her face heating as she stared up at this boy who she didn't like but did. The same boy she knew so little about but got the sense she shouldn't be around him any more than she had to. He was, after all, a Walker.

The only problem now was that she suddenly didn't want to be anywhere else.

Two

♥ Monday, October 8, 1962 ♥

If you woulda told me that Curtis Walker would carry my books to school, I woulda thought you were crazy. And if you woulda told me that I might actually like Curtis Walker, I woulda thought you needed to go to the loony bin for sure.

Today, both of those things happened. Curtis walked me to school, carrying my books (I still can't believe he carried my books!), and at the end of the day, he walked me home. At some point, I think I started to like him, even though I'm not sure I should. He's cute and he's fun to be around, and he has the dreamiest eyes. But besides that, he makes me feel like I always have a song playing inside me. I don't know if that makes sense, but I feel lighter when I'm with him.

Now, I just want to go to bed so I can wake up and see him again. ♥

PACING BACK AND FORTH ACROSS THE DIRT path, kicking rocks as he did, Curtis forced himself to wait a little while longer. School would be starting in a bit, but he knew Lorrie would be coming this way because Joseph had told him that she walked to school.

He remembered the conversation he'd had with Joseph last night, the one that had resulted in Joseph punching him, then Curtis punching him back. It was true, Joseph hadn't been at all pleased that Curtis had asked about Lorrie, but that didn't matter to him.

"Hey, you can't like Lorrie," Joseph spat.

"Why the hell not?"

"'Cause I like her."

"Why ain't you with her then?"

Joseph glared at him.

"She came over here to see me today. Not you."

"That ain't true," Joseph argued. "You just answered the door."

"Wrong. She told me so. Now tell me how she gets to school or I'll punch you again."

Joseph had finally caved. As far as Curtis was concerned, if his brother had really liked Lorrie, he would've staked his claim on her already.

Only then did it occur to him that Joseph could've been lying about her walking to school. Maybe Joseph was yanking his chain, sending him out here to look like an idiot. Squinting in the direction he expected Lorrie to come from, he contemplated his next move. If Joseph had been messing with him, Curtis was going to pay him back. With his fists.

Ever since yesterday, when Curtis had walked her home after they'd spent an hour down at the creek talking about nothing, really, he hadn't been able to stop thinking about her. Every single thought that flittered through his head was about her. Her pretty blue eyes. Her silky blond hair. Her smart-aleck mouth ... all of it. She was invading his brain. To the point he knew he had to see her again, and he couldn't wait until this afternoon.

Stopping, Curtis glanced in the direction of the school, then back toward where he expected Lorrie to appear. His breath hitched because there she was, walking his way, her head down as though she was lost in thought.

She looked pretty, even if her dress was not at all appealing. It was longer than the one from yesterday, and her arms were covered completely. Once again, he tried to imagine what she would look like in a bathing suit.

He watched her as she came closer, her eyes still focused on the ground in front of her.

Was she thinking about him? Had she thought about him at all since yesterday?

"Hey," he greeted when she neared.

Lorrie jumped, letting out a surprised shriek, her schoolbooks scattering on the dirt and grass around her. He rushed over, snatching them up one by one as she attempted to do the same.

"You scared me, Curtis Walker."

"Sorry," he said with a chuckle. "I thought you saw me."

"What're you doin' here?" Her tone was hesitant as she looked around, almost as though she feared someone might see them together.

"I wanted to walk you to school."

"I don't need help gettin' to school. I know the way."

That made him smile. "Didn't say you didn't."

Once they'd gathered all her things, Curtis stood. But when Lorrie tried to take the books from his hands, he held them out of her reach. "I'll give 'em to ya when we get to school."

"I can carry my own books," she insisted.

"I know you can." But he still didn't hand them to her.

Rather than let her continue to glare at him, Curtis started walking slowly, looking back at her until she started to follow. Finally, she inched her way forward, then fell in step with him.

"I don't know why you're here," Lorrie announced, her cheeks pink, as though she was embarrassed.

Curtis chuckled. "Then I guess we're even. I don't know why you were at my house yesterday."

"I don't, either."

"Did you ask your old man why he sent you over?"

"No."

"Are you gonna?"

"No."

Curtis couldn't stop grinning like a fool even though Lorrie was making this conversation as difficult as possible. That seemed to be a trend with her. He wanted to ask her a million questions, but he didn't even know where to start and doubted he would get any answers anyway. He decided to start simple.

"Do you always walk to school by yourself?"

Lorrie shook her head. "I usually walk with Kathy, but she's not feelin' good today."

Lucky him.

Unfortunately, their attempt at conversation was cut short when they arrived at the school a few minutes later. Before they stepped inside, Curtis handed Lorrie her books. "Can I walk you home this afternoon?"

Lorrie glanced around once again before meeting his eyes. "I don't think that's a good idea."

Curtis frowned, not understanding.

Rather than argue, because he'd already learned with Lorrie it would get him nowhere, he simply nodded his head and stepped out of her way.

And made the decision that he would be waiting for her after school whether she wanted him to or not.

LORRIE WASN'T SURE HOW SHE MADE IT through the school day. She'd been in a daze ever since Curtis had scared her that morning. Not only had she not seen him, she hadn't *expected* to see him, but it had been a nice surprise.

Except Lorrie wasn't the type to enjoy surprises. Usually.

And rightfully so.

Nothing good ever came from a surprise. At least not in her experience.

Because of who her father was and the fact that they didn't have any money, the kids made fun of her and her sisters. Her brothers, especially Mitch, didn't have to endure the comments and the pointing fingers because most of the kids were scared of him, but she hadn't been that lucky. It wasn't that they didn't like her, but they liked to pick on her about her clothes mostly. Sometimes they played pranks on her, too.

In fact, for most of the day, she'd been fighting her anxiety, fully expecting someone to tell her that this was all a joke. That Curtis Walker couldn't possibly want to walk her to school or carry her books or even talk to her. At one point, she'd even imagined the teacher telling her as much.

She'd never actually liked a boy before, but she'd seen some of the girls get teased when someone found out they liked one. She did not want to be that girl.

Hurrying out of the school, wondering if Curtis would be waiting for her even though she'd told him he shouldn't, Lorrie kept her head down as she always did. She rushed down the steps, then across the lawn, heading for the path that led to her house.

"Hey, Lorrie!"

Crap. She knew that voice, and she wished she could pretend she hadn't heard it, but it was too late. She'd been surprised enough to stop walking. Turning slowly, Lorrie found the source. Helen Jenkins, with her long brown hair flowing over her shoulders, was strutting toward her, hands on her curvy hips, the devil in her eye.

Maybe Helen was going to be the one to tell her all this was a big, elaborate joke. It wouldn't shock her if she did.

Lorrie had never liked Helen Jenkins. Not because she was the prettiest girl in school but because she *knew* she was and wanted to make sure everyone else knew it, too.

"Someone told me that you went to Curtis Walker's house yesterday," Helen said with a frown, tossing her hair over her shoulder and cocking her hip.

Rather than confirm or deny, Lorrie stared at Helen, keeping her expression neutral, waiting to hear what she had to say.

"So it's true?" Helen didn't appear happy with that answer, though she'd come to that conclusion on her own.

Again, Lorrie kept her mouth shut, hugging her books to her chest as she contemplated walking away.

"Well," Helen began with a huff, lowering her voice, "I should hope you know that Curtis is gonna be my boyfriend soon. Sandra heard him say that he was gonna ask me to go steady."

Lorrie didn't believe that for a minute, but she wasn't sure what made her doubt those words, so she didn't bother to argue. It wasn't in her nature to argue.

"And I'd appreciate if you wouldn't go to my future boyfriend's house. If you do it again, I'll…"

"You'll do what?"

The deep voice came from behind Helen, and when Helen spun around, Lorrie noticed that Curtis was standing there, staring back at her. She had no idea how long he'd been there, or how she hadn't seen him, but she assumed it was long enough to hear what Helen had said.

"Curtis," Helen whispered breathlessly. "Hey."

Curtis briefly glanced at Helen while Lorrie stood there like an idiot.

Please, please, please don't let them make fun of me.

Helen took a step closer, then put her hand on Curtis's arm. Lorrie wanted to smack her right upside the head.

Where did that come from?

"I was hopin' to find you," Helen said sweetly. "I thought maybe you'd wanna walk me home."

Funny. Helen didn't sound nearly as confident as when she'd been talking to Lorrie.

Curtis shrugged Helen's hand off. "I'm walkin' Lorrie home," he said frankly, as though it was the truth.

Lorrie was tempted to run the other way, and she wasn't even sure what she was running from. Curtis or Helen. Or both. Or neither.

"Come on, Lorrie," Curtis said, reaching out and taking her books from her hands before she even realized what he was doing. "Lemme walk you home."

Swallowing past the lump that had formed in her throat, Lorrie quickly glanced at Helen, noticing she was fuming. Lorrie was tempted to tell Curtis that she could walk home just fine without him, but she didn't want him anywhere near Helen Jenkins, so she kept the remark to herself. Then she did something she'd never done before, she flashed Helen an evil grin. It felt good, too.

A few minutes later, once they'd gotten far enough away that no one else could hear them, Lorrie glanced over at Curtis. "Is it true?"

"Is *what* true?" His eyes met hers.

"Are you gonna ask Helen Jenkins to go steady?"

He chuckled but didn't answer as he pulled his cigarettes out of his pocket.

"Why is that funny?" she snapped.

"Would I be walkin' you home if I wanted to go steady with Helen?"

No, she guessed not. "Well, she said Sandra told her that you were gonna ask her."

Curtis's grin tilted, a cigarette now dangling from between his lips, and she found she couldn't look away. "Don't believe everything you hear."

"So you're *not* gonna be her future boyfriend?"

"Lorrie!"

"What?" she asked, glancing over at him.

"Stop talkin' about Helen." He lit his cigarette and inhaled deeply.

"Why?"

"'Cause I don't wanna talk about her."

"What *do* you wanna talk about?" she implored.

"You."

"*Me?*"

"Why do you make that sound like such a crazy idea?" Smoke trickled from between his lips as he spoke.

She didn't know what to say to that, so she opted to stop talking altogether.

The rest of their walk was done in silence, so when they came up to her house, Lorrie didn't even know what to say to him. Thankfully, he handed over her schoolbooks, smiled that sheepish smile, and told her he'd see her in the morning because from now on, he was walking her to school.

"You don't have to do that," she told him.

"Oh, but I do."

"Why?" She was well and truly baffled by his matter-of-fact statement.

"Because, Lorrie Jameson, if I'm gonna be anyone's future boyfriend, I'm gonna be yours."

"*Me?*"

"Yes. *You.* I'm gonna find a way to win you over. No matter what it takes."

35

Curtis

With that, Curtis turned and walked away, leaving her completely stunned.

And more than a little happy.

Three

Curtis Walker is the best kisser in the world. Not that I have much to compare it to since he's the only boy I have ever kissed. He's also the only boy I ever want to kiss.

For his birthday, he said the only thing he wanted was to kiss me. I was hesitant at first, but then I let him. And as soon as he did, I didn't want him to stop. I can still feel how smooth his lips were against mine. I can still hear the rumble of his chest as he kissed me. That soft growling sound was so sexy. It was like I've seen in movies, only better. A lot better.

Oh, I almost forgot! After he kissed me, the best thing happened. Curtis asked me to go steady!! I still can't believe it, but I'm Curtis's girlfriend now. My tummy feels all fluttery just thinking about it. I don't know if I should tell anyone, though. I'm not sure what Momma and Daddy will say. I don't want them to tell me I can't see him, so for now, I think I'll keep the news to myself.

I can't wait to see him tomorrow. ♥

"HOW DOES IT FEEL TO BE SEVENTEEN?"

Lorrie's sweet tone had Curtis casting a sidelong glance her way. She was perched less than a foot away from him on the old fallen tree that had been stripped of its bark from weather and time. She looked so damn pretty, her golden hair falling down to her shoulders, that frilly white dress that she'd worn to church that morning hugging her curves.

He couldn't even understand how he'd ever thought Helen Jenkins was prettier than her. Lorrie was the prettiest girl he'd ever set eyes on.

"Not much different than sixteen, I don't guess." He found his voice was slightly rougher than usual. He attributed that to his hormones, which seemed to be out of whack when she was around.

For two solid weeks, he'd been going about his business as he always had, only now he felt as though he had purpose. This girl had waltzed into his life and sidetracked him to the point he hadn't spent any time with his friends or his family since that day she'd come to his door. And he didn't even care. The only person he wanted to spend time with was her.

Granted, Lorrie hadn't been quite as receptive to him as he was to her, but it did seem as though they'd established somewhat of a friendship during that time. Ever since he had laid it all on the line, letting her know he fully intended to win her over, she hadn't been quite so … combative. Granted, she still liked to argue with almost everything he said, but he found it cute.

"I can't imagine it does," she said. "Fourteen doesn't feel any different than thirteen, either, except…"

"Except what?"

Lorrie shook her head.

"Talk to me, girl."

Her cheeks turned pink. "Except, you know, I … like *you.*"

"Like me, huh?" He couldn't stop the grin from splitting his face.

Curtis continued to stare at her, trying to memorize everything. She wasn't wearing the little button-up sweater she'd had on earlier, and the dress she had on gave him an unobstructed view of the golden skin of her arms and a peek at her toned legs, something he found himself drawn to. He wanted to know if she was as soft as she looked, but he didn't dare touch her for fear of scaring her off. Which wasn't an easy feat. For the past couple of weeks, it was all he could think about. Not only did he want to touch her skin, he wanted to know how her lips would feel on his, her tongue moving against his.

His hormones were completely off-kilter. Sometimes he worried about how much he wanted her, all the things that he wanted to do to her. Truth be told, he'd never felt this way about a girl. Sure, he'd had plenty of fantasies about the girls at school— a few of them, anyway—but not the kind of fantasies he was having about Lorrie. He was sporting an erection damn near all day, every day.

If she knew what he was thinking when he looked at her, she would probably smack him right upside the head. He certainly wasn't a saint, nor did he pretend to be.

"If you could have anything in the world for your birthday," Lorrie asked, her blue eyes sparkling as she looked over at him, "what would it be?"

Her smile was so sweet, so shy.

Curtis considered that for a moment. Then he grinned. "A kiss," he said boldly.

"From who?" Lorrie looked confused, but he saw the way her cheeks turned pink again. She knew what he meant, but he liked her innocence.

"From you, of course."

"*Me*? Why me?" She sounded as though that were the most preposterous thing she'd ever heard.

One thing he'd learned about Lorrie was that she was incredibly sweet, probably a little too naïve. She was smart and pretty, but she didn't seem to realize that. He wasn't sure if that was her parents' doing or what. Whatever the reason, she was extremely reserved and equally innocent. Not as much as a couple of girls he knew, the kind who would slap a boy for looking at her too long. No, Lorrie wasn't quite that virtuous, but she definitely wasn't as forward as a lot of the girls. And maybe that was what he liked most about her.

"Have you ever kissed a boy, Lorrie?"

Her golden eyebrows darted downward. "No."

"Never?"

"Never," she confirmed.

"How come?"

More color highlighted her cheeks as she shrugged. "Never met a boy I wanted to kiss."

"What about me?"

Her glittering eyes darkened slightly as they slid down to his mouth, and Curtis instantly knew that she wanted to kiss him.

Just as he'd expected, she didn't answer him; instead, she turned the question back on him. "Have you ever kissed a girl?"

"Yep," he admitted truthfully, trying to keep the pride out of his tone.

"A lot of girls?"

"No." Curtis knew he couldn't say yes. That wouldn't get him anywhere. And the truth was he hadn't kissed but three or four. He'd kissed them, even had a few heated necking sessions in the backseat of his old man's car down by the lake, but again, he wasn't going to tell her that. Despite the rumors, he'd never gone all the way with a girl, either, though not for lack of trying.

"How many?"

Figuring Lorrie was not going to give up, Curtis knew he needed a distraction. Shifting, he turned so that he was facing her, straddling the tree trunk as he eased closer. The muscles in his stomach tightened as he closed the distance between them, the ache between his legs growing more insistent. He'd been ignoring his body's reaction to this girl as much as possible, but here, alone, so close … it was too much to bear.

"What're you doin'?" she asked breathlessly, lips pursed when he bumped her thigh with his knee.

"Will you let me kiss you, Lorrie?" He kept his eyes locked with hers, heard the slight hitch in her breath, saw the way her eyes widened. But she didn't say no.

Still, he needed her to say yes.

"Will you?" he repeated.

"You want to kiss me?"

"So badly," he admitted. He'd actually dreamed about kissing her, pulling her into his arms, feeling her slight body against his.

They remained like that for several painfully long seconds, neither of them looking away. His patience was running thin, his blood rushing violently through his veins, the urge to kiss her so great he could hardly contain himself.

But somehow he managed.

And when Lorrie didn't answer him, Curtis started to turn away, needing a minute to catch his breath and calm himself down. The last thing he wanted to do was rush Lorrie, but he needed some form of release, something to quench the undeniable thirst that consumed him when he was around her. He wasn't quite sure what it was about her, but he'd never felt this way around a girl before.

"Wait," she said quickly.

He turned back to face her, his hands fisted at his sides, fighting the urge to reach for her.

"You can kiss me, Curtis Walker."

Those were the sweetest words he'd ever heard.

Her eyes dropped to her lap. "But I don't know what to do."

Christ. This girl... She was so damned perfect for him. Sweet. So incredibly sweet. And innocent. Unlike the other girls, who followed him around and told him how much they liked him. She was the chase, and he found he craved that.

"I'll show you," he said simply.

With his patience at an all-time low, Curtis moved closer, wiping his sweaty hands on his jeans before he reached out and touched her arms, sliding his palms from her elbows up to her shoulders, his fingertips fluttering lightly over her smooth skin.

"So soft," he whispered. She was definitely as soft as she looked.

There was another hitch in her breath, but she didn't move away. She shivered, and he felt the goose bumps break out under his hands.

Leaning forward, Curtis pressed his lips to hers, applying the slightest amount of pressure, giving her a second to get used to him being so close. He would've pulled back, content with a chaste first kiss, but then Lorrie's hands came up to cup his face, and Curtis nearly lost every ounce of his self-control. He groaned low in his throat, wrapping his arms around her and pulling her to him almost roughly, their lips still touching as he settled her between his thighs. He wanted to slip his tongue into her mouth and feel hers, but he didn't dare.

Something told him that he had to go slow with Lorrie, even if it killed him.

And he had no doubt that it just might.

SITTING WITH CURTIS, DOWN BY THE WATER... It was the most relaxing thing in the world. Initially, when they'd first started coming down to the creek, Lorrie had been apprehensive. But that had been two weeks ago, and since that very first day, each day had gotten easier to be in his presence. In fact, she'd spent every waking moment that she was away from him wishing that she could see him, talk to him, listen to the deep rumble of his voice.

And now...

Curtis Walker was kissing her.

Her heart tumbled a couple of times in her chest as his lips pressed to hers. She couldn't stop herself from reaching for him, trying to rein in the crazy feelings now consuming her insides. She loved the way his lips felt, the way he tugged her closer, her legs hanging over his thigh, his arms banded around her body, holding her to him.

It was the closest they'd ever been, and still she wanted to be closer. Mostly, she wanted to keep on kissing him forever. More than she wanted her next breath. Since she'd never kissed a boy before, she'd known she had to tell him. Would he think she was a bad kisser? Would he make fun of her? Would he tell anyone else?

Her nerves were rioting as she sat there, her lips pressed gently to his, her hands cupping his face, waiting for him to pull back. But he didn't, and the sensations that assaulted her were far greater than anything she'd ever expected. There was a nervous flutter that had consumed her. It made her belly churn, her hands shake, her heart race. And there was an ever-present urge to climb his body simply to get closer.

His lips were warm and firm, not as soft as she'd thought they would be. When he cupped the back of her head and hugged her tighter, the breath whooshed out of her lungs, but that was the least of her worries, because she was so caught up in him, her body igniting in ways she'd only heard about, she couldn't think about anything but getting closer.

Of their own free will, her fingers slid into his silky hair, her palms moving against the slightly rough surface of his jaw. He was warm and he smelled so good. Like … Curtis.

Just when she thought he would pull back, Curtis's head shifted slightly, and his tongue caressed the seam of her lips. The action caught her by surprise, and she gasped, only to find his tongue sliding into her mouth, moving against hers. It was a strange sensation, but it was nice. Nicer than she'd imagined.

She could taste the sweetness of the gum he'd been chewing, which helped to mask the taste of cigarettes that was also there. She didn't mind it, actually. It was sexy.

Rather than pull away, Lorrie leaned into him, allowing Curtis to deepen the kiss. Their tongues mingled, sliding together effortlessly. The way he groaned, the rumble of his chest against her arms… It caused the butterflies in her belly to take flight.

Before she wanted it to end, Curtis pulled back, and he was staring down at her. He looked as dazed as she felt, but neither of them said anything, and her fear that she'd done something wrong began to take over. Right up until he smiled.

"That was the best birthday gift I've ever gotten," he whispered, his hands falling down to his sides as she leaned back.

Lorrie had no idea what to say to that, but she secretly hoped that he would kiss her again. His eyes raked over her face, briefly meeting hers before falling back to her lips.

"You wanna go steady?" Curtis blurted.

Lorrie couldn't hide her surprise, nor could she stop the face-splitting smile that took over. Without hesitation, she said, "Yes."

"Really?" It was Curtis's turn to be surprised, apparently.

"Did you think I'd say no?"

"I didn't know what you'd say."

Lorrie grinned to herself, her heart filled to overflowing as she looked at this boy who was now … well, technically, if they were going steady, that made Curtis Walker her boyfriend. She wasn't sure she'd ever been this happy in her entire life.

Four

It's true. Curtis Walker is the nicest, most wonderful boy I know. Even though we see each other every day, he doesn't act like it. He says he's just as excited to see me as I am to see him. Today, we went down to the creek, and he brought some blankets. Although it was cold, we curled up and talked for hours. He told me that he got a letter from his brother Gerald, who's in the Army. He seemed a little conflicted. I thought it would make him happy, but he said that Gerald really wants him to join the Army when he turns eighteen. He doesn't know if he wants to or not. But he did seem happy to hear from Gerald, and he said it made his momma happy, too.

Oh, and you won't believe it! Kathy got mad at me today. She told Momma and Daddy that Jeff Anderson wants to take her to the movie. They told her she couldn't go out with a boy because she's too young. She argued with them and said that it wasn't fair that I got to go out with Curtis. I thought they would say it was because I was fourteen, but no, they said I was allowed to see Curtis because he was a Walker. I don't know what they meant by that, but as long as they let me see Curtis, I don't really care.
♥

Curtis

Curtis keeps asking me if he can take me on a real date. I told him I don't need to go anywhere, that I'm happy just being with him. We go to get ice cream or root beer floats at the diner, and he has taken me to the library, so that feels like a real date to me. He said he wants to take me out and spend money on me, like at a real restaurant or the movie theater. He told me I'd really like the drive-in movies, too. It's nice of him to offer, but I like when we get to spend time alone. I like the way he kisses me, the way he makes me feel when he holds me in his arms. He told me I'll have to go on a date with him sooner or later.

Maybe. One day. ♥

Five

♥ Friday, February 8, 1963 ♥

Curtis took me on a date. A real one.

He said I didn't have a choice because it was an early Valentine's Day present, so I gave in and agreed. I got dressed up in my favorite church dress, and we went to the drive-in movie in Austin. I haven't been before. It was nice. I had a wonderful time. But honestly, I didn't pay much attention to the movie. I couldn't stop thinking about Curtis sitting so close to me and smelling so good. It felt different from when we're at the creek, but I don't know why that is. He makes me jittery, but in a good way. In a way that I want to experience over and over again.

I think he wants to go all the way with me. Every time he kisses me, his hands start to wander. Sometimes I think I like it more than I'm supposed to. Other times I get nervous and he stops. I don't think I'm ready for that yet. I mean, I love him and I like kissing him (I wish I could kiss him forever), I even enjoy his touch on my skin, but I'm confused by the way he makes me feel. I don't know if it's normal to have all these feelings inside me. Everyone (teachers, Momma, the pastor) says that sex before marriage is wrong, but what Curtis makes me feel doesn't feel wrong. But I still don't think I'm ready. Not yet. ♥

CURTIS COULD STILL REMEMBER THAT FIRST KISS he'd shared with Lorrie down by the creek all those months ago. It had been the first of many. For five months, they'd been going down to the creek, talking and necking, sometimes sitting for hours, always touching, trying to get close, but not too close. A few times, he'd even kissed her in the barn when she had helped him with some of his chores.

But the kissing was as far as they'd gotten, and Curtis was getting antsy. Every second he spent with her was undoubtedly the best moments of his life, but they were also the most painful. Physically, anyway. His body wasn't on the same page as his brain. His balls ached so damn bad sometimes that the only thing he could do was rub one out to relieve some of the tension.

He refused to take things further with Lorrie even though he dreamed about slipping his hand up her shirt, touching her bare breast, tasting her taut nipple. He wanted to push his fingers into her panties and make her feel good, listen to her raspy voice when she said his name. And he wanted her to touch him in return, to feel her soft, smooth fingers running over every inch of his body. He'd gone so far as to imagine sliding deep inside her body. He wanted to kiss every inch of her, listen to her moan and whimper and cry out his name as he did. As a matter of fact, he spent far too much time thinking about it. Hell, it was the only thing he dreamed about. And thoughts like that were the reason he was masturbating every night. Sometimes twice a day, yet the relief was always short-lived.

It was safe to say, she was killing him slowly.

So many months had passed since that first kiss on his seventeenth birthday, and Curtis wasn't sure how he was going to survive much longer. And though they'd kissed for hours and hours since then, that was the extent of their time together. They needed to do something else, something that would take his mind off all the things he wanted to do to her. He had yet to take her on a real date, one that required them to leave Granite Creek, mainly because she said she didn't want to, but tonight he intended to remedy that.

"Where d'ya think you're goin'?" his mother slurred when he walked into the living room to find her sitting in the dark, a bottle in her hand.

"Out," he told her.

"Where?"

"Doesn't matter." Wasn't as though she'd remember even if he told her.

"You can't take the truck."

"I'm takin' the truck," he insisted, keeping his tone firm.

"You're just like your father," Mary Elizabeth screamed. "Always doin' exactly what you wanna do. Leavin' me all alone." A sob escaped her, but Curtis didn't say anything.

Never did she commend him for doing all the chores, for keeping up with the horses, for taking care of the ranch now that his dad was gone. Not once had she had an ounce of concern for that. He feared that if it were up to her, Mary Elizabeth would lose the ranch and the house and all the land that had belonged to the Walkers for generations.

Curtis wasn't going to allow that to happen. Unfortunately, since Gerald was off in the Army, he was the second oldest, so all of the responsibility fell on him. Every now and then, he could get Joseph or David to help, but they always wanted to bitch and moan, so he found it easier to do it all himself. Somehow, he'd managed to keep things moving, to keep the hired hands working, but he wasn't sure how much longer he'd be able to do it alone.

Thankfully, his old man had been insistent that he learn what it meant to be a rancher, ever since Curtis was little. It meant long days, that was what it meant. Since his father had died, he'd busted his ass through the cold winter months, trying to keep everything running smoothly. Trying to balance that and school. It meant he got up every morning and did chores before school, then came home and did more as soon as he walked Lorrie home. All while his mother hadn't lifted a finger.

He understood that she was sad. He didn't blame her for all the tears she had shed since Frank had died. But he knew, at some point, she had to pick herself up and move on. Life wasn't going to wait for her.

So no, Curtis wasn't going to allow her to tell him what he could or couldn't do.

"When will you be back, at least?" she grumbled from the dark.

"After the movie." He was taking Lorrie to a drive-in movie for the first time—*her* first time—and the thought of being alone in the truck in the dark made his jeans tighten. "Don't wait up."

Leaving his mother with her booze, Curtis grabbed the car keys off the wall and headed out the door, eager to see Lorrie even though he'd seen her when he'd walked her home after school. It was getting harder and harder to be away from her. Curtis wanted to spend every waking moment with her, and he feared that when he graduated next year, things would only get more difficult for them.

Yet he didn't know how to fix that, but luckily he still had some time to figure it out.

FROM THE MOMENT CURTIS HAD KNOCKED ON her front door and talked to her father, Lorrie had been trying to hide the way her hands were shaking. As soon as she had mentioned that Curtis was taking her to a drive-in movie, her sister Celeste, who was only eleven, had been asking her a million questions, every one of those still pummeling her brain.

"Will you make out with him?"

"Do you think the windows will steam up?"

"Are you going to go all the way?"

"Do you love him?"

Lorrie wasn't even sure how her little sister knew what going all the way meant. Nor did she want to know.

Although Celeste seemed entirely too curious, Kathy was still a little peeved that Lorrie got to date and she didn't, but apparently she was more inquisitive than angry, because she'd urged Lorrie to answer.

Maybe.

She didn't know.

No, of course not.

Absolutely.

Lorrie didn't share the answers to any of those questions with her sisters. Except for the last one. She did love Curtis and she didn't care who knew. She loved him more than she loved anything in the world, and she wasn't even sure how she'd gotten to this point, but when she was around him, nothing else mattered. Nothing except him and the way it felt to be in his arms, to listen to his heartbeat against her ear, to hold his hand, to feel his mouth on hers. They talked about anything and everything, from what it was like growing up in Granite Creek to the fact that neither of them ever wanted to leave the small town. She had told him about how mean her father was, and in turn, Curtis had said his father wasn't as mean as people thought, but he had been one to dole out punishments to keep the kids in line.

With every word, every kiss, she was falling in love with him a little bit more.

And now here they were, alone in his daddy's fancy truck on their very first date.

"Come here, darlin'," Curtis urged, sliding his arm over the back of the seat after he affixed the speaker to the window.

Lorrie moved closer, allowing her leg to press up against his as he placed a soft kiss to her temple. She loved when he did that. He was always so affectionate, and it made her feel good. It was new to her since her mother and father didn't kiss each other like that. Her daddy didn't even hug them or kiss them good night, and he never had. For the first time in her life, she felt ... loved.

She didn't know what the movie—*The Raven*, Curtis had said—they were seeing was about, nor did she care. It didn't matter that this was her first time at a drive-in theater, either. Her parents used to go from time to time, and she'd heard about it from when Mitch talked about his dates, but it was a new experience for her. Her family didn't have money, so the luxuries that other people had weren't available to her. They didn't have a television, no record player or radio, and they never got to go anywhere. For the most part, Lorrie felt as though she knew very little about anything outside of Granite Creek.

And still, the only thing she could think about was how close Curtis was, how good he smelled, how she enjoyed the warmth of his arm over her shoulder and the easy way his thumb grazed her skin from time to time.

"You warm enough?" he asked, his mouth close to her ear, his words loud enough to hear over the tinny sound coming from the speaker box in the window.

Not quite sure her voice would work, Lorrie nodded. Still, Curtis hugged her closer as she attempted to focus on the screen, her eyes inadvertently going to the windshield, wondering why the glass fogged up when people were in cars at the drive-in. That had her attention straying to other cars and trucks nearby. Were their windows fogged up? If so, what were they doing? Did she even want to know?

Finally, Lorrie managed to relax, leaning into Curtis and resting her head on his shoulder and her hand on his thigh as she tried to focus on the movie. She felt the muscle beneath her palm flex and relax, flex and relax. She wondered if he was as nervous as she was. This was the first time they'd been away from Granite Creek together.

Halfway through the movie, she was again having a difficult time paying attention. While her hand still rested on his leg, his arm around her shoulder, his other hand had moved to her thigh, gently grazing her skin right beneath the hem of her skirt. She liked the way it felt to have him touching her like that. Chill bumps broke out along her arms, her heart was beating as fast as a wild Mustang, and her breath was rushing in and out of her chest.

Although she knew it was wrong—according to her mother, girls were not to be touched like this before they were married—Lorrie didn't want Curtis to stop. So, when his lips caressed her neck, Lorrie turned her head, giving him better access. His hand inched a little higher on her thigh, and her legs moved apart without her meaning to.

His touch was … perfect. His rough fingers brushed over the sensitive skin of her inner thigh while his lips sucked on the skin of her neck.

Oh, God. She wanted more. She wanted him to touch her everywhere.

The thought came out of nowhere, shocking her that she could even think like that.

An involuntary moan escaped her, and embarrassment caused her entire body to flush. She tried to pull away, but Curtis stilled, holding her right where she was.

She was panting, her skin hot, a strange but not unpleasant ache between her legs that made her want more, although her brain was telling her she shouldn't.

"Shh," he mumbled. "It's okay, darlin'. Nothin's gonna happen. I promise. I just want to hold you."

God, she wanted that, too. And more. But she had no idea what was happening to her. How she could feel this way. So good and so ... dirty. Like she wasn't supposed to enjoy what he was doing to her. But she did. So much. Her body was hot from the inside out. Her skin craved his touch.

"I love you, Lorrie," Curtis whispered. "It's too soon, baby, I know."

Was it too soon? Yes. It was. It had to be, because that's what her momma had told her. Her brain knew it was too soon, but her body didn't seem to understand that. "Curtis, we ... can't."

"I know, darlin'. I'll never rush you, I promise."

And she knew he was telling the truth. His hand had stopped moving, his lips, as well. The only thing she felt was his warm breath against her neck.

"You want me to take you home?" he asked, clearly sensing her distress.

Lorrie nodded, still embarrassed by her reaction to him. She needed to go home, to be alone. She didn't understand why she felt like this or what it even meant. Whenever she was with Curtis, she felt as though a lightning storm had developed inside her body, currents of sensation moving through her, and she didn't know how to handle it. She wasn't supposed to feel like this, was she? These warring emotions were confusing her.

"All right, darlin'. Lemme get you home."

An anvil of disappointment landed on her chest, but at the same time, a sigh of relief escaped her.

Six

From the moment I opened my eyes this morning, I knew today was going to be different. Not necessarily in a good way, either. It was just an eerie feeling I had.

I was right.

Daddy went over to talk to Curtis today. I don't know what they talked about because I haven't seen Curtis yet. I'm not sure I'll ever be allowed to see him again. Daddy said I couldn't, but he won't tell me why.

I don't understand why he can't see that Curtis and I love each other. We haven't done anything wrong, so Daddy's out-of-the-blue anger scares me. I want to ask Momma why he's doing this, but I know she won't tell me. She always does what Daddy says, and she doesn't argue with him.

I didn't know it was possible for my heart to hurt this much. ♥

CURTIS WAS OUT IN THE BARN TENDING to the horses when he heard the sound of tires on gravel. He peeked out to see a familiar old Ford pulling up to the house. Grabbing his hat, he placed it on top of his head and then went to greet the visitor. His mother was passed out somewhere in the house, and Carol had taken Daphne, Frank Jr., Lisa, and Maryanne over to the park. He had no idea where David or Joseph were, but he figured David was probably planted in front of the television and Joseph was over at Helen Jenkins's house now that he was chasing after her instead of Lorrie.

Just like when he'd asked Joseph how Lorrie got to school, his brother hadn't been happy when Curtis had finally told him that Lorrie was officially his girl. There had been a moment when he'd thought they might throw down in the yard, which would've been a way to settle things for good, but it'd never come to that. Still, Curtis knew Joseph wasn't happy with the decision, but Curtis couldn't change the outcome. He didn't want to.

"Mr. Jameson," Curtis greeted Lorrie's father hesitantly as he approached the porch. "Can I help you, sir?"

Philip Jameson was an average-looking man whose time out in the brutal Texas heat showed on his weathered face. His usually light brown hair was gold from the sun and currently peeking out from under the straw hat he wore. Curtis didn't know how old Mr. Jameson was, but he couldn't have been but a few years younger than Curtis's old man before he'd died. If he had to guess, he'd say somewhere around thirty-seven, give or take a year. Still, he looked significantly older than that.

"I need to have a word with you, boy," Mr. Jameson growled.

Curtis frowned, moving closer. He'd been taught to respect his elders, and that was the only reason he didn't get defensive. Yet. "Yes, sir?"

He found it odd that, for the past year, Curtis had been seeing Lorrie nearly every single day, and never once had Mr. Jameson felt the need to have a talk. Not until Curtis had taken Lorrie to the drive-in movie back in February had he shown any interest at all. But even when Curtis had attempted to ask Mr. Jameson's permission to take her out that night, the man hadn't cared to talk to him, telling him to *do what he needed to do*. Whatever that meant.

And since then, they had probably said all of ten words to one another.

Curtis was definitely confused when it came to Mr. Jameson. The irritable old man acted as though he didn't like him, but he seemed adamant that Lorrie date him. Curtis figured there had to be a reason, but he didn't care enough to ask.

Not even now, when Mr. Jameson was standing less than two feet away, looking fired up.

Lorrie's father glanced around, then his hard gaze narrowed on Curtis once more. "I know you and Lorrie have been seein' each other for a while now."

"Yes, sir." Everyone knew that.

Mr. Jameson looked a little hesitant as he once again studied their surroundings before looking up at Curtis again.

"What are your intentions with my daughter?"

"Sir?" Curtis suddenly wondered if Lorrie was okay. He hadn't talked to her yet today, but he had intended to go to her house after he finished his chores. It would've been a hell of a lot easier to talk to her if she had a phone, but her father was apparently too cheap for that, so Curtis had to go see her anytime he wanted to talk.

"I don't want rumors to start about you and my daughter. I know you've been seein' her for almost a year, but I'm unclear as to what your intentions are."

Funny how Mr. Jameson hadn't thought to come to Curtis about that before now. However, it wouldn't have mattered, because Curtis didn't know what he was supposed to say. At the moment, his intention was to see her again. That was about as far as it went. "I'm not sure I understand, sir."

Mr. Jameson thrust his hands into the pockets of his overalls, cocked his head to the side, and frowned. "Let me put it this way. If you don't have any intention of marryin' my daughter…"

The brief pause, not to mention the reference to marriage, made Curtis uneasy, but he managed to keep his mouth shut.

"Then I don't want you seein' her no more."

Curtis managed to tamp down the rage that started a slow boil in his veins. He opted to keep his cool and to keep Mr. Jameson talking. "Marry her, sir? But she's only fifteen." In fact, she'd just celebrated her birthday a couple of weeks ago.

"I don't need you tellin' me how old she is."

Curtis shifted, unable to keep the defensiveness from his tone when he said, "Have I disrespected her in some way?"

Mr. Jameson didn't answer his question. "I know what your intentions are."

Well, that was strange since he'd just asked Curtis what they were. Since Curtis hadn't answered, he wasn't sure how Mr. Jameson knew. But Curtis wasn't an idiot. Mr. Jameson was talking out of both sides of his mouth. This didn't have a damn thing to do with Curtis's intentions; it had to do with what Mr. Jameson wanted.

"Do you plan on marryin' my daughter?"

Yep. And there it was. The second reference to marriage.

Before he could answer, Mr. Jameson continued, "Because if you don't, then you need to consider yesterday as the last time you see her."

That rage in his veins started bubbling faster, hotter.

Curtis hadn't mapped out his future, didn't quite know what he planned to do after high school other than to run his family's ranch. And okay, maybe he'd thought about marrying Lorrie, but it had only been a brief fantasy. She was too young to get married. She was too young to even understand what these feelings were that she was having. Last night, in his truck, when he'd taken her down to the lake, he'd heard the way she was breathing, known he'd excited her with barely a touch, but as soon as he'd tried to take things a little further, she had panicked. The same way she had panicked the first time at the drive-in movie and every time since. Months had passed, and yet she still wasn't ready for all the things Curtis had in mind for her, all the things a husband would want from a wife.

He wasn't in a big rush. He had every intention of making Lorrie his forever, and he didn't feel the need to push her. Sex wasn't the most important thing, but it was the defining line between married and not—in his mind, anyway.

So why Mr. Jameson was standing in his front yard giving him an ultimatum, he didn't really know.

The only thing he did know was that no man—didn't matter who they were—was going to keep him away from the girl he loved.

Not now.

Not ever.

"Do you love my daughter?"

"Yes, sir." He felt no need to hide his feelings for her.

"Do you plan on marryin' my girl?"

"Sir, I'm not sure that's a topic we should be discussin' right now."

"Why the hell not?" Mr. Jameson scowled. "You don't think you gotta ask my permission, boy? I'm her goddamn father."

Of course he had to ask the man's permission. That was how things were done where he was from. He just wasn't sure now was the time for him and Lorrie to get married. He was a senior in high school, for chrissakes. They had all the time in the world.

"You've got till the end of the day to figure it out, boy. If you ain't gonna ask my daughter to marry you, I expect you'll abide by my wishes and stay away from her."

Curtis wanted to tell the old bastard just what he thought of him, but he kept his mouth shut, fearful that he'd say the wrong thing and only make this situation worse. If that were possible.

Not that it mattered. No one would keep him from Lorrie. Not Mr. Jameson, not the sheriff. Not even his own mother. No one.

And he'd like to see them try.

"WHERE'D DADDY GO?" LORRIE TRIED TO SOUND aloof as she stepped into the kitchen, where her brother and sister were. Mitch and Kathy stopped talking, then turned to look at her.

She had overheard Momma and Daddy arguing a little while ago, and she'd been sure she had heard them mention Curtis's name, which was truly the only reason she was asking now. She didn't know why they would be talking about him. Rather than butt in where she didn't belong and risk getting a spanking for it, she had gone back to her bedroom and pretended to write in her diary, but her curiosity had gotten the best of her.

"Don't know," Mitch answered, his head lifting when they heard the baby crying.

"I heard him say he was goin' to talk to the Walkers."

"The Walkers?" she asked, hoping she sounded surprised. "You mean Curtis? What for?"

"Ain't none of my business," Mitch offered unhelpfully.

"Probably to find out when he's gonna marry you," Kathy teased.

"*Marry* me?" Lorrie was horrified by the idea. "Why would he wanna marry me?"

"'Cause he's seein' you all the time," Kathy answered. "That's what boys're supposed to do when they love a girl."

"But Mitch sees Janice all the time. And he loves her. That don't mean he's gonna marry her."

"Oh, I'm gonna marry her, all right." Mitch sounded sure of himself. "Just not till she's outta school."

Lorrie wouldn't be out of school for a couple more years, and Curtis wouldn't graduate until the end of this school year. There was no way he could marry her.

Before she could say as much, the front door slammed, and she heard her father's booming voice calling for her.

With trepidation curling in her belly, she went to meet him in the living room. "Yes, sir?"

"You ain't never allowed to see that boy again," he announced, his voice as hard as she'd ever heard it.

"What boy?" she asked, knowing exactly who he was talking about, but wanting an explanation.

"That Walker boy. He's good for nothin', and he ain't gonna ever make an honest woman outta you. So from now on, you ain't allowed to see him."

An honest woman out of her? No one said that anymore. "But, Daddy! That's not fair!"

"Life ain't fair. Get over it."

Lorrie couldn't help it, she burst into tears, her heart ripping in half right in her chest. The thought of never being able to see Curtis again was more than she could bear. Without waiting for him to dismiss her, Lorrie ran to her room and slammed the door, momentarily scared that he would come in with his belt and punish her for being disrespectful.

She didn't relish the idea of a spanking, but she would've endured a million of them if it meant she could still see Curtis.

Sobbing uncontrollably, Lorrie flopped onto her bed and pulled her pillow to her chest, trying to keep the cracked and brittle pieces of her heart from escaping. It felt as though someone had filled her chest with broken glass, the pain suffocating her. Sobs tore through her, making her hiccup as she gasped for air.

Daddy couldn't do this. He couldn't keep her away from Curtis.

What had he said to Curtis? Had he insisted that Curtis marry her? Was that what this was about? And why would he? Why would her daddy want her to get married when she was still a kid? It didn't make any sense.

Closing her eyes, Lorrie gave in to exhaustion, tears streaming down her face.

It was dark when Lorrie opened her eyes. She wasn't sure what woke her, but she didn't move from where she was. Wasn't even sure she could. Her whole body hurt from crying most of the day.

Then she heard it. Something tapped against her window.

Scrambling out of bed, she tiptoed across the room, pulled back the curtain, and peered out into the night. Since they didn't have an air conditioner, Momma always left the windows open, which allowed Lorrie to stick her head out.

"Psst."

Lorrie searched for the sound and looked down at the hedges that lined the edge of the house to see Curtis hunched beneath the window behind them.

"I need to talk to you," he said in a rough whisper.

Lorrie turned and glanced back in the room. She had no idea what time it was, but it must've been really late. It was just as dark inside, but she could make out Kathy's and Celeste's forms in their beds asleep.

Peering down at herself, she realized she was still wearing her clothes from that morning. She looked out the window again, then back into the room. She knew her sisters wouldn't tell on her if they woke up to find her gone, so she was safe there. The only thing she could hope was that Momma didn't come in to check on her. Not that she ever had before, but Lorrie had evidently missed dinner, so she might.

Without contemplating what might happen if she got caught, Lorrie slipped one foot outside and eased over the windowsill. Curtis wrapped his arms around her waist and helped her to the ground, then took her hand, and they ran from the house, heading toward the tree line that separated her parents' yard from the neighbors'.

Once they were far enough away that no one could hear them, Curtis stopped. Lorrie was out of breath, but apparently she didn't need to talk, because Curtis had pulled her into his arms, holding her tightly against his body.

She allowed the warmth of him to infuse her for a few minutes while she caught her breath and her heart started beating normally. When she tried to pull back, Curtis wouldn't release her, his lips brushing over her cheek.

"I love you, Lorrie. With my whole heart."

She wasn't sure why he was professing his love for her. She already knew how he felt. He'd told her a million times, the same as she'd told him.

"I can't stay away from you," he said softly.

Lorrie managed to put a little space between them and stared up into his handsome face. "I don't want you to stay away."

She honestly couldn't think of a worse hell than living without Curtis.

Curtis cupped her head, his gaze locked on her face. She could see his eyes thanks to the bright white glow from the moon, and what she saw in them scared her. There was a sadness that she could feel piercing her heart.

"What's wrong?" she asked, not really sure she wanted an answer.

"Do you love me, Lorrie?"

The pain in his voice mirrored the pain she could see in his eyes. "Yes," she said hurriedly. "More than anything."

"Enough to marry me?"

Lorrie took a step back, breaking his hold on her. "Did my daddy come see you today?"

Curtis nodded, but he didn't move.

"What did he say?"

Curtis didn't answer.

"Did he tell you to marry me?"

His terse nod broke her heart.

"Or what?"

"Or we can't see each other," he said on a rough exhale.

Lorrie's heart broke all over again. Her father really was trying to force Curtis to marry her.

How could he do that?

Why?

Why would he do that?

Seven

CURTIS HAD NEVER FELT THIS MUCH RAW emotion before. Not even when he'd found out his old man was dead. Then again, he'd never felt anything like the love he felt for Lorrie. It was physical in the sense he was consumed by it. His chest always felt full, as though his feelings were too much to fit inside him, growing bigger every time he saw her, until now, when he thought his chest might actually explode.

As he stood in the trees, listening to the sound of the wind through the dry branches combined with Lorrie's ragged breathing, he was consumed by everything.

Love.

Anger.

Desire.

Fear.

It swirled inside of him until he wasn't sure which was most prevalent.

The anger was directed at Lorrie's father for putting them in this position. Marrying this girl wasn't the problem. He would marry her tomorrow if she would say yes. But he wasn't sure she would say yes, and that was what terrified him. If he asked her now, she would think he was only doing it because her father had forced him to. And that was partly true. He was willing to do whatever he had to in order to make sure Lorrie wasn't taken from him.

"I don't understand," Lorrie said in a rush. "Why would he do that?"

Reaching for her, Curtis pulled her back into his arms, not wanting to let her go. He loved the smell of her hair, the smoothness of her fingers when they snuck up the back of his shirt, the crush of her breasts against his chest. He wanted to kiss her, to lay her down on the ground right here and show her how much he loved her, how much she meant to him. He wanted to make love to her a million times, to let her feel every part of him and know that there wasn't an inch of him that wasn't in love with her.

Cradling the back of her head, he held her against him, briefly wondering if she could hear the erratic beat of his heart. The fear was making his blood pump harder.

Fear that she wouldn't believe that he wanted to marry her and not because of her father.

Fear that he would never see her again.

Fear that if he didn't marry her, she would move on and end up falling in love with someone else.

The last thought was what had him tightening his hold on her, his palm cradling the back of her head perfectly as he held it to his chest.

"I love you," he whispered. "God, Lorrie. I love you more than anything. I need you. I can't imagine my life without you in it."

"Daddy can't keep us apart," she said adamantly. "He just can't do it."

But he could, and that was what terrified Curtis. "I'll be eighteen in a coupla months, Lorrie. Technically, he can keep us apart then. I'm not willin' to take that chance."

Lorrie pulled back enough to look up at him. "What are you saying?"

It was now or never.

"I'm sayin' I wanna marry you."

When she started to pull away, he kept his arms banded around her.

"Wait," he pleaded. "Let me explain."

Lorrie shook her head. "There's nothin' to explain. We're too young to get married, Curtis. And I don't want you to marry me 'cause my daddy told you to."

Curtis released her but cupped her face with his hands, forcing her to look up at him. "From the day I met you, I knew you would be my girl, Lorrie. You captivated me with your pretty blue eyes and your sassy little mouth. Even though you irritated me at the same time, it was the greatest feeling in the world. I knew you would be my girl forever and a day." He took a breath. "No man is gonna force me to do anything I don't wanna do. But more than that, no man is gonna take you away from me. You hear me? Do you understand what I'm tellin' you? I love you. With every breath I take. I would be honored if you'd be my wife."

Her blue eyes were wide as a tear trickled down her cheek. Curtis knew she was having a hard time believing him, but he needed her to. He needed her to know that he would go to the ends of the earth for her.

"Before your old man came over to my house, I'd thought about marryin' you, sure. I don't know what tomorrow's gonna bring. You've seen the newspapers. Bad things are happenin'. We're at war. My brother's over there fightin', and we don't even know if he'll ever come back. That could be me, Lorrie. When I turn eighteen, I'll be expected to go over there. It's all so messed up. I know that. You know that. But that don't mean I don't think about marryin' you all the damn time."

"I'm only fifteen, Curtis."

"That doesn't make a damn bit of difference to me." Although it really did. Curtis knew Lorrie wasn't ready for marriage. She wasn't ready to be in his bed, to sleep by his side, to allow him to slide inside her body. He needed that to quench his desperation for her, but he could and would wait for her.

What he wouldn't do was sit back and let anyone take her away from him.

LORRIE COULDN'T KEEP THE TEARS BACK. THEY were streaming down her face in rivers. Curtis's words had pierced her heart and broken the dam. It was no wonder she loved him so much. She knew in her heart that she would never find a man who would love her the way that Curtis did. Never find a man who would protect her, keep her safe. She could feel it deep inside, knew that he wasn't simply telling her these words because they sounded good.

Although he wasn't her lover yet, he was her best friend, the person she confided in, shared her hopes and dreams with. She couldn't imagine herself with any other man. Ever.

"I love you, Curtis Walker," she said between sobs.

"Then marry me. Be my wife. We'll go tomorrow. To the justice of the peace. I heard that Billy Elks did that. He went to the courthouse, and they married him that same day. He wasn't even eighteen, either. I don't wanna wait, Lorrie. I don't wanna spend another second away from you."

Lorrie wanted to tell him yes, but she wasn't sure she could. What would she do about school? Where would they live? She was only in high school. Neither of them were finished yet. They couldn't just quit going. She didn't *want* to quit going.

Curtis's thumbs brushed away the tears on her cheeks as he continued to cup her face and stare down at her.

"Whatever your worries, we'll work them out together. We can do this, Lorrie."

She forced a smile.

"I've always believed for every person there was only one love that would last a lifetime. I never understood quite what it meant until I met you, though. You're it for me, Lorrie. You *are* my love that lasts a lifetime."

Lorrie felt her chest tighten, and more tears began to fall.

How she'd ever gotten this lucky, she wasn't sure. Finding a man like Curtis, one who knew what to say to ease her mind, one who didn't make promises he didn't keep... It was a dream come true. She could consider herself blessed beyond measure if she could spend the rest of her life with him.

She wrapped her arms around Curtis and held him tightly as he hugged her back. She was scared, she couldn't deny that. Just like Curtis said, they didn't know what tomorrow would bring, but she knew that if her daddy tried to keep her away from Curtis, the only thing she'd have would be a broken heart.

At fifteen, she wasn't naïve. Even though she lived in a small town, didn't know a whole lot about what was going on outside of Granite Creek, her heart knew what it wanted. She had always dreamed about marrying a good man, a strong man. Settling down, raising children, laughing, loving. Curtis Walker could and would give her that, of that she had no doubt.

"I don't wanna quit school," she mumbled against his chest. Her mother had quit school to marry her daddy, and she didn't want to end up like her.

"You don't have to quit."

"Where will we live? We can't stay with your mother."

Technically they could, she knew, but she was grateful when he agreed they probably shouldn't.

"Where then?" she asked.

"We'll work it all out, darlin'. Me and you."

Lorrie nodded against his chest. "I'll marry you."

Curtis pulled back, cupping her head in his big hands once again. When she looked up into his face, he was grinning from ear to ear. It was that radiant smile that made her laugh, made her tears dry up as she realized what they were about to do.

Married.

Holy cow.

Lorrie was going to spend the rest of her life with him. They would get married, have babies, and spend a lifetime together, loving one another. It was as simple and as complicated as that.

"It's gonna be perfect, Lorrie. You wait and see."

"It already is," she whispered back.

It already is.

Eight

AFTER HELPING LORRIE BACK IN THROUGH HER window, Curtis had come home, but he'd never gone to sleep. He'd spent the rest of the night mapping out what needed to happen for him to marry Lorrie. The actual getting hitched part was easy. It was everything else that had to be worked out.

He didn't want to live with his alcoholic mother and his horde of brothers and sisters. That was no way for a married couple to start out their life together. Since he would be eighteen soon, he did have to think about what happened next. He could work on the ranch and help his mother that way, make enough to take care of Lorrie so that she could finish school. There was an old guesthouse on the property. Maybe he could fix it up, and they could stay there until he could buy her a house.

What if Lorrie didn't want to live on the ranch? What if she wanted a house in town? His family had money, he knew that, but he didn't actually have any of his own.

A knock on his bedroom door pulled him from his thoughts.

"What?" he hollered.

"Momma wants to talk to you," Frank Jr. called out.

Curtis glanced at the window, seeing the golden rays shining in. Only then did he realize that the sun had come up. He took one last drag on his cigarette and then stamped it out in the ashtray. Getting to his feet, he tossed his pencil on the paper he hadn't even written on and headed for the living room.

"In the kitchen," Mary Elizabeth announced.

Curtis stepped into the kitchen to see Mr. Jameson sitting at the table across from his mother. Dread instantly settled in his gut. Nothing good could come from that man showing up at his house.

"Mr. Jameson came to tell me the news."

"What news?"

"That you're plannin' to marry Lorrie," she added.

Lorrie must've said something. That was the only way he would know, because Curtis hadn't yet figured out how he was going to go over there and ask for the man's permission. Not after yesterday.

As though reading his mind, Mr. Jameson said, "You didn't think anyone heard you sneak her out her bedroom window?"

Fucking bastard. The man had eavesdropped on their conversation.

"Is it true?" Mary Elizabeth questioned.

"It's true," Curtis admitted, locking eyes with Mr. Jameson. "I plan to marry your daughter."

Mr. Jameson shook his head. "I'm sorry, son. I just can't let that happen." His tone was cool and collected, the complete opposite from yesterday, when he'd driven his ass onto Curtis's property and asked what his intentions were.

A rage unlike anything Curtis had ever known consumed him. For the first time in his life, he understood the hatred that had lived inside his father.

Sparing a glance at his mother, Curtis swallowed hard before facing off with Mr. Jameson once more. "You can't stop me."

"Curtis, she's only fifteen," Mary Elizabeth pleaded. "You can't marry her without Mr. Jameson's permission."

Curtis cocked his head. "That's strange. I had your permission yesterday."

"That was yesterday. I've changed my mind."

A vision of him with his hands wrapped around the old bastard's neck blinded him momentarily.

"Unless…"

Through a cloudy red haze, Curtis focused on Mr. Jameson once more. "Unless *what*?"

From the corner of his eye, Curtis noticed Mary Elizabeth's face fall, sadness consuming her.

Mr. Jameson looked at her. "It's my understandin' that the first of your sons to marry will inherit the Walker estate. Is that true?"

What?

The red haze intensified, and for the first time in his life, Curtis contemplated killing a man.

"It's true," Mary Elizabeth said, looking up at Curtis. "Curtis would inherit it all if he were to marry Lorrie."

What the hell did that have to do with anything? He wasn't going to marry Lorrie just so he'd get the Walker land. It was already his as far as he was concerned. And Gerald's. And Joseph's. And David's. And Frank Jr's.

Mr. Jameson was looking at him once more. "I'll give you my permission to marry Lorrie provided you pay me a sum equivalent to her worth."

Curtis's fury consumed him, his hands fisted at his sides, and an involuntary growl tore up from his chest. This sorry, good-for-nothing bastard wanted Curtis to *pay* him?

"It's only fair, son," Mr. Jameson went on to say as though this was a completely rational conversation. "If she marries you, that's one less set of hands I'll have to help out at home."

Not to mention one less mouth to feed, Curtis thought, but kept it to himself.

Bastard.

"And how much do you want?" Curtis dared to ask.

"Five thousand dollars," Mr. Jameson said smoothly, as though he had this all planned out.

"Five thousand? Are you outta your fuckin' mind?" That was more money than most people made in a year. Twice as much as what the folks in Granite Creek made.

"Is she not worth five thousand?" Mr. Jameson questioned.

"Lorrie's worth more than any amount of money," Curtis bellowed, angry that her own father could imply otherwise.

"Then I don't see that we'll have a problem."

Oh, they had a big fucking problem.

Curtis looked at his mother. For the first time, he realized she was sober. And she was crying. He had no idea what she was distraught about. She had to know that he would always take care of her. But did they have that kind of money? He knew the ranch was worth a lot, but that wasn't the same as cash.

When Mary Elizabeth looked up at him, her eyes were suddenly clear. She nodded her head once, a signal for him to agree to Mr. Jameson's demands. The action shocked him, but he couldn't bring himself to deal with that right now.

"Fine," he told Mr. Jameson. "But I'm marryin' her today. And if you do anything to stand in my way, you'll never see a penny. Now see yourself outta my house."

Mr. Jameson got to his feet. "I'll expect the money before you marry her. And don't think you can gyp me, boy. You pull a stunt, and you can bet your ass you'll never see her again. I'll send her away from here for as long as I have to. I'm sure there'll be another ol' boy willin' to take her off my hands eventually."

Curtis couldn't stop himself. He grabbed the front of Mr. Jameson's shirt, jerked him forward, then slammed him into the wall, getting right up in his face. The rage blinded him, but he managed to speak. "If I *ever* hear you disrespectin' Lorrie again, I'll put my fist through your face. I don't give a good goddamn who you are. She ain't a goddamn piece of property."

Mr. Jameson's eyes widened, a hint of fear swirling in the blue orbs, but he didn't say anything, his breath rushing in and out of his lungs. It took every ounce of control Curtis possessed to keep from beating the man to a pulp.

"Five thousand," Mr. Jameson snarled. "I'm takin' you at your word."

With barely restrained fury, Curtis managed to release Mr. Jameson's shirt, then he took a step back and allowed him to pass.

"I'll tell Lorrie to pack her things. That you'll be comin' for her today."

That he would.

Even if he didn't quite know how the hell he was going to tell her about this.

Or if he even should.

"Don't leave," Mary Elizabeth whispered when Curtis started to walk out of the room after hearing the front screen door slam.

Turning to his mother, Curtis tried to tamp down his anger. His mother wasn't responsible for what happened and he didn't want to take it out on her. He expected her to tell him to bring her a drink, or go check on the kids.

"Momma? Is everything okay?" Frank Jr. asked, peeking through the doorway.

"It's fine, honey," she assured him. "Now go on. I need to talk to your brother.

Frank Jr. nodded, then disappeared.

"Please sit down." His mother motioned to the chair that Mr. Jameson had just vacated.

Taking a deep breath, Curtis sat down, pulling his cigarettes from his pocket. He lit one up and tossed the pack on the table, figuring his mother would need one, too. As he inhaled and exhaled slowly, he finally managed to calm down some. Mary Elizabeth pulled an envelope from her lap and set it on the table in front of her.

Bloodshot eyes lifted to meet his.

"I know your father wasn't the nicest man in the world."

That was an understatement. The man was a world-class bastard.

"But I loved him." A sob tore from her chest and a tear trickled down her cheek. "I loved that man with all my heart."

Curtis had never doubted that. His old man hadn't been a people person, but the love Curtis had sensed between his mother and father had always been genuine.

"And he loved me, Curtis. And the most important thing was that I *knew* he loved me. He made sure I knew."

Not sure what to say, Curtis took a drag on his cigarette and nodded.

Mary Elizabeth slid her hand over the envelope briefly.

"It's hard without him here. Not because I need him to help with you kids or with the chores." Mary Elizabeth shook her head. "I know I haven't been the best mother lately. You've taken over everything since he passed. Just as I knew you would. I always knew I could depend on you to take care of us. There was never any doubt. I think your father knew it, too."

Now *that* he didn't believe.

"Mr. Jameson is right, though," she told him, taking a deep breath. "We'd always tried to keep it quiet, but your father's will outlines everything. The first of you boys to marry receives the land and the ranch." A small smile tilted the corners of her mouth. "He always believed that love would win, Curtis. He was a hard man to live with, but he loved furiously. I think to the point he often didn't know how to deal with it, how to express it appropriately."

"I don't wanna buy Lorrie," Curtis blurted. "Not for no amount of money in return. I don't care about the land or the ranch. She's the only thing I need."

"I understand that," she said kindly. "And Lorrie understands that, too. There's no way a girl can't see the love in your eyes. It's right there, Curtis. And since the day you started seein' her, I knew she was the one for you."

"Why would you agree to pay Mr. Jameson?" That was the one thing Curtis didn't understand.

Mary Elizabeth passed the envelope over to him, her fingers trembling. He saw that his name was scrawled across the front in his father's clumsy block letters. Curtis set his cigarette in the ashtray on the table and unwrapped the string that kept the envelope closed, then pulled out a single sheet of paper.

He glanced at his mother as he unfolded the paper, resting his forearms on the edge of the table.

Curtis,

I wish I could be there right now to see you reading this. I know that I'm not, because if I were, you would be hearing it directly from me, not reading the words on paper. Just know that I'm with you in spirit.

It has always been my wish that one of my boys would take what our ancestors have built with their own hands and continue to cultivate it and grow it for future generations of Walkers. Since you're reading this, it means you're the first of my boys who will marry, and the other letters I've written aren't necessary. Truth is, I've always known that you would be the best choice, but still, I left the decision up to fate. It is my wish that the first of my sons to marry will inherit what we've worked so hard to build.

What you don't know, and what most people don't know, is that the ranch is only a small portion of what we own. There's no doubt in my mind that you haven't agreed with the way that I've raised you kids, but just like all children, you only see what you want to see. I purposely kept things from you, but know that I've never had ill intentions.

Granite Creek belongs to the Walkers. Every inch of it. From the land that our ranch sits on to the land that surrounds it. Everything. The school, the diner, the Gas n' Go. Every tree, every flower, every patch of dirt. And though I've allowed people to use the land to build their businesses and to raise their families, some pay me a fee, others live on it for free, it still belongs to the Walkers. Therefore, on your wedding day, it is being passed down to you.

Curtis looked up at Mary Elizabeth to see her watching him. She must've read the question in his eyes, because she nodded. He turned his attention back to the letter.

I wish I could be there to see you marry the woman you will spend the rest of your days with. There is nothing better in this world than the love of a good woman. I was one of the lucky ones, the blessed ones. Even I can't deny that I've been a far better husband than I have been a father. I would've gone to the ends of the earth for your mother, and sometimes I did. She'll tell you if you ask. I've ensured that she will always be taken care of. She'll never want for anything, and she knows that.

Now, son, a marriage requires a lot of work. It's never one-sided and it never should be. The woman you choose to spend your life with holds your heart in her hands, and you trust her to do so. The opposite is also true. Take care of her, and in turn, she will take care of you.

I can't say it enough. I wish I were there to see this day, but since I'm not, take these words of wisdom with you. Love furiously, son. It's the only way to live.

Dad

When Curtis looked up at his mother, this time he saw more tears dripping down her cheeks. He felt his own tears welling in his eyes, a hot ball of emotion choking him. It felt as though his father were speaking to him from the grave.

"He loved you kids. All of you. He wasn't the greatest at showing it, but *that*" — she nodded toward the letter — "is proof that he knew what love was."

Curtis swallowed past the lump in his throat. "I love her," he said.

"I know you do. And you'll do as you said. You'll give Mr. Jameson the five thousand dollars, and you'll marry Lorrie. And you'll move forward knowing that you own the land his house sits on. What you choose to do with that knowledge is up to you. Your father never flaunted it. Never wanted people to know. More importantly, he never wanted you kids to know. He believed in hard work. In earning what you want."

That he had. And Curtis respected him more for it now.

His mother smiled. "And though people didn't much care for him, what they didn't know was that he always believed in giving back. The land that their houses and businesses sit on, the land that their children walk on to get to school, the land that their cattle graze on… It all belongs to the Walkers. And as with his father and his grandfather and all before them, no one flaunted it. Instead, they chose to do right by the town they've all called home."

Curtis only wished they'd seen that side of him. But it appeared he'd only allowed one person to see it. The love of his life.

"I want you to be there," he told his mother. "At the courthouse when we get married today."

His mother smiled softly. "I wouldn't miss it, Curtis. Wouldn't miss it for the world."

Nine

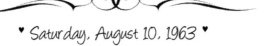

♥ Saturday, August 10, 1963 ♥

Me and Curtis are getting married!!!! Married! Today!

"I'M SO NERVOUS," LORRIE WHISPERED, HER BELLY fluttering as she stared at herself in the mirror.

She was getting married. *Today.*

"You look so pretty," Kathy told her as they sat in their bedroom, putting the finishing touches on Lorrie's hair. Celeste had been there with them, but she'd run outside to see if she could find flowers for Lorrie's bouquet. Although Lorrie had told her she didn't need one, Celeste had argued, insisting that she did.

When Lorrie had woken up that morning, she'd waited for Kathy to open her eyes so she could tell her the good news. Not long after Kathy had woken up, Celeste had, too. Then, the three of them had talked for almost an hour, whispering from beneath the blankets on Lorrie's bed, until Kathy had finally convinced her that she needed to tell Momma and Daddy. So, with her nerves rioting, she'd gone into the kitchen to find her parents sitting at the table, both of them smiling. She wasn't sure she'd ever seen them smiling that brightly before, but she didn't ask questions. The good news was that they were in a good mood, so she'd hoped her announcement wouldn't set her father off.

Unable to keep the words in, Lorrie had blurted that she was marrying Curtis. Her mother had nodded but quickly turned her attention to Linda, who was sitting in her lap, sucking her thumb. Her father had stared at her momentarily, then said, "Yes, you are."

It hadn't even registered that he'd seemed to already know; her excitement had blinded her to that initially. Lorrie still didn't know how their conversation had gone when Daddy had told Curtis that he had to marry her, but she was too happy to even care. The only thing that mattered was that she was marrying Curtis.

"Today," Daddy had said.

Today?

"That's right," Daddy had explained. "And it's time for you to go get ready. I already talked to Curtis. He'll be by to pick you up in a bit. Pack your stuff. A married girl can't live at home."

Talked to Curtis? How was that possible?

For a moment, Lorrie had been shocked. She wasn't sure how she'd gone from sneaking out, committing to marry Curtis, to actually getting married all in such a short period of time, but from the look in her father's eyes when he'd told her that, he'd been serious.

"Did you get all your stuff packed?" Kathy asked now, not meeting Lorrie's eyes in the mirror.

"I did." It was sad that everything she owned fit into a small suitcase, but she couldn't think about that due to the other pressing issues on her mind.

Like how she would get money for things she needed. Girl things. Things she was too embarrassed to talk to Curtis about.

Or how she would get more clothes when the ones she had got old and tattered. Her mother had made all her clothes up to this point, but luckily Lorrie had learned how to sew. Maybe she could make her own.

But most importantly, she wasn't sure where they would be living.

That was the scary part.

The thought of moving in with his mom and his brothers and sisters made her uneasy. What would they think of her sleeping in Curtis's bed? *Would* she be sleeping in Curtis's bed? That was what a wife was supposed to do, right?

Or would they live alone? And would that be worse? She wasn't sure how she was supposed to act around him. Was she supposed to cook his dinner? Wives did that, right? Did she have to clean his clothes? Momma handled all of that for Daddy.

A nervous flutter ripped through her again, making her hands shake.

"I'm gonna miss you," Kathy said.

She took a deep breath, swallowing her panic and forcing a smile. "I'm gonna see you at school, silly," Lorrie told her sister. She still wanted to go to school. Curtis had said she could.

"Lorrie!"

Her father's roar made her jump. Kathy ran to the window and pulled back the curtain.

"He's here," she muttered. "Curtis is here in his daddy's truck. Well, I guess it's not really his daddy's truck anymore."

No, it wasn't.

There was a knot of emotion lodged in her throat as she moved to the window and peeked out. Curtis had already climbed out of the truck and was walking up to the front door. He looked nice in his church clothes.

"He's so handsome," Kathy said wistfully. "You're so lucky, Lorrie."

That she was, but she knew there was so much more to Curtis than his good looks.

"Go!" Kathy giggled, throwing her arms around Lorrie. "Go get married."

"Yes. Okay." Lorrie laughed, but it sounded strangled. When Kathy released her, Lorrie grabbed the handle on her suitcase and lugged it toward the door, smiling back at her sister.

When she got to the living room, Celeste was the first to greet her, handing over a small bouquet of flowers she'd apparently picked herself.

"Thank you," she whispered to her sister as Celeste hugged her tightly.

When Celeste let go, Lorrie pivoted around to find Curtis standing in the doorway, his hat in his hand as he watched her. He smiled the moment their eyes met, and all of her nerves dissipated instantly. The next thing she knew, he had taken her suitcase from her.

"You look pretty," he said approvingly. "Ready?"

Lorrie nodded. When she looked back at her mother, she noticed Dorothy was crying. For a brief moment, she thought about running into her arms and hugging her, but her mother would frown on that.

"I've already signed the papers giving my consent," her father said, nodding toward Curtis.

That was it? Her father had signed papers and was just sending her on her way? Was that how it really worked?

"My mother is goin' to the courthouse with us," Curtis said, as though he could sense her tension. "The judge'll be there to expedite the marriage license, and he's agreed to marry us today."

"Okay." She didn't know what else to say. It hurt that her own parents weren't going to be there, but had she really expected them to?

"Take care of him, Lorrie. It's your job now."

Lorrie frowned as her father's words sank in.

She didn't like the fact that her father saw loving someone as a job. But that made sense now that she thought about it. Her parents loved each other; she knew they did. Even though they never acted like it. But her father did have the outlook that a woman was supposed to be at his beck and call.

As she glanced back at Kathy, Celeste, Linda, Rose, Adele, Mitch, and Bruce, Lorrie took a deep breath. Then she vowed right then and there that her husband and her children would always come first. They would always know exactly how she felt about them. Not for a single second would they ever wonder whether or not she loved them.

And with that parting thought, Lorrie took Curtis's hand and allowed him to lead her out of her parents' house and to her new life.

Part Two

"Love is composed of a single soul inhabiting two bodies."
~ Aristotle

Ten

Today is the day. The day we move out of Mrs. Walker's house. For the past two months, we've been living there, sleeping in separate bedrooms so that it wouldn't confuse Curtis's brothers and sisters. I haven't felt like I'm married yet. Things are still the same as before, except I no longer live with Momma and Daddy.

Now that we're moving into the guesthouse—just the two of us— I think it's going to feel a bit more real.

And that secretly scares me to death. ♥

THE PAST TWO MONTHS HAD BEEN HELL on Curtis. Not only because he'd spent a lot of time explaining to everyone they knew that he and Lorrie had gotten married, but also because it seemed every minute he wasn't at school, he was working. Whether it was doing the chores on the ranch that required his attention or the endless hours he'd spent fixing up the guesthouse so that he and Lorrie could move in there, every extra minute had been spent preparing for today.

But now all that hard work had paid off, and they were finally getting to move into the house.

Just the two of them.

"Are you sure it's ready to live in?" Lorrie asked as they packed the last of their things into the bed of his truck.

"I'm sure."

"What about a washer?" she asked.

He knew she was trying to come up with excuses because she was hesitant, but Curtis respected that. For the first two months of their marriage, they'd slept in separate rooms, in a house full of people. This would be an interesting transition. For both of them.

"It's bein' delivered on Monday."

"Should we wait till then?"

Curtis reached for his wife—he fucking loved the sound of that—pulling her against him on the far side of the truck, shielded from anyone's view.

He twisted their positions so that she was up against the truck, his body pressed to hers. Tilting her chin up, he stared down into her eyes, doing his best not to let his gaze drop to her mouth. "It's okay to be nervous, darlin', but we're movin' today."

"I'm not nervous," she retorted haughtily, reminding him of the first time she'd showed up on his front porch.

"Then what're you worried about?" She looked away, but he kept his finger beneath her chin. "Look at me, Lorrie."

Her eyes snapped back to his. "I'm not worried."

"Good." Not that he believed her. He leaned down and pressed a quick kiss to her lips before releasing her. "You ready?"

Lorrie glanced back at the house. "I should go say good-bye to everyone."

When she started toward the house, he grabbed her around the waist, lifting her off her feet and carrying her to the driver's side of the truck. "They're less than a minute away. They don't need you to say good-bye. Now scoot your cute little butt over so I can get in."

She did as he instructed, giggling softly, but he saw the way her hands were shaking.

After starting the truck, he put it in first gear and headed toward the small, two-bedroom, one-bath guesthouse that had once been used by some of the ranch hands before the small bunk house was built.

As he'd mentioned, less than a minute later, he was parked in front of the house. He glanced over at Lorrie. "I don't know about you, but I'm exhausted after that long drive."

She smacked his arm, this time laughing. The worry lines in her forehead finally smoothed out, but he doubted that would last for long.

"I'm gonna go in, get comfortable on the couch." He climbed out and peered into the truck. "You just lemme know if you need help with any of this stuff."

"Curtis Walker!" she huffed.

He laughed, then reached for her, pulling her out of the truck before tossing her over his shoulder and carrying her right into the house. She hadn't yet seen all the work he'd done, so he wanted to see her reaction before he started bringing their stuff in.

Setting her on her feet, he then backed away from her.

"What'd'ya think?"

Her eyes widened as she took it all in, then a small smile played on her lips. "It's … not bad."

"Not bad?" Curtis lunged for her, but Lorrie quickly evaded him, running into the kitchen and circling the table to get away from him. He nodded his head toward the stove. "You know how to use that thing, right?"

She glared at him, her cute little nose scrunching up.

"Kidding," he said quickly, pretending to go one way, then turning and grabbing her when she started to run away.

Trapping her between the wall and his body, he took her hands and linked their fingers, raising them above her head as he crushed his mouth to hers. And though he'd expected her to be a little hesitant, he was not expecting her to panic the way that she did. The way her eyes widened, her whole body shaking and her breathing raspy, he knew he'd pushed too far.

And that was his first clue that this … a house of their own … might not have been a good idea.

FREAKING OUT CERTAINLY WASN'T HER INTENTION, BUT for some reason, that was exactly what Lorrie did when Curtis pinned her to the wall. Although his mouth was warm and familiar, his hands gentle, her nerves had interrupted every signal from her brain, and she pulled back from him.

"Hey," Curtis whispered, releasing her hands and putting his arms around her. "I'm sorry, baby. I didn't mean to scare you."

Lorrie wrapped her arms around him and buried her face in his chest. "You didn't," she mumbled against his shirt. "I'm just a little nervous."

A lot nervous was more like it, but she knew she didn't need to explain that to him. He'd witnessed it firsthand.

"You know I'm not gonna push you, right?"

Clearly Curtis knew her too well if he was asking her that. "I know." And she did.

Didn't mean her brain was processing that information at the moment.

By the time they were ready for bed, Lorrie had pretty much made herself sick with worry. She knew that Curtis expected her to sleep in his bed, and she wanted to. She really did. But she wasn't ready for … sex. As much as she wanted to be ready, it didn't feel like the right time for her. And that meant that sleeping in his bed would mean she was being a tease, and she definitely did not want to be that.

"Come on," Curtis said, his tone soft as he got up from the couch.

They'd been sitting there for the last couple of hours, ever since they'd finished unloading their things and putting them in their proper place. It had seemed almost natural for both of them to be reading on separate ends of the couch since they didn't have a television, but what little reprieve she'd had from her nerves was now gone.

Knowing this was what was expected of her, Lorrie forced herself up from the couch, then took Curtis's hand when he held it out to her. She allowed him to lead her into their bedroom and right over to the new bed he'd bought for them. According to Curtis, sleeping in his old twin bed was not an option, no matter how close he wanted to be to her.

Swallowing hard, Lorrie wiped her sweaty palm on her pants when he released it.

"Get dressed for bed," he instructed.

Nodding, she did as she was told, retrieving one of her long nightgowns from her dresser, then heading to the bathroom to change. When she emerged, she found Curtis lying in the bed, propped up on a pillow with his hands tucked behind his head. Shirtless.

Her throat worked overtime as she tried to swallow the anxiety down.

"I'm dressed, darlin'. Only my shirt is gone."

She wasn't sure if knowing that helped or not.

Curtis patted the bed. "Come on."

It took a few seconds for her to convince her feet to move, but finally she managed to climb into bed, keeping a safe distance between them as she pulled the blankets up to her neck.

Curtis turned to face her, but he didn't attempt to get closer. "I'm not gonna force you to do anything you don't wanna do, Lorrie."

It sounded as though he was disappointed by her reaction, and she could see why. She was acting as though he was going to jump on her at the first opportunity. But she knew Curtis. He respected her; that she was certain of.

Still, this was significantly different than her sleeping in Gerald's old bedroom and Curtis sneaking into her room for a few minutes each night.

Which meant this was more like being married than a simple piece of paper that said they were.

Truth was, she'd thought she was fine with it until now. Thought she would be able to handle being Curtis Walker's wife in every sense of the word.

That definitely wasn't the case.

Now that it was a reality, she was just scared silly.

Eleven

Married life is not as glamorous as some probably think it is. In fact, it's not much different than not being married, except Curtis and I live under the same roof. Some of the girls at school say they envy me, others say some not-so-nice things, but I don't let it get to me. I'm happier than I've ever been in my life. Mostly.

Curtis received a letter from his brother Gerald today. It basically said that Curtis shouldn't wait to see if he gets drafted, but rather he needs to enlist. Since he graduated from high school back in May, it's a real possibility that he'll be forced to go in. This scares me more than anything, but I know how Curtis feels. He wants to defend his country and I respect that. He worries about Gerald and I understand that, too. Doesn't mean I like it.

Since we're living in the guesthouse behind his mother's house, it's a little bit lonely. Especially when Curtis is working on the ranch. I can't imagine what it'll be like if I have to be here without him if he goes away. When I asked him what he was going to do, he said he didn't know. I think he's going to sign up and not only because Gerald said he should.

I think he's thinking about it because of me.

Because of us.

Although we've been married for fifteen months now, we still haven't consummated the marriage. He keeps telling me that I'm not ready. Sometimes I agree with him, other times I don't. He's started telling me that I'm too young (which infuriates me), but I know arguing with him won't make a difference. And sometimes it's easier to think he's right. ♥

AS FAR AS CURTIS WAS CONCERNED, COMING home to see Lorrie every day rather than walking her to her parents' house seemed to be the only difference between being married and not being married. That and the fact that he was out of high school, and she had just started the new school year a couple months ago. Because he was working from sunup to sundown, Joseph was taking her to and from school with him, which was a relief.

Since the day they'd wed at the justice of the peace, they had lived together. He wouldn't lie and say it hadn't been easier when they had lived with his mother. More so than since they had moved into the small guesthouse almost thirteen months ago.

He had a wife. He had a house. He had a washing machine. And he had a shit ton of land. The latter was still odd to think about, but he couldn't seem to stop. Not only had his life changed because he'd become Lorrie's husband, he had also started working full time on the ranch and taken over the finances. Math was certainly not his strong suit, but his responsibility nonetheless, so he did what needed to be done.

It seemed he'd gone from being a relatively carefree kid to an adult way too fast. He wasn't regretting his decision, because he loved Lorrie. Loved her more than words could express, but up to this point had been hard. A lot harder than he'd thought it would be. His mother had warned him that he shouldn't have high expectations for the first few years. After all, Lorrie was still young. They both were. Mary Elizabeth had told him they should simply focus on growing up. The rest would come with time.

Except Curtis was beginning to have doubts. Doubts that he could make Lorrie truly happy. He had money, could buy her anything she wanted, but he knew Lorrie. She didn't want him to buy her things. Hell, it had taken an act of congress to convince her that they needed a new bed, that they couldn't sleep in the bed in his old bedroom. And when he had wanted to buy a television, she had put her foot down. Which, now that he thought about it, had been pretty damned cute.

"You got another letter from Gerald," Lorrie announced when she walked into the house. "Your mother asked me to give it to you."

Smiling, Curtis took the letter as he sat on the couch and stared at the wall.

"You okay?" she asked, coming to sit beside him.

Curtis put his arm around her shoulder and pulled her to his side. He loved the feel of her against him, but her proximity never failed to set his body on fire. He wanted to touch her so badly, wanted to make love to her the way a husband and a wife were supposed to. But she wasn't ready, and she'd made that abundantly clear, even if she didn't realize it.

The first few nights they'd spent in the house had been the worst, but she had finally seemed to relax. At that point, he had attempted to get a little closer, which had only set them back once again.

One night, she had even tried to convince him that they would be better off if she started sleeping on the couch. That had been his turn to put his foot down. Although he insisted that she sleep in their bed with him, Curtis had made the decision to hold off on sex until he knew she was capable of embracing it and him.

Abstaining was a hell of a lot harder than it sounded. Thankfully, Lorrie never asked why his showers were a little longer than necessary. And he didn't tell her.

"Are you gonna open it?"

Curtis glanced at the envelope in his hand. He knew what it was going to say. The same thing Gerald had been preaching to him about in every letter he'd received for the past six months. According to his older brother, it was time for him to do what was right, time for him to enlist.

Kissing Lorrie's temple, Curtis closed his eyes. He didn't necessarily want to go into the Army, or any branch of the military, for that matter. He didn't want to leave Lorrie, wasn't sure how he would survive without seeing her every day. But part of him knew that it would be for the best. He could sign up, go away, give her some time to grow up on her own, to enjoy still being a kid. Their marriage would still be intact, but it wouldn't be looming over her at ever turn.

Lorrie took the envelope from his hand and opened the flap, pulling out the thin sheet of paper and unfolding it before passing it over.

"I'll let you read it," she whispered, kissing his cheek before getting up and wandering into the kitchen.

With a heavy sigh, Curtis took the letter and peered down at the page.

Curtis,

I figure you're tired of hearing from me by now, but I'm not going to let that deter me. I talked to Momma the other day, and she told me that you and Lorrie are doing okay. I could tell by her voice that she's worried about the two of you, so I asked her why. Maybe it's none of my business, but I'm making it my business because you're my kid brother. I'm allowed to.

Curtis smiled. Leave it to Gerald to call him a kid.

I've mentioned it a hundred times, and I'm going to mention it again. You should enlist in the Army. Not only because you owe it to your country, but also because you owe it to yourself and to Lorrie. I understand the reason you married her—and I'm not saying it wasn't because you love her. Momma says that you do, and I believe her—but you have to keep in mind that she's still young. She just turned sixteen, right? She's still a kid, and she deserves to grow up before she's saddled with the responsibility of being a rancher's wife.

Curtis didn't appreciate his brother's high and mighty attitude, but he couldn't disagree. Even though he wanted to.

I'm going to give you a little advice. Don't wait for the draft. Don't wait to find out if you're going to be forced to serve for your country. That's a guaranteed two years, and more than likely you'll be in infantry. If you enlist, the chances of you seeing combat are significantly less. There are plenty of positions that you can sign up for. Doesn't mean you'll stay in the States, but at least you won't necessarily be in the infantry. Unless, of course, this is what you want.

What I'm trying to tell you, Curtis, is that you can give Lorrie time to grow up. If your love is as strong as you believe it is, it'll survive these years apart. It'll be good for you. Good for her. Please think about it.

~G

It was impossible for Curtis *not* to consider taking his brother's advice. He and Lorrie had only been married for a little over a year. Fifteen months in a lifetime was nothing, and yet it already seemed as though they'd set themselves up for failure. Curtis knew Lorrie hadn't been ready for marriage when they'd said I do, but he appreciated her love for him and the fact that she would do whatever it took to make him happy.

Setting the letter on his leg, Curtis leaned his head back and closed his eyes. And for the first time since the day he'd spoken to her on his mother's front porch, he knew that putting some space between them was the only way that this was going to work.

Which meant he had to do this. Even if it might just break her heart. And his.

WHEN MRS. WALKER HAD ASKED LORRIE TO give that letter to Curtis, she'd felt a band tighten around her heart. She'd known it was from Gerald, and she'd known what it was going to say. The same thing every letter from him had said since the day Gerald had learned that she and Curtis had married.

Gerald thought it would be best for Curtis to go into the service.

Lorrie didn't agree.

However, she had to admit that her feelings were entirely selfish. She didn't want Curtis to go away. She didn't want to have to spend her days without him. If he did go, where would that leave her? She couldn't live here by herself. She had no way to support herself. What if she had to quit school and go to work? Where would she work? What would she do? She knew how to type a little. Maybe she could do that.

As she stood in the kitchen, trying to give Curtis some privacy to read his letter, she watched him. He looked torn as he stared at the page. It broke her heart that he might be considering it, but she understood. And she also understood that it wouldn't be simply his willingness to fight for his country that would drive him away.

It was her.

It was them.

It was the fact that she was sixteen and they were married. She was still in high school, still merely a kid in so many ways, though she no longer felt like a kid.

She swallowed hard.

Regardless of his decision, she decided right then and there that she would support Curtis wholeheartedly. Whatever his decision, she would accept it, and she would make herself understand his reasons.

Because she loved him.

And nothing would ever change that.

Twelve

I don't know that I can find the words. We just heard that Gerald was shot. He's in the hospital, and they expect him to make a full recovery, but still. The thought of him so far from his family is what hurts most.

I know that Curtis has been trying to decide whether or not he would enlist, and I think this is going to push him to do it. Ever since he received the last letter from Gerald, I could sense that something was different. We've been growing apart, although we haven't really gotten close yet. Which is all my fault, I just know it.

Updated tonight

I knew it was coming, and yet I had hoped it wouldn't, but Curtis enlisted today. We had our first argument right before he left the house, and I knew it was coming as I sat in my bed and cried, waiting for him to come home.

Curtis

Curtis doesn't seem to know how long he will be gone before he gets to come home or where he will go, or if he does, he isn't telling me. He signed up for three years. Three!! I don't think I can live without him for that long. And if that wasn't bad enough, he nailed my heart to the wall when he told me it might even be more. I don't think I've cried this much in my entire life. I thought about pleading for him not to go, but I know that's selfish. He is doing this for me and everyone else.

I'm scared. Terrified, actually. I don't want to be away from him, but more importantly, I wouldn't be able to go on living if something bad happened to him. ♥

CURTIS HAD MADE THE HARDEST DECISION OF his life today. At least thus far.

As of this afternoon, he was officially enlisted in the Army.

He was still a little numb, but he knew it was the right thing to do. For him. For Lorrie. For their marriage. For... Well, those were what mattered most to him. He understood that the war with Vietnam was still underway, knew that it could get worse before it got better, but he wasn't looking forward to leaving his wife. It might be the right thing to do, it might be what they needed in order for their marriage to survive, but it still caused him a great deal of pain.

Three years.

That wasn't terrible, right?

In three years, Lorrie would be nineteen. She would be finished with school, so when he came back, they would spend the rest of their lives together, making a family, running the ranch. Being a soldier wasn't the worst thing in the world. It offered him an opportunity to acquire some skills he otherwise wouldn't be able to get.

"I'm gonna miss you so much," Lorrie sobbed, her head resting on his shoulder as they sat on the couch together.

"I know, darlin'," he whispered, cradling her head as she cried. "I'm gonna miss you, too." More than she would ever understand.

After he'd taken the necessary aptitude tests, the recruiting sergeant he'd met with had told him that he had a little more than a week until he would be shipped off to training. Nine days, to be exact. Nine days to get everything in order, to ensure that Lorrie would be taken care of while he was gone, to make sure his mother had what she needed in order to care for herself and all the kids plus keep an eye on his wife, along with ensuring that the ranch would be managed appropriately.

Nine days did not seem like a long enough time, but it also seemed like too long. He just wanted to get this over with. The sooner he was deployed, the faster he would come home.

At least it sounded good in theory.

Thirteen

I'm writing this through the tears that are still streaming down my face.

I saw Curtis off today. Mrs. Walker drove us to the location where Curtis got on a bus. I couldn't stop crying, but luckily she was with me, holding my hand after Curtis stepped out of sight. He has officially left for the Army. He said he'll be in training for almost ten weeks, but I don't know what that means. He doesn't know if he'll be back after that or if they'll send him somewhere right away. He seems to think that he'll be shipped off without the chance to come home. Sometimes I think that's what he wants. He said they are already talking about sending them to Germany. I don't want him to go that far away. I don't want him to go anywhere, actually. I want him to stay right here with me. That might make me a selfish person, but I don't care; it's how I feel. I love him. Please, God, keep him safe.

Oh, and Kathy told me today that Momma is pregnant again. They are going to have another baby. That makes nine. That means that Momma and Daddy will have more kids than Mrs. Walker does. She's got eight. One day, I hope to have that many kids. Sometimes I think about what it'll be like to have a baby with Curtis. It scares me a little, but it's the hope I'm going to cling to. ♥

Fourteen

~ 1965 ~

♥ Saturday, January 23, 1965 ♥

Sometimes I don't know how I make it through the day. It isn't easy without Curtis. I miss him terribly. I haven't heard from him at all, but he warned me that would happen. He said during training he didn't think he'd be able to make any phone calls, but he would try to send a letter. I haven't received anything yet.

I dream about him all the time, worry about him, but I know he's being careful. He promised to come back to me, and I have to keep believing that he will. I keep waiting for a letter from him. I'm desperate to hear from him.

In order to pass the time, I've been spending a lot of time with Mrs. Walker. She seems to be getting better every day and even goes some days without drinking at all. I'm trying to help Carol with the little kids when I'm not at school. Daphne helps a lot, too. She's twelve, but she acts like she's twenty. At least I have them to talk to. I have to keep myself occupied or I'll go stir crazy. Sometimes I wish I had let Curtis buy us a television. At least I'd have something to do.

Curtis

And every night, before I go to bed, I get down on my knees, and I pray that God will keep Curtis safe (and Gerald). I'm trying to be positive all the time. Mrs. Walker told me it isn't necessary, but it is. Really it is. ♥

January 28, 1965

Lorrie,

Hello, honey. God, I miss you. It hasn't been long since I've seen you, but even that short period of time feels like eternity.

It's been eight weeks since I got here. Eight weeks that I've spent getting my ass kicked into high gear by men who don't care that I'm tired or sore. The best part by far has been marksmanship, because I happen to be pretty damn handy with a gun. I won't lie, it has been hell, but it gets a little easier with every passing day. Easier in the sense that I'm actually being trained to do as I'm told. (Not easy for a Walker, most would say.)

I know you don't understand why I'm doing what I'm doing, and I get it. I do. Now that I'm in, unable to go home, unable to spend my days with you, I realize what a horrible mistake I've made. I thought about it for a whole year, and I kept trying to talk myself into it. I wish I would've listened to my true feelings.

Even though I doubt myself all the time, I know in the long run, it's the right thing to do. I have to believe that, and that's the only thing I continue to tell myself. It's my responsibility to ensure that you and our future children are safe.

I haven't spoken to Gerald, but I know he still believes in this, believes it is right. I still don't understand how he went back to work, as though he was never shot. Based on what I've heard, he could've gone home for good if he wanted to. Apparently he doesn't. I'm not sure what he finds so fascinating about military life, but I don't see it. Regardless, I'm here, and I will continue to be here until it's time for me to come home.

Just know that I love you and I think about you every minute of every day.

Curtis

Dear Curtis,

I received your letter today. I can't even begin to tell you how great it was to finally hear from you. Not quite the same as if I could hear your voice or see your face, but it was better than nothing.

I wish I could tell you that it didn't make me cry, but I would be lying. I cried. I cried like a baby. I miss you so much. My heart sometimes feels like it will explode because I miss you so much. I know I promised you that I wouldn't cry all the time, and hopefully I'll get to that point, but I'm not there yet.

School is good. At least it gives me something to do. And your brothers are trying to do all the chores, but they like to complain a lot. It makes me proud to think about how you handled everything on your own, without complaint. It proves how strong a man you are, and I love that about you.

Your mother has been great. She's very nice, always checking on me, making sure I have what I need. She asked me if I wanted to move into the big house with her and the kids. I told her I couldn't right now. I don't want to leave our little house. I can still picture you sitting on the couch, staring at the wall because there isn't a television for you to watch. It makes me smile.

Please write me back soon. I'm looking forward to the letters.

I love you!

Lorrie

♥ Tuesday, March 30, 1965 ♥

Kathy called today to let me know that Momma had the baby. I now have another brother. They named him Owen. I can't wait to see him, but I don't know when that might happen. I still haven't seen Momma or Daddy since I got married. They haven't come to see me or called me, either. Not even on my birthday or on Christmas. I know they have a phone now, because Kathy told me they did. Apparently, right after I got married, Daddy bought quite a few things. I think they've written me off completely, but I don't know why. If I'm honest, I try not to think about it too much. ♥

♥ Friday, May 7, 1965 ♥

Kathy and Celeste came over today after school to hang out. The only thing they wanted to talk about was the Beatles. The only thing I wanted to talk about was Curtis. They won. Mainly because Celeste has a bigger mouth than I do apparently. ♥

♥ Saturday, June 5, 1965 ♥

Mrs. Walker came to the house today. She said we needed to have a talk. I didn't know what it was about, but I couldn't tell her no. She told me that I needed to live my life as though Curtis was coming back tomorrow. Now that school is out for the summer, she said I can't mope around the house all the time, that I need to hang out with my friends or do something constructive. I don't want to do that, but I didn't tell her that. She also told me that it would be best if I moved into the main house with her. When she first asked months ago, I didn't want to. Now, I do. So I told her I would like that. I'm getting really lonely, and I know Curtis would be upset if he knew. ♥

June 15, 1965

Lorrie,

Hey, baby, I miss you so much! Thank you for the letters you have sent me over the last few months. I'm sorry that it has taken me so long to write back this time. There are a lot of things happening right now. We've been in Germany for nearly a month now. It's not as terrible as I thought it would be, but I still wish I was home with you. I never wanted to be a traveling man, so it takes a little getting used to. Me and a couple of guys have even left the base to check things out. I feel like a tourist, completely out of place, but it's a way to pass the time.

I talked to Momma the other day, and I wanted to hear your voice, but you weren't there to come to the phone. That's when Momma told me that she was gonna get you to move into the big house with her and the kids. I think this is a great idea. It means when I call, you'll be there so I can hear your voice. I don't like thinking about you sitting in that little house all by yourself. Unless, of course, I'm thinking about what we would be doing if I were there with you.

I miss you, baby. I miss you with every breath that I take, and I can't wait till I get to see your beautiful face again. When I get home, I plan to hold you in my arms and never let you go.

Hopefully this will make it to you by your birthday. I wish I could be there to celebrate it with you. Happy seventeenth birthday, baby. I remember when you asked me how it felt to be seventeen and I told you it wasn't much different than sixteen. That was true. That was the first birthday I spent with you, and I will never forget that. The best day of my life. Except for the day you married me.

You'll be starting school soon. Your senior year. I hope you're excited about that.

I love you.

July 22, 1965

Dear Curtis,

I was so happy to get your letter today. And yes, it made it before my birthday. Thank you for that. It's hard to think that the mail can take so long, but I guess since you are sending it from Germany, it makes a little sense.

I wish you were here, too, so we could spend the day together. Like you, I also think of all the things that we could be doing together if you were here. Mrs. Walker has told me that she has a surprise for me this weekend. I don't know what it is yet, but I'm eager to find out.

I've been thinking about you every minute of every day. Sometimes I go down to the creek and sit on our tree for hours. It's peaceful, and I enjoy thinking about all the times you and I spent there together. It's the hardest at night when I go to sleep. I'm sleeping in your old bedroom now, on your old bed, and that makes me feel a little closer to you.

It's strange to be sleeping in your mother's house again, but it's not bad. Your brothers and sisters are nice to me. And Kathy and Celeste have been coming over a lot, but I think it's more so they can watch television than to hang out with me. Kathy told me Daddy bought a television, but he doesn't let the kids watch it. I still haven't seen Momma or Daddy since the day we got married.

Did I tell you that Owen was born? Kathy says he's really cute, but I haven't seen him yet. I think about going over to their house, but then I get nervous, so I don't.

By the time you get this, I'll probably be back in school. I'm looking forward to it because it gives me something to do. If you were home, I don't know that I would care much about school anymore. I just miss you so much.

Please be safe and remember that I love you always. I'll be looking forward to your next letter.

Love,

Lorrie

Fifteen

♥ Saturday, July 24, 1965 ♥

Curtis called today.

My heart is still pounding so hard it's hard to write anything at all. ♥

"Lorrie! Telephone!"

At the sound of Mrs. Walker's voice, Lorrie looked up from the book she was reading. As she processed her mother-in-law's words, she got to her feet and headed for the kitchen.

"Who is it?" she asked, confused.

"Here," Mrs. Walker said, not bothering to answer her as she held out the phone. It didn't even register that she was smiling from ear to ear.

Fully expecting it to be Kathy asking if she could come over, Lorrie put the receiver to her ear. "Hello?"

"Hey, honey."

The instant she heard his voice, her throat closed up, tears sprang to her eyes, and her heart started a full sprint in her chest. She couldn't breathe, couldn't get a single word out to respond.

"Lorrie? Baby?"

A sob tore from her chest as she fell apart. Hearing his voice...

"It's okay, darlin'. Please don't cry."

Lorrie shook her head, knowing he couldn't see her. It wasn't okay. She hadn't heard Curtis's voice in two hundred thirty-five days. She knew because she'd been counting. And now that she had, she wasn't sure she could hold herself together.

"Talk to him, Lorrie," Mrs. Walker urged sympathetically. "I'll be in the other room if you need me."

Lorrie nodded, trying to swallow past the lump in her throat.

"I only get a few minutes, baby," Curtis said into her ear.

"I love you," she blurted. "God, I miss you so much." She was a blubbering mess, but she couldn't help it.

Curtis chuckled. "I know you do. I love you and miss you, too."

"Are you doing okay?" she asked, trying to think of all the things she wanted to ask him.

"I am," he said reassuringly. "Better now that I got to hear your voice."

Lorrie sobbed again, her throat tight from all the backed up tears.

"I know it's not until Monday, but I wanted to call and wish you a happy birthday, baby."

More tears poured down her face, so many that she stopped trying to dry them. She couldn't stop them. "Thank you," she whispered hoarsely. "Is this the surprise your mother promised me?"

Another chuckle echoed through the phone. "Probably so."

"I love you so much," she said again.

"I love you, too, darlin'. I gotta run, though. I'm outta time. I'm so glad I got to hear your voice."

She wasn't ready to let him go yet. She hadn't gotten to hear his voice long enough. "Don't go," she pleaded. "Please."

"Baby, I have to. I only get a few minutes. I love you, though, and I'm thinkin' about you always."

"I love you, too," she whispered.

"Bye, baby."

A horrific sob tore through her, and she whispered good-bye before sliding down the wall to the floor, the phone receiver falling from her hand and left dangling from the cord.

The next thing she knew, Mrs. Walker was sitting beside her, her arm around Lorrie's shoulders. "Shh, honey. Don't cry. I know it's hard."

Hard didn't even begin to describe it. Having finally heard his voice after all this time… It was as though she'd been sliced open and forced to relive the pain from the day he'd left all over again.

And God only knew how long it would be before she got to hear his voice again.

Sixteen

Mrs. Walker bought a new television. This one is even bigger than the last one. She said I could put the other one in our house if I want to. Since I'm not living there right now, I told her we could keep it here. She's so nice to me. And she makes sure that I don't have too much idle time. She says it's not healthy to sit around and wait. I've been trying not to, but it's not easy. I finally convinced Carol to teach me how to cook. Although it's not her usual job, I heard her talking about how much she enjoys it. It's a slow process, but I'm getting the hang of it.

Every day, I keep hoping that Curtis will show up and surprise me with a visit home or, at the least, another phone call. I need to hear his voice again.

I have spent a lot of time at the library. Reading is helping a lot. And Kathy and Celeste have come over a few times to watch television with me, although they don't let me pick what we're gonna watch. Now that we have a bigger television, I'm sure they'll be over here even more. I wonder if Curtis will be happy that we'll have a television when he gets home. When he first gets home, I don't think it'll matter. I secretly look forward to making love to him for the first time. I know he thinks I'm not ready, but I am. Or I want to believe I am, anyway. I just want to feel his arms around me, holding me tight. My body gets excited when I think about it. Not that I want anyone to know that. ♥

Curtis

♥ Thursday, October 21, 1965 ♥

Today is Curtis's twentieth birthday, and I hate that I don't get to spend it with him. I made him a cake, hoping it would make me feel better. It did while I was baking, but not so much after. Only because he isn't here to have any. I had hoped he would call today, but he didn't. Mrs. Walker assured me that he's busy doing what he needs to do so that he can come home to me. That didn't make me feel any better. ♥

♥ Thursday, December 2, 1965 ♥

It's been a whole year since I've seen Curtis. To be honest, I don't know how I made it all this time. Even though Mrs. Walker surprised me and I got to talk to him on the phone (hearing his voice was both the best and worst thing that has happened to me all year), it still hurts that I can't see him.

At times, I think he's avoiding me. That he doesn't want to talk to me. Maybe because it hurts too much knowing that we can't be together. I feel the same way, but my heart still longs for him.

I can't wait to get another letter from him. ♥

December 14, 1965

Lorrie,

God, baby, I miss you so much. I can't stop thinking about you. I lie here on my bunk at night and think about holding you, touching you, kissing you, making love to you until the sun comes up. Sometimes, I think about you so much that my heart hurts.

Ever since I heard your voice, I haven't been the same. It's so hard knowing that you are there, that me being away is so hard on you. I even cry sometimes, which makes me feel weak. Still, I can't help it. I'm going crazy because I think about you all the time. I wish that I could come home, but at least I'm busy here. I'm undergoing some additional training right now. Turns out that being a mechanic is a pretty big deal. Good thing I know a lot about engines, huh? If everything goes well, I might be sent somewhere else, which is something to look forward to. We don't know yet if we're being sent to Vietnam. It's a possibility, but then again, anything is a possibility. I like it here, but I really think I need something more to do.

I'm attaching a picture. It's one they took of me by one of the vehicles we're working on. I thought maybe you'd like to have it.

If you can, please send me a picture of you.

I love you.

Curtis

Seventeen

January 24, 1966

Dear Curtis,

I think I actually squealed when I got your letter and I saw the picture. It was the first time I've seen you in more than a year, and I broke down and cried again. But these were good tears, because I now have something that I can look at every day. Your mom got me a picture frame, and now I have it sitting on my nightstand, where I can look at you every night before I go to sleep. I got your mom to take a picture of me, and I'm putting it in the envelope.

Your mom got a letter from Gerald. He's doing well, she says. Since he was wounded, they gave him the opportunity to come home, but he refused. Says there is so much he needs to do, that he isn't willing to sacrifice what he's already given up just yet. He's still not coming home, and I think that makes her sad. I can't imagine what she's going through having two of her sons away from home. I know if I were her, I'd be sad, too.

Oh, and I forgot to tell you, I got to ride a horse for the first time. Joseph taught me. It's now one of my favorite things to do. Once the weather warms up, I'm hoping to start riding more. If your mom will let me. According to your sister (Daphne), your mom is a little overprotective, so it might take a little coaxing on my part.

Miss you and love you always!

Love,

Lorrie

♥ Monday, February 14, 1966 ♥

It's Valentine's Day, a day that I wasn't really looking forward to. Not that I'm celebrating, because Curtis isn't here, which makes it so hard. I feel like I've spent too many years without him, and it's only been one. Just when I thought my life couldn't get better (when we got married), he left. According to his letters, he's doing good. He says he misses me, too.

I worry about him a lot. Worry that he's going to get hurt or… I try not to think about the worst parts, but I can't help it. What if he never came back? Where would my life be then? He's the reason I breathe, and I wouldn't know what to do without him.

I've read his letters over and over, especially the parts where he says he can't wait to come home. Sometimes he even tells me that he cries. That breaks my heart the most. I hope he knows I will always be here waiting for him. Always. ♥

♥ Wednesday, May 14, 1966 ♥

Tonight was my senior prom. I didn't go, although David offered to take me if I really wanted to go. It was sweet of him, but I know Curtis probably put him up to it. The last thing I want to do right now is dance or celebrate. I'll reserve all of that for when Curtis finally does come home. It was kinda fun to see Joseph and his date get dressed up, though. They looked happy. ♥

♥ **Wednesday, May 25, 1966** ♥

I graduated from high school today, along with Joseph. Mrs. Walker and all the kids came, as well as Kathy and Celeste. Mrs. Walker gave me a card that Curtis had sent for the occasion (which was the highlight of the day). Momma and Daddy said they couldn't make it. I hadn't expected them to, but it still hurt my feelings that they didn't make the effort. Now I don't know what I'm going to do with the free time I have. Mrs. Walker is letting me make a lot of the meals now that I've gotten a handle on the whole cooking thing, which I really enjoy doing. I'm also working on the ranch, and I'm hoping she will allow me to do that more. I think she worries about me getting hurt, but I'm careful. I just need to find the courage to talk to her about it, because I really need this. I need something to do to keep my mind off Curtis. ♥

♥ **Sunday, June 26, 1966** ♥

Oh, my goodness. You won't believe this! Helen Jenkins got married today. The boy she married isn't from here, and she won't be staying in Granite Creek (probably because she thinks she's too good for it). I wasn't invited, but I didn't expect to be. Helen has been making fun of me. Always telling me I'm wasting my life waiting on Curtis. She doesn't understand that I live and breathe for that man. I'll wait an eternity for him if I have to. ♥

July 26, 1966

Lorrie,

Hey, baby. Today is your eighteenth birthday. As I sit here and stare at your picture, I wish that I was there with you. It's weird to think that another birthday has come and gone.

I haven't been doing a whole lot lately other than staying here on base. I've gotten out with the guys a few times for drinks, but it's not the same since I can't be with you. They spend a lot of time trying to hook up with girls, but I have absolutely no interest. You are my girl, the only girl in the world for me. In fact, I'm thinking about getting a tattoo with your name on it. Those are a big deal here. Everyone wants one. What do you think about that? Would you want me to get your name tattooed on my body?

When I'm working, it feels like time flies, but when I'm here in my bunk, all I can do is think that time is crawling by so slowly. Instead of waiting for school to start, you'll be… It just dawned on me that I don't know what you want to do now that you've graduated. You're so smart; I know you could do anything you want. And Lorrie, I want you to know that I will support anything you want to do. Whether you want to go to college, or if you want to work on the ranch, or if you want to stay home and take care of the house (and ultimately all the kids we plan to have). It's up to you, baby. Anything you want.

I love you.

Dear Curtis,

Your letter made me both happy and sad, I won't lie. I could almost picture sitting on the couch with you and having that conversation about what I want to do now that I'm finished with school. But I also sensed that your letter was short for a reason. I've been hoping I was wrong, but I'm starting to think that you are purposely avoiding me. That breaks my heart.

And no, I didn't have to go back to school this year. It was a little strange to see your brothers and sisters heading out while I was still sitting in the house. I don't know what to think about that yet. In fact, I don't think much about it at all. School gave me something to do, but that's it. I really like working on the ranch. I also help Carol when I can. I can honestly tell you that I would never want a housekeeper or a cook of my own. I like taking care of my own things. The only thing that would make me truly happy would be to take care of you and our family. Maybe I'm not supposed to feel that way anymore. I don't know. I've been reading books that say women are allowed to embrace the world. For me, I am.

When we have kids, I would definitely want to stay home with them, if I can. It's not that I don't want to work. Helping out on the ranch has been thrilling. I never thought I'd enjoy it after Daddy always complained how bad it was. Maybe it's the fact that I'm working for my family. (I am, after all, a Walker now.) Whatever it is, I'm just trying to make it one day at a time.

Speaking of kids … I'm ready, Curtis. I'm ready to make love to you, to spend the night in your bed, feeling your body hovering above mine. It's all I can think about these days. Maybe this wasn't the right way to tell you, but I had to get it out there. You need to know how I really feel. And no, this doesn't have anything to do with the fact that I'm another year older. It's just how it is. You are no longer allowed to tell me I'm not ready. That's no longer your decision to make.

Love and miss you always and forever.

Love,

Lorrie

P.S. It took a long time for me to write that last paragraph. Like, two whole days.

P.P.S. I think a tattoo would be very sexy on you.

♥ *Sunday, October 23, 1966* ♥

I suggested something new today. I asked Mrs. Walker if I could cook dinner and if we could have the entire family home for it. I was surprised to see the smile that lit up her face. She agreed, then the two of us worked in the kitchen together. She told the kids that they had to be here, and everyone showed up. Afterwards, I helped her clean the kitchen, and we agreed that, from now on, we would have supper together on Sundays. I like the idea of that. I think it's a great tradition, one that I want to have with my own kids one day. ♥

Curtis

It has officially been two years since Curtis left. Two years since I've seen his handsome face (in person). He's been sending me pictures, but those are still just images on paper and not as good as the real thing. I remember when he told me he enlisted, he said he would be gone for three years. I thought I would get to see him at least once. I thought that was how it worked, but it seems as though Curtis isn't allowed to come home. He has only called a couple of times since the day I broke down on the phone, but he hasn't spoken to me, only to his mother. I can't exactly blame him. It probably wasn't easy listening to me sobbing uncontrollably, so maybe that's why he doesn't call. He knows it's hard on me. He has mentioned how much he is working, and I'm glad that he's not on the front lines in harm's way. That helps to ease my mind a little, but nothing would be better than if I got to see him. I miss him terribly. ♥

Eighteen

~ *1967* ~

Lorrie,

There are two parts to this letter. First, the details on what I'm doing. The second ... well, just keep reading.

Tensions are rising in North Vietnam. Things are escalating, and we got word today that we will likely be sent there. I know that isn't what you want to hear, but honey, this is my job, my responsibility. I would give anything to come home to you, and if we can end the war, that'll be possible. So please understand. I love you and I miss you.

Now for the second part... You mentioned in your letter that you're ready to make love to me. If you only knew what that does to me, how that makes me feel. Even now, as I write this letter, I'm so hard I can hardly see straight. Remember the day that I kissed you for the first time? You asked me if I had ever kissed a girl? What you didn't ask was whether or not I'd ever made love to a girl. I know there were always rumors going around about me, but Lorrie, I'm still a virgin, the same as you. I've never been with a woman before, and you're the only woman I ever intend to be with. I have and will always put you first, but you should know right here and now, sending me letters like that makes my dick hard. It makes me think of all the things I plan to do to you when I get home. And baby, I plan to do a lot of things.

Curtis

Now that that's out of the way, I hope you know I love you, and even before you sent that, I ached to come home to you, now even more so.

I love you.

Curtis

P.S. Hold off before you send me another letter. The address is going to change. I'll make sure you get that information.

♥ Friday, March 3, 1967 ♥

I received another letter from Curtis, but this one wasn't like the others. Then again, after the last letter I sent him, I didn't expect it to be. I had managed to get up the nerve to tell him how I feel, and in return, he did the same. As I sit here, thinking about him, my body aches for his. In ways I never imagined.

BUT... If he thought he could throw me off by adding the sweet stuff in the middle, he is sorely mistaken. Even though I loved getting the letter so I could hear how he was doing, the last few words stole all the pleasure out of it. This one made me panic. Once again, I cried like a baby, but this time my heart is filled with fear. He's being sent to Vietnam. I won't lie and say I know much about what is going on other than what I hear in town or on television from time to time. It's like the people here are turning against the soldiers, thinking somehow this is their fault. I don't like that they think that way. I think I've been too scared to really focus on it, but I know it's not good. They say the war has been going on for too long. That we will not win. I just want Curtis to come home to me.

People are dying, lots of people. I ask myself those what-if questions every day. What if he gets shot? What if he doesn't come back the same as when he went away? What if, God forbid, he dies? What if I never get another chance to tell him how much I love him? The not knowing that he will come back to me is the hardest part. He owns my heart and my soul, and I can't imagine living the rest of my life without him. Still, I try not to think about those things, but it's hard.

I know these are rough times for both of us, what with having to be away from each other and all, but I know in the end it will be worth it. He will be home one day (hopefully soon), and we can start our life together when he does. I'm trying to be a grown-up about this because I'm no longer a child. I'm married now, and I have to remember that. No matter what, I refuse to regret any decisions that we've made, because in the end, these are the decisions that will lay the groundwork for our life. ♥

♥ Monday, April 15, 1967 ♥

For just a moment, I'm going to stop pretending to be a grown-up. I miss my husband. I want him to come home. I'm so mad at him for leaving me behind. Sometimes it feels like someone cracked my chest open and is squeezing my heart. I'm trying to keep up appearances, smiling until my face hurts, laughing at everyone's stupid jokes, cooking dinner, and acting as though I'm not being gutted every minute of every day that Curtis is away. I'll keep this to myself because it doesn't do anyone any good to hear it. I definitely don't want Curtis to know. He has so much to deal with. But being without him is killing me. Slowly. ♥

♥ Wednesday, July 26, 1967 ♥

Today I turn nineteen. Not that it's any different from when I turned eighteen. I still don't get to spend the day with Curtis. I haven't received a letter from him in a while, which makes my heart hurt. I know he's okay because Mrs. Walker made Gerald find out for sure since he's the only one who calls. Gerald tried to reassure Mrs. Walker, telling her that Curtis didn't have the same privileges as an officer. I get that. Kind of. The good news, Curtis is not in combat, but he is in Southeast Asia, I'm told.

Once again, I'm starting to wonder if he is purposely not sending letters or calling. It didn't slip by me that he never responded when I stated in my letter that I thought he was avoiding me. I mentioned it to Mrs. Walker one day, and she told me to remember that this is just as hard on him as it is on me. I know that. I do. I think I might lose sight of that at times because I miss him so much.

I just want to hear from him, and the more days that pass, the harder it gets for me. I still cry every day, though not quite as much. I'm wondering if I'll ever stop crying. Then again, the day that I do might not be a good day after all. ♥

♥ Friday, August 4, 1967 ♥

I've been watching the news a lot more lately. From what I've seen, we now have around five hundred thousand troops in Vietnam, and they just sent forty-five thousand more. It hurts my heart to know that Curtis is one of them. Gerald has already been over there, fighting, even getting wounded. Curtis was right, things are escalating. Now, the only thing I seem to do is pray. I can't stop worrying that he'll get hurt, maybe killed. This is serious. They're fighting day in and day out, and it's only escalating. I need God to keep Curtis safe, to bring him home to me. ♥

♥ Monday, September 25, 1967 ♥

It's been another one of those days when I don't feel like pretending anymore. I need to hear from Curtis. I'm slowly going crazy. At times, I'm so upset I want to stomp my feet and scream until I can't scream anymore. I'm doing my best not to let anyone see that side of me, but I know I can't hide it all the time, even if I try. I can't wait until he comes home. I keep reminding myself that will be soon. I hate that I'm beginning to get angry. I told myself in the beginning that I wouldn't. I can't seem to help it, though. With him being gone, I feel abandoned. ♥

♥ Saturday, October 14, 1967 ♥

I went to see Momma today. I don't know if she was happy to see me or not. She acted like she was, but she made the comment that I hadn't bothered to come until now. She said Mitch comes by a couple of times a month. I didn't bother to remind her that she didn't go to my wedding or even my high school graduation. It's not worth arguing about. I didn't see Daddy, but that was on purpose. I made sure he wasn't going to be there before I went over.

We talked for a little while and I played with Owen. He's so cute. Kathy and Celeste weren't there. Everything seemed so different than when I left. Momma looks a lot older now. She doesn't smile very much at all. I asked her if I could come by again, and she said yes, so that's what I'm planning on doing.

I've also started counting down the days until Curtis comes home. It should be soon. It's been almost three years. I can't wait to see him. ♥

November 2, 1967

Lorrie,

It seems like it's been forever since I've sent you a letter. Maybe that's because it has been. I would like to say that it's because I'm always busy, but that isn't entirely true. If I'm being honest, I haven't been able to send letters because it hurts too much. I write them, then stow them in a box. I pull them out and read them, reliving all the things I want to say to you. I'm hoping that by not sending them, you'll focus on you for a while. Momma tells me that you're doing better, that you're actually living your life. That's what you need to do, baby. It breaks my heart to hear you cry or to know that you're hurting because of me. That's the last thing I ever want to do.

I'm not sending this letter to upset you, although I know that's what will happen. I need to tell you that you shouldn't be expecting me home in December like we planned. My three years is up soon, but Lorrie, I've volunteered to stay for longer. Please, baby, please don't be upset with me. When I first left, the only thing I could think about was coming home. But now that I've been here for so long, these people are like my family. I just can't bring myself to leave yet. These men have become my brothers, and they need me.

I'm sorry, baby. I really am. I love you more than words can say.

Curtis

Dear Curtis,

I don't even know what to say. My heart is broken, and my tears won't stop long enough for me to write you back. I wish I could say that I understand, but I don't. I thought you loved me, Curtis. I thought we were going to spend our life together.

Love,

Lorrie

Nineteen

~ 1968 ~

♥ Saturday, January 6, 1968 ♥

I wonder if I'll hear from Curtis. He should be receiving my letter soon. I'm scared that he'll be mad, but I don't regret sending it. I need him to know how much he hurt me. The fact that he volunteered to stay without talking to me first is the worst part. We're married. That's what married people are supposed to do. Talk to one another.

On top of that, I was talking to one of my friends, and she said that her brother calls often, and he even has come home while he's been enlisted. Curtis told me he couldn't. Maybe that's true, but I know he could've called me a lot more than he has. It hurts to know that he is purposely pushing me away, but I don't know how to talk to him about it. ♥

♥ **Wednesday, February 14, 1968** ♥

This might just be the worst Valentine's Day ever. I haven't
heard from Curtis since the last letter that I sent. Mrs. Walker
said she hasn't heard from him, either, but she has assured me
that he is okay. Apparently Gerald is calling and sending letters
even though Curtis isn't. But at least now I know that it isn't
because he isn't capable. He just doesn't want to. My heart hurts.
♥

♥ **Wednesday, April 17, 1968** ♥

Daddy died today. I'm told he got kicked in the head by a horse
while he was working on the ranch. Killed him instantly. I'm not
sure how I feel about that yet. Kathy came over to tell me. She
was very upset. I couldn't even cry when she told me. I haven't
seen him since the day Curtis and I got married four and a half
years ago. I've seen Momma a few times, but I don't go over
there when Daddy's home. Now, I guess I'll never get that
chance. ♥

June 15, 1968

Lorrie,

I'm not sure if you want to hear from me, but I'm writing this letter anyway. I have some things I have to tell you, things I've been bottling up inside for a while now.

Baby, I know you're upset with me, and I can't blame you. When I received your letter, I dropped to my knees and cried. Knowing that I hurt you crushed me. I never meant to. I never wanted to let you down. I've been trying to figure out how I can say this, how I can tell you without upsetting you, but there's no easy way, so I'm just going to get it out there.

When I signed up for the Army, I didn't do it because I wanted to serve my country or because Gerald encouraged me to do the right thing. I did it in order to put some distance between us, but I suspect you know that now. For the sixteen months we were married before I left, things were a little uncomfortable. I wanted to believe it was the newness of it all, but I don't think that was it. Although we both smiled and laughed, I knew deep down that you were too young for marriage. But I don't regret marrying you. In fact, I would do it all over again in a heartbeat because I'm selfish like that. Especially when it comes to you.

You are the reason I breathe. The reason my heart beats. I will go to the ends of the earth to make you happy. I hope you know that. Not hearing your voice, not seeing your beautiful face… Those are the things that tear me up each and every day. But I can still hear you crying on the phone when I did call, and your tears have the power to break me. You are my only weakness, Lorrie. I knew I couldn't do what needed to be done, knowing that you were so upset.

And when I volunteered to stay on a little while longer, it really was because I couldn't bear to leave my fellow soldiers when they needed me most. It damn near killed me to agree, but I knew it was the right thing to do.

Curtis

I am ready to come home, Lorrie. I am ready to come home and be the husband that you deserve. But what I need you to know is that I need you in every way. You told me in your letter that you were ready to make love to me. I've been away from you for a long time. My desire for you has intensified to the point I can hardly sleep, hardly eat when I think about coming back to you. I need to be able to bury myself inside your sweet body for the first time, to hold you in my arms, to feel your skin against mine. The only thing I think about is sinking deep inside you and never leaving. And that is why I put these years between us. I wanted to give you time to grow up the way you deserved.

But since I'm being brutally honest, I want you to know that when I come home, I do plan to make love to you. Day and night. Until I've had my fill. And I'm warning you, baby, I will never get enough of you. Never.

I love you.

Curtis

♥ Saturday, June 1, 1968 ♥

Mrs. Walker took me shopping today. It felt a little strange, but it was fun at the same time. I hated that she insisted on spending money on me, but she told me it was my money, not hers. She went on to explain that Curtis had made sure I had whatever money I needed, but he'd also warned her that I would never ask for anything unless it was a necessity. It's true.

But today, I got some new dresses and a new hat, and Mrs. Walker convinced me to buy some shorts. They're so cute, and I can't wait to wear them. For the past few years, I've made a few dresses, but it's not the same as buying one on the rack. I still won't get used to anyone spending money on me like that, no matter where the money comes from.

I did, however, splurge a little. I bought Curtis a Zippo lighter. Mrs. Walker explained that I could get it engraved, so I decided to do that. I've always remembered those words he said, so I had them put on the lighter. "You are my love that lasts a lifetime." I hope he'll like it. Mrs. Walker actually had a tear when I told her what I wanted it to say. I miss him so much. ♥

♥ Tuesday, July 23, 1968 ♥

Funny how I can be so angry and so hurt but one letter changes everything. One letter makes my heart soar once again. The things Curtis said to me… They weren't what I expected to hear from him, but I cherished every single word. I still blush when I reread the letter because I know exactly how he feels. I feel the same way. Maybe it has been the time apart that has made me want him so much, but I can't change that, and I don't want to. More than that, I don't want to hide how I feel for him. I never want to turn into my mother. I never want to be the type of woman who serves a man. I want to be Curtis's equal in every way. I want to love him the way he deserves to be loved. And that is exactly what I intend to do when he comes home.

I only hope he knows what he's getting himself into because I'm no longer the girl he left behind. I'm no longer scared of what he makes me feel. The war has made him grow up, but it's made me grow up, too.

It won't change the fact that Curtis went to the Army to put space between us, but in an odd way, it makes sense. Still, I'm going to let this husband of mine know that if he expects our marriage to work, communication is the key. It's no longer only up to him. He doesn't get to make these decisions for both of us anymore. ♥

Part Three

*"Being deeply loved by someone gives you strength,
while loving someone deeply gives you courage."*
~ *Lao Tzu*

Twenty

♥ Friday, July 26, 1968 ♥

Today I received the best birthday present ever.♥

CURTIS WASN'T SURE THAT HE WOULD BE able to pull off the surprise, but with help from his mother and from Joseph, his arrival back in Granite Creek had gone undetected by everyone. He'd known he was coming home since he'd sent the last letter to Lorrie on June fifteenth, but he hadn't told her that. Instead, he had told her all the things he'd wanted to tell her for the past three and a half years.

He was finally home, and it looked as though Lorrie was completely unaware, at least until the moment he stepped into his mother's living room to find her sitting on the couch in front of the television. No one said a word as he stood there with his heart in his throat while he watched as she talked quietly to his sister Daphne.

Although she'd sent him pictures, nothing prepared him for how incredibly beautiful she was. There before him was a twenty-year-old woman who had taken the place of the sixteen-year-old girl he'd left years ago. His heart skipped a beat or two in his chest, and it felt as though an anvil had been dropped on his ribs.

How in the hell had he stayed away so long?

Clearing his throat, he waited for Lorrie to turn around. He watched as she slowly pivoted on the couch, her eyes seeking the reason for the sound. When they landed on him, she inhaled sharply, tears forming in her eyes, and he found his were wet, as well.

"Curtis!" Her whisper was so rough he barely heard it.

In the next second, Lorrie was on her feet, staring at him from across the room as though she thought he might not be real. Her shaky hand went to her mouth as tears began streaming down her cheeks.

He could feel the pressure in his chest as he stared at her. He'd waited so damn long for this day.

"C'mere, baby," he said hoarsely, his voice rough with emotion.

The next thing he knew, Lorrie launched herself at him, her lips finding his instantly. The kiss surprised him so much he stumbled as he held her to him, putting his hand on the wall to keep them upright. Not caring that his mother was in the room, or his brothers and sisters, Curtis cupped her face in his hands and crushed his mouth to hers, savoring the taste of her. She tasted like heaven, so damn sweet and just as he remembered. She was still the softest thing he'd ever touched, her skin like silk against his fingertips.

When they pulled back for air, Lorrie didn't release him, instead burying her face against his chest. He cupped the back of her head and slid his other hand up and down her back as she sobbed, his heart pounding uncontrollably. God, he'd missed her so fucking much.

"Are you home for good?" she whispered, her words barely audible over her sobs.

"For good," he told her. For a while there, he hadn't thought he'd ever be able to say that, but it was true. His time as an active-duty soldier was over. It was time for him to focus on the life he'd left behind, the one he'd seemingly been running from.

Curtis looked over Lorrie's head at the others standing around. Joseph was there, grinning as though he hadn't a care in the world. While Curtis had followed Gerald's lead and gone into the Army, at twenty, Joseph had decided he wouldn't unless they made him, which they knew might be a real possibility. Until that time came, Curtis wanted the kid to live his life, enjoy every second of it. It was completely up to him how he chose to do that.

Then there was David, who looked so different from the fourteen-year-old kid he'd been when Curtis had left. Of course, Daphne was now barely older than Lorrie had been when Curtis had married her, and she looked all grown up. Too grown up, if he were being honest. Frank Jr., who'd been a royal pain in Curtis's ass, had officially become a teenager. That left Lisa and Maryanne, the two youngest of the bunch. They were watching him as though he might just disappear into thin air.

The only person missing was Gerald, who was still making a career out of being a soldier, leading his men and encouraging others to serve for their country. Not an easy task at the moment, considering the US's feelings on the war, but who was Curtis to argue? He'd done his time, he was proud of what he'd done, and he was now ready to get on with the rest of his life.

"You're home," Lorrie repeated, her body trembling as he held her.

"I'm home," he agreed.

She looked up at him with watery eyes. "I'm not imagining this, right? I'm not dreaming?"

He smiled. "Nope. I'm here, darlin'." He had acquired time while in the army, time he had never used because he'd been too scared that if he came home to see Lorrie, he wouldn't be able to leave again. And though he'd re-upped for another year, he'd completed eight months, and now he was done.

"Are you hungry?" his mother asked.

"Starving," he growled, looking down at Lorrie. He didn't bother clarifying that he wasn't hungry for food. Based on the heat he saw in her eyes, she knew.

Sliding his hand over her hair, he kept his gaze locked with hers.

The only thing he could think about was taking her to their little house and burying himself inside her all night long and never, ever letting her go. For the first time. For both of them.

His dick hardened, but somehow he ignored it.

Being with her was the main thing he'd thought about for the past painfully long three years and eight months. Making love to his wife for the very first time.

"I'm so glad you're home," she whispered.

"Me, too, darlin'."

"This is, by far, the best birthday present a girl could ever receive."

Curtis smiled. He'd wanted to surprise her, and it looked as though he had.

Mission accomplished.

Now, if he could get through the rest of the afternoon with his family, he had a few plans for Lorrie to make up for all the time they'd lost.

LORRIE FELT AS THOUGH SHE WERE WALKING around in a dream. She kept waiting for the moment when she would wake up to find that she was lying in Curtis's old bedroom, alone, hugging his pillow to her chest as she had for too many nights to count.

She did not want to wake up.

She did not want this to be a dream.

Curtis was home. He was standing here, holding her in his arms, and it was the greatest feeling in the world. So great she wasn't sure she would be able to let him go.

"Come on. Let's eat," Joseph called. "You can tell us all about the things you did."

Lorrie didn't really care to hear his stories, at least not until she had time to process the fact that he was really home, but she would give anything to hear his voice, so it didn't really matter what he talked about.

"We'll be there in a minute," Curtis replied, his arms tightening around her.

"Gotcha," Joseph said with a wink.

Curtis released her, but he reached for her hand, then led her through the living room and up the stairs, then down the hall to his old bedroom. She followed, feeling the butterflies take flight in her belly. She recalled his last letter. When she'd received it, she had read it at least two dozen times. The straightforward way he told her that he wanted to make love to her... It was all she'd thought about for days. Weeks.

Now he was home. It was as though that letter had been a way of preparing her for this moment. Maybe it had. And it had worked.

He closed the door behind them, then led her to the bed. When he took a seat on the edge of the mattress, he pulled her toward him so that she was standing between his legs.

"Lemme look at you." Curtis's voice was rough, and Lorrie knew he was overcome by the same emotions she was.

She didn't move a muscle as she allowed her gaze to rake over his face at the same time he seemed to be eating her up with his.

"I missed you so much," he mumbled.

Reaching for him, Lorrie lightly trailed her fingers over his jaw. He looked different than he had before. No longer was he the skinny kid who'd gallantly ventured into the Army to go off and protect the world. He'd come back a man. His body was harder than before, his chest bigger, wider, evident even beneath the uniform that he wore. Out of the blue, Lorrie's thoughts drifted to removing it from his body so she could see what was beneath.

Curtis's hands slid to the backs of her thighs, warm and callused as they slowly glided up, then down. Her body tingled in so many places. It seemed they couldn't look away from one another, but the tension in the room was intensifying, turning into something Lorrie hadn't felt before. There was a powerful force that was drawing her toward him, her body wanting things from him that she'd never thought she would want. But she did. She wanted them all. With Curtis.

"Did you get my letter?"

Lorrie nodded. "I did."

"Did you read it?"

Chuckling, she said, "Of course."

"And?"

"And what?" She felt her cheeks heat as a blush consumed her.

"I can't wait to make love to you."

Lorrie stared deep into his eyes. "I can't, either."

A rough growl escaped him. "Need you closer," he said gruffly.

Shifting, Curtis pulled her so that she was forced to straddle his lap, her knees on the bed on either side of his hips. She didn't even think about pushing him away when his hands slipped beneath her shorts to cup her bottom.

"Kiss me, Lorrie. Kiss me like you've missed me."

That she could definitely do. Sliding her hands behind his neck, Lorrie kept her eyes fixed on his until she was too close to see him. Then she let her eyelids lower as her lips met his. The kiss started slow and sweet, but it quickly heated, her tongue delving into his mouth as he allowed her to control the kiss. It was as though someone had replaced her blood with rocket fuel. She was hot all over, her breasts sensitive. A slow, throbbing ache had settled between her thighs. They were close, but not close enough.

"Oh, fuck." Curtis's hips pressed upward. "Lorrie. Baby," Curtis growled when she pulled back, his lips sliding to her neck.

"Did you just swear at me?" she asked, grinning.

"Not *at* you, darlin'," he whispered. "I just don't know any other way to express what you do to me. How hard you make me."

He was gripping her behind, pulling her against him, grinding against her sex where she felt the evidence of how hard she made him. She could feel the thick ridge of his erection against the sensitive spot between her legs. Not once did she think about the fact that they were in Curtis's mother's house, or that there were seven people waiting for them in the other room. It didn't matter. The only thing that mattered was Curtis was home.

The knock on the bedroom door made her jump, and then she fell over into a heap of giggles. Her heart was lighter than it had ever been before.

"Food's ready," David announced.

"Be right there," Curtis told him as he twisted to look at her. He smiled. "Let's go eat, do what we need to to appease them." His hand gripped her hip as he leaned over her. "Then, Mrs. Walker, I'm gonna take you home and strip these pretty little shorts right off you and spend the rest of the night getting intimately familiar with your body."

Although Lorrie would've blushed and shied away from those words before ... well, now, she couldn't wait. "I'm gonna hold you to that, *Mr.* Walker."

Lorrie couldn't deny that she loved seeing the heat that ignited in those blue-gray eyes that she'd dreamed about for nearly four long years.

THE *ONLY* REASON CURTIS ATE ANYTHING WAS because it was the polite thing to do.

The *only* reason he sat at his mother's dining room table and told stories and answered his brothers' and sisters' never-ending questions was because it was the polite thing to do.

And the *only* reason he didn't race out of his mother's house with Lorrie tossed over his shoulder was because it was the polite thing do to.

That and because it was Lorrie's birthday, and his family had made her a cake and had given her gifts, but now the celebration was over, and he was all out of polite.

Sure, he'd missed his mother and his brothers and sisters, he was grateful to be home, more than grateful that they'd taken care of Lorrie while he was away, but the only thing he could think about was Lorrie.

And the way she'd kissed him in his old bedroom a short time ago, the way she'd gone up in flames when he'd touched her.

Fuck. He needed to get her naked. And soon.

"You ready, darlin'?" he asked when he felt the appropriate amount of time had passed since he'd stepped foot into the house several hours ago.

"Ready," she said, sounding far more confident than the girl he remembered.

"We're gonna head out, Mom," he told Mary Elizabeth, who was in the kitchen putting the dishes in the sink. She looked good, healthy. So much better than the year that had followed his father's death. And from what Lorrie had told him in her letters, she'd stopped drinking.

"I'm surprised you lasted this long," she teased, turning to face them. "Oh, and I had David stock your refrigerator and your pantry, since Lorrie's been staying here with us. And Daphne cleaned the house from top to bottom yesterday, put clean sheets on the bed, so it should feel like home again."

"How did I not know about it?" Lorrie asked, a smile in her voice. "I have to admit, Mrs. Walker, that's pretty sneaky."

And it had worked out better than Curtis had planned.

"If you need anything, y'all know where to find us," his mother said, her eyes meeting Curtis's as tears pooled. "I'm so glad you're home."

Curtis released Lorrie's hand long enough to give his mother a hug and a quick kiss on the cheek. "Me, too, Momma. Me, too."

"Now get outta here," Mary Elizabeth joked, lightly pushing him on his shoulder. "We'll catch up more tomorrow."

Curtis smirked at Lorrie. "We might not come out of our house for a few days," he said absently.

Lorrie blushed as Curtis took her hand in his. He did his best not to drag her back to their house, and once they were inside, he even managed to release her long enough to set her gifts on the table.

Still, she didn't seem nervous, which surprised him.

"Have I told you how much I've missed you?" He reached for her, pulling her toward the couch.

"I think you might've," she replied with a smile. "But I don't mind hearing it again."

Curtis pulled her into his lap, unable to leave even a breath of air between them. He never wanted to stop touching her.

Cupping her head, he stared into her eyes. "I did," he said firmly. "I missed you every minute of every day."

Her smile was slow and sweet. "I know."

He sobered as he remembered her last letter and how upset she'd been with him. "Even if I didn't handle it in the best way."

Her eyes softened. "I understand. I don't like it, but I understand. I wish you'd've been honest with me."

"I was trying not to hurt you."

"I know that, too." Her hands wandered over his chest, and the friction through the rough fabric of his uniform was enough to make his dick hard. "But I don't wanna talk about that right now."

"Lorrie." He could barely get her name past his lips. His body was fueled with so much pent up desire he could hardly breathe.

Her smile widened.

"I'm ready, Curtis. More than ready."

He loved that she knew what he needed to hear. He loved that during the time he'd been gone, the connection between them hadn't dimmed. In fact, it had grown stronger, more powerful. It was all-consuming.

"I don't wanna rush this." He really didn't, but he feared he wouldn't be able to help himself.

"Then don't. We can take all the time we need."

Easier said than done. His dick was throbbing, a desperate ache that only her body could sate. There were so many things he wanted to do to her, so many ways he wanted to pleasure her. And he wanted to start by stripping her clothes away and kissing every glorious inch of her body.

Right now.

LORRIE HAD FANTASIZED ABOUT THIS DAY FOR ... so long. *Too* long. And now that it was here, she fully expected to be nervous, anxious, scared. She was none of those things. Not that she could tell it from the look in Curtis's eyes. He seemed worried. Then again, when he'd gone off to the Army, she hadn't been ready.

She briefly wondered whether or not he wouldn't appreciate the fact that she ached for him. Perhaps she wasn't supposed to be quite so forward. But then she remembered the letter, all the things he'd said he wanted to do.

She wanted those things. Oh, how she wanted those things.

And she couldn't bring herself to hide her true feelings, her deepest desires. They were married. This wasn't frowned upon. But even if they had been, Lorrie wasn't so sure she could've pretended otherwise. Not with him.

Leaning forward, she rested her forehead against his. "I want this," she whispered, brushing her finger along his jaw. "I want you. I want to feel you..." She swallowed, forcing the next words past her lips. "I want to feel you inside me."

A deep, rumbling growl reverberated up from his chest, and the next thing Lorrie knew, she was hanging on to him as he bolted up from the couch, his arms around her as he carried her to the bedroom.

"Woman ... I think those might be the sexiest words I've ever heard."

She could tell he thought that was a good thing, so she decided to go with it. This was what she wanted. Curtis Walker. She wanted to spend the rest of her days making love to him as he'd promised.

He tossed her unceremoniously on the bed, making her giggle again. Then his big, strong body was above her, his knee pressed between her thighs, his mouth finding hers in a brutal yet devastatingly sweet kiss. They were a jumble of fumbling hands as they rolled together on the bed, her body coming to rest atop his.

When she lifted her head to stare down at him, she saw a hunger so incandescent she thought she might go up in flames.

Curtis's hands slid up the backs of her thighs, the same way they had earlier in his old bedroom. Only this time, they didn't stop; they continued higher, his fingers slipping beneath her shorts and the edge of her panties until he was cupping her bottom, pulling her lower body against his.

Another growl escaped him.

"Are you sure, darlin'?"

"More than sure," she told him, smiling.

He rolled them once more, freeing his hands as he got to his feet, leaving her lying on the bed before him. There was a fleeting moment when she felt a little anxious, but rather than let it consume her, Lorrie moved to the edge of the bed, sitting up and putting her hands on his belt just as he reached for it.

She still couldn't believe that he was here with her. The wait was finally over, and the past had become just that.... It was behind them where it belonged, and she was so ready to move forward. With him.

His hands stopped as he watched her, his eyes wide with wonder. In that moment, Lorrie was completely uninhibited. Freer than she'd ever been in her life.

And she knew it had everything to do with this man.

Slowly, she worked the belt free from the buckle, her eyes never leaving Curtis's as he stood before her. His hand went to her neck, his thumb brushing over her bottom lip as she then freed the button and lowered his zipper.

"Oh, God," he groaned. "Touch me, Lorrie. I need to feel your hands on me."

She wanted more than her hands on him, she wanted to run her lips over his skin, but she didn't say as much. Instead, she felt bold enough to say, "Take off your shirt."

With his one hand still cupping her neck, Curtis used his other to work the buttons loose on his shirt, fumbling a couple of times while she ran her hands down the outsides of his thighs. When he removed the uniform shirt, he was left in a white undershirt, which quickly disappeared.

Lorrie had seen Curtis without a shirt before. She'd seen him when he was working on the ranch, after he would shower when they'd first married, but none of those instances prepared her for the body he revealed to her now. Her eyes instantly locked on to the tattoo on his chest, directly over his heart. Her name. He had her name inked on his body, and that was possibly the sexiest thing she'd ever seen. After brushing her fingers over the letters, she let her gaze slide to the other parts he'd revealed. His chest was broad, his muscles so well-defined her fingers itched to touch them. Allowing her gaze to move lower, she bit her bottom lip as she followed the lines that bisected his abs.

Without thinking, she leaned forward and pressed a kiss right on his navel, unable to look up at him. His hand returned to the back of her head, his fingers fisting gently in her hair. A torrent of sensation shot down her spine. She liked the way he touched her, the desperation she could feel vibrating from him. It was as though he could hardly hold himself back.

She trailed kisses over his abdomen, sliding her tongue over his skin, moaning as she did. Her hands found their way up to the waistband of his pants, but before she could pull them down, Curtis stopped her.

His finger curled beneath her chin, his thumb brushing over her bottom lip. "Darlin', I can think of so many things I want you to do with that mouth." More heat flared in his eyes. "And I fully intend to get there, but right now… Oh, fuck… I'm not sure I can handle much more than sinking inside you."

There was something about his profanity that turned her on. Perhaps it was for the reason he'd explained earlier. That he didn't know how to express himself otherwise. She found it incredibly sexy.

His words made her skin tingle, her body desperate for his by the time he helped her to her feet and crushed his mouth back to hers. Strong fingers worked the buttons on her blouse before it was falling open. She didn't release him until he pushed the fabric off her shoulders, and only then so that it could flutter to the floor, leaving her clad in only her plain white bra and her shorts. Had she known Curtis was coming home, perhaps she would've gone out to buy a nicer one, maybe worn a dress. But when he freed the clasp on her bra and it fell to the floor, she figured it wouldn't have mattered what she had on.

"Let me look at you."

His voice was so rough, so deep, it caused a shiver to dance down her spine, but she dropped her arms when he took a step back. She didn't attempt to cover herself; instead, she worked her shorts over her hips and allowed them to drop to the floor, pooling at her feet.

Never once did she take her eyes off Curtis.

Twenty-Two

CURTIS KNEW WHAT WAS ABOUT TO HAPPEN. He'd known since the second he stepped into the house that he and Lorrie would soon be naked on the bed. What he hadn't known was how forward she would be, or how open she would be to the experience.

That intrigued him. Never in his wildest dreams would he have expected Lorrie to embrace this the way that she was. Maybe it was the fact they'd been apart for so long. Made sense. What was the saying? *Absence makes the heart grow fonder.* Apparently it didn't only affect the heart.

Whatever had caused his sweet girl to get that naughty gleam in her eyes, he liked it. A lot. Hell, even when he swore, she didn't seem to mind, and that, for whatever reason, turned him on more.

He liked thinking that behind that innocent façade, there was a naughty girl underneath. He wouldn't deny the fact that he'd seen his fair share of pornographic magazines as of late, some that depicted women doing things he only dreamed that Lorrie might do. And yeah, he'd imagined that Lorrie would be open to some of those things. However, the girl he'd left behind when he'd gone into the Army could hardly stand him touching her because she didn't seem to understand what was happening between them. This beautiful woman before him was not the same girl.

It didn't take long before their clothes were discarded and Lorrie was once again in his arms, her slight body beneath his as he stared down at her.

He wanted to run his tongue over every soft curve until she was pleading for more.

"I'm gonna kiss you, baby," he said, wanting to warn her. "Everywhere."

Her eyes widened, and she smiled, a slight nod the only sign of her acquiescence.

Starting with her lips, Curtis kissed her mouth before sliding down her jaw, her neck. He inhaled her sweet, flowery scent, finding himself completely addicted to it. Her skin was so smooth, so soft. Like silk against his tongue. Her faint mewls were driving him wild, making him crazy with need. He worked his way lower, going slowly, making sure he continued to caress her with his hands as he used his mouth to trail kisses over her chest.

Part of him expected her to stop him, even if only so that she could catch her breath. She didn't. Her hands moved over his shoulders, his neck, his face, her fingers then brushing against his head, his hair too short for her to tug, so she settled for gripping his head, which was erotic in its own right.

When his lips met her breasts, she let out a soft moan, which only encouraged him to continue. Unable to resist, Curtis sucked her nipple into his mouth, watching her face as he did. Her eyes were closed, one hand clenching the sheet, the other tightening on his head as he feasted on her.

"Curtis… Oh, Curtis… Mmm…"

As much as he wanted to spend all night attending to every inch of her as he'd promised, he didn't have the self-control necessary right now. His dick was like iron, and he needed to feel the warmth of her wrapped around him. Forcing himself to release her, he made his way back up her body, hovering over her as he pressed his mouth to hers. Their tongues mingled, searching, seeking, a feeling of desperation unlike anything he'd felt before consuming him as he aligned his body with hers.

"As much as I want to draw this out for you, I can't wait. I've waited so long already…"

Lorrie pressed her finger to his lips. "Don't wait."

He pulled back and stared down at her. "Are you ready, baby?"

Lorrie nodded, her arms wrapped around his neck.

"It might hurt a little," he warned. "But I'll go slow."

Another nod.

As he pushed against her sex, finding the entrance to her body, he held his breath, watching her intently. She hissed as he pushed inside, still moving slowly, only an inch, maybe two.

Holy.

Fuck.

She felt so good. So warm. So slick. It was everything he'd imagined magnified by infinity.

"Kiss me, Curtis," she whimpered.

Crushing his mouth to hers, he allowed her to use him as a distraction while he pushed past her body's natural resistance until he was fully inside her.

Heaven Almighty.

Curtis couldn't draw air into his lungs. The feeling was so exquisite. Being inside her was … better than breathing.

They were both panting, but Curtis never stopped kissing her, pumping his hips forward, then retreating. He maintained a slow pace for as long as he could, but he felt his own release barreling down on him, and he knew she wasn't even close. As much as he wanted to let go, to give in, to take what he'd only dreamed about, he couldn't bring himself to do it. What mattered was Lorrie, bringing her the most pleasure he could.

With his mouth still fused to hers, he managed to ease his hand between their bodies until he found the swollen nub at the top of her sex. He worked it with his thumb, desperate to make her climax because he couldn't hold on much longer. Her hips bucked, her fingernails dug into his shoulders, her teeth clamped down on his lip as she pleaded for more. He couldn't hold himself back any longer. He'd waited what felt like a lifetime for this.

Shifting his hips, Curtis changed the angle, reaching for her leg and pulling her knee to his side while he continued to move in and out, slow and deep.

Fuck. "Oh, fuck." He couldn't keep the words inside. "You feel so good, baby." He groaned and grunted, the sensations intensifying, sending him higher and higher.

Unable to help it, he increased his pace, his hips thrusting forward, driving as deep as he could.

Lorrie pulled her mouth from his, her back bowing as she cried out his name over and over again. He felt her inner walls gripping him until the pleasure bordered on pain. It was then that he gave himself over to his release.

LYING IN BED WITH CURTIS, LORRIE WAS sore but completely sated, her brain obliterated by how incredible that had been. It wasn't that she was a prude. In fact, she wasn't nearly as prudish as people thought her to be. The *idea* of sex had never shocked her. Not even reference to sex. After all, she did have an older brother who was quite proud of his conquests. Her trepidation had come with not knowing, not understanding. Truth was, back then, when they'd first gotten married, she had been too young.

Maybe she'd never had sex until now, but she knew her body. She understood what caused pleasure, because reading books was enlightening. But she'd also heard some girls talk. According to them, sex wasn't great, most of the time not even enjoyable. One girl had even said that it didn't feel good for her at all, but it wasn't supposed to.

Well, apparently she hadn't been with the right man, because...

Wow.

Never would she have imagined that sex would be like *that*. And she wasn't referring to the initial discomfort. That was so miniscule it'd hardly registered. What had was the way Curtis made her feel. The intensity of it was nearly overwhelming.

And yes, perhaps she'd had high expectations. After all, for the past few years, she hadn't sat around doing nothing. She'd been reading. Devouring literature as fast as she could. Since she came from a backwoods small town, she knew that she had no choice but to soak up as much information as she could or she would one day end up like her mother, wallowing in her own self-pity while popping out children for a man who didn't respect her. And that was something she refused to do.

So, she had read books. Lots and lots of books. Some were ones that she'd read secretly in the far corner of the library when she'd known no one would find out. The ones like *The Feminine Mystique* and *The Second Sex* that made her think. They also made her fear what might be her destiny. Of course, she'd then ventured into romance novels, which were ... so much better. Basically, Lorrie hadn't checked any of those out of the library, because there was no way she wanted anyone to know what she was reading.

But nothing she'd ever experienced was as empowering (at least for her) as what had transpired between her and Curtis tonight. Though they'd been married for nearly five years, it felt as though tonight was their wedding night.

Perhaps it was.

More so than that, Lorrie had never expected to enjoy it so much. So much that she was eager to do it again.

"What're you thinkin' about?" Curtis grumbled in her ear, his warmth pressing up against her back, his arms wrapped tightly around her.

Although she was still floating from that experience, Lorrie couldn't bring herself to tell him that she was thinking about sex, so she said, "What I want to do with my life?"

"That serious, huh?" He chuckled.

"Not really, no. But I have given it some thought since you left."

"Do tell," he encouraged, pulling her tighter against him.

"I don't know just yet, to be honest. But I know that I'm not going to be like my mother." She rolled over so that she was facing him, settling against him once more.

Curtis kissed her temple. "In what way?"

"I've read books," she explained. "A lot of books. And I see women complain that they don't want to be housewives."

"Do you?"

"Yes," she said quickly. "But not because that's what's expected of me."

"It's not," he said against her ear.

"I know you don't think that way, but that's not the way of the world just yet. I've learned how to embrace being a woman. And that's how I want to live my life."

Curtis nuzzled her neck. "I like that you're a woman."

151

Lorrie giggled, his rumbling voice tickling her skin.

"I love you, Lorrie," he whispered softly. "I love you more than anything in this world. My only goal is to make you happy. Things didn't start out quite the way anyone would've planned, but I think what happened is going to help us. Sure, I could've made better decisions, but—"

"I don't need an apology," she interrupted, placing her fingers against his lips. "I need your love, Curtis. That's all I need."

She knew it wouldn't be easy for them. They'd started out young, but so had lots of other people. It still hurt her heart to know that Curtis had deceived her, that he'd purposely become a soldier in order to put distance between them. When she looked at it rationally, she understood. When she looked at it as his wife, it hurt. But most importantly, she knew he'd done it because he loved her.

And with love, she knew they could weather any storm.

Twenty-Three

♥ Saturday, September 14, 1968 ♥

I've been looking forward to today all week. For the past few days, Curtis has been teasing me relentlessly. He's making all sorts of dirty promises that keep my body humming. And now, tonight, I fully intend to make him pay up for all the torment. ♥

THE MOMENT HE WALKED IN THE DOOR after working on the ranch all day, Curtis expected Lorrie to be waiting for him. She had told him in no uncertain terms earlier in the day that he had some responsibilities to take care of when he got home. And she hadn't been referring to taking out the garbage, either.

Which was the reason he was home a little earlier than usual. He was eager to get to work.

On her.

"Where're you at, baby?" he called as he tossed his hat on the coffee table.

"In here," she hollered back.

He followed the sound of her voice toward the bathroom. That was when he noticed that the shower water was on. The door was open a crack, so he pushed it in and stepped inside.

"Curtis!" Lorrie squealed from the other side of the shower curtain. "I'm takin' a shower."

"I can see that," he told her, although he couldn't actually *see* anything. Yet. "And now you're takin' one with me."

He quickly disrobed and joined her in the tub, laughing when he saw that she was trying to cover herself. Her hands attempted to shield her most secret parts, but still she spun around so that her back was to him, and he got an unobstructed view of her fabulous ass.

"No sense in coverin' it up, darlin'. I've seen it all."

It had been nearly two months since he'd gotten back, and he'd spent the first couple of weeks ravishing her every chance he got. Then he had forced himself to slow down, mainly because he'd seen how exhausted Lorrie was. But it didn't take long for him to realize that she didn't want him to slow down, and that was the reason he'd started teasing her at every turn.

Sex was fantastic, no doubt about that. But teasing her ... tormenting her ... building her up so that he knew when he finally gave her what she needed, she would come apart in his arms ... that was the best part.

Now, he fully intended to satisfy her in every way.

"Mmm," he moaned against her neck as he moved her wet hair out of the way. He cupped her ass in his hands and squeezed, bending his knees and sliding his dick along the crease. "I've been thinking about you all day."

"How so?" she asked, her voice rough with arousal.

Another thing about Lorrie that he'd learned in recent weeks was that she loved when he talked to her during sex. The dirtier his mouth, the hotter she seemed to burn.

Standing up straight, he rocked his hips, grinding his rigid erection against the smooth skin of her back while he reached around and cupped her breasts.

"Lean back against me," he instructed.

She did without question, which made him smile.

"Have I told you how fucking nice your tits are?"

Lorrie shook her head.

Curtis pinched her nipples gently, enjoying the soft moans that came from her as he did. "They're fucking fantastic."

He continued to fondle her, enjoying the way she hissed when he rolled her nipples between his fingers, tugging on them. She was so damn sexy he couldn't get enough of her.

"Turn around," he instructed, reluctantly letting go of her.

Lorrie slowly pivoted so that she was facing him, and Curtis resituated them so that she was up against the wall. He picked up where he'd left off, tweaking her nipples, watching his fingers as he did. Her pale skin was a stark contrast against his sun-bronzed hands, and for some reason, watching made his dick throb incessantly. She seemed to be just as captivated by what he was doing, her chest heaving as her breaths grew more rapid.

"You like that?"

Lorrie met his gaze. "Yes."

"You like it when I put my mouth on them?"

She nodded.

"Tell me."

"Yes."

Leaning down, Curtis sucked one distended nipple into his mouth, flicking it with his tongue.

Her hands went to his hair, holding him to her as he feasted on her, his other hand sliding down between her thighs, over the downy-soft hair. Lorrie's legs widened as he dipped his finger between her pussy lips, gently caressing her clitoris. She was wet already, and he knew it had nothing to do with the shower.

He continued to fondle her slowly as he stood up and pressed his lips to hers. He kissed her hard, but never hurried his movements, wanting to bring her to the brink but not send her over. Not yet, anyway.

Trailing his lips over her cheek, he then nibbled on her earlobe, groaning as he dipped his finger inside her, fucking her slowly.

"You like that, don't you? You like when I finger your pussy?"

Her sharp inhale was his answer.

Anticipating her reaction, Curtis removed his fingers, then took a step back beneath the water before reaching for the shampoo. Pretending that he hadn't left her hanging, he proceeded to wash his hair. When he opened his eyes and met her gaze, he laughed.

She frowned.

"Don't worry, darlin'," he said sympathetically, grabbing the bar of soap and swiping it over his body, spending an extra few seconds stroking his erection while he watched her. "I'm not done with you yet."

Wasn't long before her frown disappeared and arousal returned to her expression as she watched him masturbate slowly.

"You like watching me, don't you?" He gripped his shaft tighter, stroking slow and easy. He didn't stop, and Lorrie didn't take her eyes off his hand working his dick.

"I like when you watch," he said gruffly, letting the water rinse the soap from his body. He took a step closer. "But what I'd like even more would be for those pretty lips to be wrapped around me."

Her eyes widened, but she didn't shy away from him. Although they'd gotten the sex part down, Curtis had opted to go slow with her when it came to all of the other extracurricular activities. There were so many things he intended to experience with her, but he knew that going slow was key.

"Get on your knees for me," he instructed, keeping his tone soft but firm.

That was another thing he'd found out about Lorrie; she liked when he took charge.

Curtis continued to stroke himself, watching as she eased down to her knees before him. He cupped the back of her head, continuing to watch her face as he stroked his dick, then stepped closer to her.

"Give me your hand," he said.

Lorrie's wide eyes shot up to his face momentarily, but then she held out her hand. He took her wrist, then placed her fingers around the rigid length of his erection, sucking in a breath when she touched him. Guiding her hand slowly, he continued to watch.

"That's it. Feels so good." He looked at her face again. "I love when you touch me. I'm sure I could come from your hand alone."

Not that he intended to.

He waited until she was doing most of the work herself, fisting his dick, slowly working her hand up and down his length. When she'd ratcheted his blood pressure up a few notches, he said, "Now use that pretty little tongue and lick me."

Without meeting his gaze this time, Lorrie leaned forward. He could tell she was hesitant, but she was also curious. Up to this point, he hadn't attempted to put his dick in her mouth, choosing instead to find a million ways to pleasure her. Not that he hadn't thought about it, but in the back of his mind, there had always been a niggling feeling that stopped him. There was the risk that she would find the act too crude, that she might turn him away and be disgusted by him, but so far, she hadn't balked at anything he'd done to her, so it was a risk he was willing to take.

Lorrie's tongue darted out past her lips, swiping the crown briefly. He hissed again, making sure she heard what she did to him. As he continued to cup her head, he urged her forward a little. "Don't stop."

She dropped her hand from around his shaft, then slowly worked him with her tongue. Using his own fist, he guided his dick where he wanted it, moaning as she lapped at him like an ice cream cone.

"Now put those pretty lips around me, baby," he instructed gruffly.

Her eyes lifted again, uncertainty in her gaze this time.

Curtis didn't want to force her, knowing she would eventually relent, but he wanted her to work out the battle in her head. He knew she'd read books, because she'd told him she had, but he wasn't sure exactly how far those stories had gone.

"Fuck," he groaned loud and long when she wrapped her sweet mouth around him, her tongue working him as she sucked. "Oh, God, baby, that's good. Oh, yes. Fuck."

With his hand on the back of her head, the more she moved, the more she sucked, the more difficult it was for him not to urge her forward, getting her to take more of him into her mouth.

She was perfection, the way she licked and slurped and moaned as though this was as much for her as it was for him.

"Oh, sweet Jesus," he growled. He couldn't take much more, and he wasn't quite ready to be done yet.

Reluctantly, he pulled out of her mouth, then reached for her, helping her to her feet before crushing his lips to hers. He kissed her long and hard, pushing her up against the tiled wall. He was at his breaking point. This woman, so damn sweet and eager, made him burn so fucking hot sometimes he didn't think he'd survive it.

Pulling back, he smiled at her as he brushed her wet hair out of her face.

"Your turn," he said urgently, making sure she saw his wicked grin.

THE WATER GREW COLD, AND CURTIS TURNED off the shower, dried them both, and returned to the bedroom before Lorrie even processed what had happened in the shower. It had been ... surprisingly enjoyable? Dirty hot?

Both?

Whatever it was, she had been completely surprised, but more so turned on by what Curtis had had her do. Again, she wasn't necessarily a prude, but she didn't have any experience, either. Nothing other than what Curtis had taught her thus far and that ... putting his erection in her mouth...

She wasn't sure what to think about it other than she had enjoyed it. The way he'd moaned when she'd moved her tongue or applied a little more suction... That was the hot part. She'd been startlingly aroused by his reaction to what she was doing to him. It again gave her that sense of empowerment.

"Sit," Curtis said, pulling her from her pornographic thoughts.

Lorrie sat.

"What are you doing?" she asked when he kneeled on the floor before her, shouldering his way between her thighs.

"It's my turn to taste."

Curtis put a hand on her chest and urged her back. Catching herself on her elbows, Lorrie remained propped up, still completely naked as she watched him. Though she wasn't entirely comfortable with being naked because of her own body image issues, she couldn't deny that Curtis always made her feel like the most desirable woman in the world.

Her breath lodged in her throat the same way it always did when he touched her. So when he used his thumbs to open her lower lips, she felt a blush wash over her. She was partly embarrassed, partly turned on. Apparently more of the latter, because she didn't move to stop him.

It wasn't that he hadn't done this before, using his tongue down there to pleasure her, but usually these things only happened when the bedroom was dark. The sun was still up, the room bright, so she could see every single thing he did.

"Curtis," she cried out when he lashed her with his tongue, sliding through her slit. She automatically bucked her hips, but he gripped her thighs and held her down, his mouth doing wondrous things to her.

Before long, her body was humming, and she was squirming relentlessly, trying to get to that pivotal point where she would be catapulted into bliss. He released one leg, his hand falling from sight, and then she felt his fingers work their way inside her. It only took a few thrusts with those skilled fingers and a few more licks by that devilish tongue before she was rocketing skyward, her body and her mind separating as pleasure assaulted her.

It was too much; she didn't know how people endured that much pleasure.

She must have recovered, because when the room came back into focus, Curtis was hovering over her on the bed, his grin wide.

"Have I mentioned how much I love watching you come apart?"

She shook her head but smiled back at him.

His smirk was replaced with something that resembled desperation as he eased between her thighs, his erection pressing against her sensitive flesh. Needing more of him and not willing to see if he intended to torment her any longer, Lorrie took matters into her own hands. Reaching between them, she guided him to her, then pulled his hips, forcing him inside.

"Lorrie," he breathed roughly, his head falling down to her shoulder as he held himself above her on his forearms. "Oh, God, baby. I love being inside you. So tight. So wet. So … perfect."

He began working his hips, sliding inside, the friction sending electrical pulses through her body. She loved the way he looked above her, his muscles flexing as he slowly penetrated her over and over.

"Such a sweet pussy," he mumbled. "I wanna spend the rest of my life right here."

She loved his dirty mouth, loved how he seemed to ramble incoherently. She hung on every word, every stroke, every exquisite sensation.

Curtis's hips slammed forward, and then he shifted, gripping her hips and changing their position so that her bottom was lifted and he was impaling her roughly. He seemed transfixed by the spot where their bodies were joined, and she continued to watch him.

"Fuck," he hissed, his fingers digging into her flesh as he pounded into her, driving her higher, these sensations new, different. Better.

It was as though he was losing control, taking her, owning her.

"Curtis! Yes… Curtis!" Another more powerful orgasm slammed through her, once again leaving her mind numb and her body sated. She clutched the sheets in her fist, never looking away from him, her body continuing to hum as he worked his way to completion, his hips driving forward, then back, over and over, before roaring as he filled her.

And while she worked on getting her breathing back to normal, she couldn't help but wonder when they would be doing that again.

Twenty-Four

My heart is broken once again, and this time I'm not sure it will ever mend completely. Mitch stopped by the house today to relay the devastating news that last night, Kathy and Celeste were in a car accident. A bad one.

Kathy was drinking and driving (stupid, stupid, stupid), and apparently she'd gone to a party. Mitch said that Celeste called Kathy before the party and asked if she could pick her up from a friend's house. I don't know why Celeste didn't call us or even Mitch or Janice. Oh, my God. If she had called one of us, this wouldn't have happened.

Mitch said that Kathy picked Celeste up, and just a few blocks from Momma's house, Kathy crashed the car into a tree. (The pain in my chest is unbearable as I think about it.) They say Kathy died on impact, probably never felt any pain. For the record, that doesn't make it any better, any easier to process. Celeste is in the hospital, and they don't think she's going to make it. Kathy is only nineteen—was. Oh, God. How could this happen to her? How could God take her so soon?

Please God, please let Celeste wake up. I don't think this family will survive it if she dies, too. ♥

"CURTIS!"

A loud knock on the front door followed the bellowing of his name. Pushing up from his spot on the couch, Curtis went to the door to find Lorrie's brother Mitch standing on the porch, his hat in his hand, his face drawn up.

He looked like hell. As though he hadn't slept in a month.

"What's the matter?" Curtis asked, stepping out and pulling the door closed behind him. Something told him this wasn't good, and he didn't want Lorrie hearing only part of whatever Mitch was about to say.

"Is Lorrie here?" Mitch looked past him as though he could see through the front door and into the house.

Curtis grabbed his smokes from his pocket and lit one up while he stood there, offering one to Mitch, who shook his head. "She is. Do you want me to get her?"

"Not yet." Mitch was gripping his hat so tightly Curtis knew something was horribly wrong. "I wanna tell you first."

Good idea. Based on the pain etched around the man's eyes and mouth, whatever Mitch was going to say wouldn't be good.

"Tell me what?"

Mitch met Curtis's gaze, and it was then that he could tell his brother-in-law had been crying. His eyes were bloodshot, his cheeks puffy.

Definitely not good.

"Kathy and Celeste..." Mitch took a deep breath. "They were in a car accident last night."

"Shit. They okay?"

Mitch's face fell, and that answered Curtis's question before his brother-in-law explained.

"Kathy was at the wheel. She'd been drinking, at least according to what the doctors said. She picked Celeste up from a friend's house. They didn't make it home. She crashed the car into a tree, not far from Momma's house." Mitch pointed, as though that would help Curtis understand where he was referring to. "Kathy died on impact. Celeste is in the hospital. They don't think she's gonna make it."

"You've gotta tell Lorrie," Curtis told him while already trying to figure out a way to shield Lorrie from the pain.

Her sister was dead.

Shit.

"I know," Mitch said, his voice rough. "I don't know how to tell her. It's gonna kill her."

Lorrie was a strong woman, but Curtis couldn't imagine how he'd handle finding out one of his brothers or sisters had died. He'd nearly lost his shit when they'd gotten word that Gerald had been shot, and that hadn't been life threatening. This... Damn. This had been fatal.

Regardless, they had to tell her, and he had to take her to the hospital so she could be with Celeste.

Curtis took a couple of drags on his cigarette, then tossed it out into the dirt. Before he turned to step inside, the door opened, and Lorrie stuck her head out, grinning. "Hey, Mitch. What are—" She didn't finish her sentence, and Curtis suspected that was because she saw the pain imprinted boldly on her brother's face. "What's wrong?"

"Let's go inside," Curtis told her, not waiting for Mitch to respond. He wanted Lorrie sitting down for this news. "Mitch'll tell you. But we need to sit down."

Once inside, Curtis guided Lorrie to the couch. He could tell she wanted to fight him, that she didn't want to sit down or wait for someone to explain things to her, but he managed to coerce her with a gentle arm around her shoulder.

"It's Kathy," Mitch said once Lorrie was off her feet, tears filling his eyes as he spoke. He didn't take a seat, simply stood a few feet away, wringing his hat in his hands. "She died last night, Lorrie."

Lorrie flinched as though the words weighed a ton, hitting her directly in the chest. Curtis pulled her to his side as she stared wide-eyed back at her brother. "No. That... No, that can't be true."

"She and Celeste were in a car accident. The car hit a tree. Killed Kathy on impact." Mitch sobbed and Curtis's heart broke for the man. And for Lorrie.

"No," Lorrie said, the word so matter-of-fact it was as though she could change the outcome by saying it.

Mitch nodded.

"No," Lorrie repeated. She was shaking her head in disbelief while tears filled her eyes. "It can't be true. No."

Lorrie tried to get up, but Curtis held her, pulling her to him.

"Celeste was with her," Mitch continued.

Curtis tried to hold on as Lorrie bolted upright, tears now streaming down her face.

Mitch cleared his throat. "She's in a coma. They don't think she's gonna make it."

"No!" Lorrie was more adamant that time. "That can't be true! It can't be true!" She turned to him. "Curtis, tell me he's lying. Tell me that my sister didn't die. Please. Please don't let it be true."

He could practically feel the fissure that broke through his heart. Seeing the devastation on Lorrie's face was enough to shatter him. Wrapping his arms around her, Curtis pulled his wife into his chest, cradling her head as she sobbed uncontrollably. He physically felt her pain, wished he could absorb it for her.

While he held her, Curtis looked at Mitch. "I'll bring her to the hospital."

Mitch nodded. "I've gotta go tell Janice. I came here first."

Curtis didn't envy the man. It was hard enough that he'd lost his sister, but to have to relive it over and over again, explaining it to everyone in his family... That had to be hell.

Without a word, Mitch left, silently closing the door behind him.

LORRIE COULDN'T WRAP HER MIND AROUND WHAT Mitch had told her. She couldn't believe that Kathy could possibly be...

No. It couldn't be true. God wasn't that cruel.

The words continued to pound inside her head like a hammer. Her entire body was shaking, the emotion so overwhelming she didn't know how to process it.

Kathy had been her best friend. They'd been so close growing up. It hadn't always been perfect, but she had been Lorrie's closest confidante, especially during the years Curtis had been away.

A sob ripped through her, and Curtis's strong arms tightened around her. She was thankful that he didn't try to hush her with empty words. Nothing he said could make this easy for her. Her sister had died.

"Let me get my boots on and we'll go up to the hospital," Curtis whispered in her ear.

Yes. Hospital. Celeste.

That was exactly where she needed to be.

Nodding against his chest, she tried to pull herself together.

"I need to let Momma know," Curtis said. "She's gonna want to be with you."

Lorrie wasn't so sure that was a good idea, especially if her mother would be at the hospital, but she knew Curtis was right. Mrs. Walker would want to know. During the time Curtis had been away, Kathy and Celeste had come over a lot, even had dinner with the Walkers from time to time. And since Granite Creek was such a small town, there was no doubt word would get out, if it hadn't already.

Sitting up, Lorrie brushed her hair out of her face, then went to the bathroom to clean herself up. She stared at her reflection, and that simple action had the tears falling once again. She wanted someone to wake her up from this nightmare. She didn't want to accept the fact that her sister could possibly be dead.

And what about Celeste? According to Mitch, the doctors didn't think she was going to make it. How would...? *God.* She wasn't sure they'd make it through this. How could you grieve for one of your sisters, much less two, and still be able to function?

She managed to take a deep breath, turned on the faucet, and splashed cool water on her face while her brain tried to process the news. The more water she doused herself in, the harder the tears fell.

"Oh, God, no," she cried out. Her legs buckled, and she reached for the sink at the same time Curtis's strong arms grabbed her, lifting her up, then carrying her to the bedroom. He set her on the edge of the mattress, then climbed on the bed behind her, pulling her down with him.

"We need to go to the hospital," she said hoarsely.

"We will," he mumbled gently. "In a few minutes. Let me have this, Lorrie. I need to hold you."

She knew he was doing this for her, only claiming it was for himself. She loved him all the more for it. Giving in, she let the tears fall, her face buried in his chest, her arms wrapped around him, her fingers clutching the back of his shirt as the horrible news took root and her soul shattered.

Twenty-Five

If I never have to go through a day like today, it'll be too soon. We laid my sisters to rest today. Both of them.

Going to the cemetery and watching as they lowered not one but two of my beautiful sisters into the ground was the most devastating thing I have ever witnessed. Most of the town showed up to pay their respects, doing their best to console Momma. She is taking it hard, but that's completely understandable. My heart is shattered and they were my sisters. I can't imagine what Momma is going through. Unfortunately, she doesn't seem to want to talk to me. I tried twice. The first time, I chalked it up to her being upset. The second time… Well, it wasn't what I expected. ♥

CURTIS WOULD BE MORE THAN WILLING TO never again have to go through what he'd gone through today. More so because seeing his wife so devastated was the equivalent of stealing his heart right out of his chest.

The past week had been brutal. Between the news of Kathy's death, then Celeste's steady decline, followed by her death, it had been a whirlwind of emotions. And because the Jamesons were going through so much, Curtis had taken it upon himself to handle the funeral arrangements, working directly with Mitch. Lorrie's brother hadn't deserved to take it all on himself, and Lorrie's mother had proved to be in no shape to deal with the details.

Although horrifically sad, it had been a nice service, and he expected the graveside service to be the same. Curtis remained with Lorrie, sitting on the first row with her brothers and sisters and mother. Dorothy had taken the seat at the opposite end, as far away from his as possible. Whether that had been intentional or not, he wasn't sure, nor did he really care to know.

He kept his arm around Lorrie the entire time, even as they lowered the caskets, holding her tight to him, her body trembling uncontrollably. She was doing fairly well composing herself, but he knew how hard it was for her. For all of them.

"I wanna go say something to Momma," Lorrie told him once the service had concluded.

Curtis nodded, taking her hand and leading her toward Dorothy.

"Momma." Lorrie's voice was hoarse from all the tears she'd shed, so the word didn't carry far enough.

"Mrs. Jameson," Curtis called, getting Lorrie's mother's attention.

Dorothy turned around, and when her eyes landed on him, the sadness disappeared, and something that looked a hell of a lot like rage filled them.

"What do you want?" she seethed.

Curtis's eyebrows darted down in confusion, not sure what he'd done to provoke this sort of response. He'd spent the entire week putting things together, not wanting any of them to have to deal with this while they were grieving, so her reaction seemed entirely out of character.

"I hope you're not expecting me to thank you," Dorothy snapped.

That had been the absolute last thing on his mind.

"Momma, come on," Mitch said, his eyes meeting Curtis's briefly. Based on Mitch's expression, it looked as though he didn't know what was going on, either.

"I don't know who you think you are throwing your money around, acting like we're your charity. It might've worked when you bought Lorrie, but you can't buy me. Or my other daughters."

He felt Lorrie's eyes on him, but he didn't look away from Dorothy. There were so many things he wanted to say to her at the moment, but he remembered where they were, what they were here for. It wasn't the time or the place.

"Momma," Mitch whispered loudly. "What're you talkin' about? *I* paid for this. Janice and I. Curtis didn't pay a dime."

He hadn't, either. He had offered it to Mitch, but Mitch had kindly declined, just as Curtis had thought he would. Mitch Jameson was a proud man. A good man. He had taken it upon himself to take care of his family after their father had died, and Curtis respected him for that. The only thing Curtis had done was handle the logistics, with the help from his own mother, who had been just as devastated by the loss of Lorrie's sisters as everyone else.

Dorothy's head snapped toward Mitch, her eyes wide. She looked horrified.

Since she'd basically revealed the fact that Curtis had paid Phillip Jameson in order to get his approval for Curtis to marry her, she should be shocked. And ashamed.

He took a deep breath and glanced down at his wife. She was staring back at him, tears in her eyes. She didn't know the whole story, but he knew Dorothy had said just enough for her to put two and two together.

Now, the only thing he could do was hope she would hear him out.

LORRIE WANTED TO CRAWL INTO A HOLE and die. As people started leaving the graveside, she felt dozens of eyes on her, all likely feeling pity. Not a lick of it was due to her sisters' deaths, either.

She didn't have a clue what her mother was talking about, but she'd heard enough to know that it wasn't good.

She tried to free her hand from Curtis's, but he held tight.

"Let me go," she hissed, trying to keep her voice low.

"No," he insisted, his grip firmer on her hand as he led her toward the car.

"What did she mean when she said you paid for me?"

"We'll talk about it when we get home," he said brusquely.

Again, she tried to yank her hand from his, but Curtis stopped abruptly, then turned to face her. "It is not at all what you think," he said, his voice low, rough. "But I expect the benefit of the doubt, and I expect you to hear me out."

"What makes you think you deserve that?" she countered hotly, fury replacing the sadness that had consumed her for days.

It actually felt good to get angry. So much better than the throbbing ache in her chest that she'd endured since the minute she'd learned of Kathy's death, followed closely by Celeste's.

"Because I'm your husband," he remarked.

Lorrie noticed people were watching them, and she knew how things worked in Granite Creek. If they thought for a second that there was trouble in paradise, the rumors would run wild. That was the last thing she needed on the heels of such a tragedy.

Composing herself, she relaxed her hand in Curtis's and allowed him to lead her to the truck. A short time later, after they had pulled into the drive of their house, before he pushed in the emergency brake, she bolted out and ran up to the door.

She was inside before Curtis even got out of the truck. Anger sparked the dry kindling of emotion still in her chest, and the only way she could release it was by screaming her hatred for the situation. It wasn't even Curtis she was mad at, although she definitely deserved an explanation. No, her hatred was at God for taking her sisters from her, for leaving her family in shambles. She wasn't sure how they would pick up and move forward without Kathy and Celeste there.

She screamed until she was hoarse, then she found herself in Curtis's arms, her face buried in his chest as he held her tightly. Her knees gave out again, but rather than move her to the couch, he lowered them both to the carpet, pulling her into his lap.

"I never wanted you to find out," Curtis said softly when her sobs quieted.

"About what?" Lorrie was too weak to even lift her head to look at him. She knew he was referring to what her mother had said.

"About what your father did."

It wasn't difficult to figure it out. Lorrie wasn't stupid. She remembered the conversations that had taken place right before Curtis had asked her to marry him. She hadn't been privy to the details, but her father had gone from forbidding her to see Curtis to shipping her off the next morning.

"You paid him." It wasn't a question. She already knew he had.

"I had to," he whispered, his voice broken.

Needing to look into his eyes, Lorrie slipped out of his lap and onto the floor, kneeling across from him. She didn't even have to ask him to explain before the words started tumbling from his mouth.

"Your father came to me, gave me an ultimatum. You already know that part." Curtis looked down at his hands. "I wasn't going to allow him to take you away from me, so I asked you to marry me. That was what he wanted, but I didn't understand why at the time. I knew I would marry you eventually, so it wasn't a big deal.

"I stayed up all night trying to figure out how we would make this work. Where we would live, how I would make money to support you. Then, out of the blue, your father showed up first thing that next morning. When I walked into the kitchen, I found him sitting at my mother's kitchen table." Curtis frowned. "I still remember the smug look on that bastard's face."

Lorrie didn't interrupt, knowing there was more.

Curtis lifted his eyes and met hers. "It was no secret that your old man hated my family. He was jealous of what we had; everyone knew that. But my father never let it bother him, and we kids never thought much of it. A lot of people didn't like us. Mostly because they didn't understand us. We were wild, often out of control. I got that. What I didn't get was how a man could walk into another man's house and blackmail him."

Lorrie's eyes widened. "What?"

She saw his Adam's apple move slowly up and down. He seemed to be processing what he was going to say.

"Just tell me what happened, Curtis. No more secrets."

"That's the thing," he replied harshly. "It's not that I purposely kept it from you because of what I did. I'd do it all over again if I had to. I didn't tell you because I didn't want you to know what your father had done."

"What did he do?"

Curtis took a deep breath, then exhaled slowly. "Your father had somehow found out about the details of my father's will. No one knows how he managed to do that, nor have I ever asked. It doesn't matter. My father stated in his will that all of his land and the ranch would go to the first of his sons to marry." He narrowed his eyes as he met her gaze. "I didn't even know about it at the time. No one did. No one other than my mother, anyway. So, he confronted my mother with that information, and she confirmed that it was true. Apparently that had been your father's angle from the beginning."

"Oh, my goodness." Lorrie's hand was on her mouth; she couldn't believe what she was hearing. It all made perfect sense, right down to why her father had insisted that she get to know Curtis shortly after Mr. Walker's death.

"Yeah," he agreed. "Your father pushed you into meeting me because he wanted to benefit from my father's will."

"But why'd you pay him?" She wasn't even sure she wanted to know how much.

"That morning, after I had asked you to marry me, he told me that he would not give his permission. That he'd changed his mind."

That didn't surprise her.

"I told him he was fucking crazy. That he couldn't do it. My mother reminded me that you were underage, and I couldn't marry you without his consent." His eyes locked with hers. "Your father was a mean bastard, Lorrie. As mean as mine."

"How much did you pay him?"

Curtis shook his head.

"Tell me," she insisted.

"Five thousand dollars."

Lorrie was up on her feet, appalled by the notion that her father would insist on that much money.

In the next breath, Curtis was standing before her, his finger curled beneath her chin, forcing her to look up at him.

"I would've paid any amount he asked, Lorrie. I was not going to lose you. Especially not because of a selfish, greedy man."

"That's why he seemed so happy that morning," she mused.

It all came back to her. The way her mother and father had been smiling when she'd come to tell them the news. She hadn't figured out how they would've known, but she hadn't cared at the time. It was her wedding day and the only thing she could think about was Curtis. Marrying him and spending the rest of her life with him.

"Where'd you come up with that kind of money?"

Curtis's eyebrow lifted.

"Do I even wanna know?"

He led her over to the couch, easing her down and sitting beside her, facing her.

"Not all of my family's money is tied up in the ranch like I'd assumed. My father willed the land and the ranch to whichever of his boys married first. What your old man didn't know was that my father owned all of the land in Granite Creek."

"What does that mean?"

"It means Granite Creek belongs to me now. Us."

"All of it?"

"Right down to the very land your momma's house sits on."

Lorrie frowned. "Did my father know that?"

"No one knows that," he said, his voice gentle. "And I don't want anyone else to know. What you and I choose to do with it is our decision to make. I hated your father for what he did, but I wasn't going to hold it against your family, so I've kept it to myself."

Of all the things she'd expected to come out of this conversation, that wasn't it. Not only had her father blackmailed Curtis and forced him to pay him, Curtis now owned Granite Creek.

Goodness gracious.

Just when she thought she had things all figured out.

Twenty-Six

I don't want to jinx it and say that things are perfect between Curtis and me, but things are going really well. It hasn't been easy the last few months, especially after Kathy and Celeste died, but the more time that passes, the easier it is to move forward. It's still hard to think about my sisters. I miss them terribly, but I know I have to keep my head up, keep moving forward. It's what they would want.

I can honestly say I wouldn't have made it through it without Curtis. He knows that I need a distraction, so he's teaching me to help him on the ranch, and I've been trying to decide if I want to go to college or not. At the moment, I would prefer to be a rancher's wife, but I want to learn everything there is about being a rancher. I don't want to sit at home while Curtis works, and I've told him this a million times. I think he finally got the hint.

Oh, and tonight we went to a New Year's Eve military ball. It was incredible. I dressed up in my prettiest dress, and Curtis wore his Army service uniform… We had so much fun.

Shh. Don't tell anyone, but we snuck into a supply closet and we had sex. I still can't believe I did it, but it was actually my idea. I don't know what Curtis has done to me, but I can't get enough of him. ♥

♥ Saturday, March 8, 1969 ♥

We got the best news today! Mitch and Janice came over to tell us they're expecting a baby. A baby! I'm so excited for them. The baby is due in October, right around Curtis's birthday. This is the sort of news we all need right now. I'm so happy for my brother. I'm going to be an aunt. ♥

♥ Sunday, June 15, 1969 ♥

We had another Sunday dinner today with Mrs. Walker and Curtis's brothers and sisters. It was the first time Curtis actually mentioned something about having Sunday dinners. Apparently he likes the idea. I told him that one day, when we have kids of our own and they are grown and moved out, I want them to come home every Sunday so we can share a meal together. It made me feel good that he agreed.

Just don't tell Mrs. Walker that Curtis took me into his old bedroom and we had sex. Up against the door. ♥

Twenty-Seven

♥ *Saturday, July 26, 1969* ♥

I think I'm dreaming. I think in a few minutes someone is going to come in and wake me up. There is no way this could be happening. The only thing that makes me think today hasn't been a dream is because there is no way I would've ever imagined something like this. Ever.

Last year for my birthday, Curtis surprised me by coming home. This year, Curtis has outdone himself. If he keeps it up, I'm not sure I'll be able to make it through another birthday. ♥

GETTING LORRIE OUT OF THE HOUSE AND away long enough for Curtis to do what needed to be done for her twenty-first birthday took far more resources than he'd intended. Initially, he had asked his mother to take her to lunch. Mary Elizabeth had been more than willing. For some reason, Lorrie had said she wasn't hungry.

First attempt: fail.

Then, he had bribed his brothers to see if she'd be willing to help out with the horses. Joseph had been fairly convincing when he told her they couldn't do it without her. For whatever reason, Lorrie had said she wasn't interested in working today.

Second attempt: fail.

Then, he had called Mitch, asking his brother-in-law to help out. Mitch and Janice had asked Lorrie if she wanted to go shopping for baby things. Completely unexpected by any of them, she had said she'd prefer to sit at home and enjoy the day.

Third attempt: fail.

Finally, Curtis had convinced his mother and his sisters to come over and drag Lorrie out of the house, simply not taking no for an answer. *Jesus H. Christ.* He loved the woman with every ounce of his being, but she definitely wasn't making this easy.

Final attempt: success.

Granted, Lorrie had promised to pay him back later, so perhaps it wasn't quite as successful as he'd hoped, but still, she was out of the house just as he needed her to be.

With help from Lorrie's sister Rose and her brother Bruce, along with his brothers, Curtis managed to get the house completely decorated for the party. Joseph went to pick up the cake they'd had made, while Frank Jr. and Bruce made sure everything was where it needed to be. And when it was time, David went to pick up a couple of Lorrie's friends who she'd gone to school with, and after a little convincing, Lorrie's mother agreed to come, bringing with her the rest of Lorrie's siblings.

The only thing left was the big surprise, which he planned to have arrive after they had cake and ice cream. A surprise on top of a surprise, kind of.

Although it hadn't started off easy, getting it all set up went off without a hitch, and now the only thing left to do was wait for her to return.

"WHAT DO YOU THINK HE'LL GET YOU for your birthday?"
Daphne asked when they were driving back from the movies.

She hadn't wanted to go out today, preferring to spend the
day with Curtis, but he'd seemed adamant that she go. It didn't
take a rocket scientist to figure out what he was doing. Clearly he
was planning to surprise her; she just didn't know with what.

Lorrie shrugged. "Don't know."

"Last year you said he gave you the best present ever," Lisa
reminded her.

At twelve, the girl sure did remember a lot.

"He did," she agreed.

"By coming home?" Maryanne asked.

"Yes." That would forever go down as the best birthday
present ever, no doubt about it. There was nothing Curtis could
possibly buy her that would be better than that.

"What do you want him to get you?" Maryanne gripped the
back of the seat, leaning forward.

"Nothing, really," she answered as she stared out the window,
watching the trees pass by.

"What about a horse?" Lisa suggested. "That's what I'd
want."

"I don't need a horse." They already had plenty of horses.
Lorrie didn't need her own.

"If it was me, I'd want a car," Daphne stated.

Mary Elizabeth cleared her throat and glanced at her
daughter in the rearview mirror.

Lorrie smiled as she peered over her shoulder at the girls in
the backseat. "I don't need a car, either. Curtis takes me anywhere
I need to go."

"Yeah, but don't you ever wanna go somewhere by yourself?
I wouldn't wanna spend all my time with my husband if I had
one."

"I like spending time with Curtis," she said, chuckling at
Daphne's comment.

When they pulled into Mary Elizabeth's drive, Lorrie didn't see anything out of the norm. As they ventured down the dirt road that led to Lorrie and Curtis's little house, she realized no one was there, either. Maybe she'd been wrong. Maybe there wasn't going to be a party.

"Y'all are home," Curtis said, stepping out onto the porch, wiping his hands on a towel. "I didn't expect you back so soon."

Her husband looked as relaxed as ever. Not like a man who had put together a surprise party after making it obvious that he was trying to get her out of the house. She tried not to be disappointed when he leaned over and kissed her on the lips, but she saw the smile on his face.

Maybe he was up to something.

"Come on inside for a bit, ladies," Curtis said to his mother and sisters.

Lorrie allowed him to steer her inside. The first thing she noticed was that the lights were off.

And then they weren't.

"Surprise!"

The eruption of noise scared her, and she actually shrieked, laughing as she stumbled back against Curtis. Although she'd been somewhat expecting it, they'd still managed to put one over on her. She glanced over her shoulder at the man she loved and smiled up at him. He had given her a surprise party, which, as far as she was concerned, was the greatest gift in the world. She continued to stare at him, completely enthralled by his handsome face and that sexy smirk, and then it registered again that Curtis was giving her a surprise party—and there were more than a dozen people in her house. She finally remembered her manners.

While she greeted everyone, Lorrie relaxed, excited that they'd come to see her. In the back of her mind, she started wondering what Curtis had gotten her for her birthday. And it had nothing to do with the fact that she even wanted something, more because she didn't want anything. But she knew Curtis. He always said he wanted to give her everything, but he never seemed to realize she already had it. Him.

"Happy birthday, darlin'," Curtis whispered in her ear as he pulled her against him. "I've got another surprise for you. But you'll have to be a really good girl to get it." His voice lowered more. "And you'll have to wait for all these people to leave, 'cause it requires you to be naked."

Her face flamed instantly as she leaned back and looked at him. Luckily no one was standing close by, and the conversation carrying on around her likely made it impossible for anyone to have heard him, but still, she was embarrassed.

And turned on.

She quickly shook off the thought.

"Come on, let's get some cake."

"Happy birthday, Lorrie."

Lorrie looked over at the sound of her mother's voice, and she nearly burst into tears. She had briefly noticed that her brothers and sisters were all there, but she hadn't seen her mother.

"Momma." A sob ripped from her throat as she went to give her mother a hug.

"My little girl's all grown up."

To hear those words from her mother's mouth made her insides shake. She'd spent the better part of the last six years wishing her relationship with her mother could be better. They hadn't spoken since Kathy and Celeste's funeral, and for a while, she had wondered if they ever would.

"Thanks for inviting me," Dorothy said to Curtis.

"You're welcome here anytime."

Suddenly, the thought of whatever gift Curtis might have in mind wasn't quite so bad because as she looked around, seeing her family and friends there with her, nothing else mattered.

"Let's get some cake for the birthday girl," someone shouted.

After they did an off-key rendition of "Happy Birthday," David offered to cut the cake, and as he passed it around, Lorrie spoke to her friends from school. Although she saw them from time to time in town, or at church, it was still exciting to know that they'd come over to celebrate her birthday.

As the conversation continued to flow while everyone enjoyed cake and ice cream, Lorrie had finally started to relax when Curtis came over and put his arm around her. "You ready for your gift?"

"Maybe." Depended on what it was.

"Come on, everyone," Curtis announced. "It's time for Lorrie's present."

The chatter ceased, and everyone started following as Curtis led Lorrie out to the front porch.

The first thing she noticed was a car coming down the narrow dirt drive toward the house.

It was a fancy car. Shiny and new.

She really, really hoped he hadn't bought her a car.

"Oh, my goodness," Lisa whispered to Daphne. "Do you think that's *her* car?"

Daphne squealed a little bit.

Lorrie shook her head. She really, really, *really* hoped he hadn't bought her a car.

Trying not to get nervous because the thought of driving a car petrified her, Lorrie stood beside Curtis, waiting for him to explain what was going on. Though she didn't want to look, her eyes were glued to the pretty, shiny car that she absolutely didn't want.

Would she have to break Curtis's heart? Would he be upset with her that she didn't want a car?

He should know her better than that. She didn't know how to drive, and though she wanted to learn one day, she didn't want it to be now.

The car stopped in front of the house, and Lorrie fought the urge to squeeze Curtis's hand.

For a second, it didn't register who had stepped out.

"Mayor Clark," Curtis greeted the man walking toward them.

Why in the world would Mayor Clark be driving her car?

"You remember my beautiful wife," Curtis said, putting his arm around her shoulder.

Lorrie shook the mayor's outstretched hand.

"So nice to see you again." He was beaming as he gripped her hand firmly.

"You, too."

"Are you ready?" Curtis asked.

No. "Yes," she said nervously.

The mayor handed a folded sheet of paper to Curtis, and he released her so that he could take it and open it. He glanced over the page briefly before handing it over to her.

Hesitantly, she took the paper, glancing at the faces around her before looking down at it.

Only two words on the page registered: Coyote Ridge.

She looked up at Curtis. "What is this?"

"It's the official document reflecting the new name of our town," the mayor explained.

"What?" Lorrie knew her eyes were as big as saucers, but she couldn't help it.

Curtis's smile grew even wider.

"Your husband came to me a while back with the request to change the name of Granite Creek. In order to do something such as this, it requires a vote from the town. We are happy to say that we will no longer be known as Granite Creek. Officially, our new name is Coyote Ridge."

Lorrie couldn't breathe as she stared at Curtis in complete shock.

"Happy birthday, darlin'," he said, pulling her into his arms.

They were surrounded by applause, but the only thing Lorrie heard was the beating of her own heart as she hugged Curtis fiercely.

Her husband had changed the name of their town.

For her.

Twenty-Eight

"THANKS FOR COMIN'," CURTIS TOLD DAVID AS his brother headed down the porch. "And thanks for all the help."

"No problem," David called back, waving as he headed toward the big house.

Finally.

David was the last to leave, and though he'd thought the house would never be quiet again, Curtis now had Lorrie all to himself.

Closing the door, he turned to see her standing there, staring back at him, the same way she'd been doing for the past couple of hours. Ever since Mayor Clark had delivered the paper showing that they had officially renamed the town to Coyote Ridge.

"I thought you bought me a car," she blurted.

He grinned, closing the distance between them.

"Yeah?" He stopped in front of her. "Were you disappointed?"

She shook her head. "Not at all. The last thing in the world I want is a car."

"No?"

"No."

"So, did you like your gift?"

"I can't believe you remember that," she said, her eyes locked with his.

He took her hand and pulled her over to the couch, then had her straddle his lap so that she was facing him.

"It's funny. The day my mother told me that the Walkers owned all the land in Granite Creek, I knew that one day I would rename the town. I had no idea what that entailed at the time, but I remembered a little blond-haired, blue-eyed girl telling me that it would've made more sense to be called Coyote Ridge."

"I'm pretty sure you made fun of me for that," she said, grinning. "Was it hard to do?"

"It wasn't as difficult as I thought it would be."

"What does it entail? Changing a whole town's name?"

"Let's just say, there are some new land owners in Coyote Ridge."

Lorrie smiled. "I really like the name. It's perfect."

"It is perfect," he agreed, reaching up and framing her face with his hands. "Just like you."

Curtis pulled her face to his until their lips met. He'd been wanting to do this all damn day, desperate to feel her against him. Her mouth was pliant as he slipped his tongue inside. When she started to squirm on his lap, his dick roared to life between them.

"What do you say we take this to the bedroom?" he asked, pulling back and looking at her.

Lorrie shook her head.

Okay, so maybe he'd misread her intentions. Rather than show his disappointment, he watched her.

"I want to stay right here," she whispered, her lips returning to his mouth.

He damn sure couldn't argue with that.

As she kissed her way along his jaw, Curtis's dick throbbed behind his zipper. This woman made him wild for her, and she seemed to surprise him at every turn.

She nibbled his ear, and Curtis's hips bucked upward as he gripped her hips in his hands, pulling her down to him. "I need to be inside you," he growled.

Lorrie nodded.

"Right here?"

"Mmm-hmm."

"Undo my jeans, Lorrie," he instructed.

She sat up straight, her eyes meeting his. He saw heat and hunger swirling in the glistening blue hue. When she reached between them and undid the button, he never took his eyes off her. It didn't take long before she freed his dick, though it required a little help on his part, forcing the denim midway down his thighs.

"Do you have panties on?" he asked.

Lorrie nodded.

"Take them off."

Curtis stroked himself as she climbed off his lap. He laughed when she teased him, lifting her dress high enough to give him a little peek before she allowed it to fall back to her thighs as she lowered her panties down her legs and kicked them to the side.

"Now the dress." He smirked. She only thought she was the one in control.

Cupping his balls, he continued to torment himself while he watched the seductive little striptease that didn't last nearly as long as he would've preferred.

"Bra," he commanded.

Lorrie unhooked her bra and tossed it away, leaving her standing naked in the middle of their living room.

"Beautiful," he whispered. "So fucking beautiful. Now come here."

He helped her back onto his lap, straddling his hips, but before she lowered onto his thighs, he stroked her pussy with the head of his dick, the wet heat sending electrical currents firing through his veins.

"You're wet for me," he said.

Lorrie nodded.

"I want you to ride me, baby."

She moaned when he pressed the head against her entrance, then, using his other hand, he pulled her hips so that she took him inside.

A rumble echoed in his chest as he groaned. She felt so damn good.

When he was fully seated inside her, Curtis released her hips.

"Ride me, beautiful. Ride my cock."

Her nipples puckered instantly, and he reached up to tweak them as she began lowering and lifting, taking him inside before pulling away.

"Rock your hips," he urged. "Take me all the way inside and rock them back and forth."

She did as he instructed, taking him deep as she rolled her hips. Her eyes closed and she moaned softly.

"So tight. So wet. I love the way your pussy grips me." He knew how much she liked when he talked to her. His sweet girl was definitely naughty, and he had no problems telling her what he liked most.

He watched her for the longest time, enjoying the friction of her smooth pussy walls along his dick. Her head tipped back as he sucked one nipple into his mouth, her whimpers only heightening the sensation.

"Curtis… I need more…"

"What do you need, darlin'?"

"I…" She whimpered again. "I need … more."

He smiled, then gripped her hips to still her movements. Her eyes snapped open, and she met his gaze.

"Let me do the work now," he said. "But I want you to touch yourself." He brushed his thumb over her engorged clitoris. "Right here."

Her throat worked as she swallowed.

"Come on, baby," he encouraged. "I wanna see you touch yourself."

Taking her hand to help her along, Curtis placed her finger over her clitoris. When she didn't pull away, he gripped her hips again and began gently thrusting up into her.

"Oh … yes…"

He'd known she'd like that.

Before long, he was entranced by the way she was rubbing her pussy while he fucked her from beneath. Her beautiful tits bounced before him, and she was by far the most captivating woman he'd ever met.

"That's it," he urged. "You like that?" He groaned when her pussy walls tightened around his dick. "Oh, yeah. Do that again. I love when your pussy grips my dick."

Again, her walls milked him.

"So sexy," he said, continuing to watch as she pleasured herself.

It wasn't long before her moans grew louder, her breaths fast and labored.

"Curtis…"

"Tell me, Lorrie," he insisted. "Tell me when you come."

Her body clamped around his cock, a desperate cry escaping her as he slammed his hips upward, driving deep.

"Yes… Oh, yes… Curtis…"

He couldn't look away as her climax ripped through her. Curtis continued to hold her hips, fucking her until he was blinded by the pleasure, and only then did he give in to his release.

Twenty-Nine

♥ *Wednesday, October 22, 1969* ♥

Oh, my goodness, I can't believe it. I'm an aunt. Mitch and
Janice are now proud parents. Their little girl, Beth, is so
beautiful. I got to hold her. And just that little bit made me want
a baby of my own so much. Curtis and I haven't started talking
about kids, but I'm thinking we should really start thinking about
it, because we could get pregnant at any time. I can't wait! ♥

♥ *Friday, April 10, 1970* ♥

Curtis talked to Gerald today. He's finally coming home. I know
this makes Mrs. Walker happy. He's been gone so long, and
though she talks to him several times a month, I know she wants
him home for good. There's only one teeny tiny problem. It
doesn't look like Gerald is moving back to Coyote Ridge.
According to what Curtis told me, Gerald met a woman, and he's
moving to El Paso to be near her. This might be interesting. ♥

Thirty

Curtis bought me a car for my birthday. It actually made me laugh because he knows how much I didn't want one last year. I still don't necessarily care to have a car, but he did tell me that when we have babies, I'll need to know how to drive. That's true, so how can I be mad at him? ♥

"WHERE ARE WE GOING?" LORRIE ASKED FOR at least the third time since he'd gotten her into the new car.

When he'd opted to buy her a car for her birthday, Curtis had had to remind himself that it wasn't *his* car. It was hers, so it needed to be practical for her.

Yeah, well, picking it out hadn't been all that easy. It was a hell of a lot easier to tell himself not to buy a cool sports car than it was to actually do it. So he had compromised. Although he would've preferred to snag one of the impressive new Dodge Chargers, he had ended up getting her a 1968 Mercury Cougar. A little big for her, maybe, but he felt safe with her behind the wheel.

Or rather, he would feel safe with her behind the wheel once he taught her to drive.

"Curtis!" Lorrie squealed from beside him. "Tell me where we're goin'."

He turned on the dirt road that would lead to the perfect spot for her to get some miles under her belt. It would be her first time driving a car, and he was taking that into consideration.

Rather than answer her question, he stopped the car, put it in park, turned off the engine, opened the door, and got out. He walked around to the passenger side, opened her door, and stared down at her.

"What?" she asked, eyes wide.

"Your turn."

"My turn?" Her eyebrows darted down. "For what?"

He cocked an eyebrow. "To drive."

She started to laugh, which only made him laugh.

"No way," she said when she caught her breath.

"Yes way," he told her, helping her out of the car. "Now go get in."

She was frowning at him, which only made him laugh more.

Rather than let her sweet-talk him out of this, he climbed in and closed the passenger door, leaving her standing on the side of the road while he waited patiently for her to get in.

Lorrie huffed when she finally dropped into the driver's seat. "I can't even reach the pedals," she complained as soon as her cute little butt hit the seat.

"Move the seat up."

"I don't know how," she argued grumpily.

Underneath that sweet exterior was still the feisty girl he'd fallen in love with, so Curtis had known as soon as he'd had the idea to teach her how to drive that she would do this. Which was why he had mentally prepared himself beforehand. He could do this as long as she wanted. "It's electric, baby."

She fumbled around for a minute, and then the chair started to move forward, bringing her closer to the steering wheel. And then closer. And closer. He laughed when she got too close and had to move back some.

"Don't laugh at me," she warned, her tone serious, which only made him laugh more. "Now what?"

This wasn't quite how he'd seen this playing out, but it worked.

"Start the car," he instructed.

She started the car without problems. That was a good thing.

"This is an automatic, so you won't need to shift gears," he explained as he walked her through the gadgets and levers near the steering wheel. He showed her where her turn signals were, which pedal was the brake, which was the gas.

"What about the radio?" she asked.

"We'll worry about that later." That was the last thing they needed to deal with now.

"But what if I wanna listen to music when I drive?"

"Later, baby," he said, trying to get her to focus. "Now put the car in drive while you have your foot on the brake."

She managed to do that without issue, but then she sat there, as though she didn't know what came next.

Curtis chuckled. "Now you're gonna take your foot off the brake and put it on the gas."

She did.

And Curtis had to grab hold of the door handle.

"Easy, baby," he yelled when the car shot forward.

She hit the brakes, damn near sending him through the windshield. He managed to put his hand on the dashboard just in time to keep from getting a concussion. "Fuck."

"I told you this was a bad idea," she said.

He looked over to see her grinning from ear to ear. She was up to something…

"You know how to drive, don't you?" he asked, shaking his head as it hit him.

Her smile widened. "A little. I mean, it doesn't look all that hard."

And to prove her point, Lorrie put her foot on the gas and drove.

Like a professional driver.

"Remind me to spank your ass when we get home," he said gruffly.

"Why?" She tossed a glance his way.

"For nearly knocking me out."

Lorrie laughed, but she continued to drive, and Curtis sat back and enjoyed the trip, allowing her to go for about half an hour before he told her to head back. When they reached the last stop sign before they would hit the road home, he directed her to take the dirt path that led down to the lake.

"Why're we goin' to the lake?" she asked, doing as he instructed.

"'Cause it's high time we broke this car in right."

"What does that mean?"

He didn't answer her, instead showing her where to park and then instructing her to turn off the engine.

They sat there for a moment in the silence while Curtis continued to watch her.

Lorrie didn't turn to face him, her attention focused out the window.

"You know," she said sweetly, "I always thought there was more to it when people went parking. This is kinda boring."

Heaven help him. This woman was something else.

"Get over here," he said firmly.

She glanced over at him but shook her head.

Definitely feisty, his girl was. "Wanna play hard to get, huh?"

Her smile was dazzling.

Curtis reached for her, tickling her sides until he managed to get her over the center console and into his lap. She was huffing and puffing when he finally stopped, but her smile hadn't dimmed at all.

"Kiss me," he ordered her, sliding his hands into her hair and pulling her toward him.

She leaned down and pressed her lips to his, shifting so that she was straddling his hips.

"Holy shit," he breathed roughly. "You make my dick so fucking hard." Curtis kissed along her jaw, then down her neck, lifting her skirt as he ran his hands up her thighs.

She moaned when he cupped her mound, teasing her through her panties.

"I can think of a million things I wanna do to you right now."

"Like what?" she rasped.

"Oh, I don't know." He turned his head and glanced into the backseat. "Maybe spread you out back there and tongue-fuck you until you're begging for my cock." He slipped his thumb beneath her panties as he spoke, rubbing circles over her clitoris, making her moan. "Or maybe I could bend you over the hood and fuck you right there by the lake."

She moaned louder and he increased the pressure of his thumb.

"Or, I could simply pull these little panties aside and let you ride my dick." That was probably his favorite thing in the world, watching her as she rode him until she came. "Which do you want, baby?" he asked, figuring he would give her the option.

It didn't matter to him which one she picked. It was a win-win, regardless.

LORRIE HAD NEVER THOUGHT SHE'D BE THE type of girl who would get hot and bothered by making out in a car. Yet here she was, and the only thing she wanted was for Curtis to do all those dirty things he promised. And she would've told him that, except she couldn't wait that long.

If she chose option one, he would tease her until she unraveled slowly.

If she chose option two, they would have to move from where they were.

But if she chose option three, she simply needed to reach down and...

Lorrie worked his jeans open and, with his help, freed his cock.

"Aw, fuck, baby," he groaned, leaning the chair back as his intense gaze continued to focus on her.

She held her skirt high enough that he could see as she slid down over him, taking him deep inside.

"Oh, yes," he groaned again. "Love watchin' my dick sink inside you." His voice was rough and sexy. "Ride me, darlin'."

Thanks to him being the wonderful teacher that he was, she had learned what he liked, and she worked her hips now just as he'd shown her. The car wasn't the most comfortable place, but she did have a little leverage, so she lifted and lowered her hips, taking him all the way inside, watching his face as his eyes remained glued to where they were joined.

She loved this side of Curtis. Loved the uninhibited man who had no shame in telling her how good she made him feel or what he wanted her to do to him. And perhaps that was what she loved most about sex. Well, other than the incredible orgasms, of course.

"Faster, Lorrie," Curtis growled. "Fuck me faster. Bounce on my dick. Take all of me."

He was breathing hard, and so was she as she continued to lift and lower, trying to go faster, but it wasn't easy in the cramped space.

"Hold that thought," he groaned, gripping her hips to stop her from moving.

Lorrie stilled when he opened the door and shifted so that his feet were outside of the car touching the ground while she still sat astride him. He didn't get up, though, remaining partially seated inside the car as he said, "Turn around, baby."

She wasn't quite sure what he wanted her to do, but she did as he instructed, his erection pulling out of her when she got to her feet. The next thing she knew, Curtis was spinning her around so that she faced away from him.

"Hold on to the door," he said, pulling her back so that she was standing between his spread legs.

She grabbed hold of the ledge by the window as he took her hips in his hands and guided her down toward his lap. Her panties shifted once more and then...

"Oh!" She cried out as he impaled her from below. Her legs were closed, which intensified the sensation, making the pressure of him inside her that much better.

"Aw, yeah," he groaned, smacking her on the bottom. "Now ride me again, baby."

This position was a little easier, especially since her feet were on the ground between his and she could use her thigh muscles to lift and lower as he rocked her onto his erection.

She could feel the warm breeze against her skin where he had lifted her skirt up.

"Fuck, that's pretty," he whispered. "Love watching my dick fuck that pretty pussy."

Her inner muscles clenched tightly as an orgasm took her completely by surprise. Maybe it was the aggressive way he was handling her, or the new position, or simply the dark rumble of his words. Whatever it was, she was grateful she had the door to hold on to.

Curtis gripped her hips and continued to impale her on his erection, pulling her down, shifting her forward, over and over again as he filled her completely.

"I'm gonna come, Lorrie. I'm gonna come in your sweet pussy, baby."

She tightened her muscles around him as another climax rolled through her at the same time Curtis found his release.

After a few minutes had passed and they'd managed to catch their breath, Lorrie smiled at him. "Okay, so maybe there is something good about this whole learning-how-to-drive thing."

Her husband grinned. "Get us home, darlin'. I'm thinkin' you might need more than one spankin' tonight."

Thirty-One

♥ *Saturday, February 27, 1971* ♥

Mitch and Janice are having another baby! I'm so happy for
them. But surprisingly, I'm actually sad for me and Curtis. I want
a baby of my own so badly, but it doesn't seem like that is in
God's plan right now. I'm trying to be positive, but it isn't easy.
Curtis tells me there's nothing to worry about, that when the time
is right, it'll happen. I hope he's right. ♥

♥ *Monday, November 15, 1971* ♥

I went to see Momma today. She said she hasn't been feeling
well. I tried to get her to go to the doctor, but she won't listen to
me. Now that Rose and Bruce are off at college, Adele, Linda,
and Owen are the only ones left to take care of her. I worry
about Momma. It doesn't seem like she's very happy these days.
♥

♥ Thursday, March 2, 1972 ♥

Mitch came over to see me today. He told me that I needed to spend some time with Momma. He finally convinced her to go to the doctor, so she did. They told her she has heart problems. They say her heart is really weak. This saddens me. But more than that, Mitch says Momma doesn't seem to care to get better. The doctors are saying she's depressed. I don't really know what that means, other than she's always sad. When I asked Curtis about it, he told me that Momma has to want to live in order to get better. I've decided I will start going to see her every week, even if she doesn't want me to. ♥

♥ Thursday, June 29, 1972 ♥

Sometimes I wonder how I can continue to function with all the sadness. When Daddy died, for some reason, I didn't grieve. But today, Mitch came over to tell me that Momma died last night. He said it was peaceful and that she died in her sleep, but now I'm worried how this will affect Adele since she was the one to find her. Mitch and Janice are going to let Adele, Linda, and Owen live with them. Since they already have children, Mitch thinks it's for the best. Beth is almost three, and Brett is almost a year old. I know this is going to be hard on them, but I think it's for the best. Owen is only seven, so this is going to be a lot for Mitch and Janice to handle. ♥

Thirty-Two

♥ *Wednesday, January 17, 1973* ♥

Curtis always knows how to surprise a girl. Only, sometimes his idea of a surprise involves very little clothing. Not that I'm complaining. ♥

CURTIS AWOKE TO THE SMELL OF BACON coming from the kitchen. He glanced at the clock on the bedside table. Five forty-five a.m.

Shaking his head, he got to his feet, not bothering to put on clothes as he stumbled sleepily into the kitchen to find Lorrie standing at the stove, frying bacon in a pan.

"What're you doin?" he grumbled from behind her, planting his hand on the doorjamb.

She didn't bother to look at him when she said, "Makin' breakfast. What does it look like I'm doin'?"

She didn't sound happy, and he couldn't imagine what could have her so upset before six o'clock in the morning.

Leaning his shoulder against the jamb, he crossed his arms over his chest, letting his gaze rake over her. She looked pretty in her long nightgown, the one that practically covered every inch of her body. She insisted on wearing it to bed since it was so cold outside, but he rarely allowed that to happen. After all, it was a proven fact that sharing body heat kept you warmer than clothing. Or that was his excuse, at least.

His eyes traveled down to her pretty little toes, then started back up again. His dick had taken notice of her, as well, and was quickly hardening, a fact he couldn't hide because he was still completely naked.

"Why're you cookin'?" he asked.

She snapped her head over as though she was about to rip him a new one, but her mouth merely made a perfect little O when she noticed he was standing there in his birthday suit.

"You're naked," she said.

"I am."

"Why?" she countered.

"Because it's too damn early to be up, and I was plannin' to take you back to bed with me."

"I don't wanna go back to bed."

"Then have it your way," he said, dropping his arms and moving toward her.

Lorrie backed up against the counter beside the stove. Without thinking about it, Curtis reached over and turned off the gas burner, then stalked her until he was pressing his body against hers.

"The bacon's gonna be ruined," she said, but there wasn't a whole lot of worry in her tone.

"I don't give a damn about the bacon."

He fisted her nightgown in his hands as he leaned in and kissed her, slowly bunching it up until he could feel the warmth of her stomach against his hard-on.

"Mmm," he mumbled, brushing his lips over hers. "Since you don't wanna go back to bed, I'm just gonna have to turn you around and fuck you right here in the kitchen."

"We can go to the bedroom," she said quickly.

"Nope." Pulling back, he smiled down at her. "You had your chance."

Before she could argue, Curtis lifted her nightgown up and over her head, then tossed it onto the kitchen table. She was still staring wide-eyed back at him, but she had yet to complain, so he kept going.

"Turn around," he ordered, planting his hands on her hips and guiding her to do what he wanted. "Now put your hands right there on the edge of the sink."

Her fingers curled over the edge.

Leaning against her, he ground his erection between them, his hands sliding over her breasts, her stomach, then lower. He stopped at the apex of her thighs, dipping his fingers into her panties.

"Curtis." She wobbled slightly.

"Don't let go of the counter."

He proceeded to tease her, circling her clitoris with his finger, then dipping two inside her while he kissed her neck and shoulder. He wasn't in a hurry, and if she wanted to be up at six o'clock in the morning, he was going to give her a reason to be.

Right now.

AS MUCH AS LORRIE WANTED TO HANG on to her anger, it wasn't that easy. Especially when Curtis was naked, standing behind her while he teased her relentlessly.

She had long ago stopped thinking that she could resist him, regardless of her mood. When the man set his sights on her, pushing him off was futile. Not that he wouldn't leave her alone if she asked, but she couldn't find it in herself to do so.

Every dirty word that came out of that man's mouth made her ache for him, desperation coiling inside, pulling tight. She could never get enough of him.

"Ahh, sweet girl. I love how wet you get for me."

Lorrie pushed back against him, wishing he would take the hint.

Apparently that was the wrong thing to do, because he pulled back, his hands disappearing. She started to turn, trying to figure out what he was doing, but he put his big, warm hand in the center of her back.

"Don't take your hands off the counter," he repeated roughly.

She gripped the counter tighter until her knuckles turned white.

His lips trailed from her shoulder, down the center of her back. Tingles ignited in her limbs, making her tremble. Her back was probably one of her most sensitive spots, and Curtis knew that.

He continued lower while she faced the window that overlooked the creek behind the house. It was still dark outside, so she saw only her reflection staring back. Her hair was a mess, but she didn't even care.

Curtis's hands gripped her hips and pulled her backward, forcing her to move her feet.

"Don't move your hands," he reminded her.

She didn't, stepping back until she was practically bent over. He stopped her, then she felt his callused fingers slip beneath her panties as he tugged them down her hips, her legs. When they reached the floor, she didn't dare move, but she didn't have to. He then positioned one of her feet farther from the other, forcing her to widen her stance.

"Mmm," he said, his voice trailing up to her ears. "Such a pretty pussy."

Sometimes she wondered if it was wrong of her to want him to say these dirty things, but when she tried to think that it was wrong, she couldn't quite convince herself. Everything he did, everything he said always made her feel incredibly good, so she'd learned to accept her sexuality, her desires.

"Oh my…!" His tongue took her by surprise, the warmth of it sweeping between her legs, lashing at her clitoris. "Curtis…" Her knees trembled, but he held her thighs, keeping her upright while he feasted on her, making her body burn hotter, brighter, until the only things she saw were flashes of light behind her eyelids, her orgasm sneaking up on her, then shattering until she was floating.

She realized she wasn't actually floating, that Curtis had wrapped his arms around her and was keeping her upright while he moved behind her.

"Stay with me, baby. Keep your hands on the counter. I've gotta be inside you. Right now."

Lorrie did her best, holding on while her butt was thrust back against his hips. In one swift movement, he was inside her, filling her so completely. His pelvis slammed forward before retreating, his hands gripping her hips hard enough to bruise, but it was exactly what she needed. Everything she'd bottled up, all of the emotions, the feelings, they were set free as he used her body, bringing her to the brink once again as he fucked her hard and deep.

"You gonna come for me again?" he asked.

"Mmm-hmm." She bit her bottom lip, keeping her legs locked, enjoying the friction, the glorious way he stretched her as he pounded her from behind.

"I wanna hear you scream my name, Lorrie." Curtis grunted, his fingers tightening a little more on her hips. "Say my name when you come, baby."

"Harder," she pleaded, her voice hardly recognizable.

"Oh, fuck, baby." Curtis continued to drive into her, over and over, faster, deeper.

Finally, her orgasm crested, a brilliant explosion of electricity that radiated outward from where he filled her. "Curtis… Oh, yes… Curtis! I'm there!"

"Fuck, yes." He continued to thrust, filling her, driving deeper, harder, several more times as his fingers dug into her flesh. And then he was groaning, mumbling her name over and over as he exploded inside her.

As she stood there, trying to remember why she'd been so upset before he'd come in, she decided it didn't matter. And if it did, she hoped he figured out the same way she had that that was a surefire way to improve her mood.

Thirty-Three

♥ *Wednesday, February 21, 1973* ♥

I'm late. My menstrual cycle has always been regular, but now I'm late. At least a week. I'm scared to tell Curtis only because I fear by doing so I'll jinx it, and I won't really be pregnant. I'm going to schedule an appointment with the doctor next week to find out for sure before I tell him.

Keeping my fingers crossed. ♥

♥ *Tuesday, February 27, 1973* ♥

Tomorrow is my doctor's appointment. I'm so nervous. I wonder if I should tell Curtis. I don't want to get his hopes up, though. And this way, I can surprise him when I know for sure. More tomorrow. ♥

Thirty-Four

I'm shaking as I write this. I'm so excited. The doctor confirmed
it! We're pregnant! ♥

BY THE TIME CURTIS CAME HOME AT the end of the day, he was exhausted, which happened to be the case most days. The only thing he wanted to do was take a shower, eat dinner, and spend some time with Lorrie before crashing for the night.

The instant he stepped foot in the house, he knew something was different. For one, there were flowers on the kitchen table, a bright bouquet in one of the glass vases that Lorrie kept. The table was set, the heavenly scent of fried chicken wafted past his nose, but his wife was nowhere in sight.

"Hey, darlin'?" he called out. "Where're you at?"

"In the bedroom," she hollered back.

Wanting to take a shower anyway, Curtis headed for the bedroom, only to encounter Lorrie in the hallway. She was smiling. A radiant, beautiful grin that pulled a smile from him in return.

"What's going on?"

"Nothing," she said quickly. "You can take a shower. Dinner will be ready in a few minutes."

Planting a kiss on her mouth, he then watched her as she practically skipped down the hall toward the kitchen. He turned to go to the bathroom, but before he made it two feet, she was calling his name.

He spun around to see her running toward him.

"I can't do it! I can't wait! We're pregnant!" she squealed as she practically jumped into his arms.

He processed the words, his entire body stilling.

Pregnant.

That meant ... baby, right?

Not sure he'd heard correctly, he cocked his head and said, "What?"

Lorrie was nodding, her smile even wider. "We're gonna have a baby."

"Baby? We're... Holy shit. We're gonna have a baby?" He couldn't believe his ears.

More nodding from her, but he pulled her into his arms, holding her tight before realizing what he was doing. "Sorry, honey. I didn't mean to..."

"It's okay," she said, giggling. "You won't hurt me." Her grin widened. "We're gonna have a baby."

"How do you know?" he asked, still wrapping his head around the idea. They'd been trying for so long he'd started to wonder if there was a medical reason she hadn't gotten pregnant already. For some reason, he'd thought they would've had kids long before now. They were going on ten years of marriage in August—although in his defense, they hadn't been trying for that long.

"I went to the doctor today," she said, her words tumbling out rapidly. "I didn't want to tell you until I knew for sure. The only way I could do that was go to the doctor."

Curtis cupped her face in his hands, then pressed his mouth to hers. This was the best news ever.

"How far along?" he asked when he released her.

"Based on my cycle, the doctor says I'm almost five weeks."

It dawned on him that he didn't know exactly how long a pregnancy was even though his mother had popped out eight kids. Obviously Lorrie sensed that he was trying to figure out the timeline in his head.

"If the doctor's right, that means the baby'll be born in mid-November."

He couldn't resist picking her up off her feet and twirling her around. When he set her back down, she was still laughing, though tears were now dripping down her cheeks, which worried him. "What's wrong?"

"Nothing," she answered quickly. "Nothing at all. I'm just really happy."

"Me, too, baby. Me, too."

"Now go take a shower," she insisted. "Dinner's almost ready."

As though someone else was in control of his body, Curtis headed for the bathroom, stripped out of his dirty clothes along the way, and managed to make it through a five-minute shower. When he emerged, he was still in a daze.

A baby.

They were having a baby.

The news was so overwhelming and so welcome he found himself sitting on the edge of their bed, his head in his hands while he cried. It probably wasn't the manly thing to do, but his tears didn't seem to care.

"Curtis?" Lorrie's voice was soft.

He lifted his head and smiled.

"Are you okay?" She frowned. "Are you ... upset?"

He reached for her, pulling her to him. "God, no. This is..." Unable to control his emotions, he pressed his face against her chest, his arms wrapped around her as more tears fell. "This is the best news."

He had never thought that there could be anything better than being Lorrie's husband. But being the father of her children... Likely the best possible thing in the world.

Lorrie pressed a kiss to his forehead, cradling his head in her hands. "I don't want you to be upset."

"I'm not, baby." He lifted his head to look at her. "I'm really not. It just caught me off guard a little. But it's good. I swear it."

Her smile returned instantly. "You ready for dinner?" she asked.

"No," he said, reaching for the hem of her dress. "Not yet."

Her eyes clouded as she watched him, not trying to stop him as he lifted her dress over her head and tossed it to the floor.

"This is okay, right?" he asked, suddenly realizing he didn't even know if they could make love. He was going to have to find a way to get some information on pregnancies. Did they make books for that?

Lorrie nodded. "Yes, it's okay."

He'd worry about reading material later. At the moment, the only thing that mattered was the beautiful woman standing before him. He unhooked her bra, letting it fall to the floor before cupping her breasts in his hands, lifting them to his mouth, her hands sliding over his shoulders.

He laved her with his tongue while working her panties down her hips, then pulling her onto the bed with him. Without much fanfare, he crawled between her legs, aligned their bodies, and sank into her. Her warmth consumed him, and as was always the case, he felt whole once again.

He needed to be one with her right now. He needed to feel every part of her against every part of him. She was what held him together, and when he felt as though he might fly apart in a million pieces, he needed her to anchor him.

LORRIE HELD ON TO CURTIS WHILE HE made love to her slowly, his hips rolling as he screwed into her deep. He was being so gentle, so sweet, it made her eyes sting. The love she felt emanating from him stole her breath.

She loved this man.

More so, she loved that this man could get so emotional because they were having a baby together. She hadn't considered the fact that she'd had some time to process the information and she'd simply thrown the news at him without warning.

"God, I love you," he whispered, his forehead resting against hers. "I love you so damn much."

"I love you, too." More than he would ever know.

Cradling his hips with her thighs, Lorrie kept a tight grip on him as he continued to penetrate her over and over. She didn't know how long it lasted, nor did she care. He seemed content to be making love to her, and she didn't want him to stop. This connection between them... It had never been more prevalent than right then.

Curtis lifted his head, peered down at her, then crushed his mouth to hers. She kissed him deeply, holding him to her, meeting him thrust for thrust. She willed him to feel how deep her love for him was. This was a new beginning for them, the next chapter.

And she was looking forward to every single second spent with this man.

Thirty-Five

♥ Friday, March 2, 1973 ♥

I don't know what it is about being pregnant, but I feel fantastic.
Maybe it's that all my dreams seem to be coming true. Curtis is
here with me every single day and we're going to be parents. I
feel like the wait has been worth it. ♥

♥ Saturday, March 10, 1973 ♥

Today, Curtis and I went to Mitch and Janice's house. I helped
Janice cook dinner, and we all enjoyed a fantastic meal. Before
we went over there, Curtis and I decided we would keep the news
about the baby to ourselves for now. We decided that we would
have a party to celebrate when we're ready for everyone to know.
Right now, the only person who knows other than us is Mrs.
Walker. I'm ready for the world to know, but I know it's early
and we have many weeks ahead of us. I'm just so excited. ♥

♥ Thursday, March 15, 1973 ♥

I stayed in bed a little longer than usual today. I'm not feeling well. I'm wondering if I'm coming down with something. I know the pregnancy will make me tired, but my stomach has been hurting a little. Maybe it was something I ate. I'll have to be more careful about that in the future. ♥

♥ Monday, March 19, 1973 ♥

I haven't been feeling well and I'm scared to tell Curtis. My insides are cramping and I've been spotting a little. I don't think this is normal, and I definitely don't think it's from something I ate. I'm so scared. I don't know what to do. ♥

Thirty-Six

Tuesday, March 20, 1973

CURTIS CAME HOME FOR LUNCH THE SAME as he did every day. Not only because he had to eat but also because he couldn't go an entire day without seeing his wife. He enjoyed checking up on her, making sure she was doing okay. For the past couple of weeks, he would usually find her moving around the house, cleaning, and doing far more than he thought she should be doing. Her excuse was always that she was so full of energy and excitement that she couldn't stop if she wanted to. Sometimes he would simply watch her, but there were times she'd send him right back out the door with a sandwich, telling him that he worried too much, but he couldn't help it.

"Baby? Where're you at?" he called when he stepped into the house and closed the front door behind him.

She clearly wasn't in the living room, so he checked the kitchen, stopping to put his cigarette out in the ashtray on the kitchen table. No Lorrie.

There was a strange sensation in his gut as he moved down the hall toward the bedroom. He tried to shake off the eerie feeling, but he couldn't. Pushing open the door, he found Lorrie lying on the bed. She was facing away from the door, her legs curled up, and she was moaning faintly, the soft sound drifting across the room.

"Honey?" he asked, moving closer.

She didn't budge.

Placing a hand on her shoulder, he leaned over to see if she was asleep. Sweat dotted her forehead and her eyes were open.

"Oh, my God, baby." He didn't need to be a fucking doctor to know something was horribly wrong. Rather than ask unnecessary questions, he picked her up in his arms and carried her right out to his truck. Not a single argument came from her, which he knew was a bad sign.

Being as gentle as he could, he set her on the passenger seat, then rushed around and climbed in. The keys were in the ignition like always, so he turned the engine over and kicked gravel behind him as he sped down the dirt drive that led to the road into town.

"It hurts," Lorrie said, her hands on her stomach. "I don't know what's wrong."

Curtis didn't say anything. He was no expert, but since the day Lorrie had told him she was pregnant, he'd started reading, and this was one of those things he'd prayed he would never need to know about. He wouldn't have jumped to conclusions so fast, except he'd seen the blood on the sheet when he'd picked her up. Whatever was happening, it wasn't good.

Rather than drive all the way to the hospital, which was a good half-hour away, Curtis stopped at the doctor in town, knowing Lorrie needed help now. Not later.

When he saw the sign that read Family Practitioner, Dr. Edward Davids, M.D., he pulled into the parking lot and right up to the front door of the small building. Doing his best not to send her through the dashboard, he parked the truck, then bolted out and around to her side, pulling her into his arms and carrying her inside.

"Can I help you?" the woman at the desk asked, her eyes wide.

"We need the doctor to see her," he told her. "Now."

"Sir, the doctor's in with a—"

"I don't fucking care," he snarled. "Show me to a room and get the damn doctor."

Without waiting for her to instruct him, Curtis turned to the only door in the waiting area. He'd been here before, but not since Dr. Davids had taken over the practice. He managed to heave it open, even with Lorrie still in his arms. She had her head buried in his neck, her arms wrapped around him, and she was sobbing hysterically.

There were only two doors, and one was open, so he went there. It was a patient room, so he deposited Lorrie on the small padded table, then turned and headed right back out. He ran smack into the doctor just outside the door.

"Mr. Walker? Can I help you?"

Curtis looked at the doctor, recognizing him from church. He'd never been to see the man, wasn't even sure if a *family practitioner* could help her, but at the moment, he was the only option they had.

"Not me. My wife. She's pregnant. And she's … bleeding." Curtis helped the man along, pushing him into the room.

A nurse soon joined them.

"Mr. Walker, I need you to step outside," the doctor said firmly.

"I'm not goin' any-goddamn-where," he growled.

"It's okay, Curtis," Lorrie said, her voice choppy. "I just… Please."

He swallowed hard but nodded his head. "I'll be in the hall."

Turning, he managed to make it out the door before he realized he was shaking uncontrollably.

THE PAIN IN HER ABDOMEN WAS UNBEARABLE, but not nearly as overwhelming as the fear consuming her. When she'd woken up that morning, she had started cramping, which was the reason she'd gotten back in bed, hoping that she could sleep it off and everything would be all right.

"Lorrie, I'm Dr. Davids. Remember me?"

Lorrie recognized the name. She went to church with his family, and she'd even gone to school with one of his sons. "Yes," she managed to squeak.

"Good. Now, I need you to tell me how far along you are."

"Eight weeks," she rasped, her eyes closed.

"Is this your first pregnancy?"

"Yes."

"Have you been seen by a doctor?"

"Yes."

"How long have you been bleeding?"

"Since yesterday," she said, feeling ashamed. She should've gone to the doctor before now, but she'd been too scared. She knew in her heart what they were going to tell her, and that was the last thing she wanted to hear.

"I'm not an obstetrician," he told her, then his voice faded as though he was facing away from her. "I don't have any equipment here, but I can do an examination of the cervix."

Lorrie nodded, keeping her eyes squeezed shut, not even caring what he had to do or who he was talking to. She just wanted him to save her baby.

"Has the bleeding gotten worse?" the doctor asked, his voice closer now.

Lorrie nodded again.

"I need to do a pelvic examination. Is this okay with you?"

"Yes," she said, now crying violently.

Tears streamed down her cheeks as the nurse touched her arm. "We need to get you into a gown, Lorrie."

Another nod and a lot more tears were all she had to offer.

CURTIS REMAINED OUTSIDE LORRIE'S DOOR, LEANING AGAINST the wall, his fingers tapping against his thighs as he nervously waited. He could only hear the deep rumble of the doctor's voice but not what he was saying. Part of him was grateful he didn't have to hear, but the other part needed to be in that room with his wife, holding her, consoling her.

God, please don't let Lorrie lose this baby. We'll be good parents, I swear it.

While he sent up silent prayers, he closed his eyes and hoped for the best.

I'll quit smoking, I'll stop cursing, I'll do anything at all. Just please, don't take this baby from us. We've waited so long for this. Please don't...

He heard Lorrie's muted moan through the door, and he knew she was in pain. They'd been in the room for nearly twenty minutes, and he wanted to know what they were saying, what was going on, but he was terrified to find out.

Just a couple of days ago, he and Lorrie had been talking about the house and how they needed a bigger one. One with more bedrooms, a bigger kitchen, another bathroom, extra space for all the toys they would eventually have. Curtis had even mentioned that his mother was tossing around the idea of moving out of the big house because it was too much space now that Maryanne and Lisa were the only two still living at home. Hell, Curtis had even envisioned which room would've been the baby's.

There was more deep rumbling as the doctor spoke, followed by an ear-splitting cry. This one he knew wasn't due to physical pain, but the emotional pain that came along with the devastating news.

He didn't need to be in the room to know that their precious baby didn't make it. His legs gave out, and he slid down the wall to the floor. He placed his face in his hands and bawled, not even caring who saw him.

Thirty-Seven

♥ *Friday, April 6, 1973* ♥

These past two weeks have been the hardest of my life. All I do is cry, even when I know it's not fair to Curtis. He's hurting, too, but he's so strong. He continues to push through, taking care of me when the only thing I want to do is sleep. He assures me that it will get easier over time, but I'm not sure this is something I will ever recover from. ♥

♥ *Sunday, May 20, 1973* ♥

We went for Sunday dinner at Mrs. Walker's house today. I've avoided going over there for the past couple of months, ever since… Until now, it has been too hard to be around people. It has been two months since we lost our baby. I'm no longer crying all the time, and sometimes I feel guilty about that. I named her Susanna; although we don't know for sure that she would've been a girl, it's just a feeling that I have. Curtis agreed that's a beautiful name. He seems to be holding up fairly well, though I think he thinks I blame him. It wasn't his fault. It wasn't even my fault. I know that now, but it hasn't been easy. ♥

Curtis

Curtis took me out to pick the peaches off the trees today. I didn't know it, but he's been maintaining the trees for the past few years, and he said this has been the best year yet for the fruit. I didn't even know the trees were there. It's so exciting. He told me that he knew that peaches were my favorite, so he wanted me to have all I ever wanted. Mrs. Walker is teaching me how to make peach preserves. I think Curtis knows that I need this, something to look forward to. ♥

Thirty-Eight

♥ *Saturday, June 30, 1973* ♥

If ever I had doubts—which I have had many over the past three months—I don't have any about Curtis. After all I've put him through recently, he has proven to be the strongest, most amazing man I have ever met. ♥

AFTER TAKING CARE OF THE NECESSARY CHORES for the morning, Curtis made a quick stop at his mother's house before going home to Lorrie. Without knocking, he pulled open the screen door and found his mother standing in the living room, smiling.

"What're you doin'?" he asked, baffled because she appeared to be staring at air.

"I'm thinkin' about all the incredible memories that've been made here. Did you know I had eight babies in this house?"

Curtis smiled. "I wasn't around for all the births, but I'd heard a rumor."

"Y'all lost your first teeth here," she noted.

"I knocked one of Joseph's out if you're keepin' count." He laughed at the memory.

Mary Elizabeth's smile widened. "Smartass."

"Momma!" Curtis covered his mouth dramatically, eyes wide as he stared at her. "Did you just swear?"

"Oh, hush your mouth," she said with a giggle. "Are y'all ready to move in here?"

"I haven't told Lorrie yet," he said, watching her face closely.

Not telling his wife that he had decided that they would be moving into Momma's house was a risk he'd been willing to take. For the past few months, things had been tense between them. Although he'd grieved for the loss of their baby, it was taking Lorrie a lot longer. And he understood completely, which was the reason he thought that moving into the big house—making it their own in the process—was the right thing to do.

The guest house had been a temporary plan in the beginning. Now that they'd lived there for the last five years—since he'd returned from the Army—he figured a new start was what they needed. It wouldn't make up for the loss they'd endured, but he hoped it would be a way for them to start moving forward.

"Have I mentioned how proud I am of you?" Mary Elizabeth asked as she passed him on her way to the kitchen.

"Not lately, no."

He couldn't deny how happy he was to see his mother's spirits up. He could still remember those dark days after his father's death, the way she would drink herself stupid from morning until night, not even bothering to get dressed most days. These days, she was a much different woman, so healthy, so vibrant. She'd told him more than once that he had Lorrie to thank for that. While he'd been gone, the two of them had bonded, and Mary Elizabeth had found a ray of sunshine in all the clouds.

"Well, I am." She smiled. "I'm proud of all my kids, but I've seen you go through so much, and I've envied your strength."

"I have my moments," he joked.

"Don't let it go to your head." Mary Elizabeth leaned back against the counter.

There was no kitchen table to sit at any longer because all of the furniture had been moved to his mother's new house, a nice little three-bedroom with a small fenced yard closer to town. She'd told him about it as soon as it had come on the market, and he'd immediately taken her to check it out. Curtis was fairly certain she'd fallen in love with it instantly, although he doubted she would ever admit as much. His mother didn't want anyone to think that she hadn't loved the big old, drafty house she had raised her children in.

Curtis leaned against the doorjamb.

"Thank you for helping to get us situated," she told him. "But you're not off the hook for mentioning to Maryanne that we could get a dog."

He grinned. "A dog'll be good for you."

"Not for me," she said quickly, laughing. "I'm makin' your sister take care of it. I've raised enough kids. I don't need a four-legged one on top of the eight I have." Her smile widened. "I think Lorrie's gonna love it here. I remember back when you were gone, she would talk about all the things she would do to this place if she had a house like it."

"It's a big house," he told her. "But I plan to fill it with kids one day." He felt the ghostly ache in his chest as he said the words. According to the doctor, there was no reason they couldn't expect to have full-term, healthy babies one day. Still, when he thought about Susanna, his eyes filled with tears. He missed her so much, and he'd never even had the chance to meet her.

"And I'll be right down the road, ready to spoil 'em rotten," Mary Elizabeth stated, pulling him from his thoughts.

"Of course you will. And you'll be right down the road so we can drop 'em off to spend the night at Grandma's."

"Maybe I'll mention puppies."

Curtis shook his head. "Don't even think about it."

Mary Elizabeth stood up, grabbing her car keys from the counter. "I guess I better head on back to the house." She chuckled. "It sounds a little funny sayin' that."

He could only imagine. "I'm gonna go home and get Lorrie. I wanna surprise her tonight. Thought maybe we'd camp out on the floor."

"You can always drag your old mattress out here."

He'd forgotten about that. Everything in the house was gone with the exception of the furniture in his old room. His mother hadn't had a place to put it, so she'd told him it now belonged to him. Since there were six bedrooms in the house, he didn't think he'd have an issue finding it a permanent home if Lorrie decided to keep it.

"That's not a bad idea." He glanced around.

"All right, kiddo. I'll be at home if you need me." She giggled again. "Still strange to say."

Curtis hugged his mother after walking her out to her car, then he stood there for a minute after she pulled out of the driveway. He looked at the big house, then in the distance to the guesthouse they'd been living in. He was definitely ready for this change. It felt right.

And he only hoped it would feel right to Lorrie, as well.

"WHERE'RE WE GOIN'?" LORRIE ASKED WHEN CURTIS ambled into the house and told her to be ready to leave in five minutes. He hadn't bothered to elaborate, even as he headed right past her, where she'd been relaxing on the couch.

"It's a surprise!" he called from the bedroom.

"You better tell me what it is," she insisted, following him into the room.

She watched as he opened the closet door, then reached for a box at the top. It was her box of scarves. He pulled it down, lifted the lid, and pulled out a dark red one before putting the box back where he found it.

"You do know it's summer, right?" she asked, bemused.

"You don't say." His smile was wide as he came toward her.

"And red's not a good color on you," she added, still watching him. Red was actually a really good color on him.

"You got three minutes left. You ready?"

No. She nodded, then shook her head.

Crap. Figuring she would find out what he was up to soon enough, she ran to the bathroom, brushed her teeth, combed her hair, and tried to make herself presentable. She was wearing an old T-shirt and a pair of denim shorts. She contemplated changing into a dress, but then decided not to. If he was only giving her five minutes, he had to deal with how she looked as she was.

She ran to the closet, pulled out a pair of sandals, and pulled them on as she stumbled back to the living room. Lorrie found him waiting by the door, the red scarf draped over his shoulder.

"Ready?"

"Not really," she mumbled, unable to keep from smiling.

"Come on then."

He took her hand and led her out to the truck. After opening her door and helping her inside, he then moved closer.

"What're you doin'?" she asked when he wrapped the scarf around her neck. She tried to move away, but he grabbed her thighs with his big hands.

"Turn around."

She frowned at him only to have him respond to it with a smile. He didn't say anything more, though, so she eventually gave in and turned around, giving him her back.

He situated the scarf over her eyes, tying it behind her head.

"Curtis Walker…"

"Don't worry, darlin'. I've got you."

She knew that to be true. In the almost eleven years they'd been married, he'd proven he could and would take care of her. Rather than argue the way she wanted to, Lorrie nodded, then allowed him to turn her so that she was once again sitting in the truck correctly.

She heard the door close, then the driver's side squeak open before the seat moved when he got inside. The engine started up, and the truck started rolling forward while she kept her hands in her lap, fidgeting.

Less than a minute later, the truck stopped.

"Why're we at your momma's house?" she asked, but he didn't answer. They hadn't driven far enough to be anywhere else.

The door opened, closed. Then her door opened, and he was helping her out, holding her hand as he then led her down the dirt drive and across the small gravel path that led to the big wraparound porch. She could tell they were going to the front door rather than the back door that led to the kitchen. She didn't say a peep as he guided her up the stairs.

"It's not my birthday," she told him, trying not to smile.

"Nope, it's not."

"It's not *your* birthday, either," she added.

"Nope."

"It's not Valentine's, Easter, or Christmas," she said, ticking the holidays off on her fingers.

"Correct again."

"Then what's goin' on?"

Curtis led her into the house, stopping in the foyer, and she heard the front screen door gently close behind her.

"Curtis Walker…" She didn't finish her sentence because she heard the way her words echoed in the space. It was as though there was nothing else in the room.

He moved away from her.

"Leave it on for a minute," he warned when she reached to remove the scarf from her eyes.

"Curtis…"

"It's okay, darlin'. I promise."

His words were echoing, and she could tell he was moving farther away from her. For a good minute, she stood stone still, listening, trying to figure out what might possibly be going on around her. The only thing she heard was the random scuff of his boots against the hardwood floor.

"Okay, take off the scarf."

Hesitantly, Lorrie reached up and pulled the scarf down, allowing it to circle her neck.

Her eyes widened as she stared at the empty room, moving deeper into it. Well, it was empty other than Curtis standing there, grinning like a fool.

"What d'ya think?" he asked.

She did a slow circle, taking it all in. It was *completely* empty. Not a lick of furniture. No flowery couch, no television on the far wall, no picture frames on the mantel. The drapes were even gone from the windows. She leaned over a little and peered around the wall. The dining room was nothing more than hardwood floors and wallpaper.

"What's going on?" She wasn't sure she wanted to know. A sadness consumed her as she thought about what might've happened. She'd just seen Mrs. Walker last Sunday. Surely...

"My momma's all right," he said reassuringly, as though reading her mind.

"Then why is her house empty?"

"'Cause it's not her house anymore," he stated, moving closer.

Her eyes widened in horror. "You kicked your momma out of her house?"

Curtis nearly fell over laughing. "God, no, baby. I got her a new one."

Lorrie was confused. She didn't understand.

Curtis moved closer, taking her hands in his and then leading her farther into the living room. He turned her to face the mantel, his hands on her shoulders, his chest pressed against her back.

"This is your house now, Lorrie. *Our* house." He kissed her temple. "A house big enough for us to have a hundred kids running around if that's what you want."

Lorrie's legs felt weak, her heart beating a little too fast.

He held her tightly as he explained. "Momma wanted a smaller house, and we knew this would be perfect for us. And you can do to it whatever you want. I'm willin' to work to make it ours, darlin'."

Tears filled her eyes, but she fought them back. She couldn't believe he'd done this. For her.

Then again, she shouldn't have been surprised. The man had renamed an entire town for her.

"Mrs. Walker's okay with this?" she asked, her throat tight.

"She's happy we're gonna make it our home," he said. Curtis moved, coming to stand in front of her. His big hands circled her face as he tilted her head back. "Are you okay with it?"

She nodded, trying to hold the tears back. "It's ... more than I ever dreamed of."

And it really was.

With Curtis there, her life was more than she'd ever dreamed of. Despite the hard years, despite the loss of their baby... This one man still completed her in ways she had never imagined. And the fact that he still held out hope that they'd have a house full of children...

She smiled, her heart filled to overflowing. "I love you, Curtis Walker."

He tugged the scarf, pulling her closer before leaning down and brushing his lips over hers.

"And I love *you*, Lorrie Walker."

Thirty-Nine

♥ **Tuesday, December 25, 1973** ♥

For some reason, this has been the best Christmas yet. Perhaps it's because we spent it in the new house, or maybe it's because my heart is once again settled. I don't know why exactly, but it has been a wonderful day. Curtis and I have been doing the work on the big house ourselves, actually living here now that the bedroom is redone. That took a while, but I have to admit, watching Curtis work … mmm. Probably my new favorite pastime. Merry Christmas! ♥

♥ **Friday, August 9, 1974** ♥

I am an aunt once again. Mitch's third child was born today, a sweet little boy they've named Seth. He's precious. I have to admit, today was bittersweet. Part of me was hoping we'd be pregnant again by now, but the other part of me is scared. I can't go through what we went through before. Losing a baby… I never dreamed it could be so hard. On another positive note, Curtis's brother Joseph announced that he is getting married in a small, private ceremony on New Year's. He's been with Rosalynn for almost a year and a half, and they're trying to keep it secret, but she's pregnant. The baby is due in May. ♥

♥ Saturday, April 5, 1975 ♥

Today was an incredible day. Gerald and his new wife came to visit. Although we just saw them back in February at their wedding (it seems all of the Walker men are getting hitched these days), it was so great to see them again. The whole family was together for lunch, and let me tell you, that was a lot of people. I asked Gerald if they'd considered moving back to Coyote Ridge, but he says he's quite content where he is. His wife, Sue Ellen, was born and raised in El Paso, and she says she wants to stay there with her parents and siblings. I can't blame her for wanting to be close to them. ♥

♥ Wednesday, July 16, 1975 ♥

Once again, another precious child has been brought into this world. Joseph and Rosalynn had their baby today. A little dark-haired boy they named Wade. We went to the hospital for a little while, but when we came home, I broke down and cried. I know it's selfish of me to do. I'm happy for the proud parents; I simply want a child of my own. I know Curtis hates to see me cry, but I can't seem to help it. ♥

Forty

Well, it's officially been twelve years (tomorrow) since Curtis and I got married. And it has officially been the first time I've been inside a bar, the first time I've had a "real" drink (and maybe the last time, too). At twenty-seven, I think it might be safe to say that I've taken my time getting to this point. ♥

"YOU READY, BABY?" CURTIS CALLED TO LORRIE from the living room.

He'd helped a couple of the hands take care of a few things that afternoon, then come home, showered, and changed, all in preparation for tonight, only to realize that women needed a hell of a lot more time to get ready than a man.

He'd been ready for the past hour and a half. Lorrie had been getting ready for twice that amount of time. And yet he was still the only one ready to go.

"One more minute!" she hollered.

Yeah, he'd heard that already. About twenty-five times.

Knowing it would be pointless to rush her, Curtis flopped down onto the couch and was about to light a cigarette when he looked up to see Lorrie stepping into the living room.

His world came to a jarring halt.

"Holy shit," he mumbled under his breath.

The woman standing before him, glammed up like he'd never seen her before, made his dick jump to attention. Her hair was straight, falling over her shoulders and midway down her back. She was wearing cowboy boots and a frilly skirt that hung above her knees, along with a black shirt that she had tied beneath her breasts, showing off a glimpse of her stomach.

He damn near came right there in his jeans.

"You said to dress sexy," she said, looking at him sideways.

"Well, woman, you nailed it," he mumbled, getting to his feet. "I'm just not so sure I wanna take you out in public lookin' like that. Don't wanna have to hurt a man for looking at you too long."

What he said seemed to please her, because she smiled brightly. "Well, I'm ready when you are."

He'd been partly serious when he'd said he wasn't sure he wanted to take her out in public. The woman made his mouth water looking like that, and he knew she would draw attention wherever they went. But since one of David's high school buddies was officially opening his new bar tonight, Curtis had promised his brother he'd go, and he wasn't about to go without her.

Sending up a silent prayer that he wouldn't get in a fight tonight, Curtis walked Lorrie out to the truck, admiring the sexy sway of her ass every step of the way.

Twenty minutes later, they pulled into the gravel lot of Moonshiners—what had previously been known as Gary's Bar. Since no one knew who Gary was, one of David's buddies from high school had bought the bar from the previous owner and decided to rename it Moonshiners. Fitting name, Curtis thought.

"Why did he name it Moonshiners?" Lorrie asked as they walked through the parking lot.

"If I had to guess, it's because he's been makin' his own liquor up to this point." Living in the country had its perks. It helped that the sheriff was quite fond of moonshine.

"Really?" She peered up at him.

Curtis nodded and opened the door to the bar, allowing her to go in before him. T.G. Sheppard's "Devil in the Bottle" crooned from the jukebox, heard over the sound of muted conversation. The place wasn't crowded, but then again, in a town the size of theirs, it wasn't expected to be. It looked no different than when it had been Gary's Bar, except for the sign that spouted the new name.

"Curtis," a deep voice rumbled from across the room.

"Robert," Curtis replied, taking Lorrie's hand and leading her over to the bar. "You remember my beautiful wife, Lorrie."

"I remember," Robert said with a grin, holding out his hand to her. "Good to see you again." His eyes returned to Curtis. "Thanks for comin' tonight."

"Thanks for invitin' us. How's your brother?"

"Who, Mack?" Robert chuckled. "That boy ain't got a lick of sense."

Curtis laughed, but only because they all knew the opposite to be true. Turned out Robert Schwartz's kid brother Michael—everyone knew him as Mack because even at twelve he was as big as a truck—was some sort of genius. Not that you'd ever know it to talk to him. Apparently he preferred to keep that tidbit of information to himself.

"Good to hear," Curtis teased, glancing down at Lorrie. "You want somethin' to drink, darlin'?"

Lorrie nodded.

"What can I get ya?" Robert asked, his eyes hopeful.

Lorrie shrugged. "What's good?"

Only then did it occur to him that his wife had never had a drink before. At least not that he knew of.

"I'm thinkin' you look like a Tequila Sunrise girl," Robert suggested, glancing at Curtis for approval.

Curtis nodded. He hadn't a clue what was in it, but why the hell not? "I'll take a beer."

"Comin' right up. We got billiards and darts in the back if you're interested."

Following Robert's direction, Curtis led Lorrie to the *back*—which was really only a few feet away from the *front*—to check out the billiards table. He wasn't much for the game, but he didn't mind sitting and watching. He found an empty table in the far corner, pulled out a chair, and waited for Lorrie to take a seat before he took the seat next to her.

"What d'ya think?" he asked her as she continued to look around.

"Nice place," she said sweetly.

"You don't have to be nice on my account," he teased.

"No, I like it. I've just never been to a bar before, so I don't have much to compare it to."

Curtis frowned. "I guess I shoulda been takin' you out before now, huh?"

Lorrie shook her head. "You know me; I'd much rather be at home."

"Well, tonight we're gonna enjoy ourselves. Have a coupla drinks, maybe do a little dancin'." He smirked at her.

"You? Dance?"

There was a first time for everything.

Robert brought their drinks over, then disappeared quickly.

Curtis watched as Lorrie peered into the glass in front of her before leaning down and sniffing the drink. Her cute little nose curled up the way it normally did. She met his gaze and whispered, "What's in this thing?"

He had no clue. "You probably don't wanna know."

She took a tentative sip, her nostrils flaring as she did, but then her eyes lit up, and he knew tonight was going to be a good night.

Well, if he could get her home in one piece, it would be.

AFTER JUST ONE OF THOSE FRUITY DRINKS, Lorrie was feeling good. Better than good, actually. Her fingers were a little numb, as were her lips. Maybe her ears, too. The effect the alcohol had on her was interesting. She wasn't sure how much she liked it, but for now, she was going to enjoy.

Not only was it making her worry less, it was also affecting her libido. She'd found herself needing to be closer to Curtis, so rather than sitting in her own chair, she'd taken to sitting in his lap while he talked to several people who'd come to say hello. Apparently, as she'd always suspected, Curtis was a rather popular guy. A lot of people who'd come tonight knew him, which wasn't at all surprising. She enjoyed sitting there, listening to them chat.

Rather than interrupt, she'd decided to watch people, enjoying the music and the laughter, wondering why they hadn't done this before. Then she remembered, they hadn't gone out like this because she always came up with an excuse not to. But now that she was here, Lorrie knew that this was the sort of place she could get used to. Although it was a bar, it had a homey feel. Everyone knew everyone else, and the conversations were about family and friends and all things Coyote Ridge.

"You want another drink?" Robert asked, passing by their table on the way back to the bar.

Figuring what the hell, Lorrie nodded.

Robert tapped the table and smiled. "Be right back."

She felt Curtis's warm breath on her neck as he moved her hair back. "Are you gonna get drunk tonight, Mrs. Walker?"

"I might," she said, smiling although she still couldn't feel her lips.

His voice was low as he whispered into her ear. "I'd definitely like to see my naughty girl drunk."

She wasn't so sure about that. As it was, she was feeling a little frisky already. If the alcohol continued to work, she might just want to sneak Curtis into the bathroom and have her wicked way with him.

Robert brought her drink back, striking up a conversation with Curtis and ending their teasing session. Because her tongue was also numb, the second drink went down a lot easier than the first, but she tried to drink it slowly, knowing that too much alcohol wasn't a necessarily a good thing, no matter how great she felt at the moment.

"You 'bout ready to head home?" Curtis whispered to her.

Almost an hour had passed since the last drink, and she was still tipsy, not quite sure she could stand on her own. They'd attempted dancing, which she'd learned Curtis was actually good at, but when the room had begun spinning, he'd insisted on sitting back down.

"Ready when you are," she told him.

"We're gonna head on out," Curtis told whomever he was talking to.

Lorrie hadn't been paying attention to half of what they were saying, choosing to enjoy simply being out of the house with Curtis. She liked the fact that he was so popular, that everyone seemed to like him and want to chat. More than that, she liked that he didn't want to be too far away from her, pulling her back into his lap when she had tried to give him a little breathing room earlier.

"Come on, darlin'," Curtis said, putting his arm around her. "Let's get you home."

Lorrie nodded, though he hadn't asked her a question. The action made her smile, which then made her laugh, and before she knew it, she was giggling uncontrollably as Curtis helped her into the truck.

"I think it's official, darlin'. You're drunk."

Maybe so.

When Curtis climbed into the truck, Lorrie took a deep breath, then rolled down the window to get some air when he was pulling out of the parking lot.

"Did you have fun tonight?" he asked.

"Yep," she said quickly, looking over at him. Once again she was smiling, and the numbness had spread throughout her body.

"Sorry you didn't get to do much. Next time we'll try the dancin' thing before you knock one back," he said, his eyes on the road.

"Well, I can think of somethin' I can still do," she slurred, leaning over so that her head was in his lap.

Curtis's hand came to rest on the back of her head. "Honey, what're you doin'?"

His voice was rough, and she knew he didn't need her to answer, because she was already unbuckling his belt buckle and then undoing his jeans, freeing his erection.

"Baby…"

Feeling emboldened by the alcohol, Lorrie took Curtis's penis into her mouth, sucking him just the way she knew he liked.

"Aw, fuck, darlin'," he growled. "This ain't safe, you know that? Your mouth feels too damn good. Hard for me to focus."

Lorrie didn't let up, slurping him into her mouth, licking him with her tongue, teasing him the way he'd always teased her. She loved the sound of his voice as he continued to talk while he drove, apparently not as distracted as he'd said he was.

When the truck came to a stop, she knew they were home, yet she still didn't release him from her mouth. She liked the warmth of him against her tongue, the way his hand fisted in her hair, the deep rumble as he encouraged her to continue.

"I'm thinkin' we need to take this inside, darlin'."

Still feeling daring thanks to the alcohol, she shook her head, releasing him from her mouth before sitting up. "Not ready to go inside."

Curtis's sexy smirk made her wet. Yep, she'd said it. Or thought it. One or the other.

"Then what d'ya propose we do?" he asked.

"I think you should return the favor," she told him, nodding toward the erection he was now stroking slowly.

God, that was hot.

"But you didn't make me come, darlin'."

Ready to remedy that, Lorrie moved over him again, but Curtis quickly stopped her with his hand on her forehead, laughing.

"I ain't ready to come yet, baby," he said, his voice gravelly. "But I can damn sure return the favor."

Lorrie squeaked when he urged her onto her back. There wasn't a lot of room in the truck, but apparently there was enough for him to lean over, his head between her thighs as he shifted her panties to the side and slid his tongue through her slit.

"Oh, God!" she cried out, scrambling to hold on to something as the sensations overpowered her.

"Is that what you want, dirty girl? You want me to eat your sweet pussy right here in the truck?"

She nodded, her head falling back as he put his mouth to her again. It felt so good, the way his tongue teased her, flicking that sensitive bundle of nerves before spearing into her. He continued to torment her until she was begging him.

"Curtis, please…"

"Tell me, baby," he growled. "Tell me to make you come. Say it."

"Please…" She tried to get the words out, but she couldn't.

"Tell me, Lorrie. Tell me to make you come, and I'll give you what you need."

His tongue lashed at her again as he licked her repeatedly, sending her higher and higher, but not quite to that pivotal point.

He paused again, his finger dipping inside her, going deep, then curling until he was pressing on that sensitive spot only he knew about.

"Curtis! Pleasepleaseplease!" She was rambling; she knew it, but she couldn't help it.

"Say it!" he commanded, his voice deeper, rougher. "Tell me you want me to make you come."

"Yes! Make me come, Curtis! Please make me come!"

As soon as the words were out of her mouth, that was exactly what he did, sending her spiraling out of control.

"Don't pass out on me yet, baby," Curtis growled.

Lorrie opened her eyes to see him standing at the passenger door.

When had he gotten out of the truck?

"Let's finish what we started," he crooned, helping her to sit up, then get to her feet.

He led her up to the porch, but rather than go inside, Curtis pulled her around to the side of the house and backed her up against the railing.

"Right here, darlin'. I wanna fuck you right here."

Lorrie nodded, wanting that, too. Apparently the alcohol was making her lose her mind, but she was feeling too good to care.

"Turn around," he instructed. "Hold on to the rail."

Lorrie turned and gripped the rail while Curtis pulled her panties down her legs. She stepped out of them, then spread her legs wide, welcoming him.

"You're ready for me to fuck you, huh?"

"So ready," she whispered, though she was pretty sure it had come out much louder than she'd intended.

"You've got me too worked up, darlin'. I'm not gonna go slow."

Lorrie shook her head. She didn't want slow. "Fast and hard."

"Fuck," Curtis grumbled at the same time he pushed into her.

Her muscles clenched around him as she leaned over. He stretched her so deliciously she never wanted him to stop.

Curtis began thrusting into her, growling and grunting as he did, obviously not caring that they were outside. It was a good thing they didn't have any close neighbors or they might be the hot topic at church on Sunday.

The thought made her giggle.

Curtis's fingers gripped her hips tighter. "Stay with me, baby."

Oh, she was with him, all right. "Curtis."

He slammed into her, his hips pumping faster and harder. She had to lock her elbows to keep from falling over.

"Oh, yes," she squealed. "Harder. Please. Harder."

He muttered something that sounded like, "You're gonna be the death of me, woman," but she wasn't sure. Regardless, he did as she asked, nailing her over and over, faster, harder, deeper. His fingers dug into her hips, the pain mixing with the pleasure until her head was buzzing and her body was trembling.

Her orgasm rocketed through her, making her knees weak.

"Yes, baby," Curtis crooned, his mouth close to her ear.

She felt him pulsing inside her as he came.

"Not sure how I feel about you drinkin', but darlin', we can certainly do that again anytime you want."

Lorrie smiled. "What about tomorrow?"

Curtis was shaking his head as he led her inside the house. "Let's get you to bed, you dirty, dirty girl."

Forty-One

♥ Tuesday, October 21, 1975 ♥

Today is Curtis's thirtieth birthday. We decided to go down to
Moonshiners. Since it's Tuesday, it wasn't that busy, but still, we
had fun. Then again, I think his idea of fun is getting me tipsy,
then taking me home. But since it was his birthday, I decided to
finish him off this time in the front seat of the truck. After all, it
was only fair being that it's his birthday and all. ♥

♥ Monday, May 31, 1976 ♥

In order to keep myself busy when I'm not helping Curtis on the
ranch, I decided to start volunteering at the library. It's not a big
place, considering how small the town is, but I have so many
fond memories of it. I was in there the other day, and after
speaking with Marjorie (the librarian), she said she would be
happy to have my help. When I told Curtis, he encouraged me to
do it, so that's what I'm going to do. ♥

Curtis

♥ *Sunday, November 7, 1976* ♥

Curtis and I rode the horses down to the creek today. It was such a nice day, but what made it even better was when he tossed some blankets on the ground and we made love in the same spot where we'd first kissed. Well, not exactly the same spot considering our first kiss was on a tree, but close. The man continues to make me wild for him, and he doesn't even have to try. ♥

♥ *Saturday, January 22, 1977* ♥

It's a good thing Curtis taught me to drive a while back. Today, I took a trip into Austin because I needed to pick up a few things. I've decided with Valentine's coming up, I'm going to surprise Curtis this year. He's always the one to surprise me, so I figure it's only fair. ♥

Forty-Two

I'm gonna do it. Tonight, I'm surprising my husband for the first time. Yes, I'm incredibly nervous, but I think I can get through this. For him, I can get through anything. ♥

SINCE LORRIE HAD INFORMED HIM THAT THEY would be having a special Valentine's dinner at home this year, Curtis had made sure he was up early so he could take care of the chores, come home and shower, then go into Austin to pick up the present he'd ordered for her. Knowing Lorrie, she would tell him he didn't need to buy her anything, but this... This was something long overdue.

"Hey, baby!" he called when he came in through the back door that led into the kitchen.

He noticed that the lights were all off, which seemed a little odd. It was four o'clock. When she'd said early dinner, he'd just thought...

Yeah. Whatever he'd *been* thinking, it was long gone now as he stopped short.

"Lord. Have. Mercy," he hissed through clenched teeth the moment he stepped into the living room.

"Do you like it?"

Curtis swallowed hard as he let his eyes rake over the most stunning woman to ever have graced the earth. "It's... Uh..." He was speechless. "Holy shit."

Lorrie's smile grew. "I always know it's a good thing when the only thing out of your mouth is swear words."

Good didn't even begin to describe what was standing before him.

Lorrie had her hair up, the golden locks piled on her head, revealing the sexy curve of her neck, and she was wearing the sexiest lingerie he'd ever seen. Not that he'd seen much other than in a few clothing ads, but still.

"I was looking for pink when I went in the store," Lorrie said, still standing a few feet away. "But the kind saleslady told me that black was sexier."

"Darlin', I don't think it matters what color. *Everything* is sexy on you." He couldn't take his eyes off her. The black lace bra was completely see through, so he got a glimpse of her perfect nipples. The tiny panties looked as though they were held together by strings, and the garter belt she wore was attached to black silk stockings that showcased her beautiful legs.

Yeah, he didn't give a damn what color it was, she was breathtaking.

"Please tell me this is my present," he breathed roughly.

Lorrie nodded as he moved closer.

"Good, because I'm gonna enjoying unwrapping every inch." He leaned in close to her ear. "Very, very slowly. With my teeth."

Her body trembled as he placed his hands on her back, sliding them upward over the exposed skin.

"What made you wanna buy this?" he asked, pressing his lips to her neck, inhaling her sweet scent.

"I wanted to give you something special, something that would make you as wild for me as you once were."

That caught his attention, and he stood up, looking down at her. He couldn't hide his frown. "Baby, trust me, I still want you just as bad. Hell, probably more than I ever have. If I could spend the entire day lodged inside your sweet body, I assure you, I would."

The blue of her eyes darkened as she watched him.

"You better not think otherwise," he said roughly. "I might just have to spank your sweet little ass if that's the case. Speaking of… Turn around so I can see that sweet little ass."

Another shiver racked her body as he guided her so that she was facing away from him.

"Heaven help me," he mumbled, taking her in once again. "I can die a happy man," he told her, as he pulled her back around to face him, fusing his lips to hers while he cupped the perfect rounded globes and gently squeezed. "Fuck, Lorrie," he mumbled against her mouth. "You make my dick so hard."

She looked up into his eyes. "Show me."

If he hadn't been shocked to find his incredibly beautiful wife standing nearly naked in their living room, those two words from her innocent little mouth definitely did it for him.

"Here?" He glanced around the room.

"Yes. Here," she confirmed.

"And then what?" he asked as he quickly pulled his shirt over his head and tossed it to the floor. He loved the way her eyes instantly slid to the tattoo of her name on his chest, over his pectorals, then down to his stomach.

"It's your present," she said sweetly, her gaze once again finding his. "Do with it what you want."

"Mmm." He definitely liked the idea of that. "If that's the case…" While he finished disrobing right there, he looked around the room, trying to come up with an idea of how he wanted to do this.

Should he toss a blanket on the floor, start a fire in the fireplace, and make love to her there?

He kept looking.

Or maybe he could set her on the stairs and ravish her on the steps.

Or … maybe he should…

His mind went blank. He wanted to do so many things to her, and he was so damn eager he could've simply bent her over the arm of the couch and ridden her long and hard, but he wanted this to last a while.

She'd gone through so much trouble for him, what with buying the outfit and all. The least he could do would be to drag out her pleasure as long as he possibly could.

WHEN THE SALESLADY HAD TOLD HER THAT the black lingerie would make her husband drool, Lorrie hadn't quite believed her, although she had expected it would do what she intended. It wasn't that Curtis didn't seem to find her attractive, but now that they'd been married for almost fourteen years, she wanted to reignite that spark in his eyes. The look on Curtis's face, however… Far more than she'd expected.

Though she was extremely self-conscious standing there nearly naked, draped in only a few scraps of lace, the way he looked at her, so much heat in his eyes, eased some of her nerves. That simple look also made her nipples harden to points, her breath come in rapid pants, and a chill dance down her spine.

"Fuck it," Curtis finally mumbled, his eyes once again on hers.

The next thing she knew, he was on his knees before her, his hands cradling her thighs as his heated gaze caressed every inch of her.

"I fucking love this outfit," he mumbled, pressing kisses to her belly. "So damn much."

Yeah, well, she was beginning to love it, too.

As his mouth trailed lower, Lorrie steadied herself by placing her hands on the top of his head, sliding her fingers through his silky hair. She admired the sleek muscles in his shoulders as he moved his hands down her body, his palms once again cupping her bottom, squeezing, then sliding to her hips.

A soft moan escaped her when his finger pulled her panties aside, his warm breath intimately fanning her lower lips. When he used his thumbs to spread her open to his gaze, she nearly stumbled and fell, but he grabbed her thighs at the last second.

"On second thought…" Curtis was on his feet, lifting her and carrying her to their bedroom.

She'd thought he would want to make love somewhere other than their room, which was how she'd ended up in the living room. But this worked, too.

He put her on her feet at the end of the bed, directly in front of the wooden bench he'd built for her. She watched as he lifted the lid and pulled out a blanket before tossing it on the top.

"There. Sit," he commanded roughly.

She sat, taking a moment to take him in. Every glorious muscle, every hard angle of his body was close enough to touch, but she didn't move, waiting for him to instruct her. Curtis was by far the sexiest man alive. The way he stood, the way he carried himself, the sexy rumble of his voice… He did it for her in every way.

He kneeled on the carpet before her.

"Now where was I?" His blue-gray eyes lifted to meet hers. "Oh, yes."

His fingers once again pulled her panties aside before his mouth returned, his tongue stroking the swollen bundle of nerves at the top of her sex as he shouldered his way between her thighs, forcing her to spread her legs to make room for him.

He gently lapped at her while she watched, her chest heaving as the sensations assaulted her. Every exquisite brush of his tongue against her made her flinch. She was so sensitive, so eager for him.

"Lean back," he instructed.

Lorrie leaned back against the end of the bed, trying to steady herself as he placed his hands behind her knees and lifted her legs up and out until she was spread open for him.

"Much better," he drawled.

"Oh…" She moaned when his mouth returned, his tongue buried inside her as he consumed her, making her body tremble as her climax steadily built.

"Such a pretty pussy," he mumbled.

Those dirty words did it; they sent her over the edge when he suckled her clitoris between his lips, flicking his tongue against the sensitive bundle of nerves. She couldn't hold back, crying out his name as her body and mind fragmented.

"Oh, yes," he moaned, crawling up her body.

Before she had regained her breath or her strength, Curtis was pushing inside her, his body leaning over hers. The position couldn't have been comfortable for him. He was so much taller than her, but based on the expression on his face, he didn't care. So she didn't, either.

"God, yes," he groaned. "Squeeze my dick, Lorrie. Fuck, you're so tight, baby."

Again, her body began a steady ascent, climbing higher and higher as he began thrusting harder and deeper, one of his arms curled around her back, holding her in place, while his other was pressed to the mattress, keeping him up.

"I could do this all night," he panted, the muscles in his chest and arms flexing. "Feel your sweet body milking me."

His pace increased, and Lorrie held on, taking all he was giving her and loving every second of it. They'd needed this. For so long, they'd been making love, but Curtis had been so gentle with her. She knew it was due to the things that had taken place, but she wanted this as much as he did. She wanted to make him lose control, to send him careening into the abyss with her.

"Aww, baby," he groaned. "I'm gonna come, Lorrie."

The deep rumble of his voice mixed with the glorious sensation of him stretching her drove her right to the edge and then over once again.

"Curtis!" She dug her fingernails into his back as her orgasm raced through her.

His body stilled and she smiled against him. She hadn't noticed until now that he hadn't removed any of her clothes, only his. And since he had yet to unwrap his gift completely, she knew the night wasn't over yet.

After cleaning them both up, Curtis carried her into the living room, making her laugh as he did.

"You know I can walk, right?" she asked.

He smiled. "I know."

"Granted, my knees are a little weak." She felt her cheeks warm as she said the words. It was one thing for him to talk dirty, something else entirely for her to insinuate, although she had made a point to do it from time to time. She loved the way his eyes turned glassy when she spoke her naughty thoughts aloud.

"That's always a good thing," he said, grabbing his jeans off the floor. "If your knees aren't weak, I haven't done my job."

At first, she thought he was going to get dressed when he picked up his pants and shook them out, but instead, he pulled something from his pocket, then tossed the denim back to the floor.

"Are you hungry?" she asked, trying to get to her feet. "I've got dinner warming in the oven."

"Starving," he replied as he crawled over her, forcing her to her back. "But dinner can wait."

"What're you doing?" She saw the mischievous twinkle in his eyes and knew he was up to something.

"I got my present; now it's time for you to get yours."

"See, I'm thinking I already got my present," she said with a giggle. After what he'd done to her, it was safe to say that would last her for quite some time.

At least until tonight, anyway.

Curtis settled on the couch beside her, one arm sliding beneath her head. She was staring up at him while he fidgeted with something in his other hand.

"Give me your finger," he told her.

She held up her right hand.

"Other hand," he instructed.

Lorrie switched hands.

His big fingers touched the tip of her ring finger, and something cool slid over it before he pushed it all the way down past her knuckle.

There were tears in her eyes before she even looked at it. She didn't need to see it; she knew what it was. They'd been married for so long now, the fact that she'd never had a ring hadn't bothered her. Their wedding had been spur-of-the-moment, and though he'd promised he would get her one, she had told him it wasn't necessary. As far as she was concerned, a marriage didn't have anything to do with rings or paper or anything else. It was the two hearts joined as one that mattered most.

"It's simple," he said, keeping her finger covered. "Because I knew you'd smack me upside the head if I bought you a big diamond." He smiled sweetly. "I've always wanted you to wear my ring, Lorrie. And I know you never would've asked for one, but I had to do this."

While she stared at the glistening gold and the sparkling diamonds in a pavé setting, wrapping around the entire band, Lorrie felt the tears pool, but she fought them. She didn't need to cry right now. This was a happy moment, one she would cherish for eternity. "Thank you," she whispered, then looked him in the eye. "But what about you? I want you to wear my ring."

His smile was slow and sexy, then he held up another ring, this one much bigger than the one on her finger. "I knew you'd say that."

She laughed, taking the ring, then sliding it over his big finger.

Curtis leaned down and pressed his lips to hers softly. "You are my love that lasts a lifetime, Lorrie. No matter what obstacle we encounter, no matter what path life leads us on, you will always be the most important thing in my life. I'll give you the moon if you want it. And don't tell me I can't, woman, because I'll damn sure find a way if that'll make you happy."

Lorrie laughed. He knew her so well. "You're all I need," she replied. "All I'll ever need."

And that was the moment she accepted that she would live her life one day at a time, the way she had in the beginning. Back when the only thing that had mattered was Curtis's love. Everything else would work out the way God planned. And until then, she would be eternally grateful that she'd been blessed with the greatest thing in the world already.

A love that lasted a lifetime.

Forty-Three

After fifteen years of marriage, the man is still teaching me things I never thought I'd enjoy. And at thirty-two, Curtis Walker still has it going on. ♥

"HAVE YOU SEEN LORRIE ANYWHERE?" CURTIS CALLED to one of the ranch hands as he headed toward the barn to see if she was there. He'd searched the house prior to coming out here, a little concerned when he hadn't found her.

"Not since lunch," was the answer he received.

"Thanks," Curtis called back.

He knew she wasn't at the library, because she hadn't kissed him good-bye and they made it a point never to leave the house unless they did so. It wasn't something that he'd ever thought about; it simply was a habit.

When he reached the doors to the barn, he heard a soft sound, almost like a deep, shuddering breath.

He looked up at the loft.

He smiled to himself, making his way over to the wooden ladder that led up to where they stored hay. Trying not to make a sound, he ascended the steps slowly. When he reached the top, he found Lorrie lying on a blanket that had been tossed over the hay.

"What're you doin' up here?" he asked, grinning.

She looked so pretty lying there, all relaxed with her hair spread out around her, knees bent, dress lifted slightly but still keeping her decently covered. He wanted a picture of her just like that.

Her eyes widened and she instantly shoved something beneath the blanket.

Naughty girl.

"Are you hidin' somethin' from me, darlin'?" He had to bend over to keep from hitting the beams above him as he made his way toward her.

"No," she said hurriedly. "I was just reading."

"What're you readin'?"

"Nothing."

That made him laugh.

Rather than let her get out of it, he moved closer, then dropped to his knees, crawling forward and hovering directly above her as he stared down into her eyes.

"Are you lyin' to me?" he teased.

She shook her head.

"What if I wanna know what you're readin'?"

Her eyes were still wide, her face flushed, and that was when he knew.

"Is it somethin' I'd like?" he probed.

She shook her head, but not a sound came out of her. He knew.

"You're readin' a dirty magazine, aren't you?"

She didn't have to say no; the blush on her cheeks was all the answer he needed.

"You dirty, dirty girl."

Taking her hands, Curtis lifted them over her head, pinning her to the blanket beneath his body. He pressed his nose against her neck, brushing his lips over the sensitive skin and inhaling her. A rumble emerged from deep within him. She brought out the animal inside, and all it took was her scent.

"If I slip my hands in your panties right now, you'll be wet, won't you?"

Lorrie didn't respond, but the way her breaths were coming faster told him what he'd already known.

"Is that what you want me to do? Want me to slip my hand in your panties and finish you off? Make you come on my hand?"

She moaned, a sound so damn sexy Curtis's cock jumped behind his zipper.

But as intriguing as that sounded, he actually did want to know what she was reading. While he continued to tease her, trying to get her mind off the magazine, he released her hand and then reached for it.

"Curtis!" Lorrie squealed when he grabbed it and sat up on his knees, flipping through the pages.

"Damn, baby. I can see why you like this one."

He peered over the edge of the magazine to see her staring back at him.

"I just wanted to see why *you* liked it, that's all," she huffed.

"Me?" Curtis flipped the magazine closed so he could look at the front. "Baby, this ain't mine."

"It's not?"

He shook his head. "No. But now that I know you like 'em, I'll be doin' a little shopping next time I'm in town."

"Whose is it?" she questioned.

He shrugged. "Where'd you find it?"

"Behind the tools," she said, nodding down to the main floor of the barn.

"Interesting." If he had to guess, one of the ranch hands was doing some light reading on his off time.

Figuring he might as well have some fun with it, Curtis fell onto the blanket beside her and opened the magazine, looking at the pictures, making sure he held it so that she could see them, as well. He could tell she was trying not to look, but her eyes still slid toward the pornographic images.

"What are you doing?" she whispered loudly.

"The same thing you were doin'. Readin'." He wasn't reading, that was for damn sure.

When Lorrie went to move, he grabbed her arm and pulled her down beside him.

"You ain't goin' nowhere yet, darlin'. I haven't figured out what your punishment's gonna be."

"My punishment?" She sounded outraged.

Curtis reached down and ground his palm against the rigid length of his dick. He was hard as fucking stone, and it had nothing to do with the pictures he was looking at. Okay, well, mostly nothing. Her eyes followed his movement, focused on his crotch.

He held up the magazine, which reflected a picture of a woman going down on a man, his big dick inside her mouth. "Is this what you like to look at?"

Lorrie's cheeks turned red.

Interesting.

"Come over here, baby," he said firmly, pointing to the spot between his legs. "I'm not sure I'm gettin' the full effect of this. Maybe you can demonstrate."

Knowing he could very well push the limit with his wife, Curtis made sure she saw the heat in his gaze. More than anything, he wanted to feel those pretty lips wrapped around his dick.

She did as he said, crawling between his legs, kneeling there, but not moving.

"Take my cock out," he instructed, keeping his tone low and gentle.

To show her he was more interested in her, he dropped the magazine when she reached for the button on his jeans. He sucked in a breath when she managed to free his dick. She kept her eyes locked on his face as her soft hand slid over his rock-hard length.

"I love your hands on me, but I love that sweet little mouth, too."

Her gaze slipped to where she was currently jacking his dick, then back to his face. A sexy smirk curled the edges of her pretty lips.

"Fuck yes, baby," he whispered, sliding his hand in her silky hair when she bent over and took him in her mouth. "Damn, you don't even know how good that feels."

Curtis watched as she worked his dick with her mouth, sucking him as she moaned softly. The vibrations went straight to his balls.

He brushed his thumb over her cheek. "Such a sweet mouth. Take more of me, baby."

She eased down until she gagged, then promptly pulled back. The sight alone made his dick jump.

"Fuck, you make me so goddamn horny." He reached for her, pulling her over him before crushing his mouth to hers, holding her head as he thrust his tongue past her lips, her teeth, fueling the flames that had started from that dirty magazine.

Lorrie whimpered as she began humping his thigh.

"Is that what you need? You need me to make you come?"

She nodded.

He nibbled her ear. "You want my dick or my mouth, baby?"

"Both," she whispered, her voice raspy with need.

"I can definitely do that," he assured her. "But I'll only do it if you strip that pretty little dress off."

He knew he was asking for a lot. They were in the barn, and it was the middle of the day. The ranch hands could show up at any time, which for him only heightened his desires, made his dick throb harder. The idea of them possibly getting caught was hot as hell.

He just wasn't sure she'd given that any thought.

"Come on, baby. Lemme see those sweet tits. Lemme tease 'em with my mouth."

Lorrie sat up and stared at him.

And just when he thought he'd gone too far, his dirty girl proved she was definitely naughty.

LORRIE DIDN'T KNOW WHAT HAD COME OVER her. She wasn't even sure what had prompted her to pick up the magazine when she'd seen it beneath a pile of rags on the floor near the tack. But she had and here she was.

When Curtis had found her, she'd been embarrassed to the roots of her hair, not sure what he would say when he realized what she was doing. Truly, she had thought the magazine belonged to him. The fact that it didn't wasn't even her concern. What mattered was how turned on she'd gotten by looking at the images. She'd always heard that women were more visual than men and that was proven by how her body had responded to looking at those dirty pictures.

"That's my girl," Curtis grumbled when she pulled her dress up over her head, tossing it to the side.

Without waiting for instruction, she removed her bra and panties. She was burning from the inside out, desperate to feel him, aching for his touch.

She shivered, only partly because of the cool air that wafted over her skin.

"Lemme warm you up," he said, reaching for her hand and pulling her forward.

Before she could lean down to kiss him, Curtis stopped her, shifting so that he could take her right breast in his mouth. She groaned as the warmth of his tongue along her flesh sent an electrical current directly to that aching spot between her legs.

Curtis pulled back momentarily. "You gotta keep quiet, baby," he said faintly. "You wouldn't want one of the hands to hear you."

Oh, God. She hadn't even thought about that. Hadn't considered the fact that they were in the barn and at any moment someone could walk in. Oh, no. Someone could even come up to the hayloft and find them…

Curtis's mouth was on her again, sucking her, teasing her nipple, and every thought momentarily fled her mind. The only thing that mattered was what he was doing to her, how incredible he was making her feel.

He released her nipple with a light pop and looked up at her, grinning.

"Now I need to taste your pussy."

Her body trembled, the dirty words hitting that spot the same way they always did. How those crude words could make her body burn hotter, she didn't understand, never really had, but she'd never questioned it, either.

Curtis took control, repositioning her so that she was straddling his head. She started to pull away, embarrassed by what he was going to do out in the barn, but he held her thighs firmly but gently.

"Don't move."

She was paralyzed in place. The husky rumble of his voice made her skin tingle at the same time his tongue made other parts of her body tingle. He lapped between her thighs, licking her, sucking her, thrusting into her until she was wild with the need to come apart. Only it wasn't enough. He was keeping her on the edge, holding her there, tormenting her in the most exquisite way.

Just when she was about to tell him she needed more, she heard voices coming closer.

Curtis stopped what he was doing, shifting her off him, and she thought for a moment he was going to hand over her dress so she could cover herself, but he didn't. His hands were rough as he repositioned her so that she was on her belly, leaning over a bale of hay that the blanket was covering, her bottom sticking up in the air.

Her naked bottom.

His warm body covered her, his shirt buttons scraping her bare back, the denim of his jeans brushing the insides of her thighs, his mouth by her ear. He was fully dressed still.

"Shh," he whispered. "Don't say a word. I'm going to slide inside you right here and now."

Okay, now that was hot. Knowing that she was naked and he wasn't...

The head of his erection pressed against her entrance and she panicked. She tried to shake her head, scared that she wouldn't be able to keep quiet, but he didn't pay her any mind, his erection nudging her entrance, then slowly filling her.

Her hands gripped the blanket as the intense pleasure made her head spin.

What if they got caught? What if one of those ranch hands came up here for some reason?

Curtis's teeth nipped her ear. "Do you know how fucking hot this is? Me fucking you like this while they're down there working?"

She shook her head, but she did know. It was hotter than she ever could've imagined.

The voices grew louder, and she knew there were men in the barn now, yet Curtis continued to slowly penetrate her, over and over, his breath soft against her ear, his body still covering hers.

"Remember to keep quiet," he reminded her when she whimpered.

The warmth of his body disappeared at the same time his hands gripped her hips and he began thrusting deeper, harder, faster.

Her climax was immediate, slamming into her, stealing her breath. It took every ounce of control she had not to cry out his name as she splintered into tiny pieces.

Curtis didn't stop; he continued to thrust into her, filling her, pulling another orgasm from her while the men downstairs continued to work. She had no clue what they were saying, only that they were there. But it didn't matter, because she knew Curtis would take care of her as he always had.

She allowed herself to succumb to the pleasure once again, and moments later, Curtis's hips thrust forward, once, twice, and one final time before she felt him release inside her before his body again covered hers.

He pulled her down with him, wrapping his arms tightly around her as they both came down from that incredible sexual high while the men downstairs went about their business, none the wiser.

Forty-Four

I want to cry, I want to laugh, I want to dance … and I'm so, so scared. But at the same time, I'm so, so happy. The one thing I am going to do … talk to my husband. ♥

"HEY, BABY!" CURTIS CALLED WHEN HE WALKED into the house. He'd been out in the barn when one of the ranch hands had told him that Lorrie was looking for him. He was told it wasn't urgent, but he knew if Lorrie had asked one of them to find him, it was important.

So, here he was.

"I'm in the bathroom!" she called back.

Well, that sounded peculiar.

"What're you doin' in—" Curtis turned the corner to see Lorrie standing in the bathroom, fully dressed, staring at a hodgepodge of crap on the bathroom counter. "Is that..."

"Pee," she said, a smile on her face.

Well, okay. Definitely awkward.

"Do I even wanna know?"

She turned to face him. "I would think so, since, according to this"—Lorrie waved her hand to encompass the little dropper and tubes sitting before her—"it means we're pregnant."

Out of all that, he heard only one word.

Pregnant.

When she turned to look at him, he held his breath, forcing the words past his dry lips. "We're having a baby?"

She nodded, and as she did, tears began trickling down her cheeks. "I'm scared to believe it. But I wanna believe it."

"We should get you in to see the doctor," he blurted.

Again, she nodded. "I've already called and scheduled an appointment. They can see us on Friday."

"Oh, my God, baby," he whispered, grabbing her and pulling her into his arms. He didn't know the first thing about all the crap spread out before him, but if Lorrie said she was pregnant, he believed her. But along with his joy came a shit load of trepidation.

It had been almost five years since...

"We're gonna have a baby," he rasped, willing it to be true. He wouldn't think about the bad things, only focus on the positive. That was how he had to handle it. For all of their sakes.

LORRIE HAD WOKEN UP THAT MORNING WITH her heart set on taking this pregnancy test. It was a new thing she'd read about in an advertisement. She'd picked it up at the drugstore last week—a full week *after* her period was supposed to start. Once she had the test at home and had read the directions at least two dozen times, she'd then waited what seemed like forever, wanting to ensure enough time had passed. According to the test instructions, it was best to wait at least ten days after her missed period, so she'd waited another week. It had been fourteen days as of yesterday.

Which was the reason she'd come to the bathroom this morning both anxious and excited.

Then, careful not to mess anything up, she had done everything exactly as the little paper had instructed, and now, two hours later…

Based on the results (which the box warned were only ninety-seven percent accurate) they were going to have a baby. As excited as she was, Lorrie was also terrified.

Terrified that the test would be wrong even though she'd missed her period.

Terrified that they'd have to relive what they'd gone through before.

Yep, she was scared to death, but the only thing she could do was hope and pray for the best. If this was God's plan, it would be.

Turning to Curtis, Lorrie smiled. "Oh, and one more thing."

His eyebrow quirked.

"I think it's time you quit smoking."

Forty-Five

That husband of mine is as stubborn as they come. Doesn't he know that when a woman asks for sex, she really wants it? I can see it in his eyes, he wants it, too, yet he's so hard-headed. Hmm. I'll have to think of a plan. ♥

CURTIS HAD FINISHED THE DISHES, HELPING OUT because Lorrie had mentioned her ankles were swollen, and rather than let her steamroll right over him and do the dishes herself, he had forced her to go sit down and put her feet up.

"Curtis!"

At the sound of his name, Curtis dropped the dish towel and ran through the living room and down the short hall to their bedroom. Throwing open the door, he came to an abrupt halt when he found his wife sitting on the bed, looking…

"Where're your clothes?" he asked, bewildered.

Lorrie nodded toward the floor. "Down there."

"And why did you take them off?"

"Because if you're not gonna willingly make love to me, then I'm not gonna willingly wear clothes anymore. See how you like that."

He grunted, then moved toward the pile of clothes she'd discarded on the floor.

"Don't you dare touch those," she huffed.

"Woman." He took a deep breath, doing his best not to look at her beautiful, very naked body.

"You're not gonna hurt me. The doctor said it's perfectly okay to have sex at this stage of the pregnancy."

He knew that. She'd told him that several dozen times, but now that he could see the slight protrusion of her belly, he was scared that he was going to hurt her or the baby. Why it had been different before she was showing, he couldn't explain, but it had.

"If you don't find me attractive anymore, just say so," she said, a slight hesitation in her tone.

He met her gaze, frowned. "Baby, trust me, that ain't it." The evidence was throbbing incessantly behind his zipper. Even fully clothed, the woman aroused him with a simple smile. Without a stitch of clothing… It was highly likely that he was going to bust a nut in his jeans.

"Then what is it?" she questioned.

Figuring she wasn't going to give up until he explained, Curtis walked around to his side of the bed, then climbed on beside her.

"I don't wanna hurt you or the baby," he told her honestly, lying on his side and facing her.

"You won't."

"You don't know that," he argued. No one knew why she'd miscarried their first baby, but he did not want to be responsible for doing something that might cause that again.

"Curtis." Her tone was no longer soft and sweet. "I'm pregnant, which means my hormones are all over the damn place. I'm horny, and I'm tired of you thinking I'm gonna break. I'm sixteen weeks. The doctor has assured me that everything is going well with the baby. We can make love."

He found her rant adorable. So adorable that he couldn't resist kissing her just to get her to shut up. That was his first mistake, because kissing her had always driven him stark raving mad. This time was no exception.

When she managed to crawl on top of him, straddling his hips, he knew he was done for. Resisting her these last few weeks had been hell. He'd been jacking off repeatedly, always thinking about her when he did. Before she was pregnant, Lorrie had been stunning. Now that she was ... she was the most beautiful, radiant woman in the world, and he wanted nothing more than to make love to her every minute of every day.

Lorrie reached for the button on his jeans, then worked it free before lowering his zipper.

He groaned, pretending that he wasn't enjoying every second of it.

When she started to work the denim down his hips, he helped her along, and the next thing he knew, she was once again straddling him, only this time there was nothing between them. He slipped a hand between their bodies and grazed his knuckle against her clitoris, loving the soft moan that escaped her.

"Feels good," she whispered, pressing more firmly against his finger.

With his free hand, he pulled her head down, pressing his lips to hers once more. He savored the sweet taste of her, his tongue gliding against hers while he worked her into a frenzy.

"More," she said against his mouth. "Inside me, please."

For the love of God. There was no way in the world he could resist this woman.

Before she could ease down over him, he gently shifted her to her back and positioned himself between her legs.

"Promise you'll tell me if I'm hurtin' you?"

"I promise," she whispered.

As he slid into the hot depths of her body, he was overcome by sensations, so many that he thought for a moment his head was going to explode.

"WHAT'S WRONG?" LORRIE ASKED WHEN CURTIS STILLED inside her.

"Nothin'."

"Doesn't sound like nothin'," she said, laughing at the strangled sound of his voice.

"Don't laugh," he warned.

That only made her laugh harder.

"I'm gonna come, Lorrie. Keep it up and I'm gonna come before you ever get yours."

That hushed her right up. She'd been waiting too long for this. For several weeks now, Curtis had been finding one way or another to put her off when she mentioned sex. She knew he was worried. She'd been worried, too. For the first few months, she'd spent every minute of every day scared to death. Because of her previous miscarriage, she was seeing the doctor more regularly than if she hadn't lost a baby, and each time she'd gone, the doctor had assured her the baby was doing just fine. In fact, the baby was on target to be as big as Curtis eventually, which, honestly, was scary in its own right. She wasn't all that big, so having a big baby…

Okay, so she'd have to think more about that later.

"Make love to me," she whispered, framing his face as he hovered above her. "Slowly."

His hips began to rock, and Lorrie relaxed, holding on to him although he kept his arms locked so that he wasn't pressing against her belly. It was more proof that he was scared he would hurt her or the baby.

"Turn over," she insisted when it was clear he was trying too hard not to hurt her.

"What?" he asked, his hips stilling.

"I said turn over. On your back."

Shifting her legs, she forced his erection to fall from her body, which resulted in a disappointed grunt from Curtis, but he did what she asked. Finally.

"Now don't you dare move," she commanded, once again straddling his hips.

She leaned down, kissing his lips, trying to get him to focus on her.

"Touch me, Curtis. Put your hands on me."

His hands slid up her back, and she was surprised she didn't purr like a cat, they felt so good against her skin. While she kissed him, her tongue stroking his, she tried to control the urgency. With Curtis, it wasn't easy. She wanted him so badly, needed him to do all those naughty things he'd done to her before, but she knew that would be pushing it.

When he was good and distracted, she slid her hand between their bodies and guided him home.

"Oh, baby," he groaned into her mouth. "I love bein' inside you."

Lorrie sat up, her hands on his chest as she began to rock her hips, doing all the work while he watched. The man was so damn sexy. All that sun-bronzed skin covering sleek muscle, her name tattooed proudly on his chest. He was a work of art.

At thirty-two, Curtis was even sexier than he'd been at nineteen, and back then, she hadn't thought it possible.

"So beautiful," he breathed, his hands on her hips.

Lorrie began rocking faster, taking him deeper, until she knew he wouldn't be able to handle slow and easy anymore. He urged her forward, and she leaned down, her breasts crushed to his chest as he began to thrust into her from beneath. It didn't take much before she was hanging on the razor-sharp edge of bliss, wishing he would go over with her.

Lorrie met his gaze, hanging on as long as she could. "Come for me, Curtis."

He groaned, thrusting harder, faster, until her orgasm detonated, nearly leveling her at the same time he grunted his release.

Forty-Six

♥ Saturday, July 15, 1978 ♥

Though there have been many moments in my lifetime, today is
by far the best yet. I have given birth to the most precious little
boy I've ever seen. Yes, I might be a little biased. Though Curtis
thinks he looks like me, I think he looks just like his daddy. So
handsome. So perfect. ♥

"CURTIS!"

It took a moment for his groggy brain to wake, but he instantly registered Lorrie's voice, her tone. She wasn't screaming, but she was whispering awfully loudly.

"What is it, baby?" he asked, rubbing the sleep from his eyes.

"I think we should go to the hospital," she said, a smile in her voice.

He was up out of the bed with his jeans tugged on before he realized he was standing. "Is everything okay?"

It took a moment to see that she was standing up, already dressed, hair brushed, looking as though she hadn't a care in the world.

"Everything's perfect." Her grin faltered momentarily as she put her hand on her belly. "But my water broke and I'm having contractions, so I think it's time."

Her water had broken.

Contractions.

Christ.

He was frozen in place.

"Curtis, you should probably finish getting dressed. Then maybe, you know, grab the suitcase."

Right.

Shirt.

Shoes.

Suitcase.

Truck.

Hospital.

Shit.

They were having a baby today!

An hour later, they were checked in and Lorrie was resting comfortably in the room.

"Unghh. Oh, it hurts."

Okay, maybe not comfortably. According to the nurse, the contractions were about two minutes apart and lasting a lot longer. Now, they were waiting on the doctor, who had already been called and was on his way.

"Well, well, well," the voice said from the doorway. "Looks like you're going to have a baby today and right on time, too."

Lorrie squeezed Curtis's hand, and he leaned over the bed, kissing her forehead.

"Let's check out your cervix, see how much you've dilated."

Curtis focused on Lorrie while the doctor stuck his hand beneath the sheet, between Lorrie's legs. She squeezed his fingers numb for a few seconds, then let go.

"I don't think this one is going to be all that stubborn," the doctor said. "You're fully dilated. It's time to get this show on the road."

Already? Curtis had heard horror stories about labor lasting hours and hours and hours. Sometimes days. Hell, even Joseph had spent at least eight hours with their firstborn.

"You ready for this?" Lorrie asked, her voice weak.

"I've been ready for this my whole life," he said reassuringly.

A couple of nurses joined them in the room, and the next thing Curtis knew, the doctor was telling Lorrie to push. Curtis didn't know what he was supposed to do, but he knew to keep his mouth shut unless he was encouraging her, so he did. He held Lorrie's hand, brushed her hair back from her face while she scrunched up her cute little nose and attempted to push a human right out of her...

"I can see the head," the doctor said.

Okay, well, looked as though she was further along than he'd thought.

"Give me another good, hard push, Lorrie," the doctor urged.

Lorrie did as she was told, once again attempting to squeeze Curtis's fingers right off his hand. Not that he gave a shit. She could break every bone in his body and he'd still be standing there, still loving her with his whole heart.

"That's it," the doctor said. "One more."

Lorrie once again pushed as Curtis divided his attention between Lorrie's face and the doctor's. And that's when he saw it. The doctor's smile made his chubby cheeks bunch up, but Curtis considered that a good sign.

"Congratulations," the doctor said, holding up a slimy, wrinkled little body. "It's a boy."

It took everything in his power to remain on his feet. The news was so welcome he wasn't sure how he was still standing.

Lorrie started to laugh, then she started to cry. Then more laughter. It was all so confusing for Curtis, but he remained stoically by her side until they placed the tiny little bundle against Lorrie's chest. He wasn't as slimy anymore, thank God. Curtis stared down at the little thing wrapped in a little blue blanket.

"Oh, my God, Curtis," Lorrie whispered. "He's perfect."

Yes. He was definitely that.

Forty-Seven

♥ Saturday, July 15, 1978 ♥

TRAVIS GLENN WALKER.

My first thought when I looked at him… The doctor is wrong. He might not think this precious little boy will be stubborn, but a mother knows these things. My prediction is that Travis will be as strong-willed as his father. Which isn't a bad thing. He's absolutely perfect. Ten fingers, ten toes, his father's nose, and his father's dark hair. We're truly blessed. Welcome, and thank you for expanding our little family, Travis. ♥

♥ Wednesday, May 21, 1980 ♥

SAWYER ANTHONY WALKER.

My first thought when I looked at him… This one is going to be a handful. Although Travis has given us a run for our money these last couple of years, I have a funny feeling that Sawyer is going to be the wild one in the bunch. A mother knows these things. And just like his brother, Sawyer looks like his father. Same nose, same dark hair. Such a sweet, sweet boy. Welcome to the family, Sawyer. ♥

♥ Saturday, March 21, 1981 ♥

KALEB ALLEN WALKER.

My first thought when I looked at him… He's going to be the level-headed one. I don't know how I know that, but I do. Maybe it was the fact that I was in labor for far longer than with the first two. I think Kaleb was waiting for the right moment to arrive. Yes, I have to say, I predict he'll be just like his father, making sure things are managed even if his older brothers want to be in charge. A mother knows these things. And just like Sawyer and Travis, Kaleb looks like Curtis. Well, maybe he looks a little like me. Welcome to the family, Kaleb. ♥

♥ Monday, December 17, 1984 ♥

BRAYDON JOSHUA AND BRENDON MATTHEW WALKER.

My first thought when I looked at them… Oh, heavens, I don't know how I'm going to keep up with two at one time. Three is more than a handful; adding two more to the mix… I'm likely going to go crazy. Still, I find myself smiling. They are precious in every way. I think Curtis and I have done a fine job with Travis, Sawyer, and Kaleb so far, so I think we'll be just fine with two more. I only hope Mrs. Walker is willing to help out, because it's safe to say that we're gonna need the extra hands. Welcome to the family, my sweet twins, Braydon and Brendon. ♥

♥ Monday, November 17, 1986 ♥

ETHAN THOMAS WALKER.

My first thought when I looked at him… This sweet little boy is going to be the strongest of them all. I predict that he'll need us to look over him, but we won't be able to let him know we are. He'll be independent like that, thinking he should carry the weight of the world on his shoulders. I can say, he'll never have to worry because we'll always be there for him. No matter what he needs. And just like the others, we'll need to make certain he understands that love is unconditional. Welcome to the family, Ethan. ♥

♥ Friday, April 28, 1989 ♥

ZANE MICHAEL WALKER.

My first thought when I looked at him… Sawyer will meet his match with this one. I predict that Zane's going to be as easygoing as my pregnancy has been with him. He's going to float through life, do what he pleases. A mother knows these things. But just like with his brothers, we'll make sure he knows right from wrong, that he understands it's important to stand up for what you believe in. He's going to keep everyone on their toes, not just us. And that … that I look forward to.

Although I thought one day we might have a little girl, I can't say that I'm disappointed with all boys. And since seven is a lucky number, we've decided this little guy will be our last.

Welcome, and thank you for completing our family, Zane. ♥

Part Four

*"To love abundantly is to live abundantly,
and to love forever is to live forever."*
~ Henry Drummond

Forty-Eight

March 15, 2016

CURTIS AMBLED INTO THE KITCHEN, DRAWN BY the enticing aroma of fresh-baked something or other and coffee. It was the same smell he'd been roused by for the last … oh, forty-some-odd years or so.

"Mornin', darlin'," he greeted his wife, kissing her smooth cheek as he silently inhaled her sweet scent. She smelled better than the biscuits, no doubt about it. He'd been addicted to her scent since the very first day he'd met her—a lifetime ago—and he found he still couldn't get enough of her. Last night, for instance…

Okay, so maybe now was not the time to think about last night and the sexy way his wife had been moving against him. Only because the light, flowery fragrance wasn't the only thing he noticed about his beautiful wife this morning.

Taking a step back, he took a good long look at her, studying her face. "You okay? Your face is warm."

Lorrie shook her head as she said, "I'm good."

Her tone was a little less enthusiastic than he'd expected. Not that he thought his wife of fifty-two years was going to jump up and down because he'd made an appearance, but he had grown accustomed to her cheerful tone.

"Do you feel all right?" he probed, taking the cup of coffee she offered before moving toward the table.

Lorrie nodded. "Just a little sluggish."

"Kidney again?" For the past year, Lorrie had been experiencing a series of kidney infections that had left the doctors baffled. And because they continued to treat them with antibiotics, the infection would clear up, then a couple of months later, it would return. No one seemed to know why.

"I don't think so." Lorrie turned to him and forced a smile that didn't quite reach her pretty blue eyes. "Now quit worryin' about me and eat your breakfast."

Even forced, her smile was radiant—Lorrie had always had the brightest, most beguiling smile he'd ever seen, and she'd only gotten prettier over the years—even if there were lines near her eyes that reflected the pain she was in. The pain she was pretending *not* to be in. That was Lorrie, always looking out for everyone else, oftentimes at her own expense.

But Curtis knew his wife better than he knew himself. For more than half their lives, she'd been putting him first. Always.

Well, maybe not always. If he recalled correctly, it had taken him a little while to win her over back in the beginning. He smiled at the memory.

"Come join me, honey," he urged, nodding toward the empty seat beside him as he focused on her.

"As soon as I clean up—"

"I'll do the dishes," he interrupted.

Lorrie's head turned, her questioning gaze pinning him in place.

"What?" he grumbled, the corners of his mouth twitching as he tried to hide his smile. She always gave him that same look when he offered to do something she thought him incapable of doing. "I can do the dishes."

It was true. He could. Even if she rarely allowed him to. Then again, he thought they had a fancy little automatic dishwasher for just that purpose. But it wasn't his ability to clean them that was the issue, or so he'd been told. Apparently he didn't put them in their proper place. If you asked him, a cupboard was a cupboard was a cupboard.

"Please, darlin'," he drawled, cocking his head to the side, giving her that smile she always seemed to warm to.

It apparently worked, because she gifted him with another grin, accompanied by a brief eye roll, then poured herself a cup of coffee—added one sugar and a drop of milk, as usual—then joined him at the table.

"Have you heard from Travis?" He leaned back in his chair as he watched her. She was moving slower than usual, and when she eased into the chair, Curtis knew something wasn't right.

But for the time being, he pretended not to notice.

Lorrie nodded. "Yep. Kylie went for her prenatal checkup, and she's doin' good. She's officially fourteen weeks along, and the baby's doin' good."

"Is it a girl?"

"How would I know?" Lorrie asked, grinning—a full-blown smile this time.

Fine. If Travis, Kylie, and Gage didn't want to know the sex of the baby, then neither did he. "And Braydon?"

Another nod. "Yep. Jess went for her checkup last week. Looks as though we're gonna have two more grandbabies at almost the same time."

Not long after Christmas, Travis had announced that Kylie was pregnant with their second child, followed by Braydon's announcement that Jessie was pregnant, despite the fact that their wedding hadn't taken place until February. According to his boy, he'd gotten tired of waiting. Made sense.

And those announcements had been the whipped cream topping on a damn good year. After all, the Walker family had grown by two more when Vanessa had given birth to Reid, making Zane a proud papa back in July, as well as Kaleb and Zoey bringing their second little one, Kellan, into the world only a month later. Now that their oldest grandchild, Mason, was two, Lorrie was at the boys to keep giving her more grandkids to spoil. It seemed to be working.

"And Kate?" he asked, referring to Travis's sixteen-month-old daughter.

"Just a cold. And she's better. Back to keepin' her fathers on their toes according to Kylie."

That he believed. Since he and Lorrie had only boys, Curtis had a hard time around little girls. Granted, Kate was their only granddaughter, not to mention, the cutest thing he'd ever laid eyes on, but he couldn't deny that all that pink made him nervous.

Lorrie winced, and Curtis instantly sat up straight, reaching for her hand. "What's wrong?"

"Nothing," she insisted, her voice strained.

Yeah, he'd been down this road before.

"That's it, woman. I'm takin' you to the doctor." He was on his feet and heading for the phone before she could argue. When he turned back, he noticed she was looking paler than before, which worried him. Reaching for the receiver on the wall, he quickly dialed the phone and waited for the doctor to answer.

LORRIE WASN'T AT ALL SURPRISED WHEN CURTIS got to his feet and headed for the telephone. She'd learned long ago not to bother arguing with her husband. For one, it wouldn't do her any good. When the stubborn old fart set his mind to something, there was no way to change it, and arguing would just prolong the inevitable.

So, once he'd called the doctor and convinced them that she needed to be seen right away—the man had always been persuasive—she had changed clothes, climbed into the truck, and let him take her to her appointment.

That had been the easy part of the day.

When the doctor had run some tests, then advised her that she had another kidney infection, along with a bladder infection, Lorrie hadn't batted an eye. When he'd insisted that she go see a specialist and then arranged for her to get in immediately, she'd kept her composure then, too.

And when the new doctor with all the fancy initials after his name had kindly written out a prescription for more antibiotics, she'd accepted that, too.

But when the doctor had said that she needed surgery… Okay, technically it wasn't surgery, but her brain didn't seem to be processing that fact. What it was processing was the little bit of panic that had set in as soon as the doctor had explained what would happen.

No, maybe a *lot* of panic.

And not just her own.

Which explained why her house was full of people.

All of her boys were there, along with their significant others, the grandbabies, as well as a couple of her nephews. Oh, and the dogs. Couldn't forget them. Not that she minded a house full of people. She'd spent the better part of her life making sure her family stuck together through thick and thin. But when they were all looking at her with concerned eyes and clasped hands, Lorrie would've preferred they be at their own houses, cherishing their families and making happy memories rather than sitting in her living room worried about her.

"I could make cookies," she offered, wishing for something to do other than sit there and wait for the questions to come.

"Mom," Travis said, his tone slightly chastising. That was Travis. Not only was he her oldest son, he was also—just as she'd predicted he would be—a worrywart like his father.

"It's gonna be fine," she told him, glancing around from one set of eyes to the next. "The doctor said it's not a difficult procedure. They're gonna go in with a laser to break up the stone."

"A laser?" Zane asked at the same time Zoey said, "They don't think it'll pass on its own?"

"Based on the size of the stone and the location, along with the infection, he said the laser was the best way to go," she said, glancing down at her hands. She really didn't think all this talking was necessary.

"The blockage is causing the infection," Curtis informed them.

Lorrie cast a quick look at her husband, noticing the crease in his forehead. Ever since the doctor had started talking in big words and mentioning general anesthesia, he'd been on edge. They all knew that Curtis portrayed the laid-back country boy as well as anyone, but when it came to her, he worried. A lot. That was one of the many, *many* reasons she'd fallen in love with him all those years ago.

"Now y'all better turn those frowns upside down," Lorrie finally said, planting a smile on her face as she got to her feet. "It's routine. They do this all the time. Who wants cookies?"

Mason and Derrick hopped up and ran toward her as she'd expected, jumping up and down, insisting that they get cookies.

As she turned away, urging the little boys toward the kitchen, Lorrie hoped no one saw the way her hands were shaking. There wasn't much in the world that scared her—after all, she had raised seven rambunctious boys—but anything related to doctors or hospitals was sure to send her nerves into a tizzy.

"Momma, you really okay?"

Lorrie turned to see her youngest boy standing behind her. Zane had evidently followed her into the kitchen.

"I'm good, honey. I promise."

Zane nodded, but it didn't appear as though he believed her.

"Don't you go gettin' worried for nothin'," she told him.

"I'm cool, Momma. Promise."

"I know you are," she said, wrapping her arms around him when he reached for her. Although he was twenty-six, towered over her by almost a foot, not to mention married with a baby of his own, Zane would always be her baby boy.

When she took a step back, she put another smile on her lips. The last thing she wanted was for anyone to worry. Everything was going to be fine.

Didn't mean she wouldn't be saying a few extra prayers in the coming days.

Forty-Nine

ONCE THE HOUSE CLEARED OUT A SHORT time later, Curtis lounged in his recliner, staring blankly at the television screen, smiling to himself as the memory of the first time he'd actually spoken to Lorrie started playing in his head. It was a memory he relived all the time.

He'd known the feisty woman all his life, being that they'd lived in the same small town, gone to the same school, attended the same church... But the day he'd actually met her... That was a day he would never forget. But there had been so many days after that he still relived over and over again. Like the time they'd gotten a dog at Lorrie's insistence, only to find out she was allergic and couldn't be around it for long. Travis and Sawyer had *not* been happy about that. Luckily, Mitch had taken that little pup off their hands.

Or the time when he'd been kicked off one of the horses and Lorrie had thought for sure he'd broken his leg. The instant she'd found out, she'd been livid. Then worried. Then angry all over again. It wasn't until the doctor had confirmed it was just a sprained ankle that she'd relaxed. Right before giving him hell. He'd had to toss her onto the bed and make love to her just to get her to stop yelling at him.

That memory made him laugh.

He also recalled the births of all his boys. Though they'd suffered a devastating loss with the miscarriage of their first child, and it had taken years before they'd actually gotten pregnant again, they'd finally been blessed with Travis. It had been another emotional time for them both, and it wasn't until they'd neared the due date that either of them had released the breath they'd seemed to be holding for most of those months.

Then six more kids had followed, even two at the same time.

Although he was seventy, and sometimes he couldn't remember what he'd done last week, Curtis had never forgotten one single memory of the life he'd shared with Lorrie. Not the important ones, anyway.

And to think it had all started what that first conversation on his mother's front porch.

"Why're you here?"

"Because my daddy told me to come over here."

"To do what?"

Lorrie shrugged.

"So your old man forced you to come over here?"

"Yep."

"To see one of my sisters?"

"Nope."

"My mom?"

"Uh-uh."

"My brother?"

"Wrong again."

"Then who? Me?"

"Mm-hmm."

That gutsy little blond-haired, blue eyed girl had come to see him that day though it would take a while before they ever figured out why. Still, he reflected back on that as one of the best days of his life.

Lorrie Jameson had come to his house that sunny October day, unwilling to tell him why she was there, and still she'd managed to suck him right into her orbit. And that was the day his entire life had changed.

AFTER EVERYONE LEFT AND THE KITCHEN WAS once again clean, while Curtis sat in the living room watching television, Lorrie disappeared into her bedroom as she did every night. It was her quiet time; the few minutes every day that she took just for herself. A time to reflect.

Going into her walk-in closet, Lorrie grabbed the small diary and the pen beside it from her shelf, then started to carry it back into their bedroom but stopped. Glancing at one of the white banker's boxes on the floor, Lorrie leaned down and lifted the lid, pulling out the oldest book inside, then carried both back to her bedroom and took a seat at her little desk. She settled in with her diaries, trying to gather her thoughts.

The one on the right was worn and tattered from age. Its blue cover had been scribbled on time and time again with doodles by a teenage girl who had just started experiencing life at fourteen years old. The other, new and crisp, with a fancy leather binding, had been a Christmas gift from Curtis last year. Inside, it held the musings of a much older, much wiser woman.

The only person who knew Lorrie had been keeping diaries for the majority of her life was her husband. Not even her children were aware that every single day since she was fourteen years old, Lorrie had taken the time to jot down her thoughts. In fact, it had been the very day that she had gone over to Curtis's house and talked to him for the first time that she'd decided to start writing. Sometimes a paragraph, sometimes several pages, depending on the events that had taken place. And over the course of fifty-three years, there were a lot of words written in dozens and dozens of books. All of them kept in those boxes in her closet.

As she sat there, trying not to think about her visit to the doctor or the impending procedure scheduled for Friday, Lorrie carefully opened the first diary she'd ever written in. It wasn't anything fancy, because they'd had no money back then. Daddy had made just enough to pay the bills; Momma had stayed home to take care of the kids. If she recalled correctly, Owen hadn't even been born yet. According to Daddy, there had always been too many mouths to feed, so Lorrie had never asked for anything extra. Instead, she'd taken one of her schoolbooks without them knowing. Just a simple notebook with lined paper. And it had worked just as she'd needed it to.

Using her index finger to guide her, Lorrie started reading the first page.

♥ Sunday, October 7, 1962 ♥

I can't believe Daddy made me go over to the Walkers' place today. On my way over there, I hoped that no one would be home and I could come back and tell him so. I didn't get that lucky. ♥

Continuing to stare down at the page, Lorrie reflected back on that day, the rest of her worries disappearing for a few brief moments. Her life had been an emotional roller coaster, a ride she had never wanted to get off of. No one ever knew what the next day would bring, but it had all brought her to where she was now.

The bedroom door opened, and Lorrie looked up to see Curtis standing there, watching her with those same intriguing blue-gray eyes she'd fallen in love with all those years ago.

"You writin' in your book?" he asked.

"Yes."

"Okay, then. I'm gonna take a shower."

Lorrie nodded, watching as he made his way into the bathroom. Her thoughts drifted back to that day more than fifty years ago, and she couldn't help but smile. Five decades later and that man still made her girl parts sing.

Grinning, Lorrie picked up her pen and her current diary and began to write.

♥ Tuesday, March 15, 2016 ♥

Blessed. That's how I'm feeling today.

Although things aren't exactly perfect at the moment—my health is a little rocky, I think—I feel incredibly blessed. It is during times like these when I see how important family is. We've stuck together through thick and thin, and I'm incredibly grateful.

My boys have grown into such fine men, now all with families of their own, lives blossoming and a full road ahead of them. Watching them grow up has been one of the greatest gifts I could've ever received. And I have their father to thank for such a beautiful life.

If someone were to ask me if I could go back in time and change anything, I can

honestly say that I wouldn't. Every decision I've ever made has led me to here. Right where I am today. A life full of love and laughter and hope. And I've had the greatest man at my side along the way. No one can ask for more than that. ♥

Fifty

CURTIS HAD BEEN PACING THE HALLS, HIS boots clomping on the tiled floor, his head snapping up anytime a person walked by him or a nurse moved behind the nurse's station desk. He knew he was irritating everyone who worked there, but he truly didn't give a shit.

He was waiting for his wife.

To get out of surgery. Or procedure, or whatever the hell they wanted to call it.

He absently rubbed his chest as he continued pacing. If they didn't like it, then they damn well better get over him walking back and forth because he had no intention of stopping until they told him he could go see her.

"Mr. Walker?"

Curtis spun around so fast his seventy-year-old body could hardly keep up with his momentum, but he managed to put a hand on the wall to keep from falling over. "Yes?"

"There're some people in the waiting room. They're asking for you."

Curtis glanced down the hall, then back to the nurse.

"I promise, Mr. Walker. The second I get the word that she's being moved to recovery, I'll run right out there and get you."

He nodded, trusting the young woman's kind eyes. He did need to go out and talk to the kids, let them know that so far everything seemed to be going fine. It wasn't a long procedure, but every second that passed was like a decade to him.

Pushing open the doors, Curtis stepped into the brightly lit waiting area, finding Sawyer, Travis, Kaleb, Ethan, Brendon, Braydon, and Zane all staring back at him. All of his boys, standing shoulder to shoulder, watching him intently.

"We told y'all you didn't need to come," he said quickly.

Travis frowned, as he'd expected him to. Didn't matter how simple they'd explained the process to be, his boys still worried.

"How is she?" Sawyer asked.

Curtis planted a smile on his face. "So far, everything's goin' as planned. She should be out any minute."

"You need anything, Pop?" Brendon asked.

Yes, he needed his wife to smile back at him and tell him that she was fine and dandy and all this worrying he'd been doing was a great big waste of time. But he didn't tell the boys that. "I'm good, son." Curtis glanced around. "Anyone else here?"

Travis shook his head. "They all wanted to come, but we figured seven of us was enough." He grimaced. "Since you told us not to come and all."

Curtis chuckled. "Smartass."

But yes, seven was probably enough. Especially when those seven were intimidating men all standing at least six foot four inches tall. It wasn't often that all his boys were out in public together, other than in town, but when they were … it sometimes made people nervous.

Kaleb thrust his hands into his pockets. "Zoey's over at your house, cleaning up and changing sheets."

Lord. Sometimes Curtis wasn't sure what he'd do without his family. The last thing on his mind had been worrying about getting the house in shape for Lorrie to come home. It was a day surgery, they'd told him. Which meant, provided everything went as planned, she would be spending the night at home just as she had last night. Thank God.

"Mr. Walker?"

Curtis turned around again, finding the same kind-eyed nurse holding open the waiting room door. "Yes?"

"They're bringing her out now. I'll take you back."

"Go, Pop," Ethan ordered. "We'll be out here. When they say we can go back, we will."

Curtis nodded, then hurried after the nurse, following her down the long hallway. He tried to ignore the overwhelming smell of antiseptic, focusing on putting one foot in front of the other.

"She's still groggy from the anesthesia, but everything went as expected. I'll let the doctor fill you in."

When they finally turned the last corner and Curtis saw Lorrie lying on a bed, her eyes closed, her chest softly rising and falling, he released the breath he'd been holding. The one that had lodged in his chest the second they'd wheeled her out of his sight.

Without waiting for permission, Curtis hurried around to the side of the bed and put his hand over Lorrie's. Her pale skin was a stark contrast to his much darker hand, and her dainty fingers slid beneath his perfectly, just as they always had.

"Hey, honey," he whispered, leaning over and kissing her forehead.

He wasn't sure she could hear him, so he didn't say more, simply content to watch her, knowing she was all right.

Someone cleared their throat, and Curtis looked up to see the doctor standing there.

"How'd she do?" Curtis prompted.

"She did great. We were able to go in and dissolve the stone, extracting the pieces we could. The tiny pieces will wash out of the kidney on their own. We did put a stent in place to help the kidney drain. This is temporary, and we'll remove it when she comes for her follow-up visit in two weeks. We've inserted a Foley catheter to collect the urine."

"Stent?" Curtis frowned. He recalled hearing something about that, but for the life of him, he couldn't remember.

"Yes. She'll come back to my office in a couple of weeks to have those removed. Basic procedure, nothing to worry about. She just needs to keep taking the antibiotics and drink a lot of fluids."

Still holding Lorrie's hand, he felt her squeeze, and he turned to look at her. She was smiling up at him, and that was when the tight band around his heart released. For a second, he felt a little light-headed.

"Hey, darlin'. Doc says you did great."

"Was there ever any doubt?" Lorrie teased, her soft voice rough. "I'm a strong woman. I've put up with you all my life, haven't I?"

Her joke made him laugh and he suspected that was her intention.

The doctor went on to explain everything again so that Lorrie would understand. A few minutes later, when he finally left them alone, and after a nurse came in to check her vitals, Curtis sat down in the chair and fought the urge to cry. He couldn't remember the last time he'd cried, but the relief he felt was so damn overwhelming he could hardly contain it.

"I'm okay," Lorrie whispered, sliding her hand over the top of his.

"I know, baby. I know." Using his other hand, he brushed her hair off her face. "I love you."

That beautiful smile beamed back at him when she said, "I love you, too." And once again, all was right in his world.

"I'm so tired," she whispered.

"The anesthesia's going to keep her groggy for a little while," the nurse said. "It'll wear off in a bit."

Curtis nodded, then looked at Lorrie. "Sleep, honey. I'll be right here when you wake up."

As though that was what she needed to hear, Lorrie closed her eyes and drifted off while Curtis vigilantly sat by her side for the next couple of hours.

ZOEY WALKER STOOD AT THE STOVE, STIRRING the pot of canned stew after she set the glass lid on the pot of instant rice. It wasn't the greatest dinner in the world, but with two kids, a husband, and a bustling resort to tend to, it would suffice. That or frozen chicken nuggets, and since they'd had those twice this week, stew sounded much better.

The back screen door slammed, and she glanced over to see Kaleb standing there. He hardly had a chance to get his hat off before Mason was running into the room, hollering as he launched himself at his father's legs.

"What's up, little man?" Kaleb glanced her way as he swung Mason up into the air. "Smells good. What is it?"

"Dinty Moore," she said with a grin.

"My favorite." The man was easy to please when it came to food. For that she was grateful, because, though she could hold her own in the kitchen thanks to years of being taught by Lorrie, they didn't usually have much time for gourmet meals.

Speaking of... "How's your mom?" she asked when Kaleb cupped her chin, tilting her head up so he could kiss her lips.

"Good. Pop got her home and she's all settled in. She said to tell you thank you."

"No thanks necessary." Zoey would do anything for Curtis and Lorrie, just as she knew they'd do anything for her and her family.

"So, how was your day?" Kaleb asked, placing Mason on his feet.

"Well, I managed to keep Mason from tearing up your parents' house. Just barely."

Kaleb chuckled, watching as Mason tore ass out of the room at full speed and his loudest decibel level.

Flipping off the burner, Zoey stepped out of the way and allowed Kaleb to grab the two pots from the stove and take them to the table. She pulled plates and silverware out of the dishwasher—since she'd forgotten to empty it that morning—before joining him.

"Mason! Dinner!"

"Where's Kellan?" Kaleb asked.

"Sleeping. I think he's got another tooth coming in."

"Aww, hell." Kaleb helped Mason into his high chair before snapping the tray in place.

"Yep. More sleepless nights," she said as she scooped food onto each of their plates. "Oh. That reminds me."

Kaleb's eyebrows lifted and that mischievous smirk tilted his sexy mouth.

"What in the world could you possibly find dirty in that?" she asked.

"You said sleepless nights. I know a few proven methods to keep you up at night."

Zoey smacked his arm, then sat down beside him. "Did you know your mother keeps a diary?"

"A diary?" He looked puzzled.

"Yeah. You know, those books people write their personal thoughts in."

"I thought it was a journal."

"Same difference. But did you? Know?"

Kaleb settled his elbows on the table, spooning food into his mouth as he shook his head.

"I didn't mean to, but I stumbled upon them when I was looking for sheets for their bed. She's got several boxes of them in her closet."

"Why does she keep sheets in boxes?" he asked, staring back at her blankly.

"Not sheets, dummy. Diaries."

"You lost me, babe."

"It looks like your mom's been writing in a diary for years and years. I don't know how many there were, but there was one sitting out on one of the boxes, and it had *1962* written on the front."

"Did you read it?"

"God no." Zoey chuckled. "That's an invasion of privacy."

"I woulda read it."

"Whatever." Zoey didn't believe that for a second. "What if your mom wrote about having sex with your dad? You wanna read about that?"

Kaleb sat up straight. "Hell no."

"Hell no," Mason mocked.

"Shit," Kaleb said, glancing over at Mason.

"Shit," Mason echoed.

Great. "Not helping," Zoey told her husband, laughing at the two of them.

"So women write about sex in their diaries?" Kaleb inquired once he got Mason distracted with his green beans.

"Not only women keep diaries," she told him.

"Yes, they do. We men don't write down our thoughts."

Figuring it was easier to appease him than argue, Zoey said, "And yes, women write about everything in their diaries."

"Wait a minute." Kaleb turned to her, his face serious. "Do you keep a diary?"

She didn't, but she said, "Maybe."

"Do you write about sex? 'Cause if you do, I wanna read it."

Men.

Shaking her head, Zoey focused on her food.

Fifty-One

Two weeks later, Friday, April 1

CURTIS SAT IN THE WAITING ROOM OF the doctor's office, doing his damnedest to pay attention to the ratty magazine in his hand. Truth was, he didn't give two shits about any of the articles in *Guns and Ammo*, though it had been a smidge better than picking up the one with some half-naked woman on the front of it. Then again, he wasn't interested in any of it anyhow. His mind was off in the room with Lorrie, wishing he could be back there with her while she went through the procedure.

The appointment was to remove the stent in her bladder, along with the Foley catheter she'd been boldly managing for the past two weeks without complaint. She was definitely a better person than he was. No way would he have gone fourteen days with that shit strapped to his body. But he'd never once heard her complain.

Now, the only thing he could do was wait and try to focus on something other than storming through that door to find his wife. Curtis prided himself on his patience—he was, after all, a backwoods country boy at heart—but there was no doubt he wasn't all that patient when it came to Lorrie. She was the center of his entire world.

His phone vibrated in his pocket, and he fished it out, squinting down at the screen.

Ethan: How's the appointment going? You a nervous wreck yet?

His kids knew him too well.

He hated the damn phone, especially the whole texting thing. His fingers were too big to punch those little buttons, which made responding too damn difficult. However, he had to admit, it was a little convenient that he could have a conversation without anyone else in the waiting room hearing all the gory details.

Curtis: When have you ever known me to be nervous?

He waited for a response, watching his phone intently. The first thing to pop up was some little monkey face that looked as though it were laughing at him. He didn't know how to send all that shit, but his boys sure as hell enjoyed it.

Ethan: I'm gonna go with always.

Curtis: Shouldn't you be working, boy?

Ethan: I am working. Wanted to check in, that's all.

Curtis: She's in with the doctor. Once I know more, I'll let you know.

Ethan: Okay. Now do us all a favor and relax a bit, would ya?

Easier said than done.

"Mr. Walker?"

Curtis lifted his gaze from his phone. He glanced over at the door to see a nurse standing there, smiling at him. "Mrs. Walker is ready for you to come back now."

He shot up out of his chair, shoving his phone back in his pocket as he fought the urge to run. His old-ass legs wouldn't get him there that fast, anyway, but his brain didn't seem to realize that.

LORRIE FELT BETTER THAN SHE HAD IN forever. Lighter maybe. Even now, as she positioned herself in the hardback chair, waiting for Curtis to come into the room to get her and for the nurse to return with a prescription for more antibiotics.

The doctor had said it'd all gone well, only a minor hiccup with the procedure, but nothing that she needed to worry about. He'd told her she shouldn't feel any discomfort while he removed the stent and for her to lie still, which she'd done. So when she'd felt a slight stabbing feeling, she had flinched and cried out. The doctor had looked up at her, his smile forced as he explained that he'd nicked her bladder with whatever tool he'd used to remove the stent, causing a slight tear, but the oral antibiotics she was on would ensure no infection, and he'd get her a refill for a few more days to make sure. Since the doctor didn't seem worried, neither was she. The only thing she wanted to do was get out of there.

When Curtis walked in, she smiled at him, ensuring he knew she was okay.

"Hey, darlin'," he greeted, moving toward her slowly as though he was scared she would break. "How're you feelin'?"

"Perfect," she told him, getting to her feet. "Better than perfect. I was thinking maybe you could take me to dinner tonight."

"Anything you want," he told her, the lines on his face easing somewhat. He glanced around. "Are you all done? Did the doctor say anything?"

"I'm just…" She didn't get to finish her sentence when the nurse scurried in, handing her a sheet of paper. Lorrie promptly thanked her and was told she was free to go.

"Looks like we're good to go," Lorrie told Curtis.

"Well, then." Curtis's face lit up as though that was a relief he hadn't been expecting.

After grabbing her purse from the counter, she allowed Curtis to take her hand and lead her out of the small room. They stopped at the reception desk to ensure they didn't need to do anything more. The kind woman reminded her that the doctor said to call if she had any issues. Lorrie hoped she wouldn't have to call. She just wanted this to be behind her. Being sick for months on end had been a nuisance she was ready to be rid of.

Forty-five minutes later, they were seated in a booth at Mama's Diner, Curtis beside her with glasses of iced tea in front of them. The small restaurant was relatively busy for a Friday afternoon. The sounds of silverware clinking along with the soft drone of conversation were music to her ears. For nearly two weeks, Lorrie hadn't ventured out of the house unless it was to go to church.

"Are you really feeling better?" Curtis asked as he stacked the menus, pushing them to the far side of the table. Didn't matter what day they went to the diner, they always ordered the special, so there wasn't any decision-making necessary.

"Much," she assured him. And it was no less than the truth. She felt like a brand-new person. No pain, no discomfort. And most of all, no strange medical devices on, or in, her body.

Curtis leaned over and kissed her temple. "I'll call the boys when we get home. Let 'em know you're all right."

"You could just send them a text." Lorrie knew Curtis wasn't all that fond of texting, but she liked giving him a hard time about it. She had ensured that she kept up with the times, though Travis still enjoyed giving her crap when she messed things up, sending him texts on accident from time to time. Little did he know, but sometimes she did that on purpose. Accidentally on purpose.

Curtis frowned. "You know I ain't good with that stuff."

He would've been if he'd ever given it a chance, Lorrie thought. But if Curtis wanted to call the boys and tell them, she would let him.

"You want me to mention Sunday dinner?"

For the past two Sundays, Lorrie hadn't felt up to having a house full of people, so she'd had to let them all down. She could only remember a handful of Sundays when they hadn't all gotten together to share a meal since the boys had started moving out, and though it had only been two weeks, Lorrie missed them all terribly.

"Yes. Maybe Zoey can come over and help me cook."

"I'm sure she'd be happy to."

"Then it's settled." Lorrie was looking forward to things getting back to normal now that she felt better. "Maybe we can go out and check on the horses when we get home."

Curtis's gaze held a hint of concern. "You sure?"

"I wouldn't mention it if I wasn't." Lorrie smiled at him. "And then, if you're nice, maybe I'll give you a little surprise at home."

That wicked gleam she'd seen for the past five decades was back, and it still had the same effect on her now. People who claimed sex after a certain age wasn't possible hadn't been with a Walker man, that was for sure.

"I don't wanna hurt you," he said tenderly.

"You won't, I promise. I'm all fixed up. The doctor told me so."

"Then we'll do whatever you want, darlin'. Whatever you want."

Fifty-Two

Sunday, April 3

"POP!" TRAVIS CALLED OUT TO HIS FATHER when they walked into the crowded emergency room waiting area. There were people scattered about from one side of the room to the other, some talking, some who looked to be sleeping.

He noticed his father looking around as though he didn't know where he was or who was calling him. Then again, the frantic voice mail Curtis had left had nearly sent Travis into a panic. The only things keeping him together were the woman and man standing at his side keeping him that way.

"Dad? You okay?" Travis asked when they approached.

His father looked dazed and confused, as though he couldn't focus on who Travis was.

It only took a moment before the fog seemed to clear and Curtis was back with them.

Damn, this place smelled like disinfectant and disease, which wasn't at all appealing by any means. For a second, he wondered if maybe Gage and Kylie should take Kate home. He doubted it could be good for his pregnant wife or his little girl to be in there. Then again, he knew Kylie. She wouldn't leave until she knew what was going on. According to Curtis's message, they'd needed to get their asses down to the hospital and quick.

Here they were.

"Where's Mom?" he asked, trying not to be too gruff, but his fear was overwhelming him. He could handle a lot of shit, but he didn't hold up too well when it came to something being wrong with a member of his family. He recalled back when Zane had been beaten and hospitalized… He hated thinking about that shit.

"Tests," Curtis grumbled, his eyes scanning the faces around them. Once again, Travis felt as though his father was somewhere far away. That or he was panicking, which was likely the case.

"Dad, you need to sit down," Kylie instructed, her small hand curling around Curtis's arm as she guided him toward a chair. The woman didn't even realize she held his heart right in her hands.

Gage's firm hand came to rest on Travis's shoulder, a silent message that he was right there, ready to catch him if he fell. God, he loved that man.

"Breathe," Kylie told Travis's father. "Just breathe."

"Where're your brothers?" Curtis asked, meeting Travis's eyes.

"They're on the way. I called them as soon as I hung up with you. Did the doctor say anything before they sent you out here?"

"Something about infection…" Curtis was shaking his head as though he couldn't recall what they'd told him.

Travis gave his father's shoulder a strong, comforting squeeze. "From the kidney stone?"

"They said that shouldn't have caused it."

Travis looked up at his husband and his wife, feeling a little off-kilter. His mother was somewhere in this hospital, and they didn't seem to be telling his father what he needed to know.

His heart broke when his father put his hands over his face, breathing deeply. Travis had been there before, that space where you were trying to breathe through the emotional pain, trying to hold your shit together, and knowing it wasn't going to matter. Falling apart was inevitable.

"Hey, Trav. Pop."

The sound of Ethan's voice drew his attention toward the door. Travis saw some of his brothers and their significant others coming toward them. Ethan and Beau, Kaleb and Zoey, Sawyer and Kennedy. All of their faces reflected the same concern and fear that Travis felt.

"What sort of tests are they doing?" Kylie asked, her hand still resting on Curtis's arm.

"Blood tests and a CT scan."

Probably standard tests, Travis thought.

"What happened?" Kennedy asked, his sister-in-law's concern palpable.

Travis stepped back when his father sat up straight, gripping the arms of the chair until his knuckles turned white.

"She woke up this mornin', said she felt horrible," Curtis explained. "She couldn't eat, and if she tried, she couldn't hold anything down. Her temperature was one-oh-three…"

Ethan squatted down in front of Curtis, placing his hand on their dad's knee. "When did this start?"

"When she went to bed last night, she said she didn't feel well. Thought maybe she was coming down with the flu."

"The flu?" Ethan frowned, his eyes cutting to Travis's briefly. "But she's been better since Friday?"

Curtis nodded. "For a bit, yes. Then this morning, her skin was kinda ashy. Finally, she told me to get her to the hospital."

Well, hell. If his mother had asked to go to the hospital, it had to be bad. Lorrie wasn't the type to enjoy going to hospitals, regardless of who was there. One of those unexplainable phobias, she'd always told them.

Travis needed to get more information. He hated that his father had been sent out to the waiting room when his mother was somewhere back there being poked and prodded. She needed her husband to be with her.

"Be right back." Travis patted Curtis's shoulder, then nodded to Gage before he trekked over to the nurse's desk.

He glanced over to see Braydon and Jessie, Brendon and Cheyenne, as well as Zane and Vanessa, coming toward them. Good. All his brothers were there, just as they should be.

"Hey, Trav," his cousin Jared called out, coming toward him.

"Hey."

"Any news?" Jared asked as he hiked his son, Derrick, up on his hip.

"That's what I'm hopin' to get now," he explained, nodding toward the desk.

"I'll go keep an eye on your old man."

Travis nodded, then turned to the nurse's desk. A young woman looked up briefly, then turned her attention back to the desk.

It appeared she was going to ignore him. He'd see about that.

"I need information on my mother," he told her firmly, not giving a damn if she was busy doing something else.

"Due to HIPAA laws, we can't give out—"

That was the same bottled response he'd expected. "Family," he told her.

"What?" Her brown eyes widened when she looked up at him.

"That's the code you're gonna ask me for, right? To be able to share information with me. Well, now you've got it, so share away."

"Sir, I'm sure the doctor'll be out shortly—"

"That's not what I asked," he grumbled.

It wasn't that he enjoyed being an asshole—most of the time—but he damn sure wasn't going to sit back while his father fell to pieces worrying about his mother. She shouldn't be back there by herself, no matter what the damned doctors thought.

Her eyes narrowed. He'd seen that look before. She was weighing her options. Trying to decide whether or not it was worth the time and effort to argue with him. It wasn't.

"Her name's Lorrie Walker. She's my mother." He waved his hand behind him. "The entire family's out here, including her husband. We need to know what's going on."

She gave a terse nod, then got to her feet. She didn't look at all happy, but thankfully, she headed in the opposite direction, which he took as a good sign. That or she was going to get security. He'd had that happen a time or two.

While hopefully she went to get information, he headed back over to his father and the rest of his family. He walked up in time to hear his father mumbling to himself, "I need to see her."

"You will," Kylie assured him. "Travis'll make sure of it."

Damn right he would.

"She'll be okay, Pop," Ethan said, his voice low.

All eyes fell on him and he nodded toward the nurse's desk. "They're going to find out what's going on."

"How long has she been here?" Brendon asked their father.

Curtis shrugged. "Coupla hours, maybe."

Too long for him to have been exiled out here, that was for damn sure.

"Walker family."

The shrill voice sounded from behind him, and Travis turned to see a nurse searching the faces. Curtis was on his feet instantly, and everyone converged on the poor, unsuspecting woman.

"I'm Lorrie's husband," Curtis told her.

"She just came back from the CT scan, and they're getting her settled. Once they're done with that, someone will come get you and take you back to her."

"Why can't he go now?" Travis asked. This was bullshit.

The woman's gaze scanned all the faces, and Travis knew how it looked. It was pretty intimidating when the Walker men converged. They weren't small men, and they tended to take up a lot of space. She didn't seem to know what to say.

"Where's the doctor?" Travis asked, hoping to move this along. "We'd like to speak to him."

The woman nodded. "Of course."

Glancing over at Kylie, Travis nodded, giving her the signal to take his father back to sit down. He was shaking, whether he realized it or not.

Gage passed Kate off to Kennedy and remained at his side while Ethan and Beau joined him.

"It sounds bad," Ethan said, his voice low.

They didn't know enough to make that assessment just yet, but yeah, Travis couldn't deny that it sounded bad.

"I stopped by the house on Friday night," Beau told them. "Just to check in, make sure they didn't need anything. They were watching a movie in the living room. She seemed to be doing well."

Travis knew that jumping to conclusions was never a good thing. He could sit here and try to come up with a million reasons as to what had made her sick, but he knew it was a waste of time and energy.

"Mr. Walker."

All heads turned toward the voice coming from behind them. Travis glanced at Gage. "Go get Pop."

The doctor came to stand directly in front of them, waiting to speak until Curtis was there. "We're running some blood tests and we did a CT scan. The initial results are pointing to a large infection."

"What does that mean?" Ethan asked.

"We need to narrow down to the source of the infection. At that point, we'll be able to determine a treatment plan."

"Is it bad?" Travis blurted.

The doctor's eyes softened. "It's not good, I can tell you that much. She's vomiting a lot. We've given her some anti-nausea medicine to help with that, and we're giving her fluids intravenously. We're admitting her to ICU for now. She should be moved in the next couple of hours."

Intensive care unit. Yeah, that was bad.

Sensing there wasn't any additional information, Travis nodded his head and turned to look at his father. "You wanna ask him anything else?"

Curtis frowned. "Yes. When can I see my wife?"

The doctor turned to look behind him as a little blond nurse was hurrying toward them. Her eyes met Travis's, then slid to his father's. She looked as though she expected one of them to tackle her at any minute.

"Mr. Walker," she said, looking directly at Curtis. "Mrs. Walker is asking for you."

"I'll follow you back," Travis told his dad. "That way we'll know where you are."

They headed down a wide area of curtained-off rooms that circled around a large nurse's station. The nurse stopped in front of one of the curtains, pulled it back, then headed in the opposite direction as fast as her legs would carry her.

Travis watched as his dad hurried into the small space. He got a good look at his mother for the first time, and his heart broke. She looked so pale and weak lying there in the bed. Despite the fact that she forced a smile when Curtis leaned over and kissed her on the forehead, Travis could tell she was hurting.

"What did they say?" Curtis's deep baritone resonated out into the common area.

"Something about high white blood cell counts from the preliminary tests," Lorrie explained, her voice weak. "They've put me on more antibiotics while they wait for more tests to come back."

When his father eased into the chair beside the bed, seemingly oblivious to Travis still standing there, he knew he needed to give them a minute.

"I'm so tired," his mother whispered.

"I know, darlin'. Close your eyes and rest. I'm right here."

"You won't leave me?"

"Not in this lifetime."

Travis knew that no truer words had ever been spoken. His father would remain by her side, which meant Travis needed to step up and help out.

Knowing they would be okay, he headed back out to talk to the others, to figure out what they wanted to do for now. Because of the little ones, not everyone could stay at the hospital, but Travis knew he wasn't going anywhere until they knew for sure what was going on.

Fifty-Three

"ANY NEWS, POP?" ZANE ASKED, WORRY CREASING his brow as Curtis joined them in the waiting area.

Glancing around, Curtis noticed that the group had grown smaller over the last few hours. Since they had rug rats who needed to be put to bed, he completely understood. But there, sitting in a line against one wall, were all seven of his boys, plus Beau and Gage, who were additions to his family who he considered his own. As he neared, they all got to their feet.

"They did more blood work and the doctor came in to talk to us," he told them. He was doing his damnedest to keep his composure, but it wasn't easy.

"And?" Sawyer prompted.

"The doctor called it sepsis," he explained, although he didn't really have a clue what the hell that meant.

As soon as the word was out of his mouth, Zane was on his phone, and Curtis knew he was looking up the definition and probably what doctors did to treat it. Curtis had a fairly decent understanding based on the way the doctor had described it, and the one thing he'd taken away from it all was that it wasn't good.

"Something about a complication from infection," he said, trying to recall the long, drawn-out explanation the doctor had given.

"But she'll be all right?" Ethan asked.

That, Curtis honestly didn't know, but he'd said enough prayers since the doctor had told him that he hoped like hell God was listening. "It can be life-threatening," he relayed, hating the looks he received. The last thing he wanted to tell his boys was that their mother might not survive this, but he'd always believed in telling it to them straight.

"What does that mean?" Travis questioned, his tone relaying his lack of acceptance of a fatal outcome.

Curtis took a deep breath. "The chemicals that her body naturally releases to fight the infection have caused inflammation throughout her body. He said that this series of changes within her body has the potential to cause her organs to fail."

"Fuck," Gage mumbled.

Curtis couldn't have said it better. "Like they said, they're getting ready to move her to the intensive care unit. She's still really sick, can't stop vomiting."

Braydon's eyes widened and Curtis could feel his son's pain.

"How do they treat it?" Kaleb asked.

"They've got her on antibiotics and fluids. They'll push those, hoping to fight the infection. The problem is, they don't know where the infection is coming from."

"How long will she be here?" Brendon asked.

All faces were staring back at him, concern etched deeply across them. Curtis could only shrug. "They didn't say. They'll do more blood work to check her white count, see if the numbers'll go in the direction they want."

"What can we do?" Beau asked.

Curtis stared back at his son-in-law. Beau had been part of the Walker family since he'd been a kid, so he knew that he was close to Lorrie. Having been Zane's best friend growing up, then marrying Ethan, Beau was as much a part of the family as any of his boys. He was grateful that he was there.

"The doctor said the only thing to do now is wait. See if the antibiotics will kill the infection."

"Can we see her?" Brendon asked.

"Sure." Curtis nodded. "No more than two at a time. I'll sit out here while y'all go back. When they get her to ICU, they said there'll be visiting hours."

"Go on back," Travis told Brendon and Braydon. "We'll wait out here with Dad."

Ethan urged Curtis toward a chair.

"Can we get you somethin' to eat?" Gage offered.

Curtis looked at Travis's husband and forced a smile. "Not hungry, but thanks."

"Pop, you have to eat," Sawyer stated, squatting down before him.

"I will," he assured him. Even the thought of food didn't sit well. The only thing he could think about was how he wanted to see Lorrie smiling and laughing, enjoying her Sunday dinners with her family, not laid up in a hospital bed. His chest tightened as he tried to fight the urge to cry. He didn't want his boys to see him break down, but the mere thought that he'd have to spend a single day on this Earth without Lorrie was too much.

Fighting the tears was useless, and the next thing Curtis knew, Travis was hugging him tight, cradling his head like a baby as he broke down, releasing the pent up emotion.

"Oh, God," he groaned, his entire body weak as the emotions poured out. He was scared. So damn scared.

Travis held him tighter while Curtis fought for breath, hating that he was falling to pieces, but he couldn't stop it. The one and only thing guaranteed to take him out would be losing her.

One minute without Lorrie … would be too long.

He wouldn't survive.

LORRIE HURT ALL OVER. HER EYES CONTINUED to drift shut although she was doing her best to stay awake. It wasn't easy, especially when she had a reprieve from the vomiting. Seemed every time she would close her eyes, her body tried to send her stomach out through her mouth. That and the pain. They'd said they would give her something, but she feared it would only make her groggier; still, she wouldn't refuse, because the pain was overwhelming.

"Hey, Momma."

Forcing her eyes open, she saw Braydon and Brendon standing on either side of her bed. She smiled. At thirty-one, her twins were still identical, although she could easily tell them apart. That was a mother's gift, she supposed.

"Hi," she whispered.

"How're you feelin'?" Brendon asked, his big hand settling on top of hers.

"Like crap," she said truthfully, chuckling.

Braydon gently squeezed her other hand. "Need anything?"

Glancing over to the chair on the opposite side of the small curtained-off room, then back to him, she said, "Just take care of your dad. I know he's havin' a hard time with this. But I promise, I'm gonna get well."

"We'll keep the old man in line," Brendon assured her, grinning.

"I'm not sure that's even possible," she noted.

"Probably not," he agreed.

Looking between the two of them, she didn't try to hide her pain. "Make sure he eats. And sleeps." She forced another smile. "And showers."

"He'll be fine, Momma," Braydon stated, sliding his hand on her arm. "You worry about you."

"Did he tell you what the doctors said?"

They both nodded.

"I guess they'll be moving me to a room soon?"

"That's the rumor," Brendon said.

"Hopefully it'll have a view," she teased.

Her boys smiled, but those smiles didn't reach their eyes. They were scared, as was she.

Something about this felt off. Never in her life had she felt like this. The pain seemed to be coming from everywhere, and the only thing she wanted to do was sleep. It killed her to watch Curtis trying to process what was happening to her. She knew it was tearing him up that he couldn't fix this for her. He'd always been the one who wanted to fix whatever ailed her. Although, they'd been together long enough, endured so much, he should've known by now that he couldn't fix it all. Still, she loved him for wanting to.

Before she was ready, sleep pulled her under, but not before she saw the deep worry on her boys' faces. It hurt her heart to know they were upset. That was the last thing she wanted.

Fifty-Four

Two days later

"COME ON, POP," ETHAN STATED FIRMLY. "LET'S go down to the cafeteria and grab a bite to eat. Kaleb and Zoey are gonna hang with Mom for a bit."

Curtis looked over at Lorrie, seeing that she was still asleep. She'd been asleep for almost two days straight. According to the doctor, her body was working overtime to fight off the infection. The bad news was that her white blood count wasn't improving; if anything, it was getting worse. They couldn't pinpoint the infection, so they couldn't treat it directly, which worried him. It also worried him that the admitting doctor had called in another doctor to confer with. She seemed just as baffled.

"It's not a request," Ethan said softly.

Curtis smiled. Leave it to Ethan to be the hard-ass.

"Where's Beau?" he asked, getting to his feet.

"He's at the shop. We've got a full garage at the moment. He'll be by in a bit."

Before leaving, Curtis pressed a kiss to Lorrie's forehead and whispered that he'd be back shortly. On his way out, he greeted Kaleb and Zoey, who had been practically holding vigil in the waiting room for the past two days. The family had already rallied together. Jared was keeping an eye on Mason, while Kylie and Jessie were helping with Kellan. And they were all visiting at all times of the day, even when visiting hours were closed. Luckily it was a large waiting area, because the last time he'd checked, there'd been full grown men sprawled out everywhere, all waiting for news.

There was no doubt in his mind that he had the greatest family a man could ever hope for.

"Things goin' well between you two?" Curtis asked Ethan as they headed down the hall toward the cafeteria.

"Better than I ever expected. He's a good man," Ethan replied.

Curtis grinned. "Takes one to love one."

The two of them made it through the line, and though Curtis attempted to pay for their meals, Ethan wouldn't let him. Again, the notion made him grin.

They were sitting at the table, sharing small talk, when Zoey approached.

His heart lodged in his throat as she neared, fear stealing his breath.

"She's fine," Zoey assured him quickly. "Still sleeping. Nothing's changed."

Curtis released the breath he was holding.

"Want somethin' to eat?" Ethan offered.

"No, I'm good. I just stepped out because Zane showed up. Wanted to give him some time with her." Zoey's attention turned to Curtis. "How're you holdin' up?"

No longer hungry, Curtis pushed his tray away and leaned back. "Good as can be expected, I guess."

"She's gonna pull through this," Ethan said firmly, finishing off his food and then stacking his tray on top of Curtis's.

"I'm gonna stop by your house on my way home," Zoey explained. "Clean up a little bit, though the place is already spotless." She smiled sweetly. "Is there anything I can bring you? I'll get you more clothes, but is there anything else?"

Leaning forward, he rested his forearms on the table. "Lorrie keeps a box of diaries in the closet. Each one is labeled with a year. If you don't mind, could you get the one from 1962 and bring it up here?"

"Mom keeps diaries?" Ethan asked, looking shocked.

"Ever since the day I met her," he told his son. He still remembered the first time she'd told him about the diaries. It had been years after she'd first started writing. From time to time, she would let him read through them, no longer embarrassed by what they said.

"And you read them?" This time Ethan looked appalled.

Curtis chuckled. "Your momma is proud of those diaries, boy. She's written in them every single day since the first day she came to my house."

"That's very cool," Zoey said. "And yes, I'll get the one from 1962."

"Thanks, honey," Curtis said with a smile. He hadn't read any of Lorrie's diaries in a long time, and when he had, it had only been with her permission. For some reason, he felt the need to read them. It always made him feel close to her.

"What all does she write in them?" Ethan asked, leaning back and putting his arm over the back of Zoey's chair.

"About her day, her thoughts, that sorta thing."

Ethan outwardly cringed, smirking as he did. "I'm not sure I'd wanna know what she's thinkin' about when it comes to you."

"I heard Beau keeps a diary," Zoey said, deadpan.

Ethan's eyebrows shot into his hairline. "What the hell?"

Zoey started giggling, which made Curtis laugh.

"Kidding," she said. "You'd think it was a crazy idea."

"It *is* a crazy idea," Ethan said defensively. "There's no way I want that man documenting the shit we do."

Well, that … that Curtis understood. And still he laughed.

"YOU ALMOST FINISHED IN HERE?" KALEB ASKED Zoey when he found her in his parents' room. She was fluffing the pillows although the bed was made and looked just fine to him.

"Yep. Just need to grab your mom's diary."

"You sneaky girl." He smirked at his wife. "I knew you couldn't resist reading it."

Zoey shook her head. "It's not for me. Your dad asked if I'd bring it to him."

"My dad reads her diaries?"

"Sounds like it." Zoey moved to the dresser, opened the top drawer, and grabbed a couple of his father's T-shirts. "I think it's sweet."

"Sweet? You know he's readin' it so he can see what she says about him, right?"

"Of course he is," she replied. "It's a reflection of their life together."

Kaleb hated to admit it, but he wanted to know what the diary said. Then again, if there was even the remote mention of sex, he wanted nothing to do with it.

Zoey disappeared into the bathroom, then came back out with a small blue book in her hand.

"Is that it?" His curiosity got the best of him and he reached for the diary.

Zoey quickly yanked it out of his reach.

"Oh, come on," he said, stalking her. When he backed her up against the dresser, he caged her between his arms. "I just wanna see what it says."

"Then ask your dad." She was staring up at him, the book hidden behind her back.

"I might just do that."

"Good."

God, she was feisty. He loved that she was protecting his parents' privacy. Even from him.

"Have I mentioned how hot you look?"

Zoey rolled her eyes. "I've got my hair piled on top of my head, not a lick of makeup on, and I'm wearing yoga pants."

"Is that what those're called?" He glanced down at her pants. "Then why haven't you done yoga in them?"

She smacked his chest. "That's just what they're called. It'd sound silly if I called 'em my wine-drinking pants."

"But that'd make more sense."

"Only to you."

The frustration in her tone made him laugh. "And you're still hot. Pants or no pants."

"I'm not gonna let you read it," she told him firmly.

"At the moment, reading is the last thing on my mind."

Kaleb leaned in and pressed his lips to hers. He loved the way her arms instantly went around him, her body moving closer to his as his tongue slid into her mouth. It didn't matter that they were married or that they had two munchkins already, Kaleb still couldn't get enough of this woman. He wondered if he ever would.

He pulled back, then stared down at her. "Have you heard the story about how they met?"

Zoey nodded. "I love that story." Her smile widened before she slipped around him, shoving the diary into the overnight bag she'd been packing. "Now, let's get this stuff back to the hospital. Then, if you're nice, maybe I'll let you finish what you started when we get home."

Didn't have to tell him twice.

Fifty-Five

CURTIS RECLINED IN THE CHAIR IN LORRIE'S room, the television on above him, but he wasn't paying any attention to what was on. The night nurse had come in to check Lorrie's vitals, chatting with him for a few minutes before leaving them alone. He could see the woman standing outside the window at the station by the door, doing something on the computer. Since they were in the ICU, there was a nurse assigned to Lorrie all day and night, which made him feel a little better.

The only thing that would make him feel a *lot* better was if she would get well. He wasn't sure he'd ever been this scared in his entire life, and things between them hadn't always been easy. Until now, until this very instance, Curtis didn't think he'd ever been so afraid. Considering the doctors still didn't know what was causing the problem and Lorrie didn't seem to be getting any better, the only thing they could do was sit and wait. And pray.

He reached for Lorrie's diary that was sitting on the window ledge beside him. Just seeing the book made him smile. He remembered when she'd first told him how she had kept a diary since that first day they'd met. It had affected him profoundly to know that she'd somehow known that them meeting would be life changing for both of them.

And boy, had it been.

Opening the book, he scanned the first couple of entries, and he found himself reading her entry from his seventeenth birthday.

♥ Sunday, October 21, 1962 ♥

Curtis Walker is the best kisser in the world. Not that I have much to compare it to since he's the only boy I have ever kissed. He's also the only boy I ever want to kiss.

For his birthday, he said the only thing he wanted was to kiss me. I was hesitant at first, but then I let him. And as soon as he did, I didn't want him to stop. I can still feel how smooth his lips were against mine. I can still hear the rumble of his chest as he kissed me. That soft growling sound was so sexy. It was like I've seen in movies, only better. A lot better.

Oh, I almost forgot! After he kissed me, the best thing happened. Curtis asked me to go steady!! I still can't believe it, but I'm Curtis's girlfriend now. My tummy feels all fluttery just thinking about it. I don't know if I should tell anyone, though. I'm not sure what Momma and Daddy will say. I don't want them to tell me I can't see him, so for now, I think I'll keep the news to myself.

I can't wait to see him tomorrow.

That day would forever be imprinted on his brain. He skimmed a few more pages, then his eyes caught on the first sentence of the entry from Sunday, October 28, 1962. That would've been a week later.

Have I mentioned how great a kisser Curtis is? He's amazing. I never thought I'd ever say that about a boy, and certainly not him. While I'm sitting here in my bedroom, the only thing I can think about is him. I wish he would come over to see me. I'd even be willing to sneak out the window just to spend some time with him. When I think about lying with him in the grass, kissing him for hours, I hate that I'm not with him. The way he makes me feel is so incredible. Have I mentioned I love him? ♥

When he stopped reading, he realized he was smiling. Closing his eyes, he thought back to that day, but he didn't get far into the memory before he heard Lorrie's voice.

"What're you thinking about over there?"

He looked over to find her peering back at him, her head turned, a small smile on her face. She was still pale, with dark circles beneath her eyes, but even then, she was the most beautiful woman in the world. The mother of his children. The woman who had tolerated him all these years, forgiven him even when he wasn't sure he deserved it.

Rather than get up, he simply watched her. "All those days I spent kissin' you for hours and hours," he told her. "That's what I'm thinkin' about."

Her smile widened, and as with every smile she offered him, he fell in love a little more.

LORRIE WATCHED HER HUSBAND AS SHE HAD for the past few minutes. When she'd first opened her eyes, she had sought him out. It was a natural instinct after having been together for so long. She knew without a doubt that Curtis would be by her side during the times when she needed him most, and now was one of those times.

At first, when she'd seen him with his eyes closed, she'd thought he was asleep in the recliner. He'd looked so peaceful. Then she'd noticed he was holding her diary in his hand, and she'd known he was probably reliving one of their days together.

It didn't surprise her that he was thinking of their first kiss. She thought about that day often. It felt like so long ago, but at the same time, it was like it was yesterday.

"I remember that day," she said quietly, allowing the memories to come back. "I was so nervous."

"Sexy nervous," he noted.

"Yeah, I'm pretty sure there wasn't anything sexy about me back then."

"On the contrary." His grin was slow and warm. "Every single thing about you was sexy. Still is."

The man always knew the right things to say.

Lorrie peered over at the window to the hall, noticing the nurse was standing there. The same sweet girl who'd been with her at night since they'd moved her to ICU. She turned her attention back to Curtis.

"Did they say anything more?"

Curtis shook his head, then put the recliner stool down and got to his feet. He came to stand beside the bed, placing his big, warm hand on top of hers.

"Not yet. They're doing more blood tests. They'll be by to draw more blood in a few hours, like usual."

Lorrie sighed. "I just want to feel better."

"I know, darlin'. We all want that."

"Are the boys still camped out in the waiting room?" Although she spent most of her time in a medicated fog, she recalled the voices of her boys as they would come to visit throughout the day. Since they couldn't seem to pinpoint what was wrong with her and she was still battling the vomiting more often than not, the doctor had mentioned the possibility of a viral infection. The last thing Lorrie wanted was for one of them to get it, so they were keeping their distance but apparently not leaving the hospital.

"They are."

"Did you spend any time with them today?"

Curtis smiled. "A little. Kaleb brought Mason by since he was going crazy wanting to see his Meemaw. He had to settle for seein' me."

Lorrie chuckled lightly. She seriously doubted that was a disappointment. Mason loved his Pawpaw.

As her eyes grew heavy again, she held on to Curtis's hand, watching him as she once again drifted off, escaping the pain for a little while longer.

Fifty-Six

Five days later
Friday, April 8, 2016

"WHAT'RE YOU DOIN' UP?" KALEB ASKED ZOEY when he found her downstairs sitting on the couch, the small table lamp on beside her. It was a little after five in the morning, and he knew for a fact that when he'd gone to bed, his wife had been right there beside him. Since he'd spent the last two nights at the hospital, Travis had urged him to go home because he looked like hell. Never mind the fact that Zane had chimed in saying that was how he normally looked. Punk ass.

Zoey glanced up from the book she was holding, and there were tears in her eyes.

"Are you readin' one of those romance things again that makes you bawl your eyes out?"

Her smile was sweet. "No, I'm not." She held up the book for him to see.

Kaleb had to move closer to read what was on the cover. "1973?"

Zoey smiled. "It's your mother's diary."

"Really?" *Interesting.* "And you're reading it?"

She placed the book in her lap and pulled her blanket up closer to her chest. "I couldn't help it. I brought one to your dad the other day, and he let me read a couple of the entries. I asked him if it would be okay to read them. I hope your mom won't get mad."

Kaleb lowered himself to the couch beside her. "Honestly, I think she'd be honored. She kept those diaries for a reason." He wasn't quite sure what that reason was, but he doubted she'd thought no one would ever get a chance to read her life story.

"It's funny," Zoey said, her voice low, "I've lived next door to your parents my entire life, and it never occurred to me all that they went through long before you or your brothers came along." Her smile turned mischievous. "I think your old man might just be able to give you a run for your money when it comes to that dirty talk."

Kaleb frowned. "Now *that* I don't need to know about."

Zoey laughed. "Looks like they had a pretty healthy relationship. And your mom apparently liked his dirty mouth."

That was probably a fair assessment. "Let's just say, as kids, we did walk into a few situations that should've scarred us for life."

Zoey chuckled. "I can only imagine."

The last thing Kaleb wanted to do was remember those times. Specifically, *those* times when his parents hadn't expected one or more of their children to walk in on them. His mother and father, for as far back as he could remember, had been very … close.

"But it wasn't always roses for them," Zoey noted, a sadness in her tone once again. "Did you know your mother miscarried a baby a few years before Travis was born?"

Kaleb remembered his mother telling them the story once. She'd been so happy to find out she was pregnant, but she'd miscarried at week seven or eight, or something like that. Although she had reflected back on it with a warm smile, he knew in his heart that his mother still mourned the loss of that baby.

"It took her a long time after that to want to have another child," he told Zoey now.

"I can't even imagine." Her eyes welled with tears. "She's been through so much."

She had. They both had. And Kaleb knew without a doubt that they would get through this, too.

Which was why he'd spent days on end on his knees, praying that the good Lord not take his mother from him. These past few days had been hell on all of them. Especially his father.

"COME ON, POP. WE'RE BLOWIN' THIS JOINT for a little while."

Curtis's first instinct was to tell Travis that he wouldn't be going anywhere, but the look in his oldest boy's eyes told him that would be the wrong answer.

Travis shook his head as though reading his thoughts. "Come on," Travis stated firmly. "No is not an option."

There were a million and one reasons why Curtis didn't want to leave the hospital, and they all pointed right back to his wife lying in that bed, sleeping soundly for the first time today. The infection was still ravaging her body, and she was continuing to vomit profusely. Unfortunately, she wasn't making any progress, and as the minutes continued to tick by, when she wasn't throwing up, she was sleeping more and more, her body working overtime to fight the infection that was slowly and completely taking over her body. The infection the doctors still couldn't pinpoint.

"Kylie and Zoey are gonna stay here with her. If anything happens, they'll call me immediately. You have nothin' to worry about, so get up off your—"

Curtis cocked his head at his son, the look alone cutting him off. But instead of arguing, he managed to get to his feet. "Where're we goin'?" he grumbled.

"Across the street to grab a bite to eat. Everyone's waitin' on us."

"Everyone?" Curtis frowned.

"Yeah, you know, the other six who you donated sperm for."

Curtis shook his head in disbelief. Some of the things that came out of his boys' mouths.

He stopped by Lorrie's bedside, leaned down, and pressed a kiss to her forehead. "I'll be back in a bit. Love you, baby."

She didn't respond but he hadn't expected her to. She was sleeping soundly, mostly due to the drugs they were feeding her for the pain.

On his way out the door, Kylie appeared, hugging him quickly before sending him on his way. He caught up to Travis, following him out of the hospital and directly to Travis's truck. Just as his son had promised, they didn't go far, only to the small Mexican food place across the street.

"You hangin' in there, old man?" Travis asked as they walked through the parking lot.

Not nearly as much as he was letting on, but Travis didn't need to know that. "I'm tryin'."

"She's gonna get well," Travis assured him.

Curtis only hoped his boy was right. It had already been a week, and they were no closer to identifying the source of the infection, and the antibiotics didn't seem to be working. The doctors had called in more doctors, everyone scratching their heads as they tried to determine what the issue was.

"Hey, Pop," Ethan greeted as they approached the table.

Curtis nodded, taking a seat.

"Jared's on his way," Sawyer noted. "I invited him."

Although Jared hadn't been in Coyote Ridge but for a few years, having grown up in El Paso with his mother and father and gaggle of siblings, it was good to have the boy there with them. Gerald had called Curtis right after the big falling-out between Jared and his ex-wife, asking if Curtis could keep the boy preoccupied. Since Travis had just opened the resort and Curtis knew they were all moving toward handling that and less and less at Walker Demolition, it had seemed the natural thing to suggest. That was how Jared had come to Coyote Ridge.

And the good news was that it looked like the boy was there to stay.

"So, there's a rumor goin' around," Brendon stated after the waiter had brought tea and chips.

Curtis looked up, realizing his son was speaking to him. "About?"

"About diaries Momma kept," Braydon added.

Curtis smiled. "What about 'em?"

"Did she really keep a diary since she was fourteen?" Zane asked.

"She did," he told the boys, reaching for a chip.

"I heard Zoey's readin' them?"

Curtis nodded. His daughter-in-law had asked, and after he'd okayed it with Lorrie, he'd given her the go-ahead. He was proud of the life they'd lived and he knew Lorrie was, too.

"You think that's a good thing?" Zane's question was directed at Kaleb. "Your woman readin' about Pop's dirty mouth? I heard her talkin' about it."

The group laughed, and Curtis shook his head.

"I can totally see Momma writin' that in there," Sawyer added. "I remember when I was little"—Sawyer glanced at Travis—"I think I was, like, three or four. Trav came into my room one night and told me I wasn't allowed to get outta bed 'cause Momma and Daddy were makin' lots of noises and they didn't wanna be bothered."

Oh, Lord.

Curtis felt a blush creep up his neck. He couldn't help it.

Ethan barked a laugh. "So it is true!"

"What?" Curtis asked, looking from one boy to the next. "Y'all think you were the only wild ones in Coyote Ridge?"

Kaleb turned to him. "I still can't believe you renamed the whole freakin' town for her."

"I woulda renamed the whole damn state if that's what she'd wanted," he said confidently.

"Wouldn't doubt it," Jared said, taking the empty seat beside Curtis. "Sorry I'm late. My daddy always said Uncle Curtis had it bad for Aunt Lorrie. Said he'd never seen anything like it."

Curtis didn't know about all that. It was love. Plain and simple. A love that had taken a firm grip on his heart long ago and never let go. Not much different than what his boys had found.

"There's not a whole lot you can do when love finds you," Ethan said, smiling at Curtis. "Right, Pop?"

"Nope. You just gotta give in and enjoy the ride."

Fifty-Seven

Ten days later
Monday, April 18, 2016

CURTIS WAS PACING THE FLOOR, WAITING FOR the doctor to show up for his morning rounds. Lorrie had had an exceptionally bad night, and he wanted to know that the hell they were doing to get her well. They were going on three weeks in this place, and so far nothing they'd tried was working, and he was growing tired of the runaround. Something had to be done. Someone had to make her better, because he couldn't sit back and watch her get worse.

"Mr. Walker."

Curtis looked up at the sound of the doctor's voice. He was walking toward him in his crisp white coat, holding a chart in his hand as he scanned the pages. The only thing that stopped Curtis from railing on the guy was the concerned look on his face when the man finally met Curtis's gaze.

The doctor nodded toward Lorrie's room. "Let's go in and talk."

Swallowing hard, he followed the doctor into the room.

"Lorrie," the doctor greeted, his tone a tad more cheerful than before. "How're you feeling?"

Lorrie was sitting up in bed for the first time in what felt like days, but she looked weaker than Curtis had ever seen her.

"Not good," she rasped, her voice brittle.

"We got the result of the bloodwork from this morning. Still no improvement." The man's face softened. "Truth is, it's not looking good at all."

They had asked him not to sugarcoat things, but Curtis wasn't exactly thrilled with the way the doctor was relaying his concerns. Especially not directly to Lorrie.

"I don't understand," Curtis barked. "Why the hell can't you find what's causing this?"

Lorrie's hand landed on his, her way of pulling him back from the ledge. The doctor seemed to understand, because he didn't take offense to Curtis's outburst. Instead, he set the chart down on the table beside him and leaned against the wall.

"I'd like for you to walk me through exactly what happened since"—he briefly glanced at the chart—"Dr. Willow removed the kidney stone."

"We've been over this already," Curtis stated, his frustration growing stronger.

"I understand that," the doctor confirmed. "But I'm hoping if we go over it again, maybe I'll pick up something that I missed before."

Curtis started to answer, but Lorrie beat him to it.

"Dr. Willow said it was a normal procedure," she explained. "They blasted the stone, removed it, sent me home with a Foley catheter and a stent in my bladder. Two weeks later, I went in and they removed that, and they sent me home with a clean bill of health. Curtis took me to dinner, and two days later I'm here."

That was the exact same story they'd told repeatedly to everyone who asked.

"He didn't say anything else? Nothing he was worried about?"

Curtis wondered why the doctor didn't bother to call Dr. Willow and get the scoop for himself. Or maybe he had and that was the problem. There were no more details to the story. "That's it," Curtis acknowledged. "But you said it's not her kidney, right?"

"It's not her kidney," he confirmed, his face once again masked. "What about after that? What did you eat? Did you go anywhere?"

Curtis looked down to see that Lorrie had once again drifted off. She'd been so out of it lately, both from the drugs and the infection brutalizing her body.

Curtis sighed. "When she felt better, we went to eat at the same place we've been eatin' for forty years. She wanted to spend a little time with the horses, but we didn't stay long." He glanced down at her once again. "Other than that, pretty routine. We stayed at the house, and then the next thing I know, she's pukin' her guts up askin' to go to the hospital."

"Join me outside," the doctor said to Curtis, nodding toward the hallway.

Curtis didn't want to join him outside, but he forced his feet to move.

The doctor closed the sliding glass door and turned to face him. "Mr. Walker, you asked me not to sugarcoat it, so I'm not going to. We've tried everything we know to try, and nothing's working. Her white blood cell count continues to concern me. Because we can't pinpoint it, we've been trying new things every day based on the blood work results. As you can see, nothing is helping." The doctor glanced into the room briefly, then met Curtis's gaze again. "And now there are other issues."

"What sort of issues?" Curtis felt a little dizzy.

"Her kidneys aren't functioning properly. They have significantly reduced function, and basically, her organs are all starting to slow, which indicates that the infection is winning. Sepsis will slowly tackle every organ and reduce how they function until her vitals become unmanageable."

"What does that mean?" He reached for the desk, trying to keep himself upright.

The doctor nodded down the hall. "Is the family still here? I think it might be best if I talk to everyone at once."

Curtis nodded, then somehow managed to follow the doctor down the hall and to the waiting room. For the past few days, the boys had been spending most of their time there, sleeping in the waiting room until they were allowed to come back. Everyone was getting more and more worried, not wanting to be far if something happened. Curtis couldn't blame them, though he had continued to hold out hope.

The doctor had just sucked all the hope right out of him with those few words.

When they stepped out into the waiting room, it was full of people. Probably ninety-eight percent of them Curtis's family. Even Gerald and his wife had come down from El Paso, wanting to be there for Lorrie and helping out with Curtis's grandkids so his children could be there.

Travis was the first on his feet, with Gage right beside him, both men moving toward Curtis. "What's goin' on, Pop?"

Curtis shook his head, then allowed the doctor to repeat the same thing he'd just told him, going into more detail about the deteriorating organ function. It sounded bad, really bad. As though the doctor himself was beginning to think that Lorrie could very well take a turn for the worse.

"What're you sayin'?" Zane asked, his voice harder than Curtis had ever heard it.

"I'm saying the prognosis isn't good. At this point, Lorrie's going to continue to deteriorate, and likely her organs will begin shutting down. From there, we'll only be able to make her comfortable until…" The doctor took a deep breath. "Basically, we need to prepare ourselves because we are losing this battle."

Curtis's legs went out from under him and the world began to spin.

"Dad!" Travis yelled at the same time Curtis felt strong arms grab him.

Travis and Kaleb lowered him into a chair, but Curtis hardly noticed. He'd gone completely numb. He heard voices continue to speak as the boys fired off questions, voices rising, emotions beginning to be set loose.

This couldn't be happening.

It couldn't.

Curtis wouldn't know what to do without her.

And with that thought, he started to cry and he couldn't stop.

THIS COULDN'T BE HAPPENING. NO WAY COULD this actually be happening.

Zoey couldn't hold back the tears, but she wasn't the only one. When Curtis broke down, the room suddenly went silent, other than the horrific sound of his broken sobs. Travis and Gerald took the doctor out into the hall and were talking to him, while everyone else in the room was either in tears or damn close.

"Come here, baby," Kaleb said, his voice low and gentle.

He wrapped his arms around her and she hugged him back, tighter than ever.

This couldn't be happening. Lorrie was the foundation of this entire family. It was her love that kept things running smoothly. It was her voice of reason, her kind heart, and yes, even her stern side when things weren't being managed appropriately that kept this huge, wonderful family together.

What would they do without her?

Curtis's devastating sobs grew louder and Zoey managed to release Kaleb. "Go to your dad. Please. He needs y'all right now."

Kaleb nodded, tears in his eyes.

As she stood back, she watched as all seven of Curtis's sons as well as Beau, Gage, and Jared rallied around him, trying to keep him together while he fell apart. His desperate pleas to God broke her heart.

V, Kylie, Jessie, Kennedy, and Cheyenne came over, and the six of them clung to one another while they stood and watched the most horrific scene as the Walker men crumbled.

This couldn't be happening. Something had to be done. Someone had to figure out how to fix this, because these men— these proud, strong, stoic men—would never be the same if something happened to Lorrie.

Hell, none of them would.

Fifty-Eight

Three days later
Thursday, April 21

"MRS. WALKER, IT'S ME, JEANNIE. HOW'RE YOU feeling this morning?"

Lorrie forced her eyes open and looked at the sweet nurse who'd been by her bedside most mornings since she'd arrived however many days ago. She tried to smile, but her body was too weak. As was usual, that didn't deter Jeannie from continuing on. Lorrie liked the fact that she spent time with her, chatting about her family and the things she did outside of the hospital. It was a nice reprieve from all of the sad faces she'd been seeing lately.

The last few days had been especially hard. The doctor had given them all the grim news, and Lorrie had watched the devastated faces of her family as they'd streamed in and out of her room for the past few days. Things didn't look good, and the worst part about it, she couldn't do anything to heal their hearts. She wasn't ready to die; she wasn't ready to leave her boys or Curtis or her grandbabies. She was still fighting with every ounce of strength she had, and she would until her dying breath.

"I was talking to my mom last night," Jeannie continued. "I was telling her about you and all your kids. I've got three sisters, so my mother couldn't comprehend how you could've raised seven boys." Jeanie took Lorrie's wrist, placing her fingers over her pulse. "Then we got to talking about kidney stones. She was telling me that she had one removed a few years ago. It sounded a lot like what happened to you. They had sent her home wearing a Foley, too. She didn't remember how long she had it, but she remembered how happy she was when the doctor had finally removed it."

Something niggled at the back of Lorrie's mind, something related to this conversation. Perhaps something important.

"My mom said she still remembers leaving the doctor's office that day feeling a heck of a lot better."

"He nicked my bladder," Lorrie blurted, looking up at Jeannie.

Jeannie paused from listening to her lungs with the stethoscope. "What's that?"

She took a deep breath and explained. "When I went in to get the stent removed, the doctor nicked my bladder. Said it was only a small tear but it wasn't anything to worry about."

At that moment, Curtis walked into the room carrying a cup of coffee. He smiled back at her as soon as their eyes met. "There's my beautiful girl," he said tenderly. Despite the tone of his voice, she could see the sadness in his eyes.

"Mr. Walker," Jeannie greeted him. "Lorrie was just telling me that when she had the stent removed after the kidney stone procedure that the doctor caused a small tear in her bladder. I don't recall seeing anything about that in the chart."

Curtis had moved closer to the bed, his big hand resting over hers. "I didn't know anything about that. Baby?"

She nodded, trying to recall what the doctor had said. Her brain was so foggy. "He said it was an accidental nick and I shouldn't be worried."

Jeannie finished checking her, finally taking Lorrie's temperature, but then she excused herself. "I'm going to call the doctor really quick. I think this is information he might need to know."

Curtis nodded at the nurse, but then his attention returned to her. "Why didn't you tell me about that?"

She smiled weakly. "I actually didn't think anything of it until just now." She nodded toward the door. "Jeannie was telling me about her mother having a kidney stone removed, and it just hit me, I guess."

Curtis leaned down and kissed her forehead, whispering for her to get some sleep as once again she drifted off.

AS SOON AS LORRIE WAS SLEEPING SOUNDLY, Curtis slipped out into the hall to talk to the nurse.

"Did you call the doctor?" he asked.

Jeannie smiled, and this didn't seem like one of those forced ones that he'd seen on far too many faces as of late. "I did. And he's looking into it."

"What does that mean?"

She pivoted to face him. "It means that there's a possibility that the wound on her bladder is actually the site of the infection. If that's the case, it's no longer like looking for a needle in a haystack."

Curtis was getting the gist of it, but just barely. "So they can fight it?"

Jeannie nodded. "That's correct. If that's what's causing it, we can pinpoint the site of the infection." Her smile slid from her face. "But, Mr. Walker, that doesn't mean she's out of the woods yet. We have to confirm that this is the issue first. And we don't have a lot of time, because her kidneys are weak."

He nodded. "When will the doctor be in?"

"He'll make his usual rounds, but if he finds something before then, I'm sure he'll send instruction on what we need to do."

As soon as she finished her sentence, the phone on her desk rang. She turned to answer it, her smile returning as she turned to look at him, speaking into the phone. "Yes, sir. Right on it."

The way she was looking at him gave Curtis hope.

"That was the doctor. This might be the break we've been hoping for. He's ordered an ultrasound so we can see if this is, in fact, the site of the infection."

"And if it is?"

"Then he'll start a treatment plan immediately."

The band around his chest loosened a little. Not completely, but enough to let him breathe. This was the best news—even if it wasn't definitive—that they'd heard in all the time they'd been there.

"I'm gonna go talk to my boys," he told her as she started typing something into the computer.

"We'll be right here when you get back," she assured him.

Not wanting to keep the boys waiting when the last thing they'd heard was the devastating news from the doctor a few days ago, Curtis headed down the hall and out into the waiting area.

As soon as the door closed behind him, heads lifted, bodies shifted so that they were sitting or standing.

"Any news?" Sawyer asked, moving toward him.

Taking a deep breath, Curtis relayed everything that had just happened to the dozens of faces staring back at him. He made sure he told them that they didn't know for sure if this would work, but for the first time in three weeks, at least they had some sort of hope.

And for now, that was exactly what they all needed.

Fifty-Nine

One week later, Friday, April 29

"WHOA, MOMMA! YOU'RE LOOKIN' GOOD," ZANE TEASED when he walked into Lorrie's room. "You 'bout ready to bust outta this joint?"

Lorrie smiled at her youngest son. For the first time in a month, she felt human again. The pain was mostly gone. The infection was disintegrating thanks to the fact that the doctors had pinpointed it and knew how to treat it. She wasn't sleeping twenty-four hours a day, and as of this morning, she was officially a free woman.

"More than ever," she told him.

Yes, she was ready to get out of this place. She was ready to go home, ready to get back to living her life. These past few weeks had been difficult, but more so for her family, the ones who had lived minute by minute wondering if the worst would happen. That morning when the doctor had come in to sign her release, he'd told her that if she hadn't remembered that little detail, she probably wouldn't be with them today.

"Pop is bringin' the truck around. I'm here to make sure you're not mobbed on the way out the door. I mean, seriously, you got a town named by you."

"Oh, hush," she told her boy, giggling.

When the nurse came in a minute later, Zane grabbed her things while Lorrie got situated in the wheelchair so they could take her to the exit. She would've preferred to walk, but they insisted that she continue to take it easy, allow her body to heal completely before she tried to trek too far.

Lorrie wasn't going to argue.

Fifteen minutes later, Curtis was helping her into the truck and Zane was climbing into the backseat. When Curtis started out of the parking lot, he took her hand, linked their fingers, and remained quiet for most of the way home. Lorrie didn't mind the silence; she'd heard nothing but beeping machines and muttering voices day and night for weeks on end, so she appreciated the quiet.

"Is everyone at work?" she finally asked when they pulled into the driveway half an hour later.

"Back at it," Zane confirmed. "You know how it is around here."

She did. And she was glad that her boys could get back to their lives, back to their families. Those were the important things, and she didn't want them to miss out on a second. She certainly hadn't, that was for sure.

Curtis parked the truck, then insisted on helping her out and leading her to the front door. Once inside, Lorrie took a deep breath and… "What's that smell?"

Zane's grin went from ear to ear. "Dinner."

"Dinner?" Lorrie looked at Curtis. "It's only lunchtime."

"It is," her husband agreed, taking her arm and leading her into the living room.

And that was when Lorrie saw them.

All of them.

Her boys, their significant others, her grandbabies, the dogs, her nephews and nieces, brothers and sisters, in-laws. They were all there, crowded into the kitchen, spilling out into the living room and probably the dining room and maybe even the backyard, for all she could tell.

"Oh," Curtis said, looking serious. "Did I forget to mention that we're having Sunday dinner today?"

She pursed her lips and glared at him, unable to keep from laughing.

"Who's doing the cooking?" she asked, turning to look at the others.

She noticed a small hand go up in the air from behind the others. "I am!" Zoey announced.

"Well, in that case, let's eat."

WHEN THE HOUSE FINALLY CLEARED OUT, LONG after it'd gotten dark outside, Curtis wanted nothing more than to spend some quiet hours with his wife. He was proud of himself. For the better part of the day, he had managed not to suffocate her, but it hadn't been easy. The only thing he wanted to do was wrap his arms around her, hold her close to his body, and never let her go. Ever.

He made his way to the bedroom, finding the door open and Lorrie sitting at her desk, writing in her diary. Tapping on the doorjamb to get her attention, he smiled when she looked his way.

"Writin' in your book?"

She nodded.

"Can I read it?"

She nodded again.

After toeing off his boots, he crawled into bed.

"I thought you wanted to read it," she said, watching him from across the room.

"I do." He patted the bed beside him.

She gave a little head shake, clearly finding him amusing. Or so he wanted to believe. She got to her feet, picked up her book, then joined him on the bed. Before she could hand him the book, he wrapped his arms around her and pulled her to him, clutching her tightly, her head resting on his chest.

A tear escaped him, but he didn't try to stop it. He simply held her as tight as he dared.

"I'm sorry it's been so rough these past few weeks," she said, her words vibrating against his chest.

"It's not your fault," he told her.

"No, but I know it's been hard. I hated seeing you and the boys upset."

He ran his hand over her hair. "Honey, that's part of it."

"I know," she told him. "When you love someone, the pain can sometimes be unbearable."

"But it's worth every second," he noted.

"Yes, it definitely is. And we've had a lifetime of seconds."

He smiled. "I hope you know that's not nearly long enough. I need another lifetime with you."

She laughed.

"I love you, darlin'," he whispered against her hair. "I'm so sorry you had to go through all that. I would've given anything to take away your pain."

Lorrie squeezed him. "You can't fix everything."

"No, but I'll damn sure try."

"I know you will. And that's why I love you. That's why I've *always* loved you." She lifted her head and smiled, wiping away the tear on his cheek. "You are my love that lasts a lifetime."

"Hey…" Curtis shifted lower, pulling her closer. "That's my line. You can't go stealin' my lines."

"What're you gonna do about it?"

He grinned, and for the first time in days, he felt whole again. "I'm sure I'll think of somethin'."

"I'm sure you will," she agreed. "You always do."

♥ Friday, April 29, 2016 ♥

It feels as though I've been given another chance, more time with the only thing that matters to me. Family. It's been a rough few weeks, but I'm here, still fighting, still moving forward, just as I plan to be for years to come. I hope God knows that I'm not done here yet. I haven't gotten to spoil all of my grandkids, or my great-nieces and -nephews, to watch them grow up and become the incredible people they will become. I haven't had the chance to see our nieces and nephews get married, have babies. And I intend to be here for those moments, to share those happy memories with those whom I love, with the most incredible man at my side … for a long time to come. ♥

Epilogue

One year later...

"A FAMILY REUNION?" JARED WALKER DROPPED INTO the chair in his office and stared up at the ceiling, cell phone to his ear. "Are you fucking serious?"

For the past half hour, Jared had been humoring his cousin Travis, listening to the spiel as to why it was time the Walker family had a reunion. The last thing Jared had time—much less patience—for these days was some big-ass family get-together. At thirty-six years old and divorced, it was enough for him to deal with the day-to-day of Walker Demolition, along with being a single dad to a three-year-old little boy.

"Very," Travis confirmed, his tone gruff. "And I want it to take place next month."

Next month? The guy was getting laid too damn much these days, because now he'd lost his fucking mind and become far too optimistic. Maybe there was something to be said about the whole bisexual thing. "I think we need to be a little realistic here," Jared added.

"How long do you think it'll take to prepare?" Travis questioned, sounding genuinely curious.

Jared had no clue. He wasn't a goddamn party planner. "Do you even know where we're gonna have this thing?"

"Yep." The certainty in Travis's voice gave Jared a small measure of assurance. At least his cousin had looked that far into it.

When he realized Travis wasn't going to share the details, Jared sighed. "Where, Travis?"

"Dead Heat Ranch."

"I don't even know what that is," Jared admitted.

"It's owned by some of Cheyenne's family," Travis told him, referring to Travis's brother Brendon's woman. "Beyond that, I ain't got shit. I need you to call them, set it up."

"*Me?*" Jared sat up straight. "What makes you think I've got time to deal with this? Do you know how much business Walker Demo has at the moment?"

Travis chuckled.

Okay, so maybe he did. Jared knew that Travis probably had a finger on the pulse of every damn thing that went on with Walker Demo, not to mention the resort. And probably even the entire town of Coyote Ridge, Texas, to boot.

Unfortunately, they weren't as busy as Jared would've liked. For months on end, they'd been going ninety to nothing, and all of a sudden things had slowed drastically.

"Fine. We're not that damn busy, but still. Why me?"

"'Cause you're closer to everyone."

It was Jared's turn to laugh. "That's horseshit and you know it."

"But it sounded good, didn't it? Look, Gage just walked in, and I've gotta take care of some shit. You got this?"

Another frustrated sigh escaped him, but Jared found himself nodding. "Fine."

"Thanks. Call Cheyenne or Brendon, get the information. Let me know if you need anything."

Jared didn't bother responding. He hung up the phone and dropped his cell phone on his desk, then put his head in his hands and tugged at his hair. On top of everything, he needed a damn haircut.

He sighed.

Honestly, this was the last damn thing he needed right now, but it would help to keep his mind occupied, so that was something to look forward to. When business slowed, that was when his mind started wandering, and that was never a good thing.

Ever.

Jared sat up straight and took a deep breath. Fine. He'd do it. And if Travis wanted this shindig to take place next month, Jared needed to get started now. Reaching for his phone, he had just palmed it when it vibrated. He glanced at the screen and saw that it was Cheyenne Montgomery, the very person he was about to call.

He stabbed the screen to answer, then put the phone to his ear. "Lemme guess, Travis called you?" How that was even possible with only a minute or so passing since Jared had hung up with him, he didn't know. Then again, this was Travis Walker. The guy was quite possibly not human.

Cheyenne's husky chuckle made him smile. "Of course he did."

"And to think, he told *me* to call you."

"You know Travis, always makin' sure things go the way he wants them to."

Exactly. Which was the very reason Travis should be handling this shit. "I don't know why he's trusting me with this," Jared told Cheyenne. "I get the feelin' he's gonna handle most of it on his own, anyway."

"I wouldn't be so sure about that," Cheyenne said. "Rumor is, now that he's got two rug rats at home, he's havin' a hard time keepin' his head on straight already."

That didn't surprise Jared one bit. Travis Walker wasn't the easiest guy to get along with, and frazzled seemed to be the constant state he was in. Although he had toned down somewhat in recent years, which was a relief to everyone.

"I've got the number for you. Got a pen?"

Jared grabbed a pen. "Yeah."

He scribbled the number on his desk calendar as Cheyenne rattled it off. "You're gonna want to talk to Hope Lambert."

"Got it."

"She might have one of her sisters handle the details, but she's the best one to talk to first. They'll walk you through everything you need to know."

"I'll call her now."

"I'd offer to help, but I'm gonna be on the road for the next month."

Shit. That reminded him that he needed to try to coordinate schedules. A month wasn't nearly enough time to put this together and expect anyone to show up. Maybe he'd push it out a little.

"I'm sure I can handle it," Jared told her. "But if you could send me your tour dates, that'd help."

"I'll get them texted to you ASAP."

"Is this place close?" he asked. "This Dead Heat Ranch?"

"Not far. 'Bout half an hour from here, I'd say. In Embers Ridge. You know the place?"

"Yeah," he lied. He didn't know the place, but he figured a map would tell him. "You know why Travis picked it?" Jared hadn't wrapped his head around that part yet.

"You'll see when you call them."

Jared did not like the sound of that. "Should I be worried?"

"Nope. Just make sure you're clear on how many days you want."

"Days?" He flopped back into his chair and closed his eyes. "I thought this was a family reunion. An afternoon barbecue or some shit."

Another giggle sounded from Cheyenne. "I wish it were that simple. This is a dude ranch, Jared. My guess is Travis is lookin' for a solid week."

Dude ranch? Week?

The fuck?

He sighed again, this time in resignation. He wasn't going to get out of this, so he might as well step right in the shit and get moving.

"All right, I'm gonna call this Hope Lambert and see what she says. I'll let you know."

"Have fun!"

Right. Fun.

Because that was exactly what this *wasn't* going to be.

I hope you enjoyed Lorrie and Curtis's story. I have to say that this book was not at all what I'd anticipated it to be. It was so much better. I was nervous to write their story and at one point I wondered if I ever would, but once I started, I couldn't stop. In fact, it's the only book I've written that I never wanted to end. I wanted to stay in their world, to feel what they feel, to live what they live. It was beautiful and scary at times and I'm completely humbled by all the readers who wanted their story. So, thank you.

Curtis is the first book in the Walkers of Coyote Ridge series, a spin-off of my Alluring Indulgence series and if you haven't read about Curtis and Lorrie's seven sons, I highly suggest that you do.

ACKNOWLEDGMENTS

I want to thank Jack DeNormandie for all his help with this book. Jack, although I've never had the pleasure of meeting you face to face, I hope to remedy that in the future. The information you provided was invaluable and I can never thank you enough. You are one of a kind.

I want to thank Chancy Powley for all that you endured during the writing of this book. I thank you for sharing so much information and for talking to your dad for me. I only wish I could've seen your face when you had to ask him the hard questions. I can imagine how red your face was.

I also need to thank my mother-in-law, Carolyn, for helping me by providing diaries and pictures that gave me more insight into the 1960s.

I have to thank my husband and my children, for putting up with my craziness. From my sudden outbursts when I think of something that needs to be added or when I question why one of the characters did what they did, to the strange hours that I keep and the days on end when I'm MIA because I'm under deadline or just engrossed in a story... Y'all are incredibly tolerant of me and for that, I am forever grateful. I love you with all that I am.

My street team – The Naughty & Nice Posse. Ladies, your daily pimping and support fills my heart with so much love. You are a blessing to me, each and every one of you.

My beta readers, Chancy and Denise. Ladies, I'm not sure thanks will ever be enough. However, not only are you the ones who catch the weird things and ask the bigger questions, you've both become my friends and you keep me going.

My copyeditor, Amy. Punctuation and grammar... well, that's not my strong suit. But it is yours and you are truly remarkable at what you do. You simply amaze me and I am so glad that I found you.

Nicole Nation 2.0 for the constant support and love. This group of ladies has kept me going for so long, I'm not sure I'd know what to do without them.

And, of course, YOU, the reader. Your emails, messages, posts, comments, tweets… they mean more to me than you can imagine. I thrive on hearing from you, knowing that my characters and my stories have touched you in some way keeps me going. I've been known to shed a tear or two when reading an email because you simply bring so much joy to my life with your support. I thank you for that.

About Nicole Edwards

New York Times and *USA Today* bestselling author Nicole Edwards lives in the suburbs of Austin, Texas with her husband and their youngest of three children. The two older ones have flown the coup, while the youngest is in high school. When Nicole is not writing about sexy alpha males and sassy, independent women, she can often be found with a book in hand or attempting to keep the dogs happy. You can find her hanging out on social media and interacting with her readers - even when she's supposed to be writing.

Want to know what's coming next? Or how about see some fun stuff related to Nicole's books? You can find these, as well as tons of other stuff on Nicole's website. You can also find A Day in the Life blog posts, which are short stories about your favorite characters, as well as exclusive contests by joining Nicole Nation on Nicole's website. To join, simply click **Log In | Register** in the menu.

If you're interested in keeping up to date on any new releases and preorders, you can sign up for Nicole's notification newsletter. This only goes out when she's got important information to share.

Want a simple, fast way to get updates on new releases? Sign up for text messaging. If you are in the U.S. simply text NICOLE to 64600 or sign up on her website. She promises not to spam your phone. This is just her way of letting you know what's happening because Nicole knows you're busy, but if you're anything like her, you always have your phone on you.

CONNECT WITH NICOLE

Website: NicoleEdwardsAuthor.com

Facebook: /Author.Nicole.Edwards

Instagram: NicoleEdwardsAuthor

Twitter: @NicoleEAuthor

By Nicole Edwards

Alluring Indulgence
Kaleb
Zane
Travis
Holidays with the Walker Brothers
Ethan
Braydon
Sawyer
Brendon

The Walkers Of Coyote Ridge
Curtis
Jared
Hard to Hold
Hard to Handle
Beau
Rex
A Coyote Ridge Christmas
Mack
Kaden & Keegan

Brantley Walker: Off the Books
All In
Without a Trace
Hide & Seek

Austin Arrows
Rush
Kaufman

Club Destiny
Conviction
Temptation
Addicted
Seduction
Infatuation
Captivated
Devotion
Perception
Entrusted
Adored
Distraction

DEAD HEAT RANCH
Boots Optional
Betting on Grace
Overnight Love

DEVIL'S BEND
Chasing Dreams
Vanishing Dreams

MISPLACED HALOS
Protected in Darkness
Salvation in Darkness
Bound in Darkness

OFFICE INTRIGUE
Office Intrigue
Intrigued Out of the Office
Their Rebellious Submissive
Their Famous Dominant
Their Ruthless Sadist
Their Naughty Student
Their Fairy Princess

PIER 70
Reckless
Fearless
Speechless
Harmless
Clueless

SNIPER 1 SECURITY
Wait for Morning
Never Say Never
Tomorrow's Too Late

SOUTHERN BOY MAFIA/DEVIL'S PLAYGROUND
Beautifully Brutal
Without Regret
Beautifully Loyal
Without Restraint

STANDALONE NOVELS
Unhinged Trilogy
A Million Tiny Pieces
Inked on Paper
Bad Reputation
Bad Business

NAUGHTY HOLIDAY EDITIONS
2015
2016

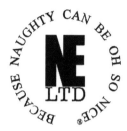

Made in the USA
Las Vegas, NV
31 October 2020

10474508R00190